Dancing

The Rise Of An English Lawbreaker Book 1

Malcolm Archibald

For Cathy

Chapter One

Kent Coast, England

FEBRUARY 1762

When the storm subsided, a litter of wreckage spread for a mile along the shore; an ugly reminder of the power of nature over man's creations. Among the spars and cordage, the fragments of shattered timber and personal possessions, a scattering of seamen proved the human cost of shipwreck. On one particular stretch of shingle, three bodies lay side by side, with the final vestiges of the wind pushing little wavelets to break around them.

Of the three, the central man was the slightest, a man in the early years of maturity, bearing scars on his back and a single brass ring in his left ear. He lay on his face, with both hands curled into the shingle and without a stitch of clothing covering him.

A lone seagull circled above the three bodies, then landed on the naked back of the man in the centre. The bird looked around before hopping onto the beach and pecked at the weather-tanned body.

"Get away," the naked man slurred the words, tried to rise, and spewed a pint of seawater onto the beach. The gull flapped a few yards away before it stopped. The man pushed himself to his feet, swore, stamped his bare feet, and stooped to inspect the men on either side.

"Both dead," he said.

"Did you know them?" A tall woman stood on the shingle, a step above the high tide mark. The wind whipped dark blonde hair across her face as she gazed at the naked man with no hint of unease.

"This fellow was James Hicks, Able seaman." The naked man turned Hicks onto his back. "He was a good sailor."

"And the other?"

The naked man prodded the body on his left. He hesitated before he spoke. "This fellow was Abel Watson, foretopman."

"Did you know them all?" The woman nodded along the shore, where each successive wave brought more wreckage and more bodies.

"Yes," the man crouched for a moment to clear his head. "They were shipmates." He unfastened Watson's trousers, dragged them from the dead man's legs and pulled them on before removing and donning Hicks' canvas shirt.

The survivor walked along the beach, checking each body. Once, he stooped to remove a belt with a sheath knife from a man's waist, and twice he muttered a brief farewell. The woman followed ten steps behind, watching everything.

"Who are you looking for?" Her voice was calm. Living beside the coast, she had seen other shipwrecks, seen the sea give up other dead men, particularly in this year of 1762, when half the world was at war.

The survivor did not reply. He crouched beside a naval lieutenant, with the early morning sun gleaming from the gold on his sodden blue coat.

"What are you doing?" the woman asked.

Sliding a hand inside the officer's jacket, the man removed a small leather purse, weighed it in his hand, and nodded. "I'll have this," he said. "Here," extracting a gold sovereign from the purse, he flicked it to the woman. "Now go away."

The woman bit the coin to test the purity of the gold, turned, and walked away. She did not look back.

The man waited for a few moments, drew his new knife, and cut the gold buttons from the officer's coat. "Any pawn shop will give me a few coppers for these."

"What the devil?" The lieutenant stirred.

"No devil," the man said. "Only me." He placed his knife against the officer's throat and pressed, slowly slicing open the flesh. The next wave washed away the blood as the survivor stood and walked on. He continued to scour the beach, removing a few coins when he could and murmuring a final farewell to men he knew.

THE PAWNSHOP OWNER KNEW BY THE MAN'S APPEARANCE THAT he was a seaman. If the checked shirt and canvas trousers had not given him away, the pigtail that extended halfway down his back would have been evidence enough.

"And what do you want, Tarry Jack?"

"A fair deal," the man said.

The pawnshop owner's eyes narrowed. "What are you pawning, Jack?"

"These." The man dropped half a dozen golden buttons onto the counter and waited for the valuation.

"An officer's buttons," the dealer said, lifting the first. "Pinchbeck, unless I am much mistaken. That's an alloy of zinc and copper mixed to resemble gold."

The man leaned across the counter. "You are much mistaken," he said. "These buttons are gold. Try again."

The dealer opened his mouth to protest, looked at his customer's bitter eyes and took the path of discretion. "I may be wrong," he said. "Times are hard. So I won't be able to pay as much as you hope."

"You don't know how much I hope," the man said. "Make me an offer."

The dealer pursed his lips, looked at the expression in the man's eyes and said, tentatively, "Ten shillings."

"Is that each?" The man asked.

"No, that's for the lot."

"Two guineas," the man said, "and you're getting a thief's bargain."

"One guinea," the dealer countered, "and that's more than you'll get elsewhere."

"One guinea and that pair of shoes there," the man indicated a pair of metal-buckled shoes the dealer had displayed behind his counter. "And a hat."

"We agree," the dealer produced a pawn ticket. "What name shall I write?"

"Smith," the man replied immediately. "John Smith."

He left the pawnbroker with his new shoes uncomfortable on his feet and found accommodation in a cheap lodging house a score of yards from the sea.

"No dunnage, Jack?" The lodging house keeper ran his gaze over Smith's spare body and ill-fitting clothes.

"No," Smith said.

"Threepence a night paid in advance," the keeper held out a grasping hand.

Smith counted out ninepence. "Three nights," he said.

"What are you staying for?"

"A burial," Smith told him.

THE ROW OF NEWLY-DUG GRAVES OCCUPIED ONE SIDE OF THE graveyard. All boasted a simple cross at the head, with the inscription. "A drowned mariner, known only to God." They lay under the whip of the wind that carried sea-salt air fresh from the Channel and within the shadow of an elder tree that raised naked branches in supplication to the closed eyes of God.

"And we consign his body to the care of the Lord." The Reverend Edmund Hood gave the signal, and the gravediggers lowered the final corpse into the grave. A handful of local people watched, with one woman surreptitiously wiping a tear from her eye, possibly in memory of a loved one the sea had taken in some half-forgotten tragedy. As the gravediggers shovelled soil into the grave, a tobacco-chewing carpenter banged in his final cross. The name Abel Watson was neatly carved into the crosspiece, with the date 2nd February 1762.

St Bride's Day, Smith thought. He stood at the gateway of the graveyard with his arms folded and a battered tricorn hat pulled low over his head. When the reverend glowered in his direction, Smith removed his hat and held it in front of him.

"You are the only person from outwith the parish who turned up," the reverend said. "Do you know this man?"

"I do," Smith said. "That's me you have just buried."

The reverend looked confused. "Who are you?"

"I am nobody. I have no name; I don't exist." Smith's smile held a vestige of humour. "After all, you have just buried my body." He placed his hat back on his head and adjusted the brim until it concealed the upper part of his face. "As I no longer exist, therefore no laws or rules apply to me."

"God's laws are above the laws of man," the Reverend Hood said, but Smith had already left.

The Reverend Hood watched as Smith stalked long-striding along the coast, with his hair — newly short of its pigtail — short and dark brown, and his back proudly erect. He walked with the peculiar gait of a seaman, as if he was compensating for the eternal swing of a ship, but with more purpose than a man casually passing his days. Hood watched for a moment and then sighed and returned to the duties of his parish.

Smith walked on, following the curve of the coast as he

headed east, automatically watching the sea with its busy ships. He stopped once to lift a piece of driftwood, which he fashioned into a staff with his knife, and walked on, relentless.

THE SINGING STOPPED THE SECOND SMITH ENTERED THE Dancing Horse Inn. A dozen faces turned to look at him as he stepped inside the door.

"Who the devil is that?" A man asked.

"The tide must have thrown it up," another replied, and a woman laughed, high-pitched and short.

Smith looked around, taking in the predatory eyes of the customers and details of the inn. The floorboards were of oak, possibly taken from a wrecked ship, while the walls were of lathe and plaster. A small fire burned in the far corner of the taproom, with an empty table on one side. On the other side sat an old man, holding a glass and scrutinising the newcomer through basilisk eyes. The scattering of men in the taproom all bore the stamp of the sea, with tarred canvas trousers or jackets, checked or striped shirts, and bright neckcloths. Some had brass or silver earrings, and two wore the old fashioned Monmouth cap. None made any move to welcome the newcomer.

Smith approached the counter, noticing the banner of a dancing white horse against a red background that hung above an array of bottles and kegs.

"Do you have a room?"

"The landlady deals with the rooms." The barman eyed the stranger up and down.

"Fetch her."

"Who the deuce are you to order me around?"

"Fetch her." Smith did not raise his voice.

"I'm here." The landlady emerged from the cellar beneath the taproom. She examined the stranger from the soles of his scuffed boots to the top of his battered tricorn hat. "You look like a seafaring man," she said, noting the weather-darkened face and the stern eyes that returned her gaze.

"Do you have a room?"

"How long for?" The landlady had spent her life dealing with men of all types. One more stranger could not unsettle her.

"Until I no longer need it."

"I'll need payment in advance."

In reply, the stranger extracted a half-sovereign from his leather purse and pushed it across the scarred oak of the counter.

The landlady lifted the gold. "And I'll need your name in case a Riding Officer asks for you."

The stranger heard the guffaw of laughter from the taproom and knew that no Customs and Excise officer would be welcome in the Dancing Horse. Riding Officers was a polite name for the Excisemen; Smith had heard them called a great deal worse. "I've come to the right place then," he said. "My name is Smith. John Smith."

"A fine name to hide behind," the landlady said. "Up the stairs and first door on the right." She handed over a heavy key.

Smith sensed the gaze of every man in the taproom following him as he ascended the stairs. He did not care. *Let them look to their heart's content, for they will see a lot more of me in future.*

The room was small, dark, and stuffy, yet compared to the fo'c'sle of a man-of-war, it was the palace of a king. Smith dragged open the internal shutters and opened the multi-paned window to allow fresh air and light inside. From the window, Smith had a view down the main street of the village of Kingsgate to the harbour, where the masts of coasters punctured the heavy grey sky. A single cart negotiated the ancient High Street, with the driver hunched forward, allowing the horse to pick its way along a road it had probably known all its life.

The bed was hard, with a straw mattress under a threadbare grey wool blanket. Smith removed the mattress, guessing it would harbour colonies of unwelcome vermin. The planks beneath were

lock of his new pistol and feeling the sharpness of the flint. "Now, madam, who did these three work for?"

The landlady began to shake her head, recognised the expression in Smith's eyes and stopped. "Who says they work for anybody?"

"They don't have the brains to organise anything," Smith eased the pistol into his belt. "Yet this inn is the centre for free trade in the village."

"Is it?" the landlady asked.

Smith touched the silk scarf around the landlady's throat, then pointed to the keg of French brandy that stood, half-hidden in a corner. "It is."

The landlady raised her eyebrows. "They work for Richard Blackwell. Captain Richard Blackwell."

Smith nodded. "Pray inform Captain Richard Blackwell that I wish to see him."

"I'll pass your message on," the landlady promised.

In the far corner, the old man looked away. For a moment, his eyes had sparkled as though the altercation in the taproom had revived a long-dormant fire. When Smith left, the old man returned to contemplating the contents of his tankard.

Chapter Two

Smith stood under the wind-twisted apple tree, staring out to sea. Over there, less than thirty miles away, the French coast marked the frontier of continental Europe. The narrow English Channel acted as a defensive moat between the two landmasses but also as a highway between two nations, Great Britain and France. The two cultures were more similar than either would care to admit, with a shared history of violence and conquest. The people of both nations owed allegiance to a man claiming royal blood, both had a crust of arrogant aristocracy, both lived by trade, and both competed for colonies across most of the nations of the world. Given all these similarities, combined with their proximity, it was natural that the two countries were rivals and enemies.

Ignoring the wind that drove cold rain against his face, Smith scanned the early morning sea, recognising the purpose of every vessel, from the fleet of local fishing boats to the Royal Navy frigate hurrying on its ceaseless patrol. Shifting his gaze, Smith looked down on Kingsgate, with the two inns set on opposite sides of the High Street, the ancient church, and the houses that straggled down to the harbour.

On one side of the High Street, the Dancing Horse was a

traditional oak-framed Kent house, with a central hall now used as the taproom and diagonal bracing supporting jutting eaves. A lookout tower thrust from one side, a virtual guarantee that smugglers used the inn as a rendezvous. Behind the inn, and accessed by a high-arched gateway, were stables for any passing traveller. Across the road from the Dancing Horse sat the larger, brick-built Hounds Rest, the coaching inn for Kingsgate, with a large courtyard at the back where horses were the innkeeper kept horses for the stagecoaches that rattled along the coast to London.

Smith nodded. The two inns encapsulated the division in Kingsgate, with the respectable establishment of the Hounds Rest and the more disreputable Dancing Horse, a centre for the broken people and those outside the framework of the law.

Smith contemplated the village. "I'm back," he said, "but I'm not me."

The memories returned, as they had so often. Smith recalled the betrayal, the humiliation, the frustration, and the sense of defeat. His hand moved automatically to his throat and fiddled with his neckcloth before he forced it back down.

Smith altered his stance under the tree and looked further inland, where Kingshunt Manor stood on its knoll, surrounded by a belt of woodland, groomed policies, and avenues of trees. Even from this distance, Smith could sense the aura of wealth, privilege, and power emanating from Kingshunt. He studied the outline of the house, noting the belvedere turret that the owner had recently added and the broad sweeping view inland.

"I haven't forgotten," Smith said. "We'll dance, Sir Francis, you and I." He felt the anger rise within him as a montage of memories ripped through his mind. Once again, his hand moved towards his throat.

"No," Smith shook himself back to the present. "This is not the time to think backwards." He looked out to sea, nodding in satisfaction.

The two-masted lugger lay a mile offshore, backing her sails against the now fluky wind.

"You'll do," Smith said.

That evening, the High Street was quiet, with rain weeping from the roofs onto the ground and people huddled against the cold wind. Smith walked through the village until he arrived at Hop Lane that extended at right angles to the High Street. A man lounged at the entrance to the lane, shielding the bowl of his long-stemmed pipe as he contemplated the view to the sea.

"It's a fine evening," Smith said.

"It's a bit cold," the man said, removing the pipe from his mouth.

"The moon will be out tonight," Smith said.

"Three-quarters moon, I reckon." The man replaced the pipe with his deep brown eyes never straying from Smith's face.

"Light enough for a run."

The man puffed blue smoke. "It could be," he agreed.

Smith lifted his head to test the wind. Somewhere in the village, a dog barked while a farrier hammered out a horseshoe. "With this breeze and the way the tide runs, Spike Cove would be an interesting place to visit."

"It may be," the man removed his pipe again, adding tobacco to the bowl.

Touching his hat with his forefinger, Smith strolled back along the High Street and leaned against the wall of the inn. As he had suspected, the man with the long-stemmed pipe vacated his position and walked casually down Hop Lane.

"Right to the Preventative men," Smith murmured in satisfaction.

The dog had stopped barking now as the farrier gave a final few blows to his horseshoe. Quiet returned to Kingsgate, the peace before the storm struck.

AT ONE TIME, THE SPIKE HAD BEEN AN IMPORTANT, THOUGH small, manor house. Local legend claimed that its origins extended to the days when the Jutes had first landed on Britain's southern shores, centuries before England existed. Smith did not know if local lore was correct. Nor did he know that the Spike had flourished in the sixteenth and seventeenth centuries. The owner had chosen the losing side in the Civil War, and now the Spike was a ghost of itself; a sad, wind-buffeted ruin that overlooked Spike Cove. Only furtive lovers and stray sheep used the crumbling stones for shelter, but that evening Smith settled himself in a corner of tumbled masonry and watched events unfold.

First to arrive were the Riding Officers, the mobile strike force of the Excise Service that patrolled the coast watching for signs of the Free Traders. They rode with their cloaks billowing behind them, and their hats firmly pushed down on their heads until they took up position in Kittiwake Wood to the east of the cove. When a stray gust of wind nearly blasted the leading rider's cloak, Smith saw the holstered pistol at his saddle.

"Three men, well mounted, but insufficient for the task in hand," Smith said to himself.

Hurrying behind the riding officers were a group of tidewaiters, the foot soldiers of the Excise.

"Underpaid, overworked, and never appreciated," Smith murmured. "You are the front line and the most vulnerable of the Excise."

Next to arrive were the infantry, King George's final say in maintaining law and order in his realm. Half a company of redcoats, each man with a long-tailed coat on his back and a Brown Bess musket pressed against his shoulder.

"Fifty men, well-drilled, but slow-moving and with rigid discipline long since removing any flexibility of mind," Smith said.

After the infantry came the Collector, fresh from his home and headquarters in Hop Lane, riding with his Churchwarden-smoking assistant at his side.

"Two men dedicated to collecting taxes for the king's revenue," Smith told himself. "One an incomer to the village, the other a paid informer, a local man without friends."

Behind the Excisemen rode their escort of five dragoons, with their equipment jingling and their horses' hooves churning mud from the track.

"Five proud horsemen, sabres at the ready, happy to cut and thrust," Smith said. "Heavy men on heavy horses, with heavy blades."

Behind the dragoons rode a tall, vibrant man. He sat upright, with a pair of pistols at his saddle and a whip in his hand.

"And there rides the squire," Smith felt the hatred build up inside him, "the brains and the heartbeat of the king's presence in Kent. Sir Francis Selby, squire of Kingshunt Manor." For the next few minutes, Smith studied Selby, committing every detail of the squire to his memory, from the square jaw to his seat on the high-stepping brown stallion.

Twenty minutes after the squire's arrival, a slow convoy of wagons lumbered from the village and surrounding countryside, rocking and jolting on the rutted road.

"The carriers," Smith said. "Transport for the law-breakers, the lifeblood of free trade here in the deep south. Fifteen wagons, drawn by twenty-nine horses, all empty and all hoping to return full."

Lastly, a small body of country folk and villagers arrived, some on foot, a few mounted, with the three principals well-known to Smith. They followed the wagons down the steep track to Spike Cove, which sheltered in a gap between hundred-foot-high cliffs.

"Now, all we need is Captain Blackwell and his lugger," Smith said, "and the stage is set for the dance."

As the sun set, the lugger unfurled her topsails and eased towards Spike Cove, where the wagons congregated to carry away her cargo. Men clustered, smoking and talking, some chewing tobacco, others sitting on rocks. One extended a brass telescope and watched the lugger ghost landward. They were relaxed, with nobody thinking to post a sentry and one man even scraping out a tune on a fiddle.

Perched in his eyrie at the Spike, Smith watched as the redcoats emerged from Kittiwake Wood and marched across the fields, scattering the sheep. They formed a semi-circle quarter of a mile from the cove and rested on their muskets, a thin scarlet line waiting for orders. Only when they were in position did Sir Francis Selby and his retinue, including the Riding Officers, leave the wood to ease down the steep track to Spike Cove.

"The musicians are tuning up," Smith murmured. "The band is ready."

Although gathering darkness hid much of the drama from Smith, he could judge what was happening from the sounds that drifted towards him. He heard the bellow of a command and the high, surprised shouts of defiance as the Free Traders refused the order to stand.

"Stand in the King's name!"

"Bugger off!"

"Run for it, lads!"

The crack of a pistol startled the night, followed by a ragged volley and the hollow drumbeat of hooves as the dragoons cantered across the foreshore to the landing spot. Smith heard more shooting, with the flash of the muzzle flares bright in the night, and then, dimly, he saw a confusion of men hurrying on the track from the cove, with unladen carts and wagons among them. Carters used their whips as they strove to escape the forces of authority, with the sound of sporadic gunfire coming from the shore.

Chapter Three

The landlady passed across Smith's tankard without a word and glanced fearfully at the door. Three women sat in the taproom, trying to comfort a fourth who wept uncontrollably. The old man in the corner watched everything, said nothing, and sipped at his beer.

"You're quiet tonight," Smith said.

"Didn't you hear the news?" The landlady snapped.

"What news was that?"

The landlady busied herself in polishing a pewter tankard. "Sir Francis Selby and the Excise men rounded up most of the village."

"Why would he do that?" Smith sipped at his ale.

The landlady stared at him for a moment before she replied. "Sir Francis thinks they were running a cargo ashore."

"And were they?" Smith asked.

"Yes."

Smith nodded and took another swallow before he spoke again. "What happened to the villagers?"

"They're in the squire's lock-up."

"Is that why that woman's upset?" Smith nodded to the crying woman.

"Yes. Sir Francis has taken her man."

Smith took another drink. "Where is Sir Francis's lock-up?" He asked as if he did not already know the answer. "Is it in Kingsgate?"

"No," the landlady shook her head. "It's the Chapel Prison, on Sir Francis's land, close by his house of Kingshunt Manor."

Smith finished his ale, wiped his mouth with the back of his hand and nodded. "Who's the turnkey?"

The landlady frowned. "Will Archer. He's been there for years."

Smith knew the name. "We'd better see about releasing the lads, then, before Sir Francis recognises them." He stamped both feet on the sawdust-covered wooden floorboards. "He'll have them hanged, else, or pressed into the Navy, and then you'll have no customers."

"What?" the landlady looked up in astonishment, but Smith was already stepping outside the inn. The woman continued to weep, with her friends trying to console her with a glass of gin. The old man in the corner put his tankard on the table and followed Smith outside.

THE MEMORIES RETURNED AS SMITH STRODE THROUGH Kingsgate and onto Sir Francis's land. The squire had built a tall wall to keep the villagers off his property and doubtless had at least one gamekeeper on patrol, but Smith slipped over the wall with ease. Although it was well over a decade since Smith had last been on the Manor's lands, the area was familiar, and he strode forward without hesitation until he reached the lock-up. The building was ancient, a mediaeval chapel that the Selbies had grabbed during Henry VIII's purge of the Roman Catholic Church and subsequently abandoned. Sir Francis's father had strengthened the building and used it as the parish prison. Drunkards, poachers, wife-beaters, petty thieves, and smugglers knew the inside of these walls before Sir Francis's men transported them to the Maidstone or Rochester Assizes for trial and sentence. As the local justice of the peace or magistrate, Sir Francis would try the lesser cases himself, pronouncing instant and stern justice.

While the exterior of the lock-up was unprepossessing, rubble-built stone unrelieved by any surviving window, the interior was worse. Smith remembered the sour stench, the rustle of rats on damp straw, and the pervading atmosphere of gloom. The shadow of the lash, the pillory, or the noose encircled the thoughts of every prisoner.

Smith shook off the old memories as he surveyed the Chapel Prison, as the locals termed the building. He walked quietly, sure of the route, knowing the layout of the policies and the location of every building but watchful for gamekeepers and mantraps. Twenty yards from the Chapel Prison, the turnkey's cottage squatted beneath a pall of blue smoke. The house was close enough to the lock-up to be handy yet sufficiently distant for the turnkey to separate himself from the stench and misery.

Smith grunted. He knew Will Archer was a nocturnal animal, a man who seldom ventured outside during the day but infested his cottage and emerged only to lock the prisoners up and occasionally feed them. After an evening check to ensure the Chapel Prison was locked, Archer sat by his fire, reading his Bible and muttering the passages to himself.

"Praying to God to give him the strength to harass his prisoners," Smith said. "I know you, Will Archer."

Without hesitation, Smith cut a wedge of turf from immediately outside the lock-up and hoisted himself onto Archer's cottage roof. He placed the turf on top of the squat chimney, blocking the passage of smoke and slid back to the ground. Ten minutes later, the cottage door opened, and the turnkey staggered out, coughing and enveloped in smoke. Smith was waiting beside the door with his pistol in his hand. As Archer emerged,

Smith smashed his pistol barrel on the man's head, knocking him to the ground.

"Are you conscious?" Smith kicked the turnkey in the ribs. When the man did not stir, Smith dragged him back inside the cottage. The interior was austere but surprisingly neat, with a table and chairs, a box bed, and a bookcase replete with religious books. One wall held an assortment of manacles, chains, and heavy padlocks, together with a whip. Smith grunted, remembering that the turnkey also performed the task of village flogger when Sir Francis ordered such a punishment. Beside this grim array was a large bunch of keys.

"Right, you bastard," Smith said, pulled Archer's hands behind his back, and handcuffed his right wrist to his left ankle and left wrist to his right ankle. Removing Archer's boots, Smith gagged him with one of his socks. "Lie quiet now, and I hope you choke."

A glance at the bookcase revealed a leather-bound account book. Smith opened it and scanned the pages until he found the names of all Archer's prisoners, with a column noting their sentences.

Lifting the book and the keys, Smith left the cottage and shut the door, trying each key until he found one to lock the turnkey within his home. Cursing his soft heart, he scaled the roof again and removed the turf so the turnkey would not choke to death.

"You'll keep until later," Smith said as he strode to the Chapel Prison.

Without the moon, the darkness was intense, and only the call of an owl and the distant hush of the sea pierced the silence. Smith glanced over in the direction of Kingshunt Manor, momentarily tempted to walk over.

"No," he told himself. "Time enough for that later. You will keep, Sir Francis, until I decide what is best."

He arrived at the Chapel Prison, with the studded, arched

door locked before him. He tried three of the larger keys before finding one that fitted the lock.

"Is there anybody in here?" Smith shouted as he turned the key. The response came in half a dozen voices, mostly obscene.

Smith placed the book against the wall and stepped inside, rattling the keys. "Lie quiet, boys," he ordered. "We don't want to alert Sir Francis." He felt along a shelf beside the door until he reached a tallow dip. "There must be a strike-a-light here some-where." His fingers found a tinder box in the form of a pistol. It was the work of an instant to pull the trigger and create a spark to light the dip, and by its flickering light, he looked around the interior.

A score of men and three women slumped on the stone-slabbed floor, staring at him but unsure who he was in the semi-darkness.

"Out you get, people," Smith ordered, putting the tinder box in his pocket, "unless you wish to enjoy more of the squire's hospitality."

Two men remained in the lock-up once the remainder rushed outside.

"What's to do?" Smith lifted the dip higher, so yellow light pooled onto the prisoners.

In reply, one of the men rattled the chains that secured him to the wall. His eyes glittered like a fox as Smith stepped closer.

"Let me see," Smith said.

The links were rusted and old, while a heavy padlock fastened them together. When the prisoner looked up hopefully, Smith recognised his old adversary with the pockmarked face.

"We'll soon have you out," Smith said. The fourth key opened the padlock. "You're free," Smith said. "Did Sir Francis get your name? Or would he recognise you?"

"No," Pockmark shook his head. "It was dark, and he was too busy. He said he'd attend to us all tomorrow."

The second chained prisoner was the lean man. "Who are you?" he asked.

"I am John Smith; who are you?"

"Ebenezer Skinner," the lean man rubbed his wrists when Smith removed the rusted manacles. "Why are you helping us?"

"That's my business. Remain here if you wish, Skinner. Sir Francis will either create some false charge to have you hanged at the assizes or send you to the Navy for smuggling."

Skinner nodded, threw Smith a sidelong look, and slid out of the building. Smith followed, lifted the book, and tossed the bunch of keys into the quiet waters of the River Spike. He began to head back to the village, but on an impulse, he altered direction and walked towards Kingshunt Manor.

The nearer Smith came to the Manor, the more groomed the surroundings until he walked on close-cropped grass that felt as soft as a Turkish carpet. The mansion loomed ahead in an array of windows and smooth walls. Two towers thrust to the sky; a dominant tall turret from where Sir Francis could survey his lands, and a smaller belvedere tower, where he could entertain his guests.

Scattered around the grounds were marble and bronze statues, some ancient souvenirs of Sir Francis Grand Tour of Europe, and others more recent. The Classical gods and goddesses appeared relaxed in the prosperous surroundings as if Kingshunt Manor was a second Mount Olympus.

Smith stood beside a marble Venus in the centre of the lawn, looking at each window in turn, wondering which one looked out from Sir Francis' bedroom.

"Where are you, squire," Smith said. "Where is your lair?"

He paced around the house with his emotions burning within him, a mixture of anger, frustration, and hatred that he knew impaired his ability for rational thought.

Calm yourself, Smith thought. *You'll gain nothing by acting on impulse.*

When a curtain twitched in an upstairs room, Smith stood still and stared upwards. For one moment, he saw a face peering out. It had been a decade, ten hard years since Smith had last seen her, but he immediately recognised the face. He gazed at her, absorbing every detail of her features, from the broad brow to the firm chin, and then she was gone. Smith stood forlorn on the vast green lawn, with the statues mute witnesses to his discomfort.

I haven't forgotten, Smith told himself. *I will never forget.*

He turned and stalked away with his heels leaving distinct impressions on the grass. Only then did the old man shift from his position under the trees. He rubbed a hand over the grey stubble on his chin, pulled a pipe from his pocket, and chuckled.

———

"I DON'T KNOW WHO YOU ARE, MISTER, BUT YOU'RE NOT A Preventative man. I'll bet my boots on that." Skinner pushed a tumbler of gin over to Smith.

"Your boots are safe," Smith said. "I'm neither a Preventative man nor an Exciseman." He tasted the gin.

"You locked the turnkey in his house and freed the lot of us," Skinner slurred his words as a river of alcohol took control of his speech. "Sir Frankie will be apoplectic."

"I hope so," Smith sipped at his gin. "Did Sir Francis see any of your faces in the dark?"

"No, but he knows who we are."

"If the squire didn't see you, he can prove nothing," Smith said. "First thing tomorrow morning, I want you to report that a gang from another village stole all your wagons. Act as indignant as you can, request that Sir Francis organises a search for the raiders and offer the services of all the village to help the squire."

Skinner raised his eyebrows. "Do you wish us to act the injured innocents?"

"That's correct. Bluff him. How many men did the soldiers shoot?"

"They killed one man."

23

"Say he was the only villager to join the smugglers. What happened to the famous Captain Blackwell?"

"He got away, but we lost all the cargo. All of it." Skinner banged a hard hand on the table in frustration.

Smith noted that Skinner trusted him sufficiently to admit they were free traders. "Where is the cargo held?"

"In the King's Warehouse, down by the harbour."

Smith finished his gin. "Thanks for the drink. Retrieve your wagons, then get the cargo back out."

"It's the King's Warehouse," Skinner repeated. "With a military guard."

"Are you scared of a few lobsters?" Smith allowed the question to hang in the air as he stood. "Let me know when you grow a backbone."

"Where are you going?" Skinner asked.

"To bed," Smith told him. "I have a busy day tomorrow." He was aware that the landlady watched as he climbed the creaking stairs. The landlady was the lynchpin of the Dancing Horse. Smith knew that if he won her trust, he had made a significant step forward.

That process could begin the following day.

Chapter Four

"She's a Froggie, right enough." A man with a lined face sat at the lookout with the telescope fully extended and focussed out to sea. "I know that by her lines."

"A Frenchie? What the devil does she want here, Hargreaves?" Captain Blackwell asked.

Down in the taproom, Smith listened to their conversation as he scanned the newspaper and puffed smoke from his pipe.

"It's a raiding party, sure as death," Hargreaves said. "There's a second ship to the west."

"Well, rot me," Blackwell said. "Where's the Navy we pay so much in taxes for? How did the French get past the blockade and evade the frigates?" He shook his head. "No matter. Call out the men, Hargreaves."

"Are we going to fight them?"

"You're damned right we are," Blackwell said. "I want every able-bodied man gathered on the green, with whatever weapons they can find." When Blackwell ran down the stairs, shouting for his crew, Smith ascended to the lookout. He lifted the telescope and focussed on the two approaching vessels before returning to his position in the taproom. The old man in the corner watched Smith for a moment before stiffly rising to his feet.

"You'll need me, Captain Blackwell," he said.

"Sit down, you doddering old fool," Blackwell snarled. "You'll get yourself killed."

Smith sensed the old man's disappointment as Blackwell stood in the centre of the room.

"Muster every man jack at the village green," Blackwell shouted. "Where's Skinner? Where's that lazy bugger?"

"He's at home with his wife," Hargreaves said.

"Kick his arse and send him to Marsham," Blackwell ordered. Marsham was about twice the size of Kingsgate and lay three miles to the east. "Tell the army to come here fast. It's only a militia regiment, but the French don't know that." He turned to Smith. "And you — Smith, isn't it?"

"John Smith," Smith agreed, nursing his tumbler of rum and wondering if this new development would hinder his plans for the day.

"I want you as well. You have a pistol, so you can shoot a Frenchman."

Smith sipped at his tumbler. "You can go without me." He did not look at Blackwell, although he assessed Kingsgate's leading smuggler. Tall, with a strong face, Blackwell was undoubtedly a forceful man, with bright blue eyes and the look of a seaman.

Blackwell's face coloured. "You yellow bastard! Won't you fight for your country?"

Smith put his rum on the table. "I've had my share of fighting for King Geordie."

"You're a coward," Blackwell said with contempt.

Smith smiled, still refusing to meet Blackwell's gaze. "Maybe a coward, but not a fool."

"I'll see off the French," Blackwell promised, "and then I'll return for you, cully."

"You do that," Smith said, sitting still while nearly all the men and many of the women left the inn. Only the old man remained behind, looking wistfully at the door.

"You're smiling, Mr Smith," the landlady said, polishing a glass. "Are you not going to fight the French?"

"I've already fought them," Smith finished his rum.

"Do you intend to sit there all day?"

"No." Smith held out his glass for a refill. "Do you have a hiding place here?"

"A hiding place?" the landlady repeated, with a trace of anger in her voice.

"You won't keep free trade goods in open view in case the Excise calls, and you'll have somewhere to conceal seamen when the Press comes," Smith explained his reasoning.

A look of contempt crossed the landlady's face. "I didn't expect that from you." She poured out Smith's rum. "I thought better of you when you freed the prisoners from the Chapel Prison."

Smith ignored the insult. "How many men can your hidey-hole hold?"

"A dozen, if they cram in," the landlady told him. "You'll have plenty of room on your own when all the *men* are fighting."

Smith grunted. "You had better get it ready, landlady," Smith said. "These ships aren't French. They're Royal Navy."

"Royal Navy?" The landlady grasped the situation immediately. Her expression altered to alarm. "A press gang? Are you sure?"

"It's a hot press. Admiral Rodney is taking a fleet to the Caribbean, and he'll need every man he can muster." Smith swallowed his rum.

The landlady's frown returned. "Are you not going to inform the men?"

Smith sighed. "I am, once Captain Blackwell has them all gathered together." He stood up and grabbed his hat. "Get prepared for an invasion, Landlady."

Most of the male population of Kingsgate village, and a high proportion of the females, was gathered on the village green, most holding a weapon, from a simple staff to a fowling piece or musket. Kingsgate's green was triangular, with a small stream trickling into a pond at the lower end, beside the expected stocks. Blackwell stood in the centre, giving orders to defend the village.

"Men with firearms, I want you to stand in the harbour, ready to greet the French when they land. Men with cutlasses or staffs, you will charge forward only after the first volley."

"How about the women?" One bold-eyed virago asked. "We can fight as well as any man!"

"Keep out of the way," Blackwell said.

"Stand aside, Captain Blackwell," Smith demanded. "I have something to say."

"You?" Blackwell did not move as Smith stepped beside him.

"These ships are not French," Smith raised his voice. "They're Royal Navy, probably going to land a press gang."

"They're French," Blackwell said. "They wear the lilies!"

"Royal Navy," Smith repeated, "and you have all the men gathered in one place for them to scoop up."

While Blackwell's crew stood by him, other villagers began to drift away from the green.

"I don't mind fighting the French," one scrawny man said, busily polishing thick spectacles. "But I'm not going into the Navy!" He moved away. "Come on, Oby," he tugged at the sleeve of a man of mighty muscles.

"You're losing your little army, Captain Blackwell," Smith pointed out as more men followed the bespectacled man's example.

"Stand with me!" Blackwell shouted. "We have to fight the French!"

Smith stepped back. "I'll leave you, Captain Blackwell." He withdrew, knowing that he could do no more. The cautious and intelligent would leave, while the most loyal of Blackwell's crew would stand by him.

The virago watched Smith walk away. "What if it is the French?" she demanded.

"It's not," Smith told her. "Depend on it; these vessels are Royal Navy under a false flag. They know the men of Kent will gather to fight the French, and they'll snatch everybody they can."

I've been part of Royal Naval press gangs, my lady. I know how they operate.

"What's happening, then?" the landlady asked as Smith returned to the inn. About twenty women had gathered there, some seeking information and others simply nervous.

"I spread the news," Smith said. "Some of the men will go into hiding, but Captain Blackwell is adamant the ships are French."

"What will happen?" One woman asked. "My husband is with the captain."

"The press will take everybody," Smith said. "With or without Protections. If Rodney is heading to the West Indies, they'll be gone for months, perhaps years, and any complaints about taking protected men will be long forgotten by the time they return." He paused for a moment. "If they return. The death rate beyond the Line is appalling, with ague and Yellow Jack."

"Oh, God!" More than one of the women looked shocked.

"What will you do, Mr Smith?" the landlady demanded. "You seemed to be a resourceful man when you rescued the men from the Chapel Prison. Do you have something in mind?"

"I may have," Smith said. "I'll need some help, though. Are any of you ladies willing to stand by me? It might be dangerous."

"Will it get our men back?" the first woman asked.

"It may," Smith said. "I cannot make a promise."

"I'm with you," the woman said, and others either nodded or just stepped forward.

"Come with me," Smith said, with his plan only half-formed. "Let's have a look at the press."

More women joined Smith's band as they marched through Kingsgate, so he had more than thirty before he reached the beach. The Royal Naval ships had anchored well outside the harbour and sent the Press gang in six boats, three from each vessel. By the time Smith and the women reached the village green, the press had pounced on the villagers. As a ship's master, Blackwell was exempt, but the Navy had captured most of the others, knocking the fight from them with marline spikes, and was busily engaged in gathering them in a sullen, dejected group.

"Come, cheer up, my boys!" a smart midshipman crowed as an elderly lieutenant gave harsh orders. "You will fight for old England! For king, country, and religion! Damn the French, and damn the Pope!"

"Cocky little bastard, aren't you?" Smith said, counting the escort. "One snotty, one bitter, worn-out lieutenant, one experienced petty officer to keep them right, and ten smiling seamen. That's not the impress service, ladies; that's the ship's captain trying to increase his crew."

The women fidgeted. "What are we going to do about it?" a middle-aged woman demanded. "I have a foolish husband and two young sons in that crowd."

Smith nodded. "Do as I say, and we have a fighting chance. We're fortunate they're only men from an ordinary ship's company and not the official Impress Service. They won't know all the tricks."

Smith divided the women into two unequal groups. "You women," he said to one group. "You're now the Petticoat Artillery. I want you to gather stones. As many as you can. Hold them in your apron, or lift the front of your skirt and hold them there."

"You'll see my legs!" one woman said.

Smith glared at her. "I don't care a damn about your legs or any other part of you!"

The second group of women looked impatient. "What do you want us to do?" the bold eyed virago asked.

Smith's smile was devoid of humour. "You are the Petticoat

Marines, and we are going to steal boats," he glanced at the darkening sky. "And then I'm going to change you into men."

The virago glanced down at herself. "I'll need to grow something," she said and laughed.

"Are you prepared to fight for your husband?" Smith ignored her suggestion.

The virago nodded. "He's not much but better than nothing." She tossed back her blonde hair.

Other women agreed, some more enthusiastically than others.

"If you can't or won't fight," Smith said, "then return home now before it's too late."

One middle-aged, nervous woman left, followed by two others. The virago began to jeer.

"Don't sneer," Smith said. "It's better for those women to be honest now than hesitate later and put the operation in jeopardy."

"What do you want us to do?" The virago asked.

"Listen, and I'll tell you," Smith said.

The press gang had arrived in six open boats: two longboats, two gigs, and two launches. With the tide at full ebb, the water in the harbour was too shallow to float the Royal Naval vessels, which sat in the Downs, a quarter of a mile offshore. Smith studied the ships, unconsciously admiring their lines and critically examining their condition.

"The tides at full ebb," Smith said. "It will be four hours before these vessels can come closer ashore, and their boats are here."

"Is that good?" The virago had appointed herself as the spokeswoman of the Petticoat Marines.

"It means that the ship's captains cannot reinforce their men ashore." Smith looked at his two companies of women. They looked eager to fight and as fit and strong as most men with whom he had worked, with the virago watching Smith with especial intentness. "Are you all ready?"

"We're ready," the virago said.

"Oh, Suzanne!" A middle-aged woman with grey hairs said. "From what I've heard, you're always ready!"

Some of the other women gave a nervous, near-hysterical laugh as Suzanne smiled in response.

"Artillery, I want you behind the fishing fleet on the beach there. The tide is too low, and there will be no boats going out as long as the Navy's there. Get your stones ready."

The Artillery nodded and scurried away, lifting missiles as they moved.

"Marines, wait here, except you, Suzanne. We'll check on the press."

The convoy pushed slowly up the main street, with the press gang escorting the scared, bewildered, and angry captives. Smith watched from the deep shadows, noting that every man either had his hands deep in his trouser pockets or held tightly onto his waistband. The press gang had resorted to removing the captives' belts and cutting their waistbands to prevent them from running away. No man could run when his trousers fell to his ankles. Leading from the front, the arrogant midshipman strutted from the village green towards the harbour.

"That's enough, Suzanne. Let's warn the others."

Suzanne smiled and touched his arm as he withdrew to the beach. "Come on, Petticoat Marines!"

Smith measured the distance from the fishing fleet to the beached Royal Naval boats and began to walk purposely along the shore. Although he did not look behind him, he knew that the women were at his back, with their feet sliding and crunching on the loose shingle.

The Navy had left two boatmen to guard each of their boats, and every man looked up in surprise when the crowd of grim-faced women advanced toward them.

"What's the to do?" A stocky man asked. "What do you women want? Here! Steer clear, won't you?"

"No, we won't," Suzanne replied. "And you're the to do!"

Smith moved from a walk to a run. "Come on, Marines!"

The stocky man barely had time to yell before Smith was on him, knocking him to the ground and leaving him for the women before moving to the next boat. The second seaman was more prepared, lifting a marline spike and swinging at Smith's head.

"Would you, you bastard!" Smith ducked, jabbed straight fingers into the man's throat, grabbed his tarred pigtail, and banged his head off the boat's gunwale. He looked up, aware of a roar of noise as Suzanne led the women into a screaming charge at the other boats.

Although the seamen were rugged and redoubtable fighters, the outcome was never in doubt. The women were roused to fighting fury and determined to save their men. They fell on the seamen like a pack of hounds, grabbing at shirts and hair, flailing fists, and aiming shrewd kicks at groins and midriffs as the seamen retreated in bafflement.

"Don't kill them!" Smith warned. "We want them subdued, not slaughtered!"

The uneven contest was over within three minutes, with the boat guards bleeding, bruised, and under the watchful eyes of a score of women. Half a dozen women bore the marks of battle, parading bruises or cuts like battle honours. With her skirt raised high, Suzanne sat astride a tall man, alternately slapping him and asking him what he meant by trying to steal her husband.

"Where are my volunteer men?" Smith asked. "I want a dozen men." He nodded when Suzanne and most of the other women stepped forward.

"Change your clothes," Smith ordered.

"We didn't bring any man's clothing," A young woman said.

Smith indicated the captured seamen. "Take theirs. And hurry!"

"Turn your back," the young woman demanded.

"This isn't the time for foolish modesty," Suzanne said, but Smith obeyed.

Women dressed as men were a novelty that could have amused Smith in different circumstances, but he could hear the approach of marching feet and knew he had little time to spare. Taking his place in the nearest longboat, he ordered the women to keep the captured seamen lying in the bottom of their boats.

"Tie them up and gag them," Smith ordered urgently. "God knows there are plenty lengths of rope. And if any of them struggle, whack them on the head."

When the dozen male-dressed women took their places in the boats, Smith nodded to the remainder. "You people join your friends behind the fishing boats, and hurry! The press gang is nearly here!"

With the seamen tied hand and foot in the bottom of their boats, and the women trying their best to look masculine, Smith stood at the prow of the first longboat. He heard the roar of sound from the protesting prisoners and watched as the press gang approached, escorting a good proportion of Kingsgate's male population.

The jaunty midshipman marched in front, with the grey-haired lieutenant at his side and a score of seamen guarding their captives. Smith waited until the mob was clear of the village and shouted.

"Now! Artillery! Now!"

The first group of women rose from behind the fishing boats and unleashed a volley of stones at the press gang.

"Watch the villagers!" Smith warned as the women hurled their missiles with more enthusiasm than accuracy, and the stones thumped down on prisoners and press gang alike.

"Get these men onto the boats," the lieutenant took immediate action, as Smith expected from the Navy. "Mr Watt! Chase these women away, damn them!"

Smith waved his hand, encouraging the press to rush their captives forward. "Come on! Hurry!"

Smith's Petticoat Artillery threw another volley of stones and ran forward, making as much noise as possible, as Smith had demanded.

"You men!" Smith shouted to his disguised women. "Get these volunteers on board! Handsomely now!"

The wiry petty officer pushed the first of the pressed men towards Smith. "Take this ugly bugger!"

Smith caught the man and winked. "Get in the boat!" He ordered.

"Who the devil?" the man asked until Suzanne grabbed him by the collar.

"Get in the boat, Joe!"

Joe was not quick in the uptake. "What are you doing here?"

"Saving you, you useless bugger!" Suzanne slapped him across the head. "Get in the bloody boat before the Navy realises what's happening!"

As the first group of women charged the press and the beach became the scene of a free-for-all, Smith and the disguised women encouraged the pressed men onto the boats. "Get in!" Smith ordered, with the women urging their men.

"That's a woman!" the wiry petty officer belatedly realised that all was not well. "What's going on here?"

"You're right," Smith agreed. "It is a woman." He hit the petty officer with a belaying pin, knocking him to the shingle. He raised his voice to an Atlantic bellow. "Get these men on board! Handsomely now!"

The fight on the beach was going badly for the women, with the press gang, men selected for their toughness, pushing them back.

"Push off!" Smith ordered. "Let the men take the oars and dump the sailors over the side."

"Where are you going?" Suzanne asked as Smith stepped away from the boats.

"To help the artillery," Smith told her. "Head for Spike Cove, then run the men back to Kingsgate and get into the Dancing Horse. The landlady will hide you."

As the women hauled the still-bound seamen out of the boats and dropped them, less than gently, onto the beach, Smith strode towards the battle of the beach. "The boats are leaving!" he yelled. "The boats are leaving!"

The lieutenant glanced over his shoulder, and a look of fury crossed his face. "Get back here, you damned fools! We're still ashore!" He strode towards the boats, with some of his men following. Taking heart, the Petticoat Artillery charged again, temporarily pushing back the press gang.

Smith stepped back as Midshipman Watt ran into the sea, shaking his fist, and other seamen cut free the boat guards. Leaving the Navy to sort itself out, Smith ran towards his artillery.

"Break off!" he shouted. "Get back to the village!"

One by one, the women began to withdraw, with the fitter helping the casualties and all bearing some mark of combat. Smith put his arm around one limping woman and half-carried, half-dragged her back towards the village.

"Well done," Smith said, yet he wondered if it had all been worthwhile. He had made his name known but had also directly opposed Captain Blackwell, and he was not yet prepared for a confrontation.

The landlady looked up when Smith pushed open the door and deposited his burden on a bench. "A brandy for this hero," he ordered. "She needs it."

"On the house," the landlady said, watching him through musing eyes. "I heard what happened." She indicated the perspiring, bleeding, vociferous women who filled her taproom.

"The men should be here shortly," Smith said.

"Their accommodation is waiting," the landlady said, "although I doubt the press will return for some time." She allowed herself a smile. "You gave them a sound drubbing, Mr Smith."

"It was necessary, landlady," Smith said.

The landlady gestured for him to come closer. "My name is Mrs Martin," she told him. "Ruth to a selected few."

"Thank you, Mrs Martin," Smith held out his hand.

"Ruth," the landlady said, and Smith knew he had made a significant stride forward.

Chapter Five

Breakfast at the inn was quiet, with only a handful of early-morning travellers in the taproom, and Ruth dishevelled as she served everybody.

Smith ate the usual mutton chop, washed it down with a small beer, and listened to the intermittent, early-morning conversation at the nearest table without much interest.

"Did you hear about Duguay?" The speaker was squat, bald, and unshaven.

There was a long pause before his companion, a fellow carter, replied. "No. Who is he?"

"Duguay, the French corsair, the privateer."

"Oh, him, God rot his liver. What about him?"

The bald man slurped at his tankard. "The Navy captured him. HMS *Partridge* caught him cruising off Folkestone."

Smith listened with more attention. Captain Duguay was one of the best known French privateers, a skilled freebooter who had been the scourge of British seamen since the beginning of the present war. If the Navy had captured him, they had delivered a grievous blow to the local French war effort.

"Does that affect me?" the second carter asked. "Is this Duguay fellow going to attack my cart or steal my horse?"

"Unlikely now that the Navy has him," the bald man said.

"No, then I care less than nothing," the second carter snapped his fingers. "That for your Duguay."

Smith tucked the information away in case he needed it at a later date, although he could not imagine how. He finished his chop, looked up at the sound of a coach horn, and knew that the twice-weekly London Mail had pulled up at the Hounds Rest across the road.

"Go and fetch the newspaper," Ruth gave the stable boy a casual slap on the backside. "Hurry now."

The boy was back within two minutes, and Ruth pinned the newspaper to the wall before scanning the page.

"I see Ambrose Grant has another success," she said casually. "He's a rising star of the Preventative Service."

"I've heard of him," Smith said. "The government send him wherever the smuggling is most rife."

"That's correct," Ruth said. "He won't be coming to Kingsgate though, not now Sir Francis stopped the last cargo." She removed Smith's empty plate. "I'll have to increase my prices unless the Free Traders get to work again."

Smith rose to his feet. "Let's hope for good news," he said and nodded to the old man beside the fire.

SHORT GREY WAVES SPLINTERED IN A LONG LINE OF SILVER-white surf on the cold shingle shore. A dozen fishing boats sat on the beach, with their crews repairing their nets from the previous night's work, while a score of disconsolate seagulls explored the pebbles for any pickings the ebbing tide had left. Smith stood at the juncture of water and land, with his hat pulled low over his forehead and the wind whipping his cloak around his legs. Only two vessels sat in the harbour, a two-masted lugger with French lines and a dirty collier unloading her

39

cargo into a succession of carts, with Skinner giving orders to the carters.

"Take your load to the Hound's Rest," Skinner said to the squat carter. "And you two," he said to the next two men, "your coal is for Kingshunt Manor. For God's sake, don't go round the front, or Sir Frankie will have your hide. The coal cellars are round the back of the house."

To Smith's right, the ancient harbour wall marked man's attempt to pacify a minuscule section of the sea while a line of buildings faced south. Their windows were small, deep-set against the weather in unpretentious walls that were more functional than aesthetic. Only two of the buildings were of any size. One acted as a grain store for Sir Francis, and the other was the customs' warehouse, known locally as the King's Warehouse.

A pair of scarlet-uniformed soldiers stood sentry in front of the latter, one an undoubted old soldier with his nose inflamed and reddened and his eyes dulled by a lifetime of heavy drinking. The second man was decades younger, with the uniform's black leather stock holding erect a chin which had barely felt the snick of a razor. His eyes darted nervously from side to side at every sound and sight.

Quite right, Smith approved. *A veteran who knows all the tricks and a youngster to learn.*

Smith had stood at the same spot all morning, oblivious of the sea that licked at his boots. He watched the sentries as they performed their duties and noted the behaviour of the sergeant that escorted the changing of the guard. At two in the afternoon, Smith stepped away from his post and walked past the King's Warehouse, wishing the sentries a good afternoon.

The old soldier ignored him while the youngster grinned an acknowledgement.

Dancing

THE OLD MAN BESIDE THE FIRE WATCHED AS SMITH JERKED HIS head towards Skinner.

"Come here," Smith ordered. "I have a proposal for you."

Skinner sidled over, with the old man straining his ears to listen.

"The sentries change every four hours," Smith said, closing a ten-minute conversation. He tapped his fingers on the side of his pewter tankard. "That's the only occasion the sergeant visits them. I've watched the King's Warehouse for three days and three nights, and the routine never varies. An officer only appeared once, and he was an ensign with the cradle marks still on his arse."

"We'll have to speak to Captain Blackwell," Skinner said doubtfully, still in shock at the audacity of Smith's idea.

Smith leaned back, resting his head against the taproom wall. "If you find Blackwell, Skinner, I'll speak to him. Bring him to me at this inn."

Skinner flinched, as Smith had expected. "Captain Blackwell won't come to you, Mr Smith. He'll expect you to go to him."

"Will he, indeed," Smith said. "Well, if the mountain won't come to Muhammad, then Muhammad must go to the mountain."

"What?"

Smith saw the reference was wasted on Skinner. Common mariners and carters were not the most educated men, although they often picked up scraps of knowledge from their travels. "Tell me where I could find the elusive Captain Blackwell."

"I can't do that," Skinner said.

"Why not?" Smith already guessed the answer.

"He'd kill me."

Smith lifted his tankard and took a draught without dropping his gaze from Skinner's face. "In that case, Skinner, pray tell him that I wish to meet him."

"I'll do that, Mr Smith."

"Do it now," Smith placed his pistol on the table as a signal that he was in earnest.

"Yes, sir," Skinner said, standing up and stumbling to the door.

Smith allowed him a full minute before leaving the inn to follow. Guessing that Skinner would check behind him, Smith crossed the road and kept in the shadows, placing his feet on the ground simultaneously with Skinner's so his quarry would not hear his footsteps.

Twice Skinner stopped to look over his shoulder, and each time Smith remained still, merging with the dark. Once a dog barked at some nocturnal sound, and Skinner jerked nervously. Only when the dog's owner snarled it into silence did Skinner move on, leaving Kingsgate to take the coastal path to the east.

As they skirted Spike Cove, Skinner glanced down the cliff at the crashing sea and moved quicker before bowing his shoulders and increasing his pace to a near run.

The village of Marsham was three miles along the coast, a huddle of houses based around the harbour with three streets stretching inland. Skinner eased past the turreted Norman Church to where a dozen larger properties stood within walled gardens, separate from the village.

Skinner glanced around him nervously before he pushed open the gate of the smallest of the detached houses.

"That'll do me," Smith said and increased the length of his stride. He was in the garden before Skinner reached the front door of the house. A board on the wall boasted the name Seahaven, while light gleamed faintly from two of the five front windows.

"Captain Blackwell's residence, I presume?"

Pushing past the startled Skinner, Smith banged on the front door. He stepped back, unsure of his reception, and placed one hand on the butt of his pistol.

"Good evening, gentlemen." The maid who answered the door curtseyed politely. She was about twenty-five years old, with a pleasant round face and neat dark hair cut short. Deep brown eyes surveyed both men as she waited for somebody to speak.

"Is your master at home?" Smith asked, removing his hand from the pistol. He realised that Skinner had fled.

"Yes, sir." The maid dropped in another, deeper curtsey. "Who shall I say is calling?"

"John Smith."

"Pray to come in, sir." The maid opened the door wider.

Despite the lateness of the hour, lamplight still shone in the hall, revealing that the house's interior was as clean and simple as the exterior. Plain, solid furniture stood against the unpainted plaster walls, and two nautical pictures added character. The maid ushered Smith into a square reception room with a long oaken table, six chairs. and a mahogany chest of drawers. An array of decanters stood on top of a polished display cabinet. The curtains had not been drawn, not the shutters closed, allowing Smith to see through the tall, multi-paned window to the darkness outside. A second door, presumably into a wall cupboard, was inset on the left and decorated with a painting of a ship in full sail.

"I shall fetch the master," the maid said, curtseyed for the third time and swept away.

Smith hardly had time to inspect the room before Captain Blackwell arrived. "What the devil do you want here, Smith?" Blackwell overtopped Smith by a good four inches.

"Good evening, Captain Blackwell." Smith eyed the captain. Nature had not blessed Blackwell with a pleasing countenance, instead giving him a long, lugubrious face with thin lips that twisted upwards on the left side. The captain appeared tense, despite being master of his home.

"What do you want?" Blackwell asked again.

Smith noticed that Blackwell remained close to the chest of drawers. "I only wish your attention, Captain Blackwell."

"You have that." Blackwell's mouth twisted further.

"You lost your cargo a few days back," Smith said. "And you nearly lost your men."

Blackwell stepped along the length of the chest of drawers and placed his right hand on top as if he were caressing the wood. "Are my affairs any concern of yours?"

"I can help you regain your cargo," Smith said.

Captain Blackwell hesitated for a moment. "Who are you to interfere, Mr Smith?"

"Call me a well-wisher," Smith said.

"I don't care for strangers interfering in my business," Blackwell said. "I could set the dogs on you or whip you out of my house." When he produced a long pistol from the top drawer, Smith had anticipated the move.

"That's not very neighbourly," Smith pointed his pistol at the captain's stomach. He heard the cupboard door open behind him and the light patter of the maidservant's feet on the floorboards. He did not expect the cold pressure of a gun muzzle against the base of his spine.

"Neither was that, Mr Smith," the maidservant said coolly. Reaching around Smith's body, she removed the pistol from his grasp. "I'll have this weapon if you please, sir."

"Search him," Captain Blackwell ordered, as the broken-nosed man from the inn entered the room and took Smith's pistol. The maid patted Smith down as if she had experience in the procedure and removed the knife from his belt.

"Nothing else," the maid reported.

"Sit down, Smith," Blackwell indicated the chair at the foot of the table.

Smith sat down. With Captain Blackwell at the head of the table, his pistol in front of him, the maidservant at the side, and Broken-nose behind him, Smith decided it were best to remain still.

"Now, John Smith, if that is your name, tell me your plan to regain my cargo."

"I'd take it from the King's Warehouse," Smith said at once, holding Blackwell's gaze.

"That will be a hanging offence," Blackwell leaned forward.

"Only if they catch you."

"I caught you handsomely enough," Blackwell said dryly. His lip curled another fraction of an inch. "And who will put his head in the noose to do the deed?"

"Who is the leader here?" Smith asked. "You? This fellow here?" He jerked his head in the direction of Broken-nose. "Or perhaps your maidservant? Does she keep you in place with curtain lectures?" Smith watched as anger darkened Blackwell's already saturnine face.

"I am the captain," Blackwell said.

"Then you must do the deed." Smith leaned back in his chair. "If your nerves are strong enough." He saw Blackwell's anger intensify, overcoming the captain's caution.

"What do you suggest?" Blackwell's fingers began to dance on the table.

"Wait until the sentries are three hours into their duty," Smith said. "By that time, they are cold, bored, and lax. Distract them with a woman or a bottle, overpower them, and break into the warehouse. Simple and direct."

"There will be repercussions," Blackwell said.

Smith smiled. Despite the guns pointed at him, he was in control of the situation. "Don't do it if you are afraid." He knew he had forced Blackwell into a corner.

Blackwell's face darkened further. "Tell me the details."

Captain Blackwell was now the supplicant. Smith stood up, dipped his finger in the decanter of French brandy, and drew a rough plan of Marsham on the table top. "Gather round," he said, "and I'll show you."

Chapter Six

Dense clouds hid the moon while a chill breeze lifted spindrift from the Channel waves. Smith checked that his pistol was secure in his belt, and the knife sat snug against his hip. He wore dark clothing with soft-soled boots, smeared soot over his face to conceal his features, and fastened a handkerchief over his mouth and nose as a further disguise.

"Is that you, Smith?" Blackwell stood in the shadow of the ancient Saxon St Dunstan's church, with the gravestones spreading beneath the creaking boughs of a yew tree and the square tower of the church thrusting to the darkness.

"There's no need to broadcast my name," Smith said.

"Dymar is here, too," Blackwell indicated Broken-nose, who hid his features behind a black kerchief and carried a brace of pistols in his broad leather belt. A cutlass slapped his left hip with every step.

"And Skinner, I see." Smith nodded to the other men. "I have met the other fellow but do not have the pleasure of his name."

"Glear," the pockmarked man said. "Mathew Glear." He touched his hat to Smith in a gesture that irritated Blackwell.

"Smith's only helping here," Blackwell snarled. "I'm in charge."

"You'll have the wagons ready, Mr Skinner?" Smith asked.

"They're ready." Skinner was surly in the presence of Captain Blackwell.

Smith held Blackwell's gaze for a long ten seconds, and then he grinned. "Let's go and twist King George's tail."

The sentries stood at their posts, the younger man visibly shivering in the onshore wind, the older as immobile and stony-faced as a granite cliff.

"The older man will be a problem," Smith said.

"I'll take care of him." Blackwell lifted his head.

Smith hid his smile. "I'll quieten the other. We'll approach from opposite sides, so we don't appear to be together."

"Don't try to give me orders, cully." Blackwell thrust a pistol into his belt and pulled his cloak closed.

"Help Captain Blackwell, Dymer," Smith ordered. "You too, Glear. Don't make it too obvious."

"What will I do?" Skinner asked. He waited slightly to the rear of the others.

"You're the wagon man," Smith said. "I want them at the door of the King's Warehouse in half an hour, with three minutes to load each wagon."

"You make it sound like a military operation."

"We're at war," Smith said. He did not tell Skinner who his enemy was.

The memories returned, crowding into his mind as if clamouring to be released from imprisonment inside Smith's past. He tried to push them away, but there were too many. Even after the passage of so many years, they were as vivid as they had always been.

The nooses swayed above him, dancing in the breeze as he looked up. Beside him, his father stood with the swelling bruise on his face and his hands shackled behind his back.

"It's a short drop," his father said, with his voice hard. "So we'll dance for quite some time before we die. Be brave."

"I will," Smith said, fighting the tears that threatened to unman him.

"Don't let Sir Francis see you are afraid," his father said. "Live bold, die game, and spit in the eye of the establishment. It's all the buggers deserve."

The cart jolted to a halt under the gallows, with the crowd surging around, some shouting encouragement, others jeering, and most merely hoping for a good spectacle, free entertainment to pass a pleasant afternoon.

Smith saw his mother near the front, hiding her tears as she watched. Between the crowd and the gallows, a line of scarlet-clad soldiers stood with fixed bayonets. A sergeant watched them, holding his halberd, while a stern-faced officer paced behind the ranks. Beyond the crowd and below Gallows Hill, the smiling fields of Kent stretched to the sea, with little villages and farmhouses a reminder that life would continue after the gallows had done its work.

"Up you get, lads," the hangman said. He helped them to their feet and placed the noose around their necks. The hemp was rough on Smith's tender skin. His father gave him a wink.

"You're becoming a man before your time," Smith's father said. "It's a damned shame for you."

The vicar came close to offer spiritual guidance, but Smith's father waved him away. "Begone, you damned hypocrite. You eat at Sir Francis's table and fornicate with his servant girls, then preach redemption and sin on a Sunday. You're worse than any of us!"

Behind the crowd, on a slight rise that formed the second hump of Gallows Hill, the local gentry sat in their carriages to watch the hangings. Sir Francis, the new landowner after his father's death, was talking to his assistant and laughing. Smith's father raised his voice to a bellow that had sounded above the roar of a Channel gale.

"Damn your eyes, Francis Selby, you murdering, lying bastard. May you never have a moment's peace from this day until Judgement day. I curse you in living and in dying, in eating and drinking, in waking and sleeping."

Sir Francis cupped a hand to his ear as if he could not hear and then gave the hangman signal. The hangman cracked his hand on the horse's rump, and the cart jerked forward, tumbling both condemned men from their perch. Smith felt the hellish pain as the rope tightened around his neck. He knew he was kicking, dancing on air, and tried to remain still. Beside him, his father was slowly strangling, with his tongue protruding and his eyes bulging.

Sir Francis shouted something that Smith did not hear, and the hangman stepped towards the gallows.

A moment later, Smith hit the ground like a sack of corn, choking and gagging. The soldiers cleared a path for Sir Francis, who sauntered towards him, eating an apple. The squire stood over him.

"The king has seen fit to grant you a reprieve," Sir Francis said. "God knows why. His Majesty has ordered you to be sent into the Navy for the remainder of your life." He bit into his apple. "I'd have told you sooner, but I wanted to see you dance first." He nodded as a hard-faced naval lieutenant hurried up with a squad of seamen.

"Here's the king's latest bad bargain," Sir Francis said. "He's a truculent young rogue, so I suggest you smarten him up with a couple of dozen of the cat before you allow him on board." He kicked at Smith's rump. "You'll not smuggle on my lands again, by God!"

Above Smith, his father danced on air, choking to death as he lost control of his bladder and bowels.

SMITH SHUDDERED, PUSHING AWAY THE MEMORIES. THAT HAD been more than ten years ago, his father was long dead, and life had altered and hardened him. Now he had a lost decade to make up and scores to settle.

Smith waited in the lee of a coasting brig, listening to the music of the wind through the rigging. He saw Blackwell make his move from the opposite side of the harbour, a tall man moving purposefully. Dymer and Glear were a hundred yards behind Blackwell, walking furtively as they kept to the shadows.

Allowing Blackwell thirty seconds to make up the extra distance he had to cover, Smith stepped away from the brig. The younger sentry was restless, shifting his feet to keep the blood flowing and moving his head to ease the pressure of the leather stock on his throat. Smith focussed his attention on the youngster, ignored Blackwell's target, and raised a hand in greeting.

"Halloa there!" He deliberately slurred his words as if he was in drink.

The sentry started and looked at his companion for guidance. The older man shook his head slightly and then looked sideways when Blackwell approached from his left.

"It's a fine night," Smith said, drew his pistol and smashed the steel barrel on the young sentry's head. Although the tricorne hat absorbed much of the blow, the youth still staggered, and Smith struck again. As the soldier slumped to the ground, Smith allowed his musket to fall, grabbed the man by the shoulders, and dragged him into the shelter of the inset doorway.

Blackwell had not been as fortunate. The older sentry, warier and much more experienced than his companion, noticed the mask on Blackwell's face.

"Stand clear, you rogue!" The older soldier lowered his musket with the bayonet inches from Blackwell's face.

Rather than speak, Blackwell sidestepped and rushed forward. Expecting something similar, the sentry swung his weapon in a sideways slash. The barrel caught Blackwell on the chest, knocking him sideways. Glear and Dymer rushed up, throwing themselves on the soldier with their fists and boots pounding.

"Don't kill him!" Smith ordered as Blackwell recovered and drew his pistol.

"Bloody lobster bastard!" Dymer said, lifting his boot and stamping on the soldier's head.

"We're not here for that," Blackwell pulled Dymer off the prone man. "Tie the bugger up!"

With the sentries bound and gagged, Smith slid the older man's bayonet from the musket and prised loose the padlock from the warehoused door.

"The door's still locked," Glear said. "And solid oak. We can't break in."

"Yes, we can." Smith began to hack at the door frame with his bayonet. "Cut around the lock with the other bayonet. The door may be oak, but the frame is only soft pine. Come on, man!"

"Hurry!" Blackwell said, looking around him. "We don't have much time!"

With two energetic men digging at the wood, the lock was soon freed, and Smith pushed the door open. Glear shoved past him to enter the building. "Out of my way, cully."

Dymer laughed and thrust in next, nearly stepping on the prostrate body of the older sentry. "I should have brought a glim," he said.

"There will be a lantern near the door." Smith felt for a shelf, located an oil lantern, and scraped a spark from his tinder box to apply to the wick. The resulting yellow glow revealed a hundred kegs, barrels, and packages.

"They've got everything ready for us," Dymer gloated as Smith lifted the lantern higher to illuminate the warehouse.

Smith walked to a desk in one corner and lit two candles. "Don't waste time," he said. "Get these kegs to the door. The wagons will be here shortly."

Glear stared at Smith. Perhaps he thought that breaking into the warehouse was the end of the business, rather than just the beginning.

"Come on!" Captain Blackwell was more practical and organised his men. "Dymer, you and Glear bring the cargo to the door. Smith and I will help the boys load it onto the wagons. Smith, help me drag these blasted redcoats out of the way."

By the time Skinner drove the first wagon along the quayside, Smith and Blackwell had a stack of kegs waiting to be loaded.

"Come on, man!" Blackwell said as Skinner looked from him to Smith. "Get these things aboard before the Excisemen come!"

Transferring the cargo from the warehouse to the convoy of wagons took the best part of an hour, but fortunately, Skinner had ensured plenty of extra hands. Smith grunted as the time passed. He watched two men load Skinner's cart with twenty-four tubs of spirits, a quarter keg whose contents Smith could only guess at, and two bags of tea. Other carts were similarly laden until they rumbled away in a steady convoy.

"Where do you store the goods?" Smith asked.

"That's none of your damned business," Blackwell replied.

"The sergeant and relief guard will be here in five minutes," Smith said as the last wagon rolled away. "Let's make it look good for him."

"What's your plan?" Blackwell was slightly dishevelled with the labour, with a trickle of sweat running from his forehead.

"Close the door and put the sentries back in place," Smith said.

His mother had run forward for a final embrace at the foot of the gallows, only for a sentry to push her roughly back. "That's my husband!" Smith's mother had said, and the sentry laughed and dropped the butt of his musket on her foot.

"Get back where you belong," he snarled.

"And my son!" Smith's mother reached out her hands. "Please!"

The sentry pushed her away. "Get back, or I'll break your head!"

"Mother!" Smith tried to help until the hangman put a hard hand on his shoulder.

"It's too late whining for your mother now," the hangman said. "You should have thought of her before you stole Sir Francis's horses."

"We didn't steal any horses," Smith said, watching as the sentry wrestled with his mother.

"Sir Francis said you did, and I'll take his word over yours!"

The soldier slammed the butt of his musket into Smith's mother's stomach then pushed her to the ground.

"We don't have time!" Blackwell complained.

"I'll do it myself," Smith dragged the younger man to his old position and propped him against the walls as if he had been sleeping. Blackwell, casting nervous glances along the harbour front, helped do the same with the older man.

"And I want their weapons," Smith said, removing both sentries' muskets and bayonets.

Only when he was satisfied did Smith step away. Rather than return immediately to the Dancing Horse, he merely retired to the shelter of the brig and watched as the sergeant marched to the King's Warehouse with the relief guard. Blackwell glared at Smith suspiciously and then joined him.

Smith grinned at the explosion of noise as the sergeant realised what had happened.

"It'll be a couple of hundred lashes for these men," Blackwell said.

"I'd imagine so," Smith said and added, "toe crushing bastards," without any explanation.

"That's a good job well done," Blackwell said. "We'll have to celebrate."

Smith nodded. "The landlady will be pleased with the extra custom."

"Not at the inn," Blackwell said. "Seahaven. We won't mingle with the crowd, Mr Smith. You and I have matters to discuss."

"I'll hide these two first," Smith lifted the muskets, "and join you within the hour."

Chapter Seven

T he dawn was grey above a grey sea, and the wind blew cold from France, rustling the grey-brown thatch of the Kingsgate roofs and causing the farm servants to pull their smocks tight over toiling shoulders. Blackwell was already in his house when Smith arrived. The maid looked tired as she opened the door to him.

"Please come in, sir. The master is expecting you." The maid gave her ubiquitous curtsey as she ushered him inside.

The front room was as Smith remembered, with the long table in the centre, the display cabinet on the left, and the chest of drawers against the opposite wall.

"Brandy, Mr Smith? Port? Or do you prefer rum, as a seafaring man?" Captain Blackwell seemed friendly, almost genial, as he gestured to the array of decanters on top of the cabinet.

Smith chose brandy and supped at his glass while Dymer, Glear, and Skinner stood awkwardly, waiting for Blackwell to lead.

"So, now, Smith, you can tell me who you are, where you come from, and what you are doing in my part of the world."

Blackwell sat at the head of the table, nursing a glass as he looked quizzically at Smith.

"My name is Smith, I'm from Kent, and I came here to join your organisation."

Blackwell swirled the rum in his glass for a moment before he replied. "You arrived from nowhere and expected to join me?" He shook his head and took a swallow of the rum. "Do you know what I think, Smith? I think that you are trouble."

"I saved your crew, and I saved your cargo," Smith reminded, with one hand on his pistol and one eye on the door behind him.

"And what price will you charge for that?" Blackwell asked.

"A fair share in your operation," Smith replied, holding Blackwell's gaze.

"The only share you'll get is six feet of Kentish earth," Blackwell said, thumping his tumbler on the table and lifting his pistol. "I don't want any rivals."

Having expected an ambush, Smith dropped to the floor, drew his pistol, and fired. His move took everybody by surprise so that Dymer was a fraction slower to pull his trigger, with Glear a few seconds later. Skinner stepped back with his mouth open.

Blackwell jerked back, staring at the blood that seeped from the hole in his chest. He coughed out blood, tried to speak, and slumped to his knees, dropping the unfired pistol from his fist.

"Shoot him, Skinner!" Glear said, furiously trying to reload his pistol.

Smith and Dymer saw Blackwell's discarded weapon simultaneously and dived forward. Smith reached it first, scooped the pistol up and kicked Dymer in the face as he rolled free.

"Skinner!" Glear dropped a ball down the barrel of his pistol and rammed it home. "Shoot the bugger!"

Lying on his back, Smith levelled the pistol. With such a short range, he did not need to aim and pulled the trigger. The gun barked, with the muzzle flare bright in the room and the cloud of powder smoke grey-white and acrid. Glear yelled as the ball smashed into his breast. The force knocked him two steps backwards into the door, and he slid to the floor, making little mewing noises as his blood spurted down his front.

While Smith had been dealing with Glear, Dymer had lifted the second pistol from Blackwell's belt.

"Damn your eyes, Smith," Dymer said and pulled the trigger.

Smith threw himself to the right, felt a searing pain across his left arm, slid across the table, and swung his empty pistol like a club. The barrel crashed into Dymer's forehead, sending him staggering.

As Smith readied for another blow, the side door opened, and the maid looked in with a heavy pistol in her hand.

"Are you all finished in here?" The maid stepped across the captain's body and looked around. "Two dead men and two injured. How about you, Dick?"

Skinner remained standing with his mouth and eyes wide open. He had not moved.

"You're not getting involved," the maid answered herself, raised her eyebrows as Dymer pushed out of the room, bleeding from a great tear in his scalp, and glanced at Smith's arm. "Is that bad?"

"I'll live," Smith replied.

"Let me see it." The maid took charge.

"What about the bodies?" Skinner asked.

"They're dead. They can wait." The maid stepped over Blackwell's corpse. "Take your shirt off, Mr Smith." She came over to help, unbuttoning his shirt and easing it from his injured arm. "It's not too serious," she said, twisting her head left and right to examine the wound. "I'll clean and bandage it." She reached for the brandy decanter. "This will sting."

Smith did not flinch when the maid poured raw brandy over the bullet wound.

"What's your name?" he asked.

"Bess," the maid said. She pulled the shirt away from Smith's shoulder and grunted. "Who flogged you? That's the claws of the cat."

"Royal Navy," Smith said.

"How many?"

"Two dozen," Smith said, remembering his introduction to the Navy. "Then six dozen."

Bess pulled a tablecloth from the chest of drawers, borrowed Smith's knife, and casually sliced off a strip to use as a bandage. "I heard that a flogging made a good man bad and a bad man worse. What had you done for the six?"

"Fighting," Smith said. "I stabbed a man."

"Why?"

"He was trying to stab me."

Marshall had yelled as Smith rejected his advances. "You little bastard! I'll teach you to respect your betters!"

Marshall drew the knife from his belt and slashed at Smith, drawing blood from his chest. In return, Smith pulled thrust, catching his attacker in the arm. Marshall screamed, falling to the deck as Perkins and Sinclair had rushed to help Smith.

"I see," Bess nodded to the dead bodies. She looked up as Skinner dived from the room. "Dick won't say anything. He'll go to his wife and keep his mouth shut."

Smith nodded. "I didn't think he was a fighting man."

Bess touched Blackwell's body with her foot. "What will we do with these two?" She did not seem upset that her employer and another man were lying dead in the room.

"They'll be unrecognisable after the fire," Smith told her.

"The fire?" Bess looked around. The grate safely contained smouldering coals within its embrace.

"It's an unfortunate waste of a fine house," Smith said, "but an excellent method of concealing the evidence. I've already been hanged, and I've no desire to repeat the experience." Smith's fingers touched the near-invisible mark around his throat and eyed Bess up and down. "You are remarkably calm."

Bess tied the bandage neatly and replaced Smith's shirt. "Your arm will ache for a while, and it'll be stiff for a few days."

"Thank you. If you have any valuables in the house, grab them now."

"I haven't a farthing to scratch myself with, but my late master, Captain Blackwell," Bess glanced at his corpse, "might have money in his study."

Smith nearly smiled, recognising a fellow spirit. "Then we'd better have a look at Captain Blackwell's study, Bess, hadn't we?"

They stepped over the bodies as Bess grabbed a candle and led the way upstairs. Smith had to boot open the locked door and found a neat room with a small, delicately carved walnut writing bureau.

"I've never been in here," Bess confessed. "This was the Captain's private domain."

"Are you the only servant?" Smith asked.

"Yes," Bess said. "The Captain didn't like people to know his business."

Smith opened the bureau. "See what you can find in the room."

"Yes, sir," Bess strode to the bureau.

They found seventy guineas in Blackwell's bureau, with a fine gold watch. Smith glanced at Bess. "Thirty-five guineas each, Bess, and then you'll walk away and start a new life."

Bess counted her money into a small leather bag. "What will you do?"

"I'll take Blackwell's place as a free trader."

Bess weighed her bag of gold. "Was that your plan all along?"

Smith weighed the watch in his hand before he replied. "I have things to do. Take whatever you can carry and a horse from the stable if you wish to ride to London or elsewhere."

"I don't wish," Bess said. "I belong in this parish."

Smith nodded. "Stay then." He lifted a brace of pistols and thrust them through his belt.

"You'll need help," Bess said.

Smith eyed her for a long minute. "If you betray me, I'll blow your brains out."

Bess held his gaze, "And if you treat me bad, I'll stab you while you sleep." She scanned Captain Blackwell's glass-fronted bookcase and removed a heavy, leather-bound journal. "Captain Blackwell's records," she explained. "Who his customers were, how much they got, and what they paid."

"I thought you hadn't been in here," Smith accused, half-smiling.

"I haven't. I helped the captain with his figuring."

Smith nodded. "How much of the profit did he give you?"

"Not as much as you will."

"How much did he give you?"

"As much as would fill a mouse's ear," Bess said. "None. I got board and lodgings and the odd few shillings when he was in the mood."

"As captain of a smuggling craft, I will get five shares of the profit," Smith said. "The mate gets two, quartermaster one and a half, full seamen and carriers one share, and all the others half a share."

Bess nodded. "And me?"

"One and a half."

"Two." Bess held up the book.

"You drive a hard bargain, Bess."

"Two, or I walk, and the accounts go with me."

"Bring them." Smith held up the watch. "We'll scrape off Blackwell's name and pawn this whenever we can." He eyed Bess up and down, wondering if he could trust her.

THEY STOOD UNDER THE ANCIENT WIND-TORTURED APPLE tree as the smoke coiled skyward, silver-blue against the dark.

"Dymar may be a problem," Bess said. "He's a man to keep a grudge."

Smith tapped the butt of one of his pistols. "I can solve that sort of problem." He sniffed the smoke as Bess pulled her cloak tight around her.

"Seahaven burns well," Bess observed.

"It does."

"What next?" Bess fingered the coins in her purse.

"Life. Where will you stay tonight?"

"In your bed," Bess stated.

Smith nodded. "Then we'll discuss tomorrow later. "I need a ship, and I need men I can trust."

Bess raised her eyebrows. "Neither are easy things to find."

"Then I might need help," Smith stated.

Bess hooked her arm with his as they walked to Kingsgate, with the acrid stench of smoke wrapping around them.

Chapter Eight

Bess woke to the sound of a lone blackbird. She looked around her, momentarily unsure where she was, and then she remembered the events of the previous evening.

"John?"

Smith was not in the room. The shutters and the door were closed, and the room was empty, with the accounts journal sitting on the table. Bess got up and stepped to the window just as Smith entered.

"I thought you had left me," Bess said.

"I had business to attend to." Smith eyed her up and down. "You'd best get some clothes on. I hear Sir Francis is due to visit today, and you must look respectable."

"What business?" Bess asked as she lifted the clothes she had worn the previous night, then replaced them on the chair.

"My business." Smith opened the shutters and stood at the window, staring at the High Street as a gleaming carriage and riders moved purposefully towards the inn.

Bess joined him, still naked. The top of her head reached up to Smith's nose. "What are you looking at?"

"The squire and his minions," Smith said, keeping the hatred from his voice.

"That's Sir Frankie's coach, right enough," Bess agreed. "And James Quinn, the parish constable at its side, with Aldred Gurnal following."

Smith noted the names for future reference. Gurnal was the man he had told about the goods that Blackwell ran to the cove, the Excisemen's informant. "A fine collection of rogues and blackguards," he said.

"Sir Frankie and his supporters," Bess confirmed.

Behind the coach and its outriders, five dragoons rode tall with their accoutrements jingling and their horses plump and glossy. Two Riding Officers made up the company, looking around them at the village.

Bess remained at the window as the Riding Officers stared up at her. "You'd think they hadn't seen a woman before."

Smith pulled her roughly back. "Get dressed," he ordered.

When the coach halted at the triangular village green, a servant leapt from the back and opened the door for Sir Francis to emerge. Tall, fit, and handsome, Sir Francis was thirty-five, ten years older than Smith, and stood outside his coach with the servant at his side. He put a large hand on the whipping post, which, together with the stocks, reminded the villagers that the king's justice ran right to the south coast. Every villager knew that Sir Francis was not loath to follow the law to its utmost vigour.

"Search the village," Sir Francis ordered. "I want every stranger and every known smuggler rounded up."

Quinn and Gurnal bowed and hurried to the nearest house, with Quinn knocking at the door and Gurnal standing slightly back with a hand on the butt of the pistol at his belt. When the occupant opened the door, Quinn thrust his foot within and began a torrent of questions.

"Where were you yesterday evening? Who is in the house? What is your occupation?"

"They'll knock at every door," Bess said, as the dragoons stationed themselves at either end of the village to prevent anybody escaping.

"They will," Smith agreed.

"They'll come to the Dancing Horse," Bess added.

"They will," Smith agreed again.

"You had better hide."

"I won't do that," Smith moved his injured arm. "You fixed my wound well. It's scarcely even stiff."

Bess checked the bandage. "You're still bleeding."

"It'll heal." Smith began to dress as Bess returned to the window. "I'll see you downstairs."

Ruth looked nervous as she served them breakfast. "It's only bread and cheese this morning, Mr Smith."

"Bread and cheese suit me perfectly," Smith said.

"Maybe you had better leave the inn, Mr Smith," Ruth suggested, "and you, Bess. Sir Francis and his men are searching for strangers."

"Bess is no stranger," Smith pointed out.

"Bess is a stranger in the Dancing Horse."

Bess glanced at Smith. "I've nowhere else to go since Captain Blackwell's house burned down," she said.

"That was a rum do," Ruth nearly dropped a plate as she stepped back. "Poor Captain Blackwell, and him such a fine gentleman. And now there's that rogue Dymar as well."

Bess started and looked at Smith again. "Dymar?"

"Of course, you won't have heard," Ruth said. "Old Thomas Carman found Dymar dead early this morning. Stabbed in seven places, Old Tom said. That's on top of that terrible fire yesterday night."

"It was a shame for Captain Blackwell," Smith agreed. "I suspect that Dymar deserved all he got, though." He took a mouthful of his bread and cheese and chewed heartily. "Do you bake your own bread, Mrs Martin?"

Everybody except Smith looked around as the door opened and Sir Francis walked in, with Quinn and Gurnal at his back.

"The Dancing Horse," Sir Francis said in his fruity accent. "The resort of all the idle blackguards in the country. It's a very sink of atrocity, and here they all are."

"Welcome, Sir Francis," Ruth ignored the squire's remarks. "What can I get you?"

"Nothing legal, I'll be bound. One day I'll close this place down. Kingsgate doesn't need two inns. Who's the stranger?" Sir Francis looked directly at Smith as Ruth curtsied. "I don't know him. He's not one of my tenants."

Smith swallowed and bit hugely into his bread before he looked up. He held Sir Francis's gaze and said nothing.

You are the same arrogant, sneering man as always. I haven't forgotten you, Francis Selby.

"Who are you?" the squire's eyes narrowed as he examined Smith. "Answer me, fellow! What's your name? And stand in the presence of your betters!"

Smith remained sitting, returned Sir Francis's scrutiny, and took a draught of the tankard of small beer that sat in front of him.

Quinn and Gurnal took hold of Smith's arms and hauled him to his feet. Smith tried not to flinch as he retained his grip of the tankard.

Sir Francis peered into Smith's face. "What's your name, fellow?"

"John Smith. What's yours? And who are you to disturb a man at his breakfast?"

"I am Sir Francis Selby, the owner of this village and the land all around. What are you doing here?"

"Trying to eat my breakfast," Smith said.

"Where do you come from?"

"I live here," Smith shook off Quinn and Gurnal's grasp.

"Sir," Gurnal said quietly. "I know this man." He lowered his voice further. "He is the fellow who informed us about the

Spike Cove landing. I believe he works for the Preventative service."

Sir Francis's eyes narrowed. Inches taller than Smith, he studied him curiously. "Do I know you?"

You will, cully, by all that's unholy, you will.

Smith sat down without replying and continued to eat while Bess held her breath and Ruth retreated to the security of her counter.

Sir Francis coloured. "You!" he pointed to Bess. "You are Captain Blackwell's servant. Why are you here?"

Bess stood up and curtseyed. "Captain Blackwell is dead, sir. He died in the fire, and this gentleman," she nodded towards Smith, "was kind enough to look after me and grant me Christian charity. I am Mr Smith's servant now, sir, if it pleases you." She curtseyed again and stood with her eyes demurely lowered.

"How fortuitous that Smith happened to be passing," Sir Francis sneered.

"Yes, sir, indeed it was," Bess agreed.

"What do you know about the fire?" Sir Francis asked.

"Why, nothing, sir, if it pleases you. I was in bed when it started, and it quite destroyed the house. Poor Captain Blackwell, sir. I was quite distraught when I realised he was gone, and Mr Smith comforted me and brought me to this inn, sir."

"Did he, indeed?" Sir Francis gave Smith a stern look.

"And where were you, Smith, when the Customs' Warehouse was raided?"

Smith looked puzzled. "I don't know, sir. At what time was it raided?"

"Two in the morning, Smith," Quinn said.

Smith shook his head. "Were there no soldiers on duty?"

"Yes," Quinn told him. "The guards said that about a score of raiders overpowered them."

"I'm glad I wasn't there," Smith said. "They sound like desperate fellows. Landlady, did you see me in the Dancing Horse last night?"

"I saw you," Ruth confirmed.

The squire grunted and left the inn without another word. Quinn and Gurnal followed, with Quinn deliberately brushing his shoulder against Bess as he passed.

When the customers in the taproom recovered from Sir Francis's visit, Bess faced Smith. "Did you tell the squire about Spike Cove?" she asked.

"What do you think?"

"I think you're a devious man, John Smith."

"The squire's in a right taking," Ruth returned from the sanctuary of her counter. "He's commandeered Captain Blackwell's ship, and he's having it searched from stern to stem."

"That must be fun for him," Smith kept his face expressionless. "Whoever recovered the smuggled brandy will have placed it in a secure place."

"It's probably in a dozen hiding places the length and breadth of Kent," Ruth said. "I only have half a dozen barrels." She drew up a chair and sat beside them, hoping for information. "I hear the Collector reported the break-in at the King's Warehouse to the king. He sent one of the Riding Officers directly to London with the news."

"I'm sure Geordie will be interested," Smith said. "It will quite disturb his breakfast to hear about smugglers when he's trying to conduct a war."

"The Excisemen are bound to increase their presence here," Ruth said and left to serve another customer.

"Sir Francis is irritating," Smith said. "I wanted that ship."

"If you still intend to take over Captain Blackwell's position, you'll need a ship," Bess agreed.

"A ship and a crew I can trust," Smith said. He finished his breakfast and stood up. "We have things to discuss upstairs, Bess."

Ruth watched as they mounted the stairs, shook her head, and cleared away the plates. What her guests got up to was not her concern, as long as they paid their bills. She looked up as the twice-weekly coach to London rattled to the Hounds Rest, with the guard blowing his long horn to clear the path, and then returned to her work.

Smith leaned back in his chair, watching Bess through hard, musing eyes. "Life appears to have thrown us together," he said.

"It does," Bess replied.

"Yet you held a pistol to me," he said.

"I did," Bess agreed, meeting his gaze without flinching.

"Would you have shot me?"

"If I had to."

Smith smiled. "How many people have you shot before now?"

"None," Bess admitted.

Smith began to stuff tobacco into the bowl of his pipe. "What do you think it feels like to shoot somebody?"

Bess pondered for a moment, watching Smith. "I don't know."

"You may have nightmares for the remainder of your life, or you may love it," Smith said. "Or you'll feel nothing."

Bess did not reply.

Smith lifted Bess's pistol, opened the window, and fired into the sky outside. "That will wake up the neighbours." He handed the weapon to Bess. "How are you with a gun? Let me see you."

"Who is making that noise?" Ruth hammered at the door.

"It's all right, Mrs Martin," Smith soothed her. "Nobody's hurt. It was only a practice shot." He waited until Ruth bustled away then returned his attention to Bess as she aimed at the fireplace.

"No." Smith shifted the muzzle until it pointed directly at his face. "Aim at me. Look me in the eyes and shoot me. It's all right; it's empty. I've just fired the damned thing, and these weapons only hold one charge."

Bess's hand trembled slightly as she lifted the pistol and pressed the trigger. The hammer fell with a slight click.

"You see how hard that was?" Bess removed the pistol from Bess's hand. "The trigger has a very heavy pull. It's hard enough for a man and harder still for a woman." He smiled, taking any sting from his words. "It's a general fault with many pistols that their triggers are so excessively stiff that it's impossible to keep the sight on the target when firing."

Bess listened, nodding.

"This weapon is ten inches long. You'd be better with a pistol about six inches in length, certainly no longer, and a 20 to 24 bore. Find one with a spring hook on the side to fit onto a belt and a trigger that is exceedingly light to pull."

"I'm as strong as many men," Bess protested.

"And many men struggle to pull a stiff trigger," Smith told her. "Choose an eminent gun maker, one on whose respectability you can place utter dependence."

Bess listened intently. "I've never heard you speak at such length."

Smith touched her pistol. "A good weapon can save your life," he said, "while one of poor quality jeopardises it." He smiled. "One thing's for certain, if you need a gun, you'll need it badly."

"I was standing right behind you," Bess said. "I could hardly miss."

"That is true," Smith agreed. "If you managed to pull that stiff trigger before I shifted aside."

Bess's brows closed in a frown. "I'd have blown a hole in your spine," she told him.

"You might be better with a blunderbuss," Smith said. "It's anything but ladylike, but it is functional and a fearsome weapon. It takes a charge of 120 grains of black powder and holds a load of musket or pistol balls. Swan shot can also be effective."

"Have you used one?" Bess asked.

For a moment, Smith was a youngster back aboard the ship, with a horde of yelling French seamen trying to board. *He held the blunderbuss in trembling hands, with the foretopman shouting at him to fire before the damned Crapauds swept onto them. He lifted the blunderbuss and squeezed the trigger, with the shot blasting into the French ranks,*

wreaking carnage as men and pieces of men dissolved in a welter of blood and flesh and torn bones. Smith screamed at the sight and cringed as the wind blew a haze of French blood over him.

Smith pushed away the memory. "Imagine how you would feel with a two-inch muzzle thrust in your face. A blunderbuss is the best weapon for creating instant respect. At forty feet, there is a spread of between twenty-four to thirty-six inches. At sixty feet, the spread can be fifty inches." Smith gave an evil grin, darkened with memory. "Now, Bess, that's hard to avoid."

Bess nodded. "Yes, and you can load a blunderbuss with scrap iron, stones, or even rusty old nails, so you don't have to waste money on shot."

Smith shook his head. "Only in an emergency. That kind of ammunition can play merry hell with the bore, and imagine if a nail was caught crosswise in the barrel? The weapon would blow up in your face."

Bess nodded, shivering.

Smith continued. "Whatever you choose, Bess, keep the flint sharp and your powder dry." He touched the pan of the pistol. "Ensure the frizzen — that's the metal the flint strikes to create a spark — does not become greasy or worn, or there'd be few sparks, and the priming powder won't ignite."

Bess nodded, with her eyes fixed on Smith and her eyes softening.

"Remember that if the touchhole between the pan and the powder becomes clogged, the priming powder might flash in the pan without the spark reaching the charge, so you'll have a misfire, and your opponent will have an advantage."

Bess put her hand on the pistol. "So keep my flint sharp, my frizzen in good condition, the touchhole open, and the priming powder fresh and dry."

"You've got it," Smith became aware that Bess's expression had altered since he had begun speaking. She was no longer looking at him like a friend or a client but with a more disturbing emotion.

Damn! Damn, damn, and double damn! I've no time for romance!

"Well, John Smith, my frizzen is in excellent condition, and my touchhole is open if your flint is sharp and your powder fresh."

Am I wrong? Does she only wish to bed me? No, not with that look in her eyes. She's moved beyond the purely physical.

Smith twisted his lips into the semblance of a smile. "In that case, Bess, let me check the condition of your frizzen."

Bess's smile was that of a woman in complete control.

"The Excise Service is the natural enemy of the free traders," Smith spoke to the wall, fully aware that Bess was listening to every word. "Excisemen on land, and the Preventative Service at sea."

"That's correct," Bess agreed.

"Tell me how it works in this parish," Smith shifted, so he sat up in bed, with the sounds of the street evident although the window was closed.

"Much the same as everywhere else," Bess told him.

"Tell me anyway."

Bess gathered her thoughts for a moment before she replied. "There is Musbie, the Collector's Clerk. You'll know him by the ink stains on his fingers. He never comes to the Dancing Horse, though. Like all the Custom staff, he drinks at the Hounds Rest."

Smith nodded. "He'll be underpaid, underappreciated, and a font of knowledge in all things to do with the Customs and Excise. I might cultivate his friendship."

"Then there are the tidewaiters or tidesmen. There are eight of them for the parish, two based in Kingsgate and the rest in Marsham. The Collector rotates them, so I don't know their names."

"The tidesmen are the lads who patrol the coasts and check

the cargoes of ships that arrive in the harbour," Smith said. "Sometimes, they travel with suspect ships."

"That's right," Bess agreed. "We only get coasting craft in Kingsgate and Sir Francis's ship for sending farm produce away."

"The tidesmen are badly paid, too," Smith said, "but they get a share of all the contraband they seize."

Bess nodded.

"If we give them a larger bribe or allow them to find part of the cargo, we can neutralise them." Smith folded his hands behind his head, watched as Bess shifted her position, and allowed his brain to ponder all the information she provided.

"Next up the ladder is the landwaiter, who supervises the tidesmen. The landwaiter also checks cargoes leaving the harbour and arriving and can enter anybody's house to rummage for smuggled goods. Above him is the surveyor, also based in Marsham, as is the comptroller, who deals with the financial matters."

"And above all is the Collector of Customs, who lived in Hop Passage, a hundred yards from the Dancing Horse," Smith said. "Thank you, Bess."

"Don't forget the Preventative service," Bess said. "The Customs sloops and cutters that patrol offshore."

"I know of them," Smith said.

"There's one man that scared Captain Blackwell," Bess said. "A fellow called Ambrose Grant. He's the best Preventative captain in the fleet, but thank God he's based up in Scotland at present."

Grant's name seemed to hang like a threat in the room until Bess slid her foot up Smith's leg. "Is your flint sharp again?"

Smith pushed thoughts of Ambrose Grant to one side and concentrated on more immediate matters.

SMITH COULD NOT JUDGE THE AGE OF THE MAN WHO SAT IN the furthest corner of the taproom. He might have been fifty, or he might have been seventy, although Smith guessed somewhere in between. The man was evidently of the sea, with a tarred canvas jacket above wide, much-patched trousers, while his face was as deeply tanned as any deep-water man should possess. To prove Smith's assessment, the brass earring in the man's right ear glinted in the firelight.

Every time Smith entered the taproom, the man sat in the same position, with his back to the wall and a small pewter tankard on the table at his right elbow, yet Smith was aware the old man had followed him on more than one occasion.

"That fellow there," Smith said to Ruth. "Who is he?"

"Thomas Carman," Ruth said at once, "and he's as interested in you as you are in him."

Smith lifted his head slightly. "Thomas Carman? I know that name," he studied the man again. "I thought he was long since dead."

"Not yet," the landlady said, "although he sits there, day after day, trying to drink himself to the grave."

Smith smiled. "Let me help him towards his destination, landlady. I'll buy him a drink."

"He drinks rum," Ruth said.

Smith shook his head. "Not today, he doesn't. Come to the counter with me, and make up what I say."

Ruth raised her eyebrows. "If you wish, Mr Smith, but Tom is not a sociable man."

"Fetch a pint tankard," Smith said quietly, "and put in half a pint of strong beer, none of your frothy light rubbish, but as hoppy, as you have, Kent beer of the best quality."

Ruth obeyed, with her eyes sceptical.

"Then add a gill of gin and quarter of a pint of sherry."

"In the same tankard?" Ruth asked.

"Yes, and then add a gill of rum."

Ruth made up the drink, screwing up her face. "I wouldn't like to drink that concoction," she said.

"It's about to get worse," Smith said. "Do you have a powder flask for your pistol?"

"I do," Ruth said, wondering.

"Pass it over, please."

Wondering, Ruth did as Smith asked and watched as Smith added a measure of gunpowder to the tankard and stirred with one of Ruth's spoons.

"That's appalling," the landlady said. "Nobody can drink that. There ought to be a law against it."

"There probably is," Smith said, "or an extra tax, but Thomas Carman can, and will, drink it," Smith said. "Put it on my account."

Smith carried the tankard across the room and placed it in front of Carman.

"What's that?" Carman looked at the tankard with basilisk-hard eyes. "And who the devil are you to bring me a drink?"

"I am John Smith, and that's rumfustian, Teach's favourite." Smith sat opposite Carman.

"How the hell do you know what Teach drank?"

"Drink it," Smith said.

"I sailed with the bugger." Carman tasted the mixture. "That was a long time ago."

"Forty years and more," Smith said. "Are you the man now that you were then?"

"Don't be bloody stupid. I'm an old done man."

"It's the spirit that makes the man," Smith said, "not his years, and you're dying of inactivity here."

Carman grunted and drunk more of the rumfustian. "This stuff takes me back."

"I heard that the authorities hanged you."

Carman licked his lips. "Did you hear that?" He glanced at the door as if expecting the heavy tread of Jack Ketch and the shadow of the noose.

"I heard they hanged you at Barbados, or maybe Jamaica."

"Is that what you heard? Are you sure it wasn't at Charleston in the Carolinas?"

Smith leaned back, aware that Ruth was watching and listening to every word. "A man who survives a hanging becomes one of the devil's children."

Carman nodded. "I met the devil, and his name was Teach." He flicked aside Smith's kerchief, exposing the neck and throat. "We share the same father, I see."

Smith replaced the kerchief. "My father is long since dead."

Carman drained the tankard. "So is mine." He gave a gap-toothed grin. "I died beyond the Line, where there was no law except what we made ourselves. Where did you die, John Smith?"

"Gallows Hill, in this parish, and the Downs, three miles off the coast of Kent."

"You died twice, yet you look alive to me. That's a rare gift."

"A man can only die a limited number of times," Smith said. "After that, his luck ends, and he must live forever."

Carman pushed forward the empty tankard. "A man can die while still alive," he said. "He can die of day after day of nothingness, killed by the grey drag of pointless time until death welcomes him with an open grave, or Davy Jones brings him home."

Smith understood. "A man can get a surfeit of excitement when he is young, and he can never return to a quiet existence again."

Carman waited while Ruth made up his rumfustian again. He peered into the tankard with his eyes three thousand miles and half a century away. "Where are the days that have been, and the seasons that we have seen, when we might sing, swear, drink, drab, and kill men as freely as your cake-makers do flies when the whole sea was our Empire, where we robbed at will and the world but our garden where we walked for sport?" He drank

more from the tankard. "John Ward said that. He was a 17th century Barbary pirate from Kent."

Smith frowned. "The world is still out there," he said, "the sea is still the sea."

"The authorities have closed down the old days, the sea is no longer open, and there is no salt to life."

"I'll soon be looking for a crew," Smith said. "I want bold men of character, men who are not afraid to stake life on the roll of a dice, and men who can look the devil of misfortune in the face and laugh."

"Where do I sign articles?" Carman asked.

Smith smiled. "Welcome aboard, Thomas Carman."

I have my first crew member. Now all I need is eleven more men and a ship, and I'll set a fire throughout Kent that no man, king, or devil, will ever douse.

Chapter Nine

March 1762

"W e're going for a walk, Bess."

The sun emerged that March morning, with the Channel a kindly blue and the sails of coasters and fishing boats hungry for even a breath of wind. Even so, the air held a whiff of the previous night's fire, with smoke acrid at the back of their throats.

Smith was silent for the first half-mile until they arrived as Spike Cove, with the gaunt skeleton of the Spike looming on the hill above and a hundred kittiwakes screaming from their nests on the cliff.

"The Channel," Smith said as if Bess was unaware of where she was. "Home of sore heads and sore hearts."

Bess looked at him, unsure of his mood. "The authorities will be looking for you," she said. "You can't escape them forever, and Sir Francis is a dangerous man to cross."

"They'll be looking for the man who robbed the King's Warehouse," Smith corrected. "And he's dead and burned to a crisp."

"Somebody will talk," Bess said. "Gossip spreads, and informants such as Aldred Gurnal earn good money."

"Only three people know the truth," Smith stood at the edge

of the land, staring out to sea. "I am one, and I don't exist; another is Dymer, who would incriminate himself, and the third is you."

"Word will spread," Bess was persistent as she took hold of Smith's arm. "Rumours and whispers grow into facts, and somebody will point a finger and hold out a grasping hand. She hunted for inspiration to strengthen her case. Look at that!" She pointed to a notice nailed to the twisted apple tree.

"*REWARD,*" the notice read.

"*For the apprehension of the Persons concerned in the robbery of the King's Customs House in the village of Kingsgate in Kent. The King and the Excise Service will pay the sum of £50 to any person who gives information about the above crime. Any man turning King's Evidence will receive a full pardon and an honourable acquittal in addition to the aforementioned sum.*

Contact Sir Francis Selby of Kingshunt Manor or any office of the Customs and Excise Service."

"Fifty pounds is a king's ransom," Bess said. "People would sell their soul for half that amount."

"Let them talk," Smith said. "Rumours mean nothing."

"They'll hang you."

Smith grunted and touched his neck. "Maybe I was born to be hanged."

"Dymer might turn King's evidence."

"I'll burn that bridge if I come to it."

When Bess moved to tear down the proclamation, Smith grabbed her arm. "Leave it," he said. "There will be a hundred others all across the south coast."

They walked down to the cove where the sea hushed in, kissed the sun-gleaming pebbles and withdrew. A Preventative cutter drifted past with an officer in the stern studying the coast through a brass-bound telescope. The officer focused on Smith and Bess for a moment, but only seeing what he believed was a courting couple, he ordered the cutter to continue.

"You need a boat and a crew," Bess reminded. "I can't help with the ship, but I know the bold men in the area."

"I have one man already," Smith said. "Thomas Carman."

"He's a bit of a dodderer, isn't he?" Bess complained. "What can he do?"

"He has more experience than half of Kingsgate put together," Smith said. "Tell me, are the Ramsleys still in the village?"

Bess frowned, holding onto her hat as the wind threatened to blow it from her head. "What do you know about the Ramsleys?"

"They were always game."

"They still are," Bess said. "The Ramsleys are game to anything that benefits the Ramsleys."

"They weren't with Blackwell's crew."

"Captain Blackwell didn't favour them," Bess said.

"All the more reason for me to talk to them." Smith watched the Customs Cutter slide away, with the wind bellying her topsails and two officers studying the coast. "They used to live in Flanders Lane."

Bess shook her head. With her hair loose around her face and her determined chin dimpled, she looked the picture of innocence, a child's nanny or a demure schoolmistress. "Not now. They've lived in Gillet Lane for years. How do you know them yet not know that?"

"I've been away. Gillet Lane it is."

"Who are you, John?"

"I'm nobody," Smith said. "I'm dead."

Kingsgate had been established long before the name was coined. It had existed before Rome's iron legions crossed the narrow sea from Gaul. Centuries later, the village suffered from the invasions of both the Jutes and the Normans. The old folk claimed that Kingsgate gained its name when William the Bastard of Normandy landed here before his famous campaign of 1066, but educated men and women sneered at the fancy.

Everybody agreed that French privateers and Dutch men of war had raided Kingsgate, and now it huddled around the harbour and threw a long main street inland. Off this High Street, a score of narrow lanes branched off at right angles, most named after people whose bones had long since disintegrated into powder and whose history had merged with myth.

Gillet Lane was one such place, a narrow, curving passage between two rows of tumbledown cottages with sinking thatched roofs.

"You don't have to come," Smith said as they stopped at the entrance to the lane. Even in daylight Gillet Lane was desolate, while the rat that scurried past seemed bolder than most of its kind.

"I'll wait here." Bess sat on a mounting block, one of two such luxuries in the village. The second, and far more used, was outside the Hounds Rest for the benefit of the mail coach passengers.

Smith touched the butts of his two pistols as he strode along Gillet Lane, avoiding the worse of the animal and human waste and instinctively watching for predatory eyes in the rundown homes. The lane curved halfway along its length, blocking the view of the lower section from the more civilised people in the High Street. The Ramsley family lived at the furthermost end, with the gable-end of their cottage butting onto the beach. In wild weather, the sea lapped the wall and lifted the thatch, so the family had to slam shut a warped wooden shutter and shelter inside, listening to the wind roaring in the chimney.

Smith rapped on the door and stepped back.

"Who's that?" A female voice called from within the house.

"John Smith."

"What do you want?"

"To speak."

"Go to the devil."

Smith knew that half the Ramsley clan would be watching

from cracks in the shutters and through secret apertures. They would know who he was and would have been aware of his progress from the minute he set foot in Kingsgate. Smith extracted a gold coin from his pocket, spun it in the air, dropped it, and swore as it rolled and bounced along the ground. He searched for a moment, shook his head as the coin remained elusive, and stomped away, pulling his tricorne hat lower over his head.

At the curve of the lane, Smith stopped, out of sight of the Ramsley's domain. He shrunk into a recessed doorway and pulled one of Captain Blackwell's fine pistols from his belt. As he had expected, the Ramsley's door opened as soon as he disappeared from their view, and a furtive-looking youth appeared, searching for the missing coin.

Aiming the pistol, Smith fired a single shot, with the lead ball flattening on the ground two inches from the youthful Ramsley's hand and ricocheting down the street towards the beach. The youth jerked back, cursing as he turned savage eyes towards Smith.

"Who are you firing at, you bastard?" The youth scurried back, glaring.

Smith strode forward, lifted the coin, and pushed through the open door into the Ramsley's cottage.

"Good morning to you all!"

Two women, four men, and the furtive youth filled the room. All shared the same dark blonde hair except one middle-aged woman, who sat on the only armed chair and looked up calmly when Smith entered. Her hair was as neat as any lady in the court of King George while golden hooped earrings extended nearly to her shoulders.

"You'll be John Smith," the middle-aged woman did not seem perturbed by Smith's dramatic entrance as she sat with her hands demurely folded in her lap.

"I am," Smith said, and the Ramsleys watched. The youth moved to block his exit.

"You recovered the free trade goods," the middle-aged woman said.

"You must be Mother Ramsley," Smith ignored the others. In this gathering, only the middle-aged woman mattered. The men were poor shadows, thin-faced creatures waiting for her orders.

The woman nodded. "What do you want here?"

"Recruits," Smith said. "Now that Captain Blackwell is gone, there is a vacancy for a smuggling master."

"You?" Mother Ramsley looked Smith up and down. "You'll need a ship, and I hear that Sir Francis has sold Captain Blackwell's *Free Enterprise*."

"I need a small number of bold men," Smith said. "And I know that the Ramsleys used to be bold free traders." He began to reload his pistol, taking his time as he rammed home the ball and wad. "That would be in your husband's day, a decade ago."

"Abe was a bold man, as you say," Mother Ramsley agreed. "How would a stranger to Kingsgate know that?"

Smith pulled back the hammer of his pistol, checked the flint was sharp, and carefully tucked the weapon under his belt. "No man is ever as bold as his father," he said.

Two more men sidled into the room. They looked rough, weather-battered, while one had the defiant, devil-damn-your-eyes stare of an adventurer.

"I shall take my leave," Smith said, having already selected the two newcomers as possible additions to his crew.

"Wait," Mother Ramsley ordered. "Who are you?" Her eyes were gimlet sharp. "You're no stranger. How did you know about my Abe?"

"People talk," Smith said, "and Abe Ramsley's name was mentioned."

"You find yourself a ship," Mother Ramsley decided, "and I'll send two of my sons."

"You can find me at the Dancing Horse," Smith told her.

"I know where you are," Mother Ramsley said. "Now leave us. Your girl is waiting for you at the top of the lane."

Smith nodded. "I want these two men," he nodded to the newcomers.

"I know you do," Mother Ramsley said. "Jake and Henry, as handy seamen as you'll ever meet between Ushant and Cape Farewell." Her smile showed perfectly white, even teeth. "But seamen without a ship are like fish on land." She moved her hands to reveal the double-barrelled pistol she had pointed at Smith's groin. "Goodbye, John Smith."

Bess was sitting where Smith had left her. She looked up when Smith arrived. "Well?"

"I need a ship," Smith said.

"Where will you get one?"

"The French will help," Smith said, "and Sir Francis will provide one."

For all her lack of height, Bess matched him stride for stride as they paced the length of the village. "The French are our enemies," she reminded.

"The French are King George's enemies," Smith corrected. "I'm not King George."

Bess sighed. "Have you got an evasive answer for everything?"

"If I had all the answers," Smith said, "I'd be living in a palatial mansion with a thousand acres of land."

Bess gave him a sideways look. "That's a different world," she said.

Smith led her to the harbour, where three coasters lay along the quay, one loading and two unloading.

"Nice looking craft," Smith said to a white-bearded watcher with one leg.

The watcher took the clay pipe from his mouth, eyed Bess slyly and nodded. "Which one?" he asked.

Smith ran an experienced eye across all three coasters. The vessels unloading were short, dumpy, and blunt, built for cargo carrying, with anything else neglected. Smith considered them seaborne warehouses at best. The two-masted lugger that was loading was longer, with sleeker lines and a sharper bow, carvel-built, and looked hungry to be set loose from the drudgery of coastal trade.

"That lugger," from his angle, Smith could not make out her name. "Is she due to sail soon?"

"First tide, the day after tomorrow," the watcher said. "If Captain Young completes her loading. The damned Navy pressed her blind on her return the last voyage, so she has a crew of old men and children."

Smith nodded and began to fish. "The Navy is like that. She'll be a Hastings vessel then."

"Not a bit of her," the watcher said, gratified that he knew more than Smith. "Sir Francis owns nearly every last inch of *Maid of Kent*."

"Nearly?" Smith queried.

"Nearly," the watcher confirmed, keeping his knowledge to himself. He thrust an empty clay pipe between his teeth, waiting for Smith to offer his tobacco in exchange for further information.

"Ah," Smith said and walked away, with Bess's arm hooked in his.

"What was that about?" Bess asked.

"I was merely curious."

"I doubt that," Bess said. "I've only known you a short time, but you're planning something."

Smith tightened his grip on Bess's arm. "I've already planned it," he said. "Although there are many possible variations."

They walked on in silence until they reached the Dancing Horse. Two men slouched outside, smoking long-stemmed pipes. One gave Bess a leer, winked at his companion, and settled back down, still watching Bess.

"I'll leave you here," Smith said.

"Where are you going?" Bess accepted the situation without question.

"Back to sea," Smith said. He faced the leering man. "This woman is mine," he said. "I'll leave her in your care. If anything happens to her when I am gone, I'll put a bullet through your brain."

The leering man winced. "She's safe with me," he said, backing away.

"Make sure she stays that way," Smith told him.

———

"AHOY, THERE!" SMITH STOOD ON THE QUAY. "I'M LOOKING for a berth."

Captain Young of the lugger *Maid of Kent* stepped forward, looking Smith up and down, assessing his worth and reliability.

Smith knew that every shipmaster was desperately short of hands in the interminable war with France, with the ever-expanding navy snapping up anybody who even looked like he could haul a rope.

"What was your last ship?"

"*Acheron*," Smith replied at once.

"River of Woe," Captain Young translated, proving he knew classical mythology. "Was she not in the Baltic trade?"

"Yes, sir," Smith replied, deliberately choosing a route with which Captain Young was unlikely to be familiar. "Arbroath to Riga."

"You're not a Royal Navy deserter, then?" Young asked shrewdly.

"No, sir."

"Then it must be a coincidence that you call me sir and stand at attention when you address me." Captain Young inclined his head. "As it happens, we're short-handed, so step on board. What name shall I call you?"

"Smith, sir. John Smith."

"An easy name to remember," Young said dryly. "I believe I've heard it mentioned in connection with the free traders."

"Smith is a common name," Smith said. "There are many of us around." He boarded the lugger. If Young believed he had caught him out in a small deception, he would not search for a larger one. "Where are you bound, sir?"

"Coast hugging, Smith. We're heading for Portsmouth with wheat for the Navy." Young gave a twisted smile. "I hope you're not branded with a D."

"No, sir." The letter D branded on a man's chest was the sign of a deserter, marked as a rogue for all time. "I will need a Protection from the Press."

Young nodded. "Come aft to my cabin, Smith."

In the cabin with its open windows, Young opened a drawer in his desk. "Sir Francis Selby is the managing owner of this vessel, and he's also the local magistrate." He produced a blank Protection certificate, already signed at the bottom with Sir Francis's flowing hand.

"By the Commissioners etc.," the certificate began,

"whereas by an Act of Parliament passed in the 13th *year of the Reign of his Majesty, King George the Second it is enacted that the persons under the Age and Circumstances therein mentioned, shall be freed and exempted from being impressed into H.M. Service "*

"All I have to do is add your name here," Young indicated the space, "and you're legal and safe from the Impress Service and any casual King's ship that's desperate for men. Common Mariners are only protected for one voyage at a time, as you'll know, while Masters, Mates, and specialists have longer spells. Be careful when we return to Kingsgate."

"Yes, sir." Smith held the Protection certificate as if it were gold. In a way, that single document was more precious than any coin of the realm, for it would ensure his freedom. Without a Protection, the Royal Navy could legally snatch any seaman and keep him until death, disability, or the end of the current war. The present war was already eight years old and showed no sign of ending, and the next would come along before people grew used to peace. War was virtually guaranteed in the eighteenth century, with France and Great Britain struggling for maritime and trade dominance and colonies and

European border posts changing hands with every temporary peace.

"Keep hold of that document," Young growled and suddenly altered from a genial new employer to a tyrant that would extract the last drop of sweat from the seaborne labourers. "Now get to work, you blasted lubber! We've a cargo to load!"

Chapter Ten

"I'm damned if I agree with you, Hargreaves. She's only a fishing boat." Captain Young addressed the mate.

"I don't think she is, Captain," Hargreaves was an elderly man with more grey than black in his hair. He screwed up his eyes in concentration. "I'd say she's a Dunkirk privateer. No fishing boat carries that volume of sail or has such a crowd of men aboard."

Young grunted. "You could be correct, Hargreaves." He looked around his craft for inspiration. With his crew of old men and young boys, *Maid of Kent* could not put up much resistance. "Smith! Have you any gunnery experience?"

"Some," Smith looked at the four-pounder that was the vessel's sole armament. "Do you have powder and ball?"

"Some," Captain Young echoed Smith's reply. "Can you cripple that vessel before she closes?"

"I can try, sir," Smith was fully aware of the advent of the privateer.

"Do your best," Young said. "I'll have the men bring you ammunition."

Smith rejected the first cannonball that an eager teenager brought him. "That's not round," Smith said. "It won't fly true."

87

The second ball was rusty, but the third was as spherical as Smith desired. Placing the cannonball at his feet and shovelled powder from the old-fashioned powder bucket into the barrel of the cannon. He was more familiar with the pre-packaged linen or canvas powder bags that the Navy used but did not expect a merchant ship to carry such material. After priming the touch-hole, he asked for the slow-match. Fortunately, Captain Young had a forked linstock, a long staff, to hold the match.

"Stand clear," Smith said, applied the slow-match to the powder in the touch-hole, and stepped out of the gun's path. He hoped his rapid calculations were accurate, for too much powder would lead to a bushed touch-hole or even an exploding gun barrel, and too little would reduce the range and impact of the ball.

A complex system of ropes and pulleys tethered the cannon to absorb most of the recoil, but still, the gun slammed back on its low-slung cast-iron trucks. Grey-white powder smoke jetted out, temporarily obscuring Smith's vision until the wind blew it clear of the ship. Although Smith tried to watch the passage of the shot, he only saw a slight splash, three cables' lengths short and well to the privateer's starboard side.

"Try again!" Young ordered.

"Yes, Captain," Smith sponged out the gun and reloaded, this time adding slightly more powder. He waited for *Maid of Kent* to rise on the swell and fired again. The shot reached the apex of its arc and dipped, passing between the enemy vessel's masts without doing any damage except to rip an elliptical hole in the mainsail.

"Good shooting," Young said and flinched as the privateer fired her bow chaser. The powder smoke had not cleared from her bow when the shot splashed alongside.

"Not as good shooting as their's," Smith loaded again, rolling in the roundshot and adjusting his aim as the French ship drew closer.

Captain Young snapped an order that saw *Maid of Kent* alter the Royal Navy to disrupt our conversation." He gave a low whistle to call back his men.

"God speed, Captain Dupon," Smith said.

The privateers did not require any further warning. One glance showed them the approaching British frigate, and they hurried to their vessel. The prospect of spending years in some British prison was not alluring. The last man cast off, and the privateer crowded on canvas and sped away, leaving *Maid of Kent* free in the Channel swell.

"Did you agree on a ransom?" The captain asked, eyeing Smith curiously.

"No need for that," Smith said. "I only had to keep him talking until the Navy arrived." He nodded towards the frigate, now more visible as the westerly wind dissipated the mist.

"How the devil did you know when the Navy would arrive?"

"I watched," Smith said. He was aware that Hargreaves was studying him through suspicious eyes. "I make it my business to know such things."

course slightly. Smith readjusted his aim, allowed the stern to rise, and fired again. The shot dislodged a spar from the French vessel, which faltered, then responded by showing her broadside and firing. A torrent of six-pound cannonballs tore towards *Maid of Kent*, raising fountains of water all around and with one shot smashing the mizzentopsail yard arm.

"Damned Frenchie!" Young looked aloft as the mizzen swayed and blocks and rigging swung loose. "Get that mess fixed, Hargreaves!"

"Yes, Captain!" Hargreaves led a team of men aloft as Smith loaded, no longer checking the shot. He coughed in the smoke, aimed again, and realised the privateer was closing rapidly with the injured *Maid of Kent*. The Frenchman's sails clouded aloft, and men were busy at her bow chaser.

Smith fired a fraction before the privateer and saw fragments fly from her bow. Then the Frenchman replied, with the shot again hitting aloft, splintering a spar, and snapping cables. A block tumbled to the deck, bounced, and fell overboard, trailing a line.

"Damn their French hides!" Young shouted. "Hargreaves! Fix that spar!"

As Young spoke, *Maid of Kent* heeled to starboard, with her mainsail flapping loose. She wallowed in the water, losing speed as the privateer closed the gap between them.

Smith shovelled more powder into the cannon and grabbed a cannonball.

"It's no good, Smith!" Young shouted. "We'll have to surrender."

Smith looked up to see the French ship only five cables' lengths away. With her broadside of six-pounders grinning at the Kingsgate vessel, and armed men lining her rail, the Dunkirk privateer had *Maid of Kent* at her mercy.

"Sorry, boys," Captain Young said. "It looks like a French prison for us."

Smith stood beside the cannon, studying the damage his shot

had done to the Dunkirk vessel. He glanced upwards, trying to judge the time. "They might ransom us," he said. "Let me talk to them, skipper."

"You?" Young shook his head. "You're only a common mariner. Why the devil should they listen to you?"

Smith smiled. "Why should they listen to any of us, skipper? We have a crippled ship with one small cannon and scant ammunition, while they have twelve six-pounders, a long nine and a crew of over a hundred men. Let me try."

Young glanced aloft, where Hargreaves and his crew were attempting to rectify the damage the French had caused. He twisted his hands together. "Do what you can, Smith."

When the French privateer drew alongside, Smith waited for them, his hands by his side and his head erect. "Good afternoon, gentlemen," he said in French.

The privateer's deck was crammed with men, at least seventy, and all armed with pistols, swords, or boarding pikes. A dozen crossed to the deck of the British ship, looking around.

"You gave us a pretty chase," one man addressed Smith. "Are you the master?"

"Not I," Smith stood firm as the privateers pressed *Maid of Kent's* crew aft at point of pike and pistol. "I am the owner's representative."

The French captain, a plump-faced man in his late forties, mouthed a string of orders before returning his attention to Smith. "I am Captain Dupon. I will place a prize crew on your ship and take her into Dunkirk."

"You could do that," Smith said, "or you could ransom us."

Captain Dupon laughed. "You carry a cargo of grain to the Royal Navy," he said. "That will fetch me a good profit in Dunkirk."

"Grain? How would you like Captain Duguay back?" Smith saw the Frenchman's expression alter.

"Captain Duguay is a prisoner in England," the privateer said.

"Duguay is the best privateer captain you have," Smith

glanced behind him, wondering if any of the ship's crew un[der]stood French. "You would be exchanging one ship's cargo for [the] prospect of many."

Captain Dupon frowned. "Are you a Frenchman, monsieur? [If] not, why do you so willingly betray your king and country?"

"I am no Frenchman," Smith said. "And I don't care that," h[e] snapped his fingers, "for King George, his court, and all hi[s] government."

They stood in silence for a while as the privateers ushered the British crew below and the French captain pondered Smith's offer. The westerly breeze increased, kicking up waves that broke against the ship's stern, splattering both men with unheeded spray, while a lone seagull landed on the taffrail, watching them with unblinking eyes.

Smith glanced aloft, judging the time by the sun. He knew where he was and had long since worked out the patrol routes of the Royal Navy frigates.

Stay with me, Dupon.

"You could free Duguay?" the French captain asked at length. "You look like an ordinary seaman!"

Smith smiled. "How many ordinary seamen speak fluent French?" He could make out the topsails of the frigate approaching above a bank of low cloud. "Think about my proposal as you flee back to Dunkirk, Captain," Smith said. "For that British frigate will catch you if you delay another ten minutes."

The frigate captain had seen the two vessels side by side and was crowding on sail, fully aware of the danger of French privateers in these waters.

The French captain glanced over his shoulder. "I regret I must leave you, monsieur, without even learning your name."

"John Smith," Smith gave a slight bow. "At your service."

"Adieu, Monsieur Smith. You played a clever game." The privateer captain doffed his hat. "I hope we meet again, without

Chapter Eleven

"The Preventative men know this is a smuggling centre," Smith said, leaning against the counter in Dancing Horse's taproom, "and sooner or later they will tear up every corner to find the goods. I presume some are sold onto regular customers, and others are stored locally."

"I believe that's how it works," Ruth said. "I store some here."

"Well then," Smith said. "We'll have to find somewhere the Preventative men won't look."

"Do you know of somewhere?" Ruth asked.

"I might do," Smith said.

Is that a cave up there? Becky asked as they sat in Spike Cove with the sea breaking silver-white on the pebble beach.

Smith looked upward, where the cliff soared above him. The path down which they had come was easy enough, but on either side, the ground fell away in a slithering descent.

"I think it is," Smith said.

"I'll wager that cave is the entrance to a passage that stretches all the way to the Spike!" Becky sounded excited. "Shall we try to reach it?"

"Yes," Smith said, with the spirit of adventure high in his blood. "Are you coming?

"*Try and stop me!*" *Becky said, lifting her skirt to mid-calf as she stepped to the base of the cliff.*

The route from the path to the cave seemed simple until they found the ground crumbled under their feet. Becky was first to stumble, with Smith catching her as she slid to the ground.

"*You'll get into trouble if you go home with your skirt covered in dirt!*"

Becky giggled, covering her mouth with a small hand. "What will mother say?"

"*Nothing good, I'm sure. Your mother disapproves of me.*"

Becky looked serious for a moment. "No, she doesn't."

"*She thinks I'm beneath you.*"

Becky shook her head. "I don't think that!"

Smith smiled, although he knew that Becky's mother was correct. The son of a minor smuggler had no business spending time with the daughter of a landowner, however limited his lands.

"*Come on, Becky, we'll try again.*"

With no purchase on the slippery ground, they made no progress and gave it up after a long afternoon of laughter and frustration. Yet when Smith looked back, it was Becky's words that he remembered. He knew that, socially, he was on a much lower lever than Rebecca Strode.

"Where?" Ruth had been waiting for Smith's reply while he drifted into his past.

"I'll have to check it first," Smith said.

Bess accompanied him to the top of the cliff, a score of yards from the outer wall of The Spike. She looked over the edge to where the sea crashed onto the beach a hundred and twenty feet below.

"It's a long way down." Bess did not flinch from the drop.

"It is," Smith agreed, "and it might be a wasted journey. Can you see the cave?"

"No." Bess shook her head.

"Good. If you can't see it, then neither can the Excisemen." Smith unravelled the rope he had brought. "I'll climb down while you act as my lookout. Sing out if you see anybody approaching."

"Be careful," Bess said.

"I will." Smith hammered a crowbar into the ground, tested that it was secure, looped the rope over it, and tied it tight. With a parting wave, he dropped the end of the rope over the edge of the cliffs and lowered himself down. After spending half his life at sea, climbing down a rope was as natural as breathing, and Smith descended without hesitation.

Looking up, he saw Bess watching him. For one instant, Becky was there with her blonde hair billowing across her face, but Smith shook away the past and concentrated on the task in hand.

He reached the cave within five minutes and swung inside, balancing with one hand as he got his footing.

"Are you all right?" Bess's voice floated down to him.

Smith looked into the cave. It was smaller than he had hoped but dry, with no seepage from the roof. The walls and ceiling were solid. *There is no passage to the Spike, Becky.* "We've found our storage site," he shouted back and stepped inside. The angle of the entrance would make the cave invisible from the sea, as the cliff made it impassable without a major effort.

Thank you, God.

"We'll need to make rope ladders," Smith said when he returned to the top of the cliff. "Not everybody can climb a rope. The rungs will be ten inches apart, of hazel or ash. We can keep the ladders at the Spike, under a pile of rubble. Nobody will search an old ruin, and if they do, they'll probably think the rope was only boys bird nesting." He smiled. "Things are beginning to come together, Bess."

"Not quite," Bess said. "Until you have a ship, you can do nothing."

"I'm sure Sir Francis will provide one," Smith said.

Classical statues occupied each niche in the great hall, staring outward through blank marble eyes. Splendid in his livery, the manservant spoke in a whisper as he addressed Smith.

"You'll have to wait. Sir Francis is engaged at present."

"Sir Francis requested that I meet him at noon," Smith reminded.

The manservant frowned. "Sir Francis is engaged," he repeated.

"Where is he?" Smith looked around the hall, with its marble staircase ascending to the upper stories and precious Turkish carpet spread over the floor.

"Upstairs, sir, in the Chess Room." The servant lowered his voice still further as though he were in church. "One does not disturb Sir Francis when he is playing chess."

"Doesn't one?" Smith asked, wondering what Sir Francis's reaction would be if he disturbed his game.

No, I won't spoil everything for one moment's diversion.

"Thank you for the advice," Smith said. "Shall I wait here?"

The servant eyed him up and down, deciding if this guest was of the required quality to place in the withdrawing room. "That would be best," he said.

Smith began to pace the hall, examining the statues and wondering at their provenance. After fifteen minutes had passed, he heard a shout from upstairs.

"Checkmate, by God!" Sir Francis sounded triumphant. "That's a hundred guineas you owe me!"

A moment later, a door opened upstairs, and a well-dressed, portly man emerged. "You're too good for me, Sir Francis," he said as he hurried away. The manservant waited with the portly man's hat, cane, and cloak.

"Ah, Smith," Sir Francis was slightly flushed as he strode down the stairs. "Come to my study. Show him up, Jenkins!"

Sir Francis eyed Smith from the opposite side of his walnut bureau. "This is the second time you've come to my attention, Smith."

The longcase clock in the corner of the study struck ten, with the mechanism whirring softly between each sonorous bell. The name Harrison was scrolled across the face while the walnut veneer matched Sir Francis's bureau.

"Yes, sir," Smith agreed.

"You helped the Preventative Service intercept a cargo of illicit spirits, and you saved one of my vessels from a French privateer." Sir Francis poured two glasses of port and passed one to Smith. "These are not the actions of a common mariner, Smith, whatever role you wrap around yourself."

"Thank you, sir," Smith sipped at the port.

Sir Francis frowned. "Yet while you were in the Dancing Horse, you were less than co-operative."

"Yes, sir. It would not be safe to be a friend of the Excise in that establishment."

Sir Francis's brow cleared. "I see! Then remove yourself to the Hounds Rest, sir! A far more salubrious inn, by any standards."

"The Hounds Rest charges more than I can afford, Sir Francis."

"Ah!" Sir Francis nodded understandingly. "It's a matter of money. I might be able to do something about that. You have extensive seagoing experience, I understand."

"I have, sir." Smith fought to keep the hatred from his eyes.

"At what level?"

"I was the mate of a coasting brig, sir, and mate of a Baltic brig, carrying flax from Riga to Arbroath in Scotland. The Navy pressed me, and I was foretopman and master." Smith included some of the truth in his list of lies.

"How would you like to command one of my ships?"

Smith looked up. "I would be honoured to command one of your vessels, sir."

"Captain Young did not cover himself in glory on his last voyage. I am removing him from command of *Maid of Kent* and will put you in charge," Sir Francis had already made his decision and took Smith's acceptance as a formality. His eyes narrowed. "I am sure I have met you before, Smith." His pleasant face creased into a smile. "Captain Smith, rather."

"I would never forget you, sir," Smith bowed before Sir Francis's memory improved further.

Sir Francis accepted the tribute as his due. "You'd better get along to your new ship, Captain Smith. I have to attend court now, with my magistrate's hat on. You know the sort of thing; poachers, petty disputes, theft," he smiled again, "but no local smuggling since you helped me smash the Blackwell gang, and that fire deprived me of the pleasure of sentencing its leader."

"Yes, sir. I am sure you do your duty admirably." Smith bowed and withdrew, aware he was trembling with hatred.

As Smith stood in the hallway of the house, with busy servants bustling around, he sensed, rather than heard, the patter of light footsteps on the stairs leading upstairs. Instinct forced him to turn.

She was on the landing at the turn of the stairs, with one hand on the varnished balustrade and the other holding an ivory fan. Five feet seven in height, with blonde curls framing her oval face, her eyes were wide and blue, as they had always been. She stopped when she recognised Smith.

"Oh!" The woman lifted her fan to cover her mouth.

"My dear," Sir Francis had emerged from his study. "There is no need for alarm. I know this man appears rather rough, but he is in my employ."

The woman lowered her fan, with only a slight tremble of her chin revealing her discomposure. "Good evening, sir." She dropped in a curtsey.

"This fellow is John Smith. I have given him command of *Maid of Kent*."

"Captain Smith," the woman straightened up, with her eyes

never straying from Smith's face. "Good evening, Captain Smith."

"Good evening, Lady Selby." Smith gave a low bow.

"You have command of *Maid of Kent?*" Lady Rebecca Selby asked, with her voice like music, slicing into Smith with bitter-sweet memories.

"As from ten minutes past the hour," Smith confirmed.

"Then you have my congratulations, Captain Smith." Lady Selby accentuated the name only slightly, but Smith understood.

"Thank you, Your Ladyship." Smith bowed again, lower this time, knowing Lady Selby would dance to any reel he chose.

Lady Selby swept past and into the front room, leaving only the lingering scent of her passage and a host of memories. When Smith had last seen her, she had been a teenager on the cusp of womanhood. Now she was a beauty, shapely, poised, and confident, somebody who knew her place in the world. Smith took a deep breath. He had returned to Kingsgate for two reasons. One had been to seek revenge on Sir Francis, and the other was to find Rebecca, yet now he had found her, he felt very unsettled.

Damn! Smith thought. *That is a further complication. Damn the man, and damn Rebecca, Lady Selby.*

———————

"You are out of sorts tonight," Bess said as Smith sat in the taproom, failing to drown his thoughts in a sea of rum.

"I have things on my mind," Smith told her.

"What things?" Bess asked.

Smith put down his glass, aware that Carman was listening from the neighbouring table. He looked at Bess, mentally comparing her to Rebecca.

"Sir Francis has given me command of *Maid of Kent,*" he said.

"You have your ship, then," Bess said.

"I have my ship," Smith agreed.

"Then I suggest you stop drinking, or you'll be in no fit state to sail her."

"Good advice, Captain," Carman said. "Listen to the woman."

When Smith looked at Bess, he saw Becky's face as it had been ten years ago. "Bloody women!"

"Bloody woman," Bess said. "There's only one of me."

"And that's more than enough," Smith said, as Carman watched, smiling from behind his glass of rum.

SMITH ALREADY KNEW HOW *MAID OF KENT* SAILED, BUT NOW he studied her with more care. She was a two-masted lugger, with the figurehead of a half-naked woman and a crew who greeted their new captain with sullen resentment. They remembered him as one of the crowd, a before-the-mast newcomer and had no intention of welcoming him as their captain.

"Everybody aft!" Smith ordered. He waited beside the wheel as the hands mustered. There were twelve men, either grey-bearded or too young to have felt the kiss of a razor. They glared at this jumped-up foremast hand with undisguised contempt.

"All right, men, and boys, you've had it easy so far. You knew me as John Smith, now I am Captain Smith, and I learned my trade in the Channel and the Navy. As from today, you will work navy-style, or you won't work at all." Smith looked over the crew, watching the dismay that replaced the dislike in their faces.

"Everybody!" he shouted. "Get up the mainmast!"

Smith led the way, cursing them to the top and racing them back down. Then he had them running around the deck, with the youngsters at his heels and the older men lagging far behind. After an hour, two of the veterans collapsed, gasping for breath. Leaving them lying, Smith continued, up and down the masts, round the deck, into the hold and out again.

"I need fit men!" Smith roared. "We have to face the sea, the French, and the damned Royal Navy! Move!"

After three hours, he had only three men at his heels, two under twenty and Hargraves the mate, with his jutting grey beard and the light of defiance in his eyes.

"We've work to do tomorrow morning," Smith told his crew as they lay gasping and sweating on the deck. "You all have shore leave. Report here at the forenoon watch. Dismiss." He watched them stagger away, knowing the majority would already hate him. They would gather in the nearest tavern, devising methods of retaliating.

Smith did not care what they thought. He had plans of *Maid of Kent*, with or without her current crew. He would prefer without, for he wanted to choose his crew, men as bold and unscrupulous as himself.

SMITH WAS WAITING ON *MAID OF KENT* BEFORE THE FORENOON watch began. He rang the ship's bell, enjoying the brassy clamour that sounded across the harbour. Of the dozen crew he led the previous evening, only three turned up. One was the elderly Hargraves who had managed to keep with him, the other two striplings under eighteen years old. Ten minutes later, Thomas Carman stepped on board, dropped his chest on the deck and looked around.

"Reporting for duty, Captain," Carman said.

"Take your place, Carman," Smith ordered.

"I need more men," Smith said, "and I need another mast on *Maid of Kent*."

"Another mast?" Hargreaves raised a quizzical eye and nodded his agreement. "That will increase her speed and improve her manoeuvrability."

"That's the idea," Smith said. "I don't intend any other French privateer to catch my ship."

Hargreaves nodded sagely while Carman's eyes explored the ship. "I understand. Does Sir Francis approve?"

"He doesn't know," Smith said. "I'll gather a suitable crew while Jackson's yard does the work."

Hargreaves smile was as wicked as anything Smith had ever seen. "The Dancing Horse is a good place to start," he said. "I'll come with you, Captain Smith. I know the kind of bold lads you desire."

"What kind is that?" Smith challenged him.

"The sons of the men who sailed with your father."

As Smith stared at him, Carman gave a brief cackle and moved to the foc'sle.

"YOU'RE MAKING QUITE A NAME FOR YOURSELF, CAPTAIN Smith," Ruth told him. "You have a way of being at the centre of things." She nodded to Smith's elderly companion. "Peter."

Hargreaves grin took ten years off his age. "Mrs Martin."

"Mind you," Ruth said to Smith. "Your choice of company leaves something to be desired. Peter Hargreaves here is a rogue and a blackguard."

"I reckoned he was," Smith said solemnly.

Ruth's eyes flickered from Smith to Hargreaves and back. "What do you plan today?"

"Peter Hargreaves is going to help me recruit a crew."

Ruth sighed. "The king is dead. Long live the king."

"Meaning?" Smith asked.

"Meaning that Captain Blackwell is hardly cold in his grave, and you're going to take his place."

Hargreaves looked around the taproom, nodding to some of the men he knew. "How many hands do you want, Captain?"

"Twelve," Smith replied. "I have six already, so I need six new men."

"Which six do you have, Captain?" Hargreaves raised his eyebrows

"Thomas Carman, the two young lads who turned up today, you, and two Ramsleys."

"That would make thirteen in the ship, including you," Hargreaves reminded. "That's an unlucky number for a seaman."

"I don't care about luck or superstition," Smith said. "I've seen the worst the world can do and shaken the devil's claws."

"Yes, Captain," Hargreaves said.

Smith chose a corner seat facing the outer door of the taproom. "You were Captain Young's mate, so you keep your position. Send your prospective crewmen to me, Mr Mate."

Hargreaves smiled. "I didn't think you'd keep me as the mate."

"I need a man who knows local conditions," Smith said. "Are you that man?"

"I've sailed these waters all my life," Hargreaves said. "And there's not much I don't know about Kingsgate." He lowered his voice. "Carman may be a bit old, Captain."

"I want him as quartermaster," Smith said. "He'll have a host of experience."

"Yes, Captain," Hargreaves agreed.

"Send me your men, Mr Mate," Smith said.

They came one by one, a collection of the disreputable, the shifty, the thirsty, and the unwanted. Some were thieves, others footpads or simply ne'er do wells, men who had worked on slave ships or privateers, Greenland whalers or south-Spainers, with a sprinkling of good seamen among the dross of Southern England.

"Who are you?" Smith looked the man up and down.

"James Hewitt," the man had the cut of a seaman, with hard hands and a face battered by ten thousand winds and the tropical sun.

"You're a seaman," Smith said. "Which seas have you seen?"

"The North Atlantic from Bristol to Newfoundland and

downward to the Old Bahamas Channel, West Africa and the Brass River, the Caribbean to the Main and the Gulf in hurricane season." Hewitt's voice was hoarse, and his eyes alternated from dead to intensely alive.

"That sounds like the triangular trade. Were you a slaver?"

"Aye, captain, a slaver and a slave."

"Tell me more."

"When I was a youngster, no more than fifteen, I sailed as a cabin boy in a slaver. When we got to West Africa, a local king decided he wanted a white slave, so the captain handed me over."

Smith grunted. "How did you get back?"

"I escaped three years later. I swam to another slaver and hid on board until we were clear of the coast."

"You won't be afraid of hard work and hard knocks, then."

"After three years of being a slave to African chiefs, praying for death to release me, anything is freedom."

"Mr Hargreaves will help you sign articles," Smith said.

Smith signed a young man named Mitchell, reputed to be the swiftest runner in Kent, and a sour-faced man named Roper, who was without fear or morality.

Smith chose carefully, looking for men with sufficient spirit to run an illicit cargo, men who would not be scared to confront the Preventative service face to face, yet men with experience of sailing in the worst weather the Channel could produce.

While the respectable merchantmen struggled to find crews in the face of threats from the impress service and French privateers, Smith realised that a smuggling captain could have his pick. His men knew that few French privateers would attack a ship that traded, however illicitly, with their country, while a fast lugger could outsail any but the speediest of Royal Naval craft.

"You've turned away some good men," Hargreaves said.

"Maybe," Smith sipped at a tankard of ale. "I have selected my crew. Now I need a cargo."

"Sir Francis will provide a cargo for *Maid of Kent*."

"The squire will provide our cover," Smith said. "We're going into the Free Trade business, Mr Mate, and we're going to astonish the country."

Hargreaves removed the pipe from his mouth. "Sir Francis won't like you using his ship for free trade."

Smith curled his fist around his tankard until he buckled the pewter. When he looked up, Hargreaves flinched from the expression in his eyes.

"Aye," Smith said. "Sir Francis." He stared at nothing, with his mouth moving silently. Nobody came near him.

"I HEAR YOU'VE BEEN BUSY," BESS SAID AS SMITH STEPPED INTO the room. She smiled at him from her seat beside the window. "Should I call you Captain Smith, now?"

Smith closed the door. "If you wish," he eyed her, again comparing Bess with Becky.

"What's in your mind?" Bess stepped towards him, studying his face. "You've changed."

"Perhaps," Smith said. He stepped to the window. "The world looks different from here."

"A captain's viewpoint?" Bess pressed against him.

Smith turned the question over in his mind. "Perhaps," he said cautiously.

"What's changed, John?" Bess forced herself in front of him. "What's happened? You're different."

"Am I?"

"Yes." Bess lifted her chin. "You've got your ship. Why are you not happy?"

Why am I not happy? I am never happy, damn it. Smith looked at Bess. She was not Becky, but she was here, and she had never let him down so far.

"You're a handsome piece, Bess," Smith allowed.

Bess studied him. "You're a worried man, John," she retaliated and put a hand on his arm. "What's in your mind?"

"The past," Smith said truthfully.

"Leave it alone," Bess said. "If you disturb the past, it may bite you in the arse."

Smith's mind cleared. "That may be good advice," he agreed.

JACKSON'S SHIPYARD AT MARSHAM WOULD GENERALLY TAKE weeks to fit a mizzen mast to a trading lugger, but Smith took Jackson the foreman aside and spoke quietly to him. "Double the workforce," Smith said. "Triple it if you wish. Work all day and all night."

"That will cost Sir Francis a pretty penny," the foreman warned.

"Let me worry about Sir Francis," Smith said.

With *Maid of Kent* in dock, while Jackson fitted the new mast, Smith could view her better. She had even finer lines than he expected, a vessel built for speed, with a flared bow to slice through the waves and a copper-bottomed hull.

"She'll be fast," Jackson said.

"I'll ensure that," Smith said. "I want the masts raked aft, with extra spars aloft."

"She's a cargo vessel," Jackson reminded. "Not King George's racing yacht."

"She might well be racing," Smith walked around *Maid of Kent*. "On our last trip, a Dunkirk privateer outsailed us. I don't want that to happen again."

Jackson ran a hand over *Maid of Kent's* keel. "She was French-built," he said. "We captured her as a prize. The French build lovely ships, faster than ours."

"Could you give the figurehead a lick of paint?" Smith said. "I like a smart figurehead.

"Do you want a blonde or a brunette?" Jackson asked, smiling.

Becky or Bess? Smith asked himself. "Make her a redhead."

Maid of Kent was ready within ten days, with her three masts thrusting to the sky and the shipbuilders looking tired but proud.

Sir Francis was not so pleased when he produced Jackson's account and slapped it down on his desk. "What the deuce is the meaning of this, Smith?"

"I need a fast ship, sir," Smith said blandly. "The Channel is alive with privateers. I reckoned it was better to pay for a new mast than lose the entire ship to some Frenchman." He lowered his voice. "I don't want any more damned Dunkirk privateers on your ship, sir."

Sir Francis lifted the account, re-read the final figure, and slammed his hand on the desk again. "I'm taking this amount off your wages."

"As you wish, sir," Smith said.

And I'll take this vessel wherever I like, Franky, and damn you for an arrogant murdering, woman-stealing bastard.

Chapter Twelve

Smith took a deep breath as he stood on *Maid of Kent's* deck. It was a massive step from serving before the mast to commanding a ship, especially with an untried crew. He stamped his feet, lifted his chin, and smiled.

Act the captain, and men will follow.

"Are we all ready, Mr Hargreaves?"

"Ready, sir," Hargreaves replied.

"Let go aft!" Smith ordered. "Let go forward!" He watched the cables snake away, and *Maid* was free of the land, feeling like a living creature under his command as he steered her out of the harbour into the fresh Channel breeze.

"Let fall! Sheet home!"

Maid responded, lively with the wind.

"Man the tops'l halliards! Tend the braces!" Men hurried to obey Smith's commands as *Maid* eased outward and westward along the coast.

You have a new life now, Captain Smith.

With her new mizzen, and her masts raked to Smith's requirements, *Maid of Kent* was fast with the wind astern or on either quarter, and Smith tested her with a full spread of sails. "She's a speedy little craft," he said with satisfaction.

"She'll outrun most French privateers," Hargreaves said.

"She will," Smith agreed. *And the Preventative cutters.* "I would wish we were better armed," he said. "One four-pounder can't keep anybody at bay, except maybe a small rowing boat."

"You could ask Sir Francis for more guns," Hargreaves said doubtfully.

"I could, but he's not forgiven me for the mizzen mast yet."

Hargreaves grunted. "Sir Francis is not a man to easily forgive."

Smith appointed Carman as quartermaster and ordered him to ensure the hands kept busy.

"Aye, Captain," Carman had lost twenty years of his age since he stepped on deck. He looked around him, joying in the feel of the wind and the music of the shrouds. "She's a fast ship, Captain."

"She is, Carman."

"Teach would like her," Carman said. "Or men in Teach's mould."

"Are you suggesting that we become pirates, Carman?"

Carman grinned. "I'm not saying anything, Captain."

As Sir Francis had a contract to supply wheat and mutton for the Navy, *Maid of Kent* sailed from Kingsgate to Portsmouth once a week. Smith tested the ship for speed on each voyage, altering the set of the sails with every change in the wind's direction, so he knew her intimately. He had the crew performing sail drill in addition to the normal routine of the ship, as Carman seemed to grow younger day by day.

The first three voyages passed without incident, but on the fourth, a suspicious sail came closer than the crew liked.

"That vessel looks like trouble, Captain," Hargreaves said. "She's French, or I'm a Dutchman."

"Steer west-south-west by a half west," Smith ordered.

"That will bring her even closer to us," Hargreaves warned.

"West-south-west by a half west," Smith repeated.

As Carman the helmsman obeyed, *Maid of Kent* eased over. "Take in the mainsail," Smith ordered. "I want us under topsails only."

Ghosting under topsails, *Maid of Kent* reduced her speed until she barely made headway, allowing the strange sail to crawl closer.

"She's French," Hargreaves said, with resignation in his voice.

"Mitchell, take over the helm," Smith ordered. "Hargreaves, send all the men below except the helmsman and Carman."

"Carman?" Hargreaves repeated.

"Carman," Smith said. "You look like a harmless old fellow. I want you to work near my cabin until I call for you."

Carman nodded. "Yes, Captain."

The strange vessel was single-masted, and when Smith examined her through his telescope, he saw she carried four six-pounders and about twenty-five of a crew. She closed with *Maid of Kent* under all sail and fired a single cannon.

"Halt!" A young man stood in the bows with long hair flopping around his neck as he spoke through a speaking trumpet. "Who are you?"

"*Maid of Kent*, Captain Smith from Kingsgate in Kent," Smith replied at once. He estimated the speaker to be in his late teens or early twenties, and although he spoke English, he had a strong French accent.

"Heave to!" the youngster wore a big grin. "I am Captain Dupon, and you are now a prize of *Marie Blanc* of Dunkirk."

"You're too late," Smith said. "We're already the prize of *Dragon* of La Rochelle, under ransom. Why do you think we didn't try to run?"

"Haul your wind," the young man sounded irritated rather than disappointed. "I am going to board."

"We're short-handed," Smith scanned the French crew. All were young men, some little more than boys. "*Dragon* took the best of my hands as hostages, but come on board if you wish, Captain."

Marie Blanc came alongside, crowded with bright, eager faces. When one of the youths threw a line, Smith secured it, and the young French captain leapt across the gap with a pistol in his hand and a delicate small sword at his left hip. Three other Frenchmen followed, looking around them at this ship they believed they had captured.

"Welcome aboard, gentlemen," Smith said. "If you would kindly step this way?" He bowed politely and led them to his cabin as Hargreaves watched wonderingly, and Carman hovered around the captain's cabin. "Pray come with me, Mr Hargreaves. Mitchell does not need our supervision." Smith nodded to Carman.

The second the Frenchmen entered the cabin, Smith lifted the pistols from the desk.

"You are now my prisoner, Captain, and your men," he levelled one weapon at the young Frenchman's head and passed the other to the grinning Carman. "Hand your weapons over to Mr Hargreaves here, or I'll blow your captain's brains all over the bulkhead."

"And I'll shoot this one!" Carman pressed the muzzle of his pistol against the cheek of the closest Frenchman.

The young privateers looked astonished, with the youngest nearly in tears. They did not resist when Hargreaves removed their pistols and swords.

"Take them below, Mr Hargreaves," Smith ordered. He stepped onto the deck, replacing his pistol in his belt, with his jacket on top.

"I thought you were in the mould of Teach," Carman said as Smith placed one foot on the taffrail.

"Your captain has decided to remain on board," Smith shouted to *Marie Blanc*. "He asks that four more men cross to take control of the ship."

Smith helped the next four Frenchmen on board, invited

them into the cabin and made them prisoner.

"Take them below, Mr Hargreaves," Smith said. "Mitchell, you have the wheel, and Carman has the deck." He followed Hargreaves below, where the rest of his crew waited.

"There is a small French privateer alongside," Smith said, "with about eighteen armed men on board." He watched the men's faces. Some looked apprehensive while the two Ramsleys stamped their feet. Jake Ramsley put a hand to the long knife at his belt. "If the Frenchie captures us, we could be prisoners for months or even years. If we capture her, we'll earn ourselves a little prize money."

The crew perked up at the thought of prize money, while an appeal to patriotism would have meant nothing to them.

"Are you with me, boys?"

When the crew roared its assent, Smith opened the arms locker and issued cutlasses and pistols.

The Ramsleys grinned and brandished their weapons, nodding happily.

"Right, lads," Smith said. "Up on deck and follow me!"

Smith dispensed with pretence and led a roaring, cutlass-waving charge from *Maid of Kent* onto the deck of *Marie Blanc*.

The Frenchmen stared at this reversal of fortunes, and only two of the French youths resisted. Smith shot the first, while Jake Ramsley thrust a cutlass through the belly of the second, twisted the blade, and hauled out the man's intestines.

"That's my boy!" Carman had followed the rest, flaunting his pistol and looking for a victim. However, he was denied when the remainder of the French surrendered, more astonished than scared, despite the two dead men on their deck.

Smith herded his prisoners down below. "And that, gentlemen, is how you capture a French privateer."

"The ghost of Blackbeard Teach walks with you," Carman said, still waving his pistol.

"Mr Hargreaves, please take over our prize and follow us home."

"Aye, aye, Captain," Hargreaves said.

HALF OF KINGSGATE ASSEMBLED TO WITNESS *MAID OF KENT'S* arrival with the French vessel as a prize. Smith came ashore to the cheers of men and women. Even Lady Selby watched from the back of her horse, lifting her hand in salutation.

Damn the woman! I don't need any complications!

Smith met her gaze for a second before looking away.

"That's an unusual sight," Bess stood slightly apart from the others as Smith pushed through the crowd to her side. "I don't recall a merchant lugger capturing a privateer before."

"I was lucky," Smith said. "She had an inexperienced crew, maybe the younger brothers, or even the sons of privateers."

"What will you do now?" Bess's attention shifted from the captured ship to Lady Selby and back.

"Sell her as a prize," Smith said, "and mount her guns in *Maid of Kent*. I feel naked sailing the Channel with only a pop-gun."

"And all legal and above board," Bess shook her head in mock disappointment. "I'm surprised at you, John. I thought you planned to be a free trader, not a respectable merchant."

"I plan a lot more than that," Smith said. "You stay with me, Bess, and you'll find out what I plan."

"Other people have plans too," Bess said. "Most of these women," she indicated the crowd, taking care to include Lady Selby and Suzanne, who stood in front of the others with her arms folded, "were devouring you with their eyes."

Smith kissed Bess full on the lips. "Let them," he said.

"Don't turn around," Bess said. "One, in particular, is very interested in you."

Smith remained still. "Describe her," he said.

"Sir Frank's lady wife," Bess kept her voice flat.

"Ah. We met in the big house."

"She's trouble," Bess warned.

"I know."

Bess was silent for a minute, and Smith knew she was returning Lady Selby's scrutiny.

"I'm going to exchange the French crew," Smith tried to distract Bess from Lady Selby. "The French are bound to hold some Kingsgate men."

"Can you do that?" Bess asked.

"I can try." When Bess took possessive hold of Smith's arm, Lady Selby kicked in her heels and rode away.

"That would make you popular with the villagers, particularly the wives."

Smith nodded. "That's the idea," he said. "I am not altruistic by nature."

Bess squeezed his arm. "Perhaps not, John, but things happen when you are around.

WHEN A LONDON MERCHANT BOUGHT *MARIE BLANC*, SMITH pocketed eighty guineas as his share of the prize money, with another forty for her cargo.

"You're rich," Bess said when Smith deposited the bulk of the gold in the bank and returned with a heavy purse.

"Not yet," Smith said, "but it's a start."

"What are you going to do with the money?"

"Pay for the mizzen mast, buy shares in *Maid of Kent*, bank the rest, and dress you like the fine lady you are."

"There is a dressmaker in Marsham," Bess said hopefully, "and more than one in Dover."

"No," Smith shook his head. "We're going to town, Bess. Hargreaves can look after the ship while you and I take the mail to London."

Bess looked at him with her mouth open. "I've never been to London."

"Neither have I," Smith admitted.

Chapter Thirteen

The mail coach was stuffy inside, with its leather upholstery and straw to keep the feet and legs warm, but Smith settled back and watched Bess stare out of the window. He listened to the guard blowing his horn to clear the road of any other traffic, looked out on the villages they rattled through, and noted where the coach stopped to change horses.

So many inns and taverns. So many potential customers.

When they reached London, Smith thought it vast, crowded, and immensely noisy. Bess stared around her, clinging to Smith in a combination of fear and excitement.

Smith booked them both into the Golden Cross at Charing Cross, between London and Westminster.

"Mr and Mrs?" The clerk asked, searching for a wedding ring on Bess's finger.

"Smith," Bess answered quickly. "And could you direct us to the nearest jeweller, please? Some blaggard stole my wedding ring, and I feel quite naked without it." She leaned across the polished counter. "Quite naked," she repeated.

"Smith," the clerk wrote their name in his ledger. "There are many jewellers in London, Mrs Smith. I am sure you will find one to replace your ring."

"Thank you," Bess said.

Smith quickly realised that clothes perfectly suitable for a maritime village in Kent were out of place in London. He and Bess looked like rustics lost in the big city, which was precisely what they were.

"We need new clothes," Smith said after half an hour walking along the Strand and Fleet Street, during which Bess gaped at the array of shops and beautifully dressed people. "I had intended to buy you one dress, Bess, but we need more."

Bess looked at him sideways. "Nobody's ever bought me a dress before." She lowered her voice. "Nobody's ever bought me anything before."

Smith agreed and put an arm around her in sudden sympathy. "Those days are past." He was surprised when Bess leaned into him. "Come on, let's find a clothes shop."

For the first few hours, Smith and Bess toured central London, staring at the architecture, like the neo-classical Hanover Square and the straight, open streets of the West End. They peered at the dark alleyways of the St Giles rookery and quickly recoiled, recognising the danger within. Barrows, waggons, and coaches crammed into the streets while open wherries carried passengers on the Thames.

Bess stopped in St James Square. "I've never seen anything so elegant," she said. "Imagine living here, John."

"I'd have to capture a few more French prizes," Smith said, watching a gloriously clad footman carry a load of packages from a carriage into one of the houses.

"What sort of people are they? How do they get their money?" Bess stared as a footman in green livery opened the carriage door, and a slim man left, followed by a woman in a skirt so wide she had to emerge sideways.

Smith watched without any expression on his face. "Lords and ladies," he said. "The sort of people who oppress their tenants to gain another few guineas to spend on selfish pleasures."

"I'd like to live like that," Bess looked down on her suddenly dowdy best clothes, with the scuffed boots she had cleaned especially for her visit to London.

"Would you?" Smith looked sideways at her.

"Yes," Bess nodded vigorously. "Wouldn't you?"

The seamen crammed into the lower deck of the man-of-war, with the hammocks so close that Smith did not have to stretch to touch his neighbour. At night, the deck was a solid mass of snoring, grunting men, and during the day, the men not on duty lived in the same confined space. They ate, played, sang, gambled, and fought together, and when in port, the wives and would-be-wives joined them.

Privacy was unknown. Everybody knew the most intimate secrets of their shipmates, and lower deck justice ensured the men were honest and fair. Bullying was rife, with anybody unfortunate enough to have a weakness or disability taunted unmercifully. The officers rarely ventured to the lower deck and only spoke to the hands to give an order. God help the man who hesitated to jump at every command.

"Yes," Smith replied. His dreams and plans did not include London, but compared to the lack of privacy, and intense discipline of a man-of-war, living in St James Square would be like entering Paradise. "We would hardly fit in, though."

Bess glanced at their rustic clothing and smiled ruefully. "You mentioned buying new clothes," she said.

I also said 'we.' Do I think of our relationship as permanent? A woman will only slow me down.

"Come on, then, Bess!"

Smith dragged the not-unwilling Bess to a dressmaker, who lifted his nose at Bess's country accent, then met Smith's eyes and co-operated with sudden enthusiasm.

"It will be a pleasure to make your lady wife a dress," the dressmaker's sweeping bow held only a hint of mockery. "Is it for a special event, sir?"

"It's for a dance," Smith told her, adding the only place he knew in London where dancing took place. "At Covent Garden."

"Ah, at Covent Garden." The dressmaker said no more.

After measuring Bess with intrusive fingers, which nearly caused Bess to retaliate, the dressmaker gave a date to collect his creation.

Bess glanced at Smith in sudden concern. "We won't be here, then," she said.

"We'll be back in two days," Smith told the dressmaker. "You'll have it ready by then."

"My girls will have to work all night," the dressmaker said.

"Then do so," Smith told him, with a hint of menace.

Smith waited for a moment as the dressmaker retired to his workshop at the back of the premises.

"We have to make this dress for a supposed lady," the dressmaker said. "And a gentleman of the four outs — without manners, without wit, without money, and without credit."

"No!" Bess pulled Smith back as he reached for his pistol. "It's only the opinion of a fool."

From the dressmaker, Smith took Bess to a coffee shop to recover, listening to the conversation about the progress of the war in Europe, North America, and Hindustan. The Londoners were more aware of current events than the villagers of Kingsgate, although they did not mention the smuggling or struggles in the Channel.

"Are you ready, Bess?" Smith asked.

"Where are we going next?"

"To buy some clothes to wear," Smith said. "Something more fitting than what we wear at present, yet not especially made for us."

London was the best shopping centre in Great Britain, and Bess marvelled at the displays in the brilliantly lit bow-windowed shopfronts. When she indicated clothes she liked, Smith pushed into the shop and bought them, waiting for the shopkeeper to make alterations while he waited. By the end of that day, both were fully outfitted and carried a dozen packages to the Golden Cross.

They ate at the Inn, slept in comfortable beds, and returned to the streets the following morning. Smith toured the gunsmiths, discarded the first three and found a small premise in Cheapside.

"This is not the most common place to find a gunsmith," Smith said and tapped a small brass plate on the wall, "but look at the sign."

Bess read the words. "Arbuthnot Moodie," she said. "A member of the Worshipful Company of Gunmakers of London."

"That means Moodie has passed his apprenticeship and will make quality guns," Smith told her.

The shop's interior was dark and smelled of gun oil, while Mr Moodie was quiet, bald, and efficient.

"A pistol for the lady," Moodie repeated Smith's request. "Is it for horseback, carriage, or carrying?"

"Carrying," Smith said. "I want it small and light."

"With a delicate trigger," Moodie understood at once. "With so many footpads and highwaymen in these troubled times, one needs to take precautions."

Moodie had a selection of pistols of various sizes, from fourteen inches long to weapons that would fit into a lady's purse.

"Remember what I said," Smith murmured as Bess looked over the weapons. "Light trigger and short barrel."

"I have a range downstairs," Moodie said and ushered them to his basement, where Bess tried out four weapons before she chose one.

"I like this gun," she said. "It feels right."

"Then make friends with it," Moodie said, "for it may save your life someday."

"That's better," Smith said, paying more than he expected, but satisfied with the quality of Bess's choice.

"Visitors to London, are you?" Moodie eyed them both. "You'll be here to see the sights. There's the lunatics at Bedlam to visit if you have a mind, or you can visit Bridewell to see the felons whipped or even a multiple hanging at Tyburn."

"No," Bess said. "None of these."

"We'll also purchase a blunderbuss," Smith ignored Moodie's list of London's attractions. "We'll collect it later."

They ate richer food than Bess had ever seen in her life and spent the evenings at a theatre in Drury Lane, where the audience bayed at the actors and behaved with less decorum than any crowd in a Kentish tavern.

"Will this be normal life for us?" Bess looked up from one of the two chairs in the room. "I mean, will we visit London often?"

"No," Smith said. "This is unusual. I have to make money, and you have to keep the books. Capturing that privateer was a bounty, an extra."

"Why spend all your money on me?"

"Why not?" Smith asked, looking at her youthful face, with eyes that could sparkle like a child's or brood over past hardships, ancient with experience.

Why not? Because spending money on a woman diverts me from my objective.

Twice Smith saw Bow Street Runners, Henry Fielding's private police force, and wondered if the idea would spread.

"I doubt it," Bess said. "The rich can protect themselves with pistols, bars on the windows, and armed servants, while nobody cares a two penny damn for the poor."

The dressmaker pretended pleasure at their appearance and fussed over Bess as though her recently purchased clothes made her a more respectable person.

"There now," he purred, patting Bess as though she were a parcel rather than a prickly woman. "You look fit to grace the royal court."

"Thank you," Smith decided not to take offence as the man ran his hands over Bess's body and wondering why fashion dictated such a strange pattern of clothing with its extra-wide hips and close bodice. He paid the price, flinched at the speed in which his store of gold was diminishing, and was glad his visit to London was nearing its end.

All that remained was the ball he had promised Bess and the opportunity for her to wear her new creation.

Then it's back to sea, thank God.

Smith ordered a sedan chair to carry Bess to the ball while he stalked at the side, holding his newly acquired cane like a sword and glaring at anybody who glanced in his direction. He felt uncomfortable in his over-tight knee-breeches and with his hat perched on his powdered wig, but London fashion demanded such extravagances.

Bess did not ask how Smith obtained entry, and Smith did not explain, yet both knew they were outsiders in such an event. They observed how the wealthy lived, and although they were present, society did not include them.

One or two of the ladies present raised their eyebrows at Bess's dress as if it were not as sophisticated as they would expect at such a function. Smith realised that Bess did not notice, as she was so taken with admiring everything she saw and listening to the music.

Next time, he vowed, *they will look at my woman with admiration.*

After an hour in the room full of swirling dresses and elegant men, a bevy of impassive servants and smiling musicians under the glitter of crystal chandeliers, Bess touched Smith's arm.

"John," she said, straining to be heard above the music and sound of dancing feet. "Look over there."

Standing in profile, Sir Francis was engaged in animated conversation with a tall, red-haired woman. As Smith watched, Sir Francis put an arm around her waist and pulled her close in an embrace.

"That's not Lady Selby," Bess said.

"No," Smith said, "it's not."

Your husband is cuckolding you, Becky. Your man is worthless.

Bess watched Sir Francis escort his female companion away from the dance floor. "Do you think Lady Selby knows?"

Smith affected unconcern. "Maybe," he said. "Let's dance, Bess."

As Sir Francis left the room with the redhead, Smith led Bess onto the floor. It seemed that everybody present was an expert, knowing all the moves for the latest dances. Smith knew the basic steps for the minuet, and compared to the others present, he knew he was clumsy, but he persevered, improving as the night progressed.

When the band began *Sir Roger de Coverley*, Bess whispered that it was the last dance of the ball.

"This dance is like a fox hunt," Bess said, "the steps are like a fox jinking from covert to covert, with the hounds on the chase."

Smith nodded, trying to concentrate on the lively dance. Although he soon picked up the steps, the company was distracting, and he did not wish to embarrass himself, or Bess, who seemed to be enjoying herself.

"That was interesting," Bess said as they left, to walk past the gathering of carriages and liveried servants.

"It was," Smith did not mention his feeling of frustrated unease. It was not the night he had planned for Bess, nor the evening he had hoped for himself. The image of Sir Francis with another woman remained with him, as did his awkwardness in the company of the more leisured classes.

"It was something I will always remember," Bess said, hooking her arm in Smith's. "I will talk about it to my grandchildren, the night I mixed with the wealthy. We were rubbing shoulders with lords and ladies, John."

And not one of them worth a queer farthing, Bess.

"We were," Smith agreed. "I am glad you enjoyed it." He said no more, being content to allow Bess to talk.

Next time, my sweetie, next time, the gentry will dance attendance on us and be pleased to sup our leftovers.

Chapter Fourteen

Kingsgate, Kent, April 1762

I t took Smith half an hour to find the simple grey gravestone. He cleared away the weeds and rank grass with his knife and cleared a path six feet by three from the stone before kneeling at the head.

"Well, mother," he said. "You had a hard life and a lonely death, but at least somebody had the decency to erect a stone for you."

Only the wind in the trees whispered a reply. Smith knelt beside the stone for a full fifteen minutes, reliving old memories and stifling half-forgotten regrets before he stood again. He was in the furthest corner of the graveyard, with the square tower of the ancient church visible above the yew trees.

"I couldn't care for you in life," Smith said, "but I'll look after you in death."

There was no reply from the quiet grave.

Smith stood a few moments longer, unsure what to say. He was a man of deeds, not words. Eventually, he clapped his hat back on his head, squared his shoulders, turned, and marched away. Only then did the woman come out from her hiding place in the shadow of the furthest yew. She watched as Smith left by the lynch-gate and placed a small bouquet of primroses on the grave. Rebecca, Lady Selby, touched the gravestone, said a short prayer, and followed in Smith's footsteps.

Sailing under a flag of truce, *Maid of Kent* lay outside Dunkirk harbour, with half a dozen small boats alongside as Smith ushered his prisoners ashore.

"Your parents will be looking for you," he told them as they boarded the boats.

Captain Dupon was the first man to board *Maid of Kent*. "That's my son," he pointed to the dejected young captain of *Marie Blanc*. "On his first independent command. My younger son was also on board *Marie*." His eyebrows raised in parental concern.

Smith allowed the question to remain unanswered. "Your elder son is a fine, spirited boy," Smith said. "He has his father's looks but lacks his guile."

"He'll learn," Dupon said, "and then he'll take his toll of English shipping."

"Of that, I have no doubt. Squabbles between kings in this troubled world provide many opportunities to learn."

"And opportunities to trade without paying the king's taxes," Dupon said. He frowned when he realised his younger son was not with the returning prisoners.

"We understand each other," Smith gave a slight bow. "My mate, Mr Hargraves, can find a ready market for silk and brandy, to say nothing of tobacco, sugar, and anything else." He paused, watching a herring gull fly between *Maid* and a French craft as if nationality and wars meant nothing to such a bird of passage. "Perhaps even some fine Parisian clothing."

"Perhaps," Dupon said with a bow. "I will need the lady's measurements and the colour of her hair and eyes."

"That can be arranged." Smith had no idea of Bess's measurements.

"I heard there were casualties among *Marie Blanc*." Dupon searched anxiously for his missing son.

"There were two young men killed," Smith replied. "Neither bore your surname."

Some of Dupon's anxiety eased. "Where will I meet you?" he asked.

"Mid Channel. Two miles SSW off the Goodwin Sands," Smith said at once. "You bring the cargo and give me credit for the payment."

"I am afraid that I cannot allow credit," Dupon replied with a smooth bow. "In times of war, unfortunate accidents occur. You may be pressed by the Royal Navy or killed by one of our cannonballs. Even knifed by a jealous husband if England has such a man."

Smith looked towards Dunkirk behind its broad beach. "Your younger son has decided to remain in England," he said casually.

"A hostage?" Dupon asked.

"A house guest," Smith replied.

Dupon stroked his chin. "You'll bring him to me?"

"As a token of my goodwill when I pick up my first cargo of brandy and silk."

Dupon bowed, agreeing to Smith's demands. "His mother will be pleased to see him."

"I will ensure he is clean and presentable," Smith said, "and unharmed."

"That will be best for all of us." Although Dupon smiled, there was no mistaking the menace behind his words.

"Now," Smith said. "I have a parcel of visiting Kingsgate men to collect."

FOR THE SECOND TIME IN HIS LIFE, SMITH SAILED INTO Kingsgate harbour to find a crowd waiting for him.

"You're becoming quite the famous man," Bess said as the freed prisoners-of-war greeted their wives and families on the quayside. They stood on *Maid of Kent's* raised quarterdeck with a tidewaiter checking the ship for illicit cargo.

"I am not a philanthropist," Smith told her. "I have my reasons for everything that I do."

"I am sure you have," Bess said. "I'd like to know her reason for being in Kingsgate."

Lady Selby wife sat within a closed carriage at the head of the quay. The window curtains were nearly closed, leaving a slight gap through which Bess could barely see the occupant.

"She's been there since before dawn," Bess said, "I've been watching her."

"Maybe she knows one of the returning prisoners."

"Maybe," Bess said. "She certainly knows you. Doesn't she?"

"Maybe she thinks she does," Smith said. *Maybe she does.*

Bess slipped a possessive arm around his waist. "Maybe nobody knows you. Come on, your ship is safe, and the tidewaiter won't steal anything." She led Smith off *Maid of Kent* and towards the coach, through a crowd eager to shake his hand or pound him on the back.

"Nobody does," Smith said. "Unless they know a dead man."

"You're not dead." Bess stopped immediately outside Lady Selby's coach, wrapped both arms around Smith's neck, and kissed him. When she stopped, Smith looked directly at the coach window. The curtains were closed.

"WE'RE RUNNING OUR FIRST CARGO NEXT WEEK," SMITH SAID as they sat in the corner seat of the taproom, with Smith's chair facing the door.

Hargreaves nodded. "What do you want me to do?"

"Arrange storage and buyers."

"I can do that," Hargreaves said. "I'll need transport."

"That's Skinner's job. I've already told him what to do." Smith leaned closer to the mate. "We'll need to ensure the route to the Preventative service is closed. Tell me who the informants are."

"There are two," he said. "Gurnal and Craddock. Gurnal is the fellow who infests Hop Lane and listens to everything before reporting to the Preventative men."

"I know that man," Smith said. "And Craddock?"

"Cradock is the man who reports to Sir Francis."

"Is he, by God?" Smith said softly. "I was not aware of that." He remembered Jim Craddock as a man in his prime, always eager to help.

Hargreaves pulled his chair further back as he saw the sudden bleakness of Smith's eyes. Sitting at the neighbouring table with a glass of rum, Carman gave a slight chuckle.

"We'll see what can be done with those two," Smith said. He tapped his fingers on the tabletop, a devil's dance that revealed something of the turmoil inside his mind. "I want to ensure there are no more informers in the village."

"Yes, Captain," Hargreaves said.

"I want to make an example that people remember for a long time." Smith felt his temper rising with the memory of past events. He controlled himself with an effort. "We'll take Gurnal first," Smith decided. "Gather me two of the wildest lads. The Ramsley brothers will do nicely. They don't care for God, the king, or the devil."

Hargreaves nodded. "Shall I bring them here, Captain?"

"No." Smith shook his head. "Bring them to the Spike."

"The old ruin?" Hargreaves did not hide his surprise.

"Tomorrow evening at seven," Smith said.

WITH HIS FACE BLACKENED AND HIS TRICORNE HAT PULLED low over his face, Smith stood at the side of the Dancing Horse, with rain weeping from the eaves to increase the puddles at his feet. He pulled his cloak tighter and watched Gurnal stand at his post at the head of Hop Lane. Gurnal appeared quite relaxed, lounging against the wall as he chewed on a wad of tobacco, occasionally ejecting a stream of tobacco juice from his mouth onto the wet ground.

Smith gave a long, low whistle, and the Ramsley brothers appeared at the other end of the street. They moved quickly, with their shoulders hunched and heads down against the driving rain. Smith waited until the Ramsleys were within twenty yards of Gurnal before he stepped into open view, walking forward.

Gurnal looked up, with his hat shading his face and one hand on the weighted cane at his side.

"Your name is Gurnal," Smith asked. "Aldred Gurnal." He had no desire to assault an innocent man.

"That's correct." Gurnal stepped back with a smile on his face. He lifted the cane, half in threat and half in apprehension. "Have you intelligence for me?"

"I have not," Smith told him.

"Then what do you want?" Gurnal lifted his cane as if to strike.

"You," Smith grabbed Gurnal's arms before the informer swing the lead-weighted end of his cane.

"You bugger!" Gurnal swore and tried to ram his knee into Smith's groin, but Smith twisted away while maintaining his hold on Gurnal's arm. "It's no good, my friend. We have you."

The Ramsleys hurried up, grabbing Gurnal from behind. While Jake Ramsley held Gurnal secure, Henry Ramsley threw a meal sack over his head and tied it around his neck.

Smith removed Gurnal's cane and tossed it away. "Now, don't you struggle, Gurnal, or it will be the worse for you."

When Gurnal kicked out, Jake Ramsley lifted his pistol and delivered a smart tap on the back of his head. "Try that again, and I'll put a ball between your eyes."

Gurnal grunted and shouted, with the sack muffling his voice. "I know you, Jake Ramsley. I'll have you before the magistrate for this night's work. Sir Francis knows how to deal with men like you."

Jake punched Gurnal in the kidneys, twisting his fist. "Is that the way of it, Gurnal? Inform on me, will you?"

"Enough," Smith said. "We want him in fair condition for where he's bound."

"Aye, aye, sir," Jake said and kicked Gurnal's backside. "Fair condition it is!" He kicked again, taking pleasure in his victim's reaction.

"This way, Gurnal!" Smith shoved the informant down the street. He saw a window shutter open, then the flicker of light from a candle before the shutter closed again. The people of Kingsgate knew when to ignore happenings in their street, and Gurnal, the informer, was never a popular man.

"Come on, you snitching bastard," Jake said, kicking Gurnal again. "We've got a surprise for you."

Hargreaves stood on the deck of *Maid of Kent*. "Is that him?"

"This is Gurnal, the informer," Smith confirmed.

"This way." The Ramsleys dragged Gurnal below and tied him hand and foot before removing the sack.

"You'll pay for this!" Gurnal threatened.

"No, we won't," Henry Ramsley said and thrust a gag in Gurnal's mouth. "How do you like that, eh?" He replaced the sack before grabbing Gurnal's hair and hauling him into the cable locker.

"Let him cool off in there," Smith said. "No food or water, and no company except his thoughts and fears. He'll be a more pliable man when he next feels God's free wind."

"The authorities will miss him," Hargreaves said. "Sir Francis might institute a search."

"He might," Smith said. "But we're on his side, remember? Sir Frank is unlikely to search a ship he owns, especially as we're famous all over the village."

Hargreaves shook his head. "You're a devious, dangerous man, Captain."

THE MINUTE HAND OF THE HARRISON LONG-CASE CLOCK wavered at the number nine as if reluctant to progress any further. Sir Francis Selby sipped at his port and looked at Smith over the rim of his glass. "A letter of marque?" he said.

"Yes, Sir Francis," Smith looked around the study. The inlaid desk was laden with the estate's documentation, while memorabilia from Sir Francis's great tour of Europe filled the room. Smith glanced at the marble busts and pieces of Venetian glass, collected when Sir Francis celebrated reaching the age of majority. Smith had celebrated his 21st birthday on the lower deck of a man of war, shivering with cold as they patrolled the edge of the Arctic ice to protect the whaling fleet.

"Twenty-one, are you?" the petty officer asked. "Well, now that you're a man, you can clean the heads to celebrate."

"Aye, aye, sir!" Smith had learned it was better to agree and obey.

"And once you've done that, you can get a holy stone and get the ice off the deck. All of it. Start at the bow and work astern." The petty officer had lifted his starter, the length of knotted rope he used to enforce his orders. "Run, you bastard!"

Leather-bound books filled the glass-fronted bookcases, busts of classical gods stood in the corners of the room, and a full-length portrait of Lady Selby faced the desk, so Sir Francis could see his wife whenever he looked up. Smith examined Becky's picture, wondering when the artist painted the likeness, noticing the signs of maturity in the face he remembered so well.

The Harrison clock ticked away the minutes in one corner, with a beam of sunlight gleaming from the walnut case.

"Do you intend to capture more French privateers?" Sir Francis had a twinkle in his eyes as he questioned Smith.

"If the opportunity arises, sir," Smith allowed the clock to tick away a full thirty seconds of his life. "Although merchant vessels may be a more valuable acquisition." He waited another few seconds for Sir Francis to digest the information. "I believe the owner of a privateer gains a percentage of the prize money."

Sir Francis's twinkle vanished, replaced by a frown. "A letter of marque gives a ship permission to capture vessels of the king's enemies," he said. "Funding such a privateer is a sign of patriotism, and I pride myself as a loyal subject of King George. I would not finance a privateer merely as a licence to increase my wealth."

"Of course not, sir," Smith said, aware he had made his point.

"There are forms and documents required to licence a letter of marque," Sir Francis said after the clock marked another passage of time.

"I have them here, sir," Smith handed over the sheaf of documents Bess had obtained for him.

"You're well prepared, damn you." Sir Francis scanned the forms, noting that Bess had filled in everything except his signature.

"Thank you, sir," Smith said. "I thought it my duty, as master of *Maid of Kent.*"

"Did you, by God." Sir Francis gave Smith a stern look as he reread the documents. "These appear to be in order." He lifted his quill and added his name on the space at the bottom. His writing was flamboyant, Smith thought.

"There you are, Captain Smith. You are now a legally recognised pirate. When you bring in the first prize, I will pay the required fee to His Majesty."

"Thank you, sir. I will try not to disappoint you." Smith held the document secure. The clock struck ten o'clock. The entire operation had only taken a quarter of an hour.

AN AUTUMNAL WIND RAISED SPINDRIFT FROM THE CHANNEL waves and eased *Maid of Kent* east by southeast. With all her lights doused and under topsails only, she sailed to the agreed rendezvous point, then cruised back and forth, with the crew ready to welcome Captain Dupon or fire a broadside at any Frenchman, at Smith's will. To the north, the tide steadily receded from Goodwin Sands, with moonlight gleaming on the yellow banks that endangered shipping in this stretch of the Channel.

"Vessel approaching, Captain," Hewitt shouted from aloft. "I can see moonlight reflecting on her sails. Damn! The moon's gone!"

Smith grunted. "Run aloft, Hargreaves. Tell me what you think."

Hargreaves scrambled aloft and focussed the telescope on the vessel. "That might be her, Captain, but it's hard to make out in the dark."

"Make the recognition signal," Smith said. "Stand by at the guns."

As Henry Ramsley lifted a lantern aloft and dipped it three times, Smith and the crew waited. If the approaching vessel acknowledged with the agreed signal, then they were safe. If not, they might face an arduous voyage against the wind and tide to return to the security of the English coast.

The return signal gleamed through the night, three red lights repeated.

"That's our man," Smith said. "Time to let our prisoner free."

Jake Ramsley dragged Gurnal on deck, blinking and cramped after three days of solitary confinement.

"Captain Smith!" Gurnal looked around, rubbing at his wrists and ankles. "Thank God it's you. Is this *Maid of Kent?*"

"It is," Smith confirmed with a nod.

"There must be some mistake, Captain," Gurnal said. "A trio of smugglers kidnapped me and bundled me aboard your ship. What's happening? Where are we?"

"We're about half a mile south of the Goodwin Sands," Smith said. "And you are about to help us transfer a cargo of spirits and wine from a Dunkirk vessel to *Maid*."

"The devil I am!" Gurnal's mouth opened in shock. "You're a smuggler!"

"Amongst other things," Smith agreed.

"You blackguard!" Gurnal saw the crew grinning around him. "The devil a bit of help you'll get from me!"

"If you refuse, I'll throw you overboard," Smith said. "Which is a lenient fate for an informer of the Preventative Service."

"I'll toss him, Captain!" Jake Ramsley offered.

"Not yet, but you may encourage him to cooperate." Smith watched as the Ramsley brothers took it in turns to kick Gurnal.

"Mr Hargreaves," Smith turned his attention away from the informer. "Bring young Monsieur Dupon on deck. He'll be eager to see his father."

"We'll miss him," Hargreaves said. "Mrs Hargreaves was quite taken by the lad, and he's picked up some English as well."

Smith nodded. He had passed Marcel Dupon to Hargreaves, who already had a brood of children and grandchildren. Marcel smiled as he emerged on deck and waited eagerly to see his father's ship.

"There's *Profiteur*," Marcel shouted, waving as the French ship approached.

"Hands to the guns," Smith ordered. He had recruited another eight men and mounted cannon from the captured French privateer. Suitably armed, *Maid* was a match for anything less than a French warship.

"Are you going to attack *Profiteur?*" Marcel asked in some dismay.

"No, Marcel," Hargreaves reassured the youngster. "We are going to ensure she does not attack us."

Profiteur hove to within ten cables' lengths of *Maid of Kent* and within minutes sent a small boat across the water. Captain Dupon leapt on board the Kingsgate vessel with two pistols in his belt and a body of armed men at his back, glaring about suspiciously. Only when he saw his son did he relax.

"You kept your word," he said to Smith.

"I did," Smith nodded. "As you will keep yours." He indicated Gurnal. "That man is an informer who needs to be encouraged to help load the cargo."

Dupon smiled, immediately understanding. "We will ensure he does the work of ten men."

Less than two hours later, the ships parted company, and *Maid of Kent* resumed her passage, with *Profiteur* sailing in the opposite direction. The crew had securely stowed the illicit cargo behind false bulkheads, and Gurnal was back in the cable locker.

Smith stood on the quarterdeck, sniffing the wind as he steered *Maid* around the Sands and headed west towards Portsmouth.

"Here's HMS *Tamar* approaching," Hargreaves lowered his telescope. "She's seen us."

Smith grunted. "She's right on time, according to her patrol route. You can set your clock by her routine."

Tamar was a 32-gun frigate that patrolled the Channel for French privateers. Smith and *Maid of Kent* passed her on every voyage between Kingsgate and Portsmouth.

"Ship ahoy!" HMS *Tamar* hailed them as she drew closer. "Who are you, and where are you bound?" A smart lieutenant stood on the quarterdeck with a speaking trumpet in his hand.

"*Maid of Kent*!" Smith replied. "Captain Smith, from Kingsgate to Portsmouth with a cargo of beef, beer, and mutton for the Royal Navy." He lowered his trumpet. "Mr Hargreaves, it's likely that they'll board us and look for unprotected seamen. Get Gurnal out of confinement, but keep him in hiding for now."

"Aye, aye, Captain."

"We're sending a boarding party, Captain Smith! Stand by!"

"Standing by, *Tamar*!"

A middle-aged midshipman stood in the stern of the launch that rowed across, with half a dozen armed seamen at his back.

"You'll find our papers in order, sir," Smith said. "All our crew have Protections, duly signed by Sir Francis Selby, the local magistrate." He gave a short laugh. "None of your Boston protections in my ship."

False Protection certificates were the bane of the Impress Service, with some English and colonial towns having a reputation for producing forged Protections at minimum cost.

"Muster your men." The midshipman had experienced such assumed joviality before when shipmasters attempted to hide unprotected seamen. "Show me their Protections."

Although it was common practice for the Royal Navy to press inward bound mariners, they would be less likely to take protected men working on a Navy contract.

The midshipman examined each man, matching them with the details on their respective Protection certificates. "Do any of you wish to volunteer into His Majesty's service? Good pay, daily beer, and the possibility of prize money."

Nobody stepped forward. Only a fool or a very naïve man would exchange the coastal trade for the dangerous uncertainly of His Majesty's service.

The midshipman's face darkened. "Search the ship," he ordered, and a petty officer split the boarding party into teams of two. After only a few moments, one pair dragged out a protesting Gurnal.

"Look what we found, sir!" A monkey-faced seaman said, laughing as he held Gurnal by the collar. "He was hiding in a storeroom pretending to be a keg of rum!"

"He don't look like rum to me," the petty officer said. "Can you drink him?"

"Wouldn't care to try!" the seaman said.

"Has this man signed articles with you, Captain?" the midshipman asked, with his eyes sharpening with interest.

Smith looked at Gurnal as if he had never seen him before. "I can't honestly say he has, sir," he said.

"These men are smugglers!" Gurnal shouted.

"Does this man have a Protection?" The midshipman asked,

happy to have found a potential able-bodied seaman to add to *Tamar*'s crew.

Smith shook his head. "This man has not signed articles, sir, and I have no Protection for him."

The midshipman smiled. "Then I shall relieve you of the cost of feeding him, Captain."

"They're smugglers!" Gurnal shouted, with a navy seaman holding each of his arms.

"That may be so," the midshipman replied, "but HMS *Tamar* is not in the Preventative service."

"Sir," Smith said, "if you insist on taking that man, I must warn you that he is a troublemaker, a liar, and a sea lawyer."

"Is he, by God?" The midshipman gave Gurnal a stern look. "If he causes trouble on *Tamar,* he'll find we have methods of dealing with his sort."

"I'm sure Gurnal will find patrolling the Channel with the Navy beneficial, sir."

The midshipman smiled again. "This is our final day on the home station, Captain Smith. Tomorrow we are outward bound for the East Indies and not due to return until the end of the war."

"No! You can't take me!" Gurnal shouted until the petty officer clipped him across the head.

"You behave yourself, my friend, or we'll have to teach you what the King expects from his sailors."

Smith watched as *Tamar* sailed away. "Gurnal won't trouble us again," he said. "It's a six-month voyage even to reach the East, and once there, Gurnal could be out for years."

Hargreaves gave Smith a look that combined respect with fear. "What do you plan to do with Craddock, Captain?"

"Something much more public," Smith said. "When it's time. First, I need a period of sustained rainfall. Now, Mr Hargreaves, we have a cargo or two to unload."

Chapter Fifteen

May 1762

By *Maid of Kent's* fifth trip, Smith had the procedure working like a machine. They loaded the cargo at Kingsgate's harbour or in any of the small creeks and ports along the Kent coast and left with the evening tide. After a quick run to Portsmouth to deliver the legal cargo with the Navy, they crossed the Channel and picked up the illicit cargo off France. Now that Smith had the operation running smoothly, he paid for the French spirits with British gold, earned from his network of customers. Between the extra mast and Smith's habit of driving the ship hard, *Maid of Kent* could make the extended voyage in the same time as other shipmasters made the simple return trip.

Once he reached the Kent coast, Smith hovered offshore and landed the free trade goods at Spike Cove, hauling some up the cliff face to store in the cave and having Skinner deliver the remainder. Every time he was home, Smith sought to expand his number of customers, moving outward from Kingsgate to Marsham and inland towards London. By keeping his prices low, Smith attracted new custom, so the kegs and hogsheads of brandy did not remain in the cave for more than a few days.

Bess checked the figures from the latest free trade endeavour and counted the extensive piles of gold on the table. "You're much more successful than Captain Blackwell was."

"It's early days yet," Smith said, spinning a sovereign, catching it, and tossing again.

"What does that mean?"

Smith pulled the account book to him. Written in Bess's immaculate hand, the columns were totalled day by day, with the payments given to each man. Bess had taken care to disguise the names with a pseudonym in case prying official eyes found her accounts.

"We're making some decent money," Smith said, "that's for sure. We pay eleven shillings in France for a three-and-a-half-gallon tub of brandy and sell it for three guineas." He nodded. "Even taking into account the expenses of delivery and the wages of the men, that's 150 per cent profit."

"We could make a lot more," Bess said. "If we diluted each tub with, say, two gallons of water and raised our price by half-a-guinea, we could easily add another fifty per cent profit."

"No." Smith shook his head. "I want to be known for good quality spirits and low prices. I want to undercut the opposition as well as giving better brandy."

"Diluting the spirits is common practice," Bess encouraged. "It's expected."

Smith looked up. "I want my reputation to spread right across Kent," he said. "Together with the privateering and honest trading, we make good money, and we'll make better when I expand from the North Foreland to the Sussex border."

"With your profit, John, you can easily lease a house," Bess said. "Like Captain Blackwell did." She looked around the single room that had been their home for months. "We can get out of this cramped accommodation in the Dancing Horse."

Smith closed the book. "Not yet," he said. "We'll get a house when I've completed my business here."

"What business, John?" Bess asked sharply. "What do you intend? Why have you come to Kingsgate?"

"I have wrongs to right." Smith did not smile.

"Maybe it would be better to continue as you are and let sleeping dogs lie," Bess suggested.

"No," Smith said. "These dogs have lain in comfort long enough."

Bess looked away. "As you wish, John, but sometimes the best victory is to achieve success despite an initial setback."

Smith could see the noose dangling above him and feel the rough touch of hemp around his throat. His father was dancing above his head, slowly dying as the young squire watched.

"I have only just begun," Smith said. "I will not allow the dogs to sleep for much longer." He stood up and looked out of the window at the street below, but his mind witnessed another scene when Sir Francis led the parish constable and half a dozen tidewaiters into the house. Smith's mother had screamed as Sir Francis and the constable subdued Smith's father with cudgels.

"Leave him!"

"He's a smuggler and a horse thief!" Young Sir Francis shouted and then pointed to Smith. "Take the cub, too!"

"I never stole a horse in my life!" Smith's father roared.

"I'll see you hanged on my oath!" Sir Francis said.

"John?" Bess held his arm. "Are you all right?"

"I will be," Smith said. "It's nothing a good hanging won't cure."

SMITH STOOD AT THE EDGE OF KINGSHUNT MANOR'S POLICIES, beside the smooth trench of the ha-ha, with the horse chestnut tree rustling above him.

Bright green with new growth, the leaves filtered the sunlight and sheltered nesting birds while a dozen rabbits scampered nearby. Smith had been watching the house since an hour before dawn, immobile, seeing everything that happened and noting every movement. He carried a pen and ink, with half a dozen sheets of foolscap paper, on which he wrote his notes. He remained there all day, not leaving until dark when he strode directly to Hargreaves's home in Fletcher's Lane and rapped on the door.

"Who is it?" A woman shouted.

"It's Captain John Smith!"

When the door opened, Smith blinked in surprise. Suzanne, the virago who helped him fight the press gang, stood in the doorway with a broad smile on her face. Younger than Hargreaves by some years, she blinked at Smith, then extended a welcoming hand. The glow of firelight behind made a halo of her hair.

"Good evening, Captain Smith," Suzanne opened the door wide to reveal a household full of children of all ages from eighteen months to fourteen years old.

"Who is it, Suzanne?" Hargreaves appeared, with his white shirt unfastened and his face unshaven. "Captain! Come in, sir, come in!"

Smith walked in, removing his hat to Suzanne. "I'm here on business, I'm afraid," he said.

Hargreaves nodded to Suzanne. "Ship business? Or other?"

"Other."

"Your mother would wish to see you, Suzanne," Hargreaves said.

"At this time of night?" Suzanne began and then understood. "Oh, yes, Peter. Look after the children."

"I always do," Hargreaves lifted a toddling little girl and balanced her on his hip.

Suzanne removed her cloak from a peg on the wall, accidentally brushing against Smith on her way to the door. "Don't be too long," she said.

Smith waited for half a minute before following Suzanne and jerking the door open. "Don't get cold out there."

Suzanne moved guiltily away from the door, smiling.

Smith closed the internal shutters on the front window. "We

have Gurnal out of the way." He sat in the chair Suzanne had vacated, opposite Hargreaves at the fire with half a dozen children staring at him. "Now, I want to remove Craddock."

Hargreaves poked at the glowing embers, holding his daughter in the crook of his left elbow. "That won't be so easy, Captain. Craddock seldom leaves his master's side."

"He has a sweetheart," Smith said.

Hargreaves put down the poker. "So I believe. The widow Dodd."

"That's the woman. Craddock meets her on Tuesday nights, and she probably tells him the local gossip to pass on to Sir Francis."

"We'll be at sea on Tuesday night," Hargreaves pointed out.

"Not this week," Smith said. "Smell the wind."

Hargreaves opened the shutters on the back window, slid up the sash window and sniffed at the wind from the sea, nodding slowly. "Coming in hard from the south, I reckon."

"I reckon you're right. We'll be wind bound in the harbour." Smith stretched out his boots to the fire. "Are you game?"

"I'm game. The same two lads?"

"The very same."

"And the same procedure? Hand Craddock to the Navy?" Hargreaves shifted his position so his daughter could snuggle into sleep.

"No," Smith shook his head. "Gurnal vanished, and people wonder what happened to him. They talk of the Impress Service but suspect me. I want Craddock to be more public. I want to send out a visible warning what happens to informers in the village."

Hargreaves began to stir the fire again, raking at what remained of the coal. He glanced at his now-sleeping daughter and carried her to the bed she shared with three of her sisters.

Hargreaves returned to his seat and added coal to the fire. "Do you mean to redcap him?"

"That's what I have in mind," Smith agreed.

"Your father was a good man, Captain."

Smith understood Hargreaves' point. "Until Craddock informed on him," he said, "and Sir Francis dreamed up false evidence of horse theft and had him hanged."

"That's what I heard," Hargreaves said, watching the flames lick over the fresh coal. "What do you want me to do, Captain?"

THE WIND ROSE FROM THE SOUTH, ROARING ACROSS THE Channel like some maritime monster, rustling the thatch on village roofs and hammering waves against the worn stones of the harbour wall. Sensible men kept indoors with their wives or sat in huddled groups around the circular tables in Kingsgate's taprooms.

"God help sailors on a night like this," Hargreaves said.

Smith did not reply. He and his followers waited at the edge of the Common, the vacant ground between the village and Kingshunt Manor's policies. Once, the Common had been four times the size, but successive Acts of Parliament, sponsored by generations of the Selby family, had seen the Selbies gradually gain the land. Each slice of common land the Kingsgate people lost added to the villagers' resentment of their self-proclaimed betters.

"Here he comes now," Hargreaves said, with the rain dripping from the point of his tricorne hat to add to the puddles on the sodden ground.

Craddock walked swiftly, a middle-aged man with his head down and his shoulders slightly bowed. He looked up when Smith stepped in front of him.

"I desire a word with you," Smith told him.

"Well, I don't desire a word with you," Craddock said. "Stand out of my way, fellow."

"Come with me," Smith spoke quietly to control his hatred.

"I will not," Craddock said. "Do you know who I am? I am Sir Francis's personal assistant. I am important in this parish."

"I know exactly who you are," Smith said, "and what you are." He produced his pistol and thrust it hard into Craddock's stomach. "Now shut your teeth."

"I'll do no such thing," Craddock said.

Smith lifted his left hand, and the Ramsley brothers emerged behind Craddock, knocked off his hat, and hit him on the head twice, catching him as he staggered.

A squat ruin sat at the side of the Common. At one time, it had been a shepherd's hut, but when Sir Francis grabbed another section of the land, too little of the Common remained for shepherding to be viable. The last shepherd had shut the door and abandoned the hut to wind, weather, and wildlife.

With five men inside, the hut was overfull, but Smith did not care. "Gag him," he said and watched as the Ramsleys followed his instructions. By the time they finished, Craddock was stirring, groaning at the pain in his head.

Henry Ramsley stuffed a rag into Craddock's mouth and tied it tight around the back of his head. When Craddock struggled, Jake Ramsley kicked him hard in the groin.

"He's trying to say something," Hargreaves said.

Smith loosened the gag. "What?"

"What did I ever do to you?" Craddock groaned.

Smith knelt at his side. "You had me hanged," he said and stuffed the gag back into Craddock's mouth. "Put a sack over his head and take him outside."

Craddock struggled to resist as Jake Ramsley hauled a canvas sack over his head and tied it around his neck.

"There you are, you bastard!" Ramsley grunted.

Writhing and kicking, Craddock could do little against four men.

"Take him to the village green," Smith said grimly. "We'll deal with him there."

The Ramsleys took an arm each and lifted Craddock to his feet, dragging him across the Common to Kingsgate.

Usually, the stream that fed the village pond was little more than a trickle of water, but after heavy rain, it overflowed its banks to flood the green and overfill the pond. At present, the pond was about half-full, with an islet in the centre, peeping above the water, but as the rain continued to teem down, it was gradually filling.

Smith stood at the edge of the pond, shaking away the memories of Sir Francis and his men dragging him away from his house, with two grinning dragoons holding his screaming mother. From his position beside the pond, Smith could see his childhood home.

"Spread-eagle him face up on the island," Smith ordered, with the image of his mother vivid in his mind. "Tie him to the sides and remove the sack, but keep the gag in place. We don't want him bellowing for help."

Smith leaned over the suffering man. "The water will rise," he said in a conversational tone, "and you'll try to keep your head above water. In time, your neck muscles will complain, and you'll have to rest your head in the water. The water will rise, inch by inch. You'll try to shout, but you can't."

Craddock writhed against his bonds, pleading for mercy with his eyes.

Smith held Craddock's gaze. "The gag will soak and expand, and you'll slowly drown." He smiled, seeing his father kicking, dancing on air as he choked to an agonising death. "If you happen to survive and mention my name, I will burn the widow Dodd alive on the village green with you watching."

Smith lowered his voice to a whisper that only Craddock could hear. "You helped Sir Francis hang my father and me." He adjusted his neckcloth to show the mark of the rope. "This is retribution."

Craddock squirmed against the ropes, straining to say something. Smith watched, but in his mind, he only saw his mother weeping in anguish and his father choking within the noose.

Smith turned to his followers. "Who has the redcap lantern?"

"I have." Henry Ramsley produced a small lantern with red painted glass. He lit the wick and placed the lantern at the edge of the pond.

Anybody seeing the red light would know that Craddock was an informer and would not interfere to save him. The process of drowning informers was known as redcapping, although it was more common to leave the victim on the beach for the rising tide.

"Goodbye, Craddock, you informing bastard," Jack Ramsley said. "Drown slowly."

Leaving Craddock in the pond with the water level rising and the rain hammering down, Smith nodded to his companions. "A drink for the boys, I think, and we'll ensure that nobody leaves the inn for an hour or two." Stepping over Craddock's straining body, Smith led the way to the inn.

Chapter Sixteen

May 1762

"**G**uilty!" *The judge said, with the black cap balanced on his wig. He pointed a podgy finger at Smith's father, with his jowls trembling, and his eyes gimlet-sharp. "A jury of your peers has found you guilty of horse theft, and I sentence you to be taken to the place from whence you came and from thence to a place of public execution."*

"No!" Smith's mother screamed from the public galleries. "My husband is not a horse thief!"

"Take that woman away!" The judge ordered. "I will not have such outbursts in my court."

Smith lifted his manacled hands and shifted forward in an attempt to save his mother, but a brace of beefy, well-fed guards held him back.

The judge watched as two hefty court officials wrestled Smith's mother out of the courtroom.

"It is the sentence of this court that you be hanged by the neck until you are dead!" The judge continued his condemnation, turning his attention to Smith.

"And you, sir, have followed the example of your father, with the same inevitable result. I sentence you to be taken to the place of public execution and hanged by the neck until you are dead!"

Smith heard another stifled scream in the audience and, for the first time, saw Becky sitting there. He saw the horror in her eyes as she sat with her hand over her mouth, and then he saw the satisfaction in her mother's face.

"Take them away!" the judge ordered.

As the guards gripped his arms, Sir Francis leaned back to talk to one of his companions, his face smug with triumph. Sir Francis caught Smith's glance, put both hands around his neck, and made choking motions.

"John!" A small hand shook Smith awake. "John!"

Smith opened his eyes and looked around the familiar surroundings of his room at the Dancing Horse. "A nightmare," he realised he had both hands on his throat and pulled them away.

"A memory?" Bess leaned over him.

"Yes," Smith said.

"Tell me about it." Bess sat up beside him, tracing the red mark around his throat. "Tell me everything."

Smith saw sunlight slant through the gap in the shutters and heard the song of a blackbird. "Maybe some time," he said, rising. "I have a cargo to load." He was aware of Bess watching him as he dressed and carefully tied the scarf around his neck.

THEY MET IN A SECLUDED CORNER OF THE TAPROOM, SMITH, Hargreaves, and Bess. One of Bess's leather-bound books lay open before them, a map at the side and tankards of small beer making fresh rings on the surface of the table.

"We have a good network of buyers in this area of Kent," Smith swept his hand across the map, "but nothing west of the marshes."

"No," Hargreaves said. "Not even Captain Blackwell ventured into that area."

"Not even?" Smith repeated the words. He felt Bess's eyes on him as her foot pressed warningly against his leg. "I'm not

Captain bloody Blackwell. I aim to control free trade operations in all of Kent."

"Holden's Sussex Gang controls the west of the county," Hargreaves said.

Smith knew of the Sussex Gang. They were long-established and notoriously violent. "Tell me more," he said, with his voice dangerously quiet.

"Holden's Sussex Gang have built up their contacts, inns, and network over the years," Hargreaves said. "When Captain Blackwell tried to expand into western Kent, the Sussex Gang killed one of his men and intimidated the innkeepers and tavern landlords. Now everything west of Romney Marsh is in thrall to Holden." He took a draught of his ale. "Frankly, Captain, everybody's terrified of the men from Sussex."

Smith tapped his fingers on the table. "What do you think, Bess?"

"I think the Sussex Gang are an unpleasant bunch of blackguards," Bess said. "They're dangerous men to cross, and I heard they bribe the Preventative men to ensure nobody interferes with their operations."

"What's this fellow Holden like?"

"William Adam Holden," Bess replied. "A one-eyed monster who would slit his mother's throat for a shilling. He's a veteran of the French wars, a cold-blooded, treacherous brute that you never want to meet. His associate is Nat Hitchens, the most handsome man who ever charmed a woman into bed or shot a man in the back."

Smith listened, unmoved. "I want to meet them." He expected the silence as Hargreaves and Bess looked at him. "Where are they based?"

Smith was not surprised that it was Bess who supplied the answer.

"The Templar's Cross," Bess told him. "At Hastings."

"Then that's where we'll go," Smith said. He touched the butt of the pistol in his belt, knowing he was inviting trouble.

148

Dancing

"GET HIM!" A GROUP OF BOYS AND GIRLS EXPLODED FROM THE lane, with Hargreaves' children to the fore. They all carried long bunches of nettles and screamed in excitement as they chased the slender form of Musbie, the Excise clerk.

"Get him, Toby!" A diminutive six-year-old squealed in excitement. "Give him what for!"

Two years older than the squeaking girl, Toby ran to Musbie's side and delivered a hefty whack with his nettles across the man's backside. "Oak Apple Day!" He shouted happily. "It's Oak Apple Day!"

Musbie gasped at the sting, raised his hand to send young Toby spinning, and realised that half a dozen grinning villagers were watching.

"Oak Apples!" The other children yelled, caught up with Toby, and began to flail at the unfortunate Musbie with their nettles. Forgetting all ideas of dignity, Musbie clapped a hand to his hat and fled to Hop Lane, with the children following, nettles in hand.

"It's Oak Apple Day," Bess said as she stood beside Smith at the window.

"I know," Smith said. Wearing a sprig of oak on the 29th of May was a sign of support for the monarchy. On that day in 1660, King Charles II had been restored to the throne after the Cromwellian commonwealth. It was a tradition in Kingsgate that children could whip anybody with nettles who failed to display such a sprig.

"I've cut us both some oak leaves," Bess said and then looked at Smith through narrow eyes. "Did you set the children on poor Mr Musbie?"

"I don't know why you would think that," Smith protested.

"You had intended to gather intelligence from him," Bess said. "Did you try?"

"We sat next to him at the church, if you recall," Smith

149

reminded. "But he's a very honest man. He refused my blandishments."

Bess nodded. "So you set the children on him." She watched as Toby led his gang in a raid on the Hounds Rest, charging inside to search for those unfortunates who had neglected to protect themselves with oak leaves.

Three minutes later, the children ran out again, with Quinn, the burly parish constable, chasing them with swings of his staff.

"There's Quinn," Bess said. "He'll be asking questions about Craddock; I'll be bound."

"I imagine so," Smith said.

With Toby's gang chased from the High Street, Quinn strode into the Dancing Horse. Smith and Bess descended the stairs in time to hear his opening statement.

"Poor George Craddock was murdered," Quinn took up space at the counter. "Some murderous blaggard tied him up in the village pond and left him to drown."

"That's terrible," Ruth said, shaking her head. "And him such a nice, respectable man too. How will the Widow Dodd live without him?"

"The Widow Dodd?" The constable asked. "Why mention her?"

"Why, sir," Ruth said in all innocence, "she was fast friends with Mr Craddock. I heard tell that they had an arrangement." She winked. "I even heard that Craddock and the Widow had an arrangement before Mr Dodd had that terrible accident that killed him."

"Oh," Quinn looked around the inn. He nodded a greeting to Smith, the respected master of *Maid of Kent*.

"Indeed, sir, people talked about Mr Craddock's arrangement with Mrs Dodd," Ruth added suggestion to suspicion.

"And her as thick as thieves with that foreign fellow, Mrs Martin." Bess joined in the conversation. "I wonder that George Craddock allowed her such latitude."

"Which foreign fellow?" the constable was clearly out of his depth in the women's conversation.

"Why, sir, didn't you hear?" Ruth affected surprise at Quinn's ignorance. "The foreign fellow what was poking around this last three weeks and more. He tried to sell his illicit brandy to Mrs Martin here until she sent him away with a flea in his ear."

"I did that!" Ruth joined in Bess's game.

"What fellow was that?" Smith asked. "Was it some damned Frenchie?"

"No! No Frenchie would dare come here. It was that man from Sussex or Surrey or some other foreign parts," Bess said. "The one-eyed blaggard, Holdme or Holdthis or Holdhim."

"Holden!" the constable supplied the name. "William Holden! Was he here?"

"Holden! That's the name!" Bess said. "I think."

"That was him," Ruth began to clean a tankard. "Do you think William Holden killed George Craddock? God knows he looked sufficiently devilish."

Quinn began to look uncomfortable. "I don't know," he said. "I've come here to gather intelligence."

"Is Holden a violent man?" Bess asked, with her eyes round with pretended interest. "You'd better arrest him, constable, before he murders somebody else."

"He's not a native of this parish," Quinn muttered as he left the inn. "I have no powers elsewhere." He closed the door with a bang.

"Well done, ladies," Smith said.

"We look after our own here," Ruth told him as Bess smiled and drew her foot across the floor. "Quinn's nobody's fool, though. He'll be back."

"Nobody will talk," Smith said calmly. He pointed to the red-glassed lantern that hung above the bar, beside the banner of the Dancing horse. "Most have too much loyalty, and the others know of the redcap."

Smith did not know who the Knight Templar had been who made his mark at the Templar's Cross Inn, nor did he care. If pressed, Smith might have known that the Templars had been a military-minded religious order of the Middle Ages. However, history did not interest him unless he was directly involved. He dismounted from his hired horse and threw the reins to a stable boy, adding a shilling.

"Look after him," Smith said.

"Yes, sir." The boy knuckled his forehead, staring at the silver coin.

Smith circled the outside of the inn to look for a rear entrance, completed the circuit and pushed inside. The Templar's Cross was quiet, with a jovial-faced, hard-eyed man behind the bar and a scattering of customers talking together. Few even bothered to look up when Smith entered. Smith ignored the courting couple engaged in an amorous embrace in the corner and allowed his gaze to pass over what was evidently a family group at a central table. He looked longer at three men who could have been cracksmen or lawyers, or perhaps both, and examined the four men who sat at the furthest corner beside the crackling fire.

"What will be your pleasure?" the barman asked.

"Rum," Smith immediately stamped himself as a nautical man. He dropped a coin on the counter, let it spin for five seconds, and clapped a hand on top. "And an introduction."

"Rum it is," the landlord said. "Who do you wish to meet?"

"Nathaniel Hitchins," Smith said. "Or William Holden, or both."

The landlord looked confused. "I don't believe I know either of these gentlemen," he said.

Smith saw that the group of four beside the fire had reduced to three. He guessed that one had slipped away to warn Holden.

"I was certain this was the correct inn," Smith said. He sipped his rum. "I'll wait to see if he arrives."

"You could be here a long time. Perhaps even days." The landlord gave an insincere smile.

"All the more custom for you," Smith said. He saluted the landlord with his rum glass and found a seat against the wall, from where he could watch the door and the trio around the table.

Within ten minutes, a smooth-faced man entered Templar's Cross. He glanced around the room, murmured something to the landlord, and sat alone at a table near the door.

Nathaniel Hitchins, I wager, Smith thought, as he called for another rum. He felt Hitchin's eyes watching him. The landlord busied himself behind the counter, evidently waiting for something to happen.

After another five minutes, a tall man wandered in, stumbled as if he were drunk, and reeled against the counter. The eye patch would have given him away, even without the respect with which the landlord treated him.

William Holden, pretending to be drunk. Let's dance, gentlemen.

Holden slouched beside Hitchins, ordered a tankard of strong ale, and grinned across to Smith.

"Good evening," Smith called out, rose from his seat, and walked across, fully aware that every person in the inn, except the amorous couple, was watching him.

"You must be William Peter Holden." Smith sat on Holden's right side to block his right hand from reaching for a weapon.

Holden did not react for a full ten seconds, but when he faced Smith, his single eye was clear and his voice unaffected by alcohol. "Who are you?"

"John Smith of Kingsgate." Smith felt the tension rise in the inn.

"What do you want here, Smith?"

"I want Kent," Smith did not temporise. "You keep Sussex, and I won't interfere."

Holden turned his single eye onto Smith. "I keep what I have."

"I want Kent."

"You'd be best to keep silent, cully, and be grateful I let you keep your heart beating."

Smith heard movement behind him and knew Holden's men were preparing to interfere. "Next week," he said calmly. "I'll take over all the inns west of Romney Marsh."

"Next week, Smith, you'll be dead," Holden said as Hitchins gave a friendly smile. Hitchin's eyes were soft as a girl's, Smith noted, with long curving lashes.

"Order your people to remain on the Sussex side of the border," Smith said.

"Some of my people are behind you now, Smith," Holden said.

"And some of my people are behind you," Smith told him.

As Smith and Holden had been talking, the courting couple had released their embrace. Mitchell held a pistol to Hitchin's head while Bess pressed a blunderbuss against Holden's back.

"Your men might kill me," Smith said, "but my people will undoubtedly kill you. A blunderbuss at one-inch range will spread your insides all over the inn. Stand up!"

When Holden and Hitchins both stood, Smith pulled a pair of pistols from his belt and presented one at each man. "Cover the others," he ordered, and Bess and Mitchell moved their weapons.

"Now we have a choice," Smith said. "We can have a blood-bath, where I'll be dead, and at least three of you will also die. Or we can all walk away. I'll keep Kent, and you, Holden, can retain Sussex with my blessing."

"Who are you, Smith?" Holden's voice was as steady as if he were discussing the weather despite the pistol pointed unwaveringly at his face. "You arrive out of nowhere and demand I split my organisation with you."

Smith thumbed back the hammer of both pistols. "Keep out

of my Kent," he said, "and I'll keep out of Sussex. If I hear of you or any of your men in my county, it will be war." Smith leaner closer to Holden. "I'm used to war, and I don't lose."

"You've made an enemy there, Captain," Mitchell said as they rode away, with Bess demurely side-saddle despite the blunderbuss in its holster at her side.

Smith glanced behind him at the Templar's Rest. "Only if he's a fool," he said.

Chapter Seventeen

"I thought I might find you here," Lady Selby dismounted, straightened her hat, and stepped towards Smith.

"I come here to think." Smith patted the rough stonework of the Spike. He watched Lady Selby walking towards him, unconsciously admiring her carriage.

"I can't remember you ever thinking much," Lady Selby said. "You were always acting rather than thinking."

"I was younger when you knew me."

Lady Selby smiled and adjusted her hat again. "We both were. What brought you back?"

"A ship," Smith said after a slight pause. *That was uncalled for. Becky has never been anything but kind to me.*

"A journey requires the will as well as the means," Lady Selby brushed a stray hair from her face. "What willed you back?"

"Home called," Smith said. *Does Becky want me to say I came back for her? That would cause unwanted complications in both our lives.*

"You've changed a lot," Lady Selby looked him up and down. "I'm not surprised that nobody recognised you."

"You recognised me," Smith said with a faint smile.

"I knew you better than most."

Smith nodded slowly. "You did."

Lady Selby patted the horse and sat on a tumbled block of masonry, frankly examining him. "You don't say much, do you?"

"How have you been?" Smith descended from his perch and sat near her, leaning his back against the wall.

"Francis married me the year after you left." Lady Selby said, indicating the wedding ring on her finger. "You know that I'd have preferred you."

"Are you happy?" Smith revealed no emotion.

Lady Selby said nothing for a few moments. "I don't want for material comforts," she said, eventually.

"Are you happy?" Smith repeated.

"Francis doesn't beat me." Lady Selby gave a weak smile. "I am fortunate that way."

Smith nodded. He understood that she was not a happy wife. "Why did he marry you?"

Lady Selby thought for a long minute. "To create an heir," she said, "and because I was your sweetheart."

Smith nodded. "Did you create an heir?"

"I gave him two sons and a daughter in three successive years."

Smith felt something twist inside him. *Am I jealous?* "Where are they? I didn't see them in the house."

"The boys are at public school. The girl, my daughter, died." Lady Selby's lack of emotion was a shield. Smith knew she was hiding her grief.

"And since then?"

Lady Selby's lips twisted into a parody of a smile. "I have fulfilled my function. Sir Francis's line is secure."

Neither of them noticed as the wind blew cold rain against the ruin. "What do you plan now?"

Lady Selby sat in silence for a long ten seconds, slowly pushing the hair from her face. "I am not in a position to make plans for my future," she said at last. "My destiny is in Sir Francis's hands."

Smith took out his pipe and stuffed tobacco into the bowl, pressing it in place with a calloused thumb. "Do you have access to money?"

"Sir Francis does not keep me in poverty."

Smith lit his pipe, puffing out aromatic blue smoke. "That does not answer my question. Do you have any savings?"

"No."

Smith removed the pipe from his mouth. "I'll give you the address of my banker. Inform him that I sent you, and start an account. If Sir Francis hands you a shilling, spend ninepence and save threepence. If he gives you a guinea, save a crown. Sell some of your jewellery and get cheap copies made. Save the profit and put aside every penny you can, my Lady Becky. You need money to gain independence."

Lady Selby listened with her eyes intent. Fine eyes, too, Smith noted, eyes that the years and experience had improved.

No! I cannot afford the distraction. One woman is sufficient for any man and too many for most.

"What do you suggest I do with the money?" Lady Selby asked.

"The money is your security," Smith told her. "A lone woman without money is a target for all men. A lone woman with money can create a new life for herself."

Lady Selby straightened her back. "I am not a lone woman."

Smith remembered Sir Francis at the ball in London. "Does your husband entertain other women?"

"Yes," Lady Selby said frankly. "All his peers do likewise. A wife is for breeding heirs. Other women are their lovers for companionship and entertainment."

Smith was aware of the twisted morality of the upper classes. "Does he expect you to be chaste, except in his bed?"

Lady Selby hesitated before she replied. "I was going to say that I don't know what he expects." Her smile was wistful. "But, honestly, I don't think he cares a damn what I do, as long as I am discreet." Lady Selby looked away. "My husband would not like me to bring scandal to his door."

Smith faced away from the wind to add tobacco to his pipe. "You are free to take a lover, in that case."

"I am."

"Do you intend to?"

"I rather hoped that you might fill that role." Lady Selby widened her eyes.

Damn the woman! And damn me for ever returning to Kingsgate.

Smith drew on his pipe, holding her gaze. "You're an attractive woman," he said. "You can find a richer, more respectable man than me. I was born to be hanged."

"You've already been hanged," Lady Selby reminded, leaning forward to touch the faint mark on his neck. "People say that lightning does not strike twice."

"They also say that the sea and the gallows refuse no man," Smith removed her hand, holding it a fraction longer than necessary. "You can catch a richer fish than me in your net of seduction."

"I don't want a richer man."

Smith leaned closer and placed his hands on Lady Selby's shoulders. He spoke around his pipe. "You don't have to want him or even like him. You possess looks, charm, and a warm body — all that a man desires in a woman. Use your gifts, and seduce a rich man. Take all you can from him and reward him with smiles and tender caresses."

She was listening, unsmiling.

"The more he gives you," Smith continued, "the more you offer him. Take his money and bank it. Take as many men as you desire, and bleed them dry until you are rich and secure."

"Is that how you see my future?" Lady Selby asked.

"It's a better future than most people will have," Smith said.

"And if, somewhere along the way, you find a good man that you wish to keep, why then, you take him and keep him." He hardened his voice. "But make sure your savings are secure. There are few good men."

"You've grown very cynical," Lady Selby sounded regretful.

"I hope you take my advice." Smith stood up, tapping out his pipe on the stonework. "Now, if you will excuse me, I have a ship to prepare. I can't leave everything to Hargreaves." He did not comment on the moisture in her eyes or the defiant lift of her chin as he walked away.

When he looked back, Lady Selby remained sitting, a lonely figure in the rain and a woman who had everything she needed except happiness.

CAPTAIN DUPON HELD OUT HIS HAND. "THAT'S ANOTHER cargo, Captain Smith."

"It is." Smith shook Dupon's hand.

"I have another matter to discuss," Dupon said.

"We know each other well enough." Smith did not mention that two of his men were waiting in the cabin, fully armed, in case the Frenchman showed any sign of treachery. Nor did he mention the rack of cutlasses and pistols hidden behind an old sail hanging over the taffrail.

Becky was correct. I have become very cynical.

"It's a matter we have already mentioned," Marcel said. "The imprisonment of Captain Duguay."

Smith glanced around, identifying each visible sail in the surrounding sea and assessing their possible threat to *Maid of Kent*. He could see no Royal Navy or Excise cutters, nor any French warships or privateers.

"He is held at Sissinghurst Castle in Kent," Smith said. "Guarded by the army."

"I would like you to bring him home," Dupon said.

Smith watched as Thomas Carman adjusted the wheel to compensate for a sudden slant of wind. "I could perhaps arrange that," he said, "but it won't come cheap."

"The townspeople have raised a fund," Dupon said. "Suitable to meet your expenses and recompense you for your efforts." He mentioned a figure that impressed Smith.

"The people of Dunkirk must be desperate to have Duguay back."

"He was the driving force behind the privateering economy," Dupon admitted frankly. "Apart from my sons and me, the seamen have lost heart. The Royal Naval victory at Quiberon Bay and Captain Thurot's defeat in the Irish Sea ruined their morale."

"Defeat can do that," Smith said. Quiberon Bay had been a significant victory for the Royal Navy, while Thurot had been the most successful of French privateers. The Scotsman, Captain John Elliot, had defeated his squadron and killed Thurot at the battle of Bishop's Court.

Dupon nodded. "If we do not have some better news soon, our captains will not put to sea."

No captains at sea would mean no free trade brandy. Dupon is manoeuvring me.

"I'll make some arrangements and see what can be done," Smith shook Dupon's hand again. "If Duguay is loose, our merchantmen will be in danger. I'm no patriot but no traitor either, so I must have something to redress the balance."

"Not from Dunkirk," Marcel said at once. "I will not give any of my friends into British captivity."

Smith noted, and approved, the absence of national feeling. "If you provide the sailing times of suitable merchantmen," he said. "I'd call the bargain square."

Dupon smiled. "We understand each other, Mr Smith."

Smith watched Dupon return to *Profiteur* before he gave orders to return to England.

Well, Devil, you and I will soon be dancing again, and Hell mend the loser.

SISSINGHURST WAS A LARGE BUILDING, A STATELY HOME IN THE Kent countryside, with a tall tower and an exterior wall. The government had housed French prisoners of war in Sissinghurst for some years, with numerous sentry boxes outside and inside and more red-coated guards than Smith expected.

This rescue will not be easy, Smith thought as he studied the building through his telescope. *I'll need some careful preparation.* He grinned to himself, snapped the telescope shut and mounted his hired horse. *I'll have to become a gentleman to gain access to Sissinghurst.* When the idea came, it was so simple that it stunned him. *Dear God in heaven! I can kill two birds with one stone and still retain everything for which I have worked.*

"You look happy," Bess said as Smith stepped into their room.

"Do I?" Smith sat on his chair and pulled off his boots. "I'll need a horse, Bess, and not a hired hack either. And I need quality clothes, tailored to fit."

"Anything else?" Bess asked.

"Yes," Smith said. "You have a better hand with the quill than I do. I want you to teach me your skills."

"My writing is adequate," Bess agreed. "As is yours."

"I know," Smith produced a document from the table. "I want you to copy that style of writing until you have it perfect."

Bess lifted the document. "What are you planning?" she asked.

"I'm going to play the devil and dance with the Army," Smith said. "Now, where can I purchase a horse?"

ONE OF THE NEW MILITIA REGIMENTS WAS ON DUTY WHEN Smith rode up on Rodney, his new brown gelding. The soldiers around Sissinghurst's walls watched him suspiciously, decided he was no threat and returned to the boredom of sentry duty.

Smith rode slowly to the furthest corner from the main entrance, where a young sentry stared into the green Kent countryside.

"Good evening to you." Smith dismounted and stamped his feet on the ground as if he was restoring circulation to his legs after a long ride.

The sentry started as if surprised that this well-dressed gentleman would condescend to address a lowly private. "Good evening," he replied at last. "I'm ordered not to talk to anybody, sir." He spoke in the accents of North Kent.

"You must obey your orders," Smith said with a smile. He knew there was a quota system for filling the militia's ranks, with many men chosen preferring to select a substitute to take their place. Naturally, the replacements were often the unwanted of the parish, the work-shy, petty-criminals and ne'er do wells that the respectable people wished elsewhere. In Smith's opinion, such men were not always blessed with great intelligence.

"Yes, sir," the sentry said.

"You'll get cold out here," Smith sipped from a small flask and passed it to the sentry.

"Drinking is against orders," the sentry said.

"It's rum," Smith said and glanced around. "Nobody's looking."

British soldiers had many fine qualities, but resistance to alcoholic temptation was not one of them. Leaning his Brown Bess musket against the side of his sentry-box, the private took the flask. "That's very decent of you, sir," he said and took a long swig. "That's the real stuff."

"Jamaica rum," Smith assured him. "None finer in the world." He looked around. "Put it inside your coat."

The sentry grinned and obeyed. "You're a real gentleman, sir," he said.

"Just a man like you," Smith said. "It must be a hard job guarding this place. A very responsible duty, keeping all these Crapauds in their place."

"We don't mind, sir," the sentry said, much more affable once alcohol had formed a bond of friendship.

"Do you treat them well?"

"We treat them as they deserve, the dirty toads!" The sentry replied.

"I heard the conditions are a bit rough," Smith produced a twist of tobacco, began to fill his pipe. and handed the rest to the sentry.

"They like to complain," the sentry said. "Why, thank you again, sir!"

"The governor, Captain Summerside, isn't it?" Smith made up a name.

"Why no, sir, it's Major Foss," the sentry said.

"Foss! That's the fellow!" Smith said. "Is he in at present?"

"He is, sir," the sentry said, then lowered his voice confidentially. "The major leaves every Tuesday, sir. Some of the boys think he's off to his club for cards, but I reckon the major has a sweetheart."

"Ah!" Smith stored the information away. "With the good Major Foss with his lady, who then is in command?"

"Why, sir, Captain Easton, sir. A fine fellow!"

Smith nodded. "Easton! Of course. Thank you for your help, private, but I must be on my way. Tell me, do you have any distinguished prisoners here?"

The sentry grinned, showing a mouthful of half-masticated tobacco. "Lord bless you, sir, yes. We have a whole host of naval officers and the like, with that pirate fellow here too."

Smith heard an NCO's snarl from further along the wall. *Damn! That will be the sergeant of the guard walking his rounds.* "Which pirate fellow private? Captain Kidd? Blackbeard Teach?"

"Why no, sir. We don't have any prisoners with those names. I mean the Duguay fellow."

"Thank you, Private." Smith remounted his horse and turned her head away so the sergeant would not see his face. "I wish you a good morning."

"Good morning to you, sir," said the sentry, still chewing.

Kicking in his heels, Smith trotted away, with the ideas formulating in his head. Now he knew the governor's name, and when he was absent, and the quality of the unit on guard.

"Sir Francis," Smith said as he patted Rodney's neck. "I think we have you."

"AMBROSE GRANT, HIS NAME IS," HARGREAVES SAID, THEN stopped to bellow at a man who was caulking the deck. "He's the best man the Preventative service possess."

Smith grunted. "Ambrose Grant. I've heard that name. Did he not smash the smuggling ring at Montrose?"

"That's the man," Hargreaves was on his knees, checking the deck. "The Montrose smugglers were all ex-Jacobites, a devious, cunning bunch who knew every trick there was, yet Grant out-manoeuvred them. He's a dangerous man to cross."

Smith grunted again, shouted to the hands to change the rigging on the foremast and watched Skinner bring a wagon-load of grain into the warehouse beside the harbour. "Montrose is a long way north of here," he said. "Let's hope the Excise doesn't send him south."

Hargreaves stood up, satisfied the deck was perfect. "The Preventative service sends Grant wherever the trouble is greatest," he said, "and rumour says he's sailing off Essex. That's far too close for my liking."

"I'll keep the name in mind," Smith said. "At present, my main concern is to get this ship seaworthy again. That last blow battered us a bit, and we have a fast passage ahead." He saw the lone horsewoman riding slowly along the quay, looking everywhere except at *Maid of Kent*, and knew she was watching him.

No, Becky, I am not interested in becoming your lover. So why did his stomach churn whenever he thought of her?

Chapter Eighteen

"I desire to see the governor!" Dressed in all the finery that Kent could provide, Smith emerged from his hired coach at the main gate of Sissinghurst.

"Who the devil are you?" The sentry was not impressed with soft clothes and a gold-braided hat.

"I am Sir Francis Selby of Kingshunt Manor." Smith rapped his cane against the sentry box. "Stand aside and let me in, fellow!"

"Oh!" The sentry hesitated. Drilled since birth to respect authority, he also had orders no to allow any unauthorised person past. Now a man of evident wealth and position was challenging these orders, putting him in a conundrum. His face cleared as he came to a decision. "If you wait here, sir, I'll fetch the sergeant."

"Fetch him," Smith ordered, feigning carelessness, and swung his cane. "But hurry, man. I don't have all day!"

The sergeant of the guard was puffed up with self-importance as he swaggered to the gate. A Maidstone baker in civilian life, Sergeant Atkinson was in his late twenties and imbued with more authority than he had ever expected to wield in his life. Placing himself directly in front of Smith's coach, he held his halberd across his chest.

"We have orders not to permit anybody to enter without direct permission from the commandant."

"Major Foss is my cousin," Smith said casually, twirling his cane to allow the sunlight to reflect from the golden top. It was only pinchbeck but appeared like gold to a less-than-knowledgeable observer. Smith did not expect any of the rank-and-file to recognise the difference. "If you wish to retain your rank, Sergeant, I'd advise that you stand out of my path."

"The major is out of the camp." Atkinson could not hide his satisfaction at using his authority.

Smith had watched Major Foss ride away half-an-hour previously. "Damn the man!" he tutted in pretended frustration. "He'll be away to meet that damned dragtail again. He's always up to something." He shook his head and took the sergeant into his confidence, sharing a secret to win the man's friendship. "He was the same at Eton, Sergeant. We both knelt over the birching block because of Charlie Foss's pursuit of an easy skirt."

Atkinson smiled as the supposed gentleman included him in his memories.

"If Charlie Foss is busy," Smith said, with a leer, "then pray tell Captain Easton that I am here. I'd be much obliged, Sergeant. Much obliged, indeed."

The sergeant's assumed authority evaporated before Smith's confidence, and he ordered the gates to be open and ushered the supposed gentleman inside and directed him to the deputy commandant's office.

"Thank you, Sergeant," Smith handed the man a crown. "Buy yourself a drink from me when next you are off duty."

"Thank you, sir," Atkinson was all obsequious smiles as he pointed the way. "That's very kind of you."

Smith marched into the office as if by right. "Captain Easton! I am Sir Francis Selby of Kingshunt Manor." He held out his hand. "Major Foss informed me of your efficiency."

Captain Marcus Easton was the younger son of a provincial banker, used to lifting his hat to even the most minor of country gentlemen. Becoming a captain in the county militia was a step or two higher in the social scale than he had ever expected. Now a titled gentleman treated him as an equal, which appealed to his vanity, as Smith had intended.

"Major Foss is a kind man, Squire," Easton said, shaking Smith's hand like a pump handle.

"Charlie always was kind, despite his unfortunate Christian name," Smith used his well-tried method of sharing a confidence to win Easton's friendship. "We were at Eton together, don't you know, while the Young Pretender was causing all the trouble up in Scotland. Poor Charlie had to use his middle name to prevent some serious ragging!" Smith laughed heartily, with Easton joining in as if Major Foss was his bosom companion rather than a superior officer.

Now that Smith and Easton were firm friends, it was easy to move onto business. "Charlie already gave his permission for me to bring out the privateer master, Captain Duguay, as a guest," Smith said casually. "I will take full responsibility for his security, of course."

Captain Easton looked doubtful for only a second. "Duguay is a most dangerous man," he said. "He was a constant threat to our shipping."

Smith swung his cane. "I know," he said with a smile. "What an honour to have such a man in my house." He lowered his voice. "And how galling for a French privateer to be so near the coast yet unable to sail." He produced a flask from inside his cloak, uncorked the lid and handed it to Easton. "French brandy, Easton. Have a taste."

Easton accepted the flask and met Smith's smile. "If the major has already agreed, then I see no reason to object, sir, no reason at all." He sipped at the flask. "Your good health, sir."

"Good man!" Smith said, holding out his hand again. "And call me Francis, Captain. There is no need for formality between friends, is there?"

"Why no, sir, Francis," Easton said.

"After all, Charlie is a mutual friend, however stodgy he can be at times."

Easton laughed again at this fresh example of a confidence between such excellent companions.

"Did Charlie ever tell you of the time we went skirt-hunting at Eton together?" Smith glanced at the clock in the corner and sipped at the brandy before handing it back to Easton. "Poor Charlie found himself a dog, a veritable dog! Her father nearly forced him into a very inconvenient marriage. He was a common farmer, Easton, a mere tenant!" He encouraged the captain to drink more of the brandy.

"There is the matter of Captain Duguay's parole," Easton suggested delicately.

"I'll write you a letter, of course." Smith had initially intended that Bess write a letter in Sir Francis's hand but realised it would be more effective to produce a letter with Easton watching. Accordingly, he had spent hours practising Sir Francis's writing and signature, taken from the Protection certificates and Letter of Marque.

"I'm sure there is no need, sir,"

"My name is Francis," Smith reminded with a smile. "A letter will keep you right if there are any questions. Now, do you have some paper, Captain?"

"I have, Francis, and pray call me Matthew."

Drawing the paper to him, Smith scribbled a note.

Let it be known that I, Sir Francis Selby of Kingshunt Manor in Kent, have taken Captain Duguay, the French privateer, under my wing this day. I take full responsibility for Captain Duguay's actions and security as long as he is in my company.
Francis Selby
18th June 1762

"Thank you, Francis." Easton placed the letter in his top drawer.

"And now, Matthew, I must thank you for a very pleasant time." Smith passed over the flask again. "If you would be so kind as to fetch the prisoner, we will be on our way." He lowered his voice slightly. "Duguay and I knew each other before the present war, you see. He supplied my cellars with this excellent brandy." Smith tapped the flask. "There is no need to inform the Preventative men, is there?"

Easton laughed. "There is no need at all, Francis" He raised his voice to a bark. "Sergeant Watler!"

A beefy sergeant appeared, slamming to attention in front of Easton.

"Fetch Captain Duguay for Sir Francis, Watler!"

"Very good, sir!" Watler left immediately.

Captain Duguay looked confused when Easton brought him to Smith.

"My dear Captain!" Smith greeted him like a long-lost friend, speaking in English. "How sad to see you in such a plight!"

Duguay stepped back a little, glancing at Easton.

Smith addressed Easton. "Do you speak French, Matthew?"

"Not a word, Francis," Easton said. "We have little need for French at home."

"I see." *Typical of the British to put a man in charge of Frenchmen without having a word of their language.* "With your permission, I'd like to speak to the Captain in French."

"Naturally, sir," Easton allowed, with a slight bow.

Smith turned to Duguay. "My name does not matter, but I am a colleague of Captain Dupon, Captain. We plan to take you home if you wish."

Duguay nodded. "I wondered. Do we know each other?"

"We are old friends. Call me Sir Francis, which is the name I am using here."

"I understand." Duguay held out his hand and spoke in English. "It's good to see you again, Sir Francis."

"I have signed a document taking you under my wing," Smith

continued in English. "Now, I wish you to give your parole not to escape. Give it to me personally."

"I will not break my parole to an English gentleman," Duguay said solemnly.

"I have a document made out," Smith pulled a folded piece of stiff paper from inside his jacket. "If you would read this, Captain Easton?" He handed it over. "I have it written in both English and French."

To whom it may concern,

I, Captain Rene Duguay, do freely give my parole to Sir Francis Selby of Kingshunt Manor in the County of Kent. Sir Francis Selby will take full responsibility for my behaviour and security as long as I remain in his care.

Signed Sir Francis Selby of Kingshunt Manor
Signed Captain Rene Duguay
18th July 1762

Easton returned the document.

"Could you sign here, Rene?" Smith asked.

"On my honour," Duguay said, signing with a flourish. He looked up, meeting Easton's gaze. "I will keep any promise I make to Sir Francis." He replaced the quill in its holder and looked up. "If you have a Bible, Captain Easton, I will swear on that."

"I am sure there is no need," Easton said. "We are all gentlemen here."

Talking like old friends, Smith and Duguay strolled out of Easton's office, with Easton accompanying them to Smith's carriage. Skinner stood beside the horses, smoking his pipe and trying to look calm. He extinguished his pipe and hurried to open the door.

"Your carriage awaits," Easton said.

As Duguay and Smith prepared to board the coach, they shook hands with Easton. Duguay gave a formal bow.

As they sat inside, Skinner cracked the reins and drove them through the open gates, with Sergeant Atkinson calling the sentry to attention. Smith acknowledged the salute with a casual flick of his hand.

"Sissinghurst is a foul place," Duguay said as Skinner whipped up the horses. "Dirty, violent, and overcrowded." He glanced through the coach window, then flicked the curtain shut. "What's all this about?"

"I have made an arrangement with Captain Dupon," Smith said. "My part was to free you from captivity and deliver you safely in France."

"And his part?" There was a sharp edge behind Duguay's humorous voice.

"Dupon's part is between him and me," Smith said. "It is a gentleman's agreement."

Duguay smiled. "Do you trust him?"

"As much as I trust you, and as far as this," Smith tapped the butt of his pistol. "If he breaks his word to me, I shall hunt him down and put a ball in his brain."

"Ah," Duguay said. "And what do you require of me?" He leaned back, regarding Smith through his disturbingly intelligent eyes.

"I wish you to write a letter for me," Smith said as the coach eased through the various shades of green that marked the Kent countryside.

"A letter?" Duguay raised his eyebrows. "What sort of letter, and to whom?"

"I wish you to write a letter to our mutual acquaintance, Sir Francis Selby," Smith said. "You will thank him for his help in freeing you from captivity."

"Ah, I see," Duguay smiled. "I will be effusive in my gratitude to Sir Francis."

Chapter Nineteen

"Who are you?" Big Tom from Hastings looked surprised when Smith dismounted from his horse outside the Royal Arms in the village of Snargate. Tom fondled the ears of his packhorse, grinned disarmingly, and hefted a keg of brandy.

"I am John Smith of Kingsgate. As from today, we will be supplying these premises with their spirits." Smith indicated the loaded wagon at his back, with Skinner on the driving seat and the two burly batsmen sitting at the tail. Dressed in men's clothing, Bess rode behind the wagon, with a blunderbuss sitting handily beside her saddle. She smiled at Big Tom and tapped the butt of her blunderbuss.

"Who are you?" Smith asked.

"Tom Goodsell," Tom said, "but people just call me Big Tom because of my size." Tom spread his arms.

"Well, Big Tom," Smith said. "I want you to return to William Holden and tell him that he's not to sell anything else in Kent. The entire county is our territory now."

Big Tom looked at Smith, the two batsmen, and Bess with her blunderbuss and decided he did not like the odds. "Mr Holden will like to hear about this," he said.

"I've already warned Mr Holden," Smith said. "And now I am warning you. If I find you, or any other of Holden's men, in Snargate or anywhere else in Kent, there will be blood spilt." He watched as Big Tom backed away, returned the keg to its position on the packhorse, and headed westward towards Sussex.

"Holden will be back," Bess said. "He won't like to have his men turned away."

"I know," Smith said. "He requires a confrontation to prove we are in earnest."

Bess pulled her horse beside Smith as he mounted Rodney. "Do you think it will come to bloodshed?"

"Without a doubt," Smith said. "We'll have to teach the Sussex men to remain on their side of the border."

Bess tapped her blunderbuss. "I might have the opportunity to fire this thing."

"I hope not, Bess," Smith said.

I am beginning to care for that woman, yet Becky is also in my thoughts. Life was simpler at sea, with no women involved. Old Jock Sinclair was correct.

"Women," Sinclair had said, with all the wisdom of age in his faded blue eyes, "are good for two things. Causing trouble and raising children."

Smith had laughed, filled with the certainties of youth. "I can think of another use," he said.

Sinclair shook his head. "Be careful, younker, for once a woman allows you into the pleasant warmth of her body, she will also expect you to share her emotions."

Smith laughed again. "I'm not so easily trapped."

"Wise word from a young mouth," Sinclair said. "I wonder how many men have thought the same."

HARGREAVES DOWNED HIS RUM WITHOUT EFFORT. "THAT fellow Grant has been busy again," he said.

"What's he done now?" Smith asked.

"You'll remember he was in Essex, last I heard," Hargreaves said.

"I remember," Smith said.

"He's finished there," Hargreaves told him. "He wrapped up Betty Totman and her gang within two weeks."

Smith frowned. "Red-haired Betty? She was a character! This Grant fellow bears some watching."

Hargreaves signalled for more rum. "He operates with two cutters, one to watch the coast and one that shadows his suspect. He stays with the free trader until he — or in Betty's case, she — makes a mistake. Then Grant moves in to trap them."

Smith grunted. "Thank you, Hargreaves. Let's hope Grant doesn't come here. Now, how did you get on talking to Sir Francis's servants?"

Hargreaves sipped at his refilled glass of rum. "My attempts failed," he admitted. "After all, who wants to talk to a wrinkled old bugger like me?"

"That is true," Smith allowed.

"So I sent Suzanne to charm them instead."

Smith nodded. "Your wife is a redoubtable woman. Was she successful?"

"She was," Hargreaves said. "She got you what you wanted." He handed over a small packet.

Smith looked inside. Three pieces of putty, each with impressions of a key. "Thank you, Hargreaves. That will do nicely."

Hargreaves looked troubled. "What do you have in mind, Captain? I wish you would concentrate on the smuggling. We understand the free trade business, but I don't wish to start housebreaking."

Smith leaned back and placed his feet on the fender of the unlit fire. "I have wrongs to right."

"You'll end up in more trouble, Captain. Let the past stay in the past and allow the dead to look after the dead."

Smith fingered the faint scar of the rope around his neck.

"No, Hargreaves. I won't." He touched the putty again, with his eyes vacant.

IN THE DARK HOURS BEFORE DAWN, SMITH BUNDLED DUGUAY down to the harbour and installed him in *Maid of Kent's* hold, behind the false bulkhead.

"You'll be a bit uncomfortable," Smith said, "but we'll have you home soon."

Duguay sat on the deck. "No more uncomfortable than I was in Sissinghurst," he said. "Thank you for the hospitality in Kingsgate, Captain."

"Don't thank me," Smith said. "Mrs Martin, the landlady, kept the room for you."

Duguay smiled. "You paid her handsomely for it."

"She deserved it. Now, you stay quiet, and we'll have you back in Dunkirk before you know it."

As the sun rose over the Channel, *Maid's* crew came on board, all grasping the Protections that Smith had obtained for them, and many hoping for more prize money.

Smith looked on them fondly. Now that *Maid of Kent* was a fully licensed privateer, any enemy vessel that crossed their path was fair game, and the crew had a possibility of making extra money. Even the ship's boy, Hargreaves twelve-year-old son Edward, would receive three-quarters of a share of any prize money, while the able seamen pocketed a full share, and Hargreaves seven shares. Smith would take home fourteen shares. As *Maid of Kent's* managing owner and the man who purchased the privateering licence, Sir Francis would pocket seventeen shares in any profit.

Am I bribing these men? Smith asked himself. *Yes, I am, and I am using them for my ends, although they're better off under my command than in most ships they've served in before.* He ran his eyes over them, noting their faces from the falsely benign expression of Carman to the sinister Ramsley brothers and all the rest.

"Cast off aft!" Smith bellowed. "Cast off forward!" He raised his voice even further so the people gathered on the quay could hear him. "Come on, *Maidens!* We're off to face the French!"

———————

CAPTAIN DUPON LOOKED AROUND AS A WESTERLY WIND kicked up spray from the Channel. "Did you succeed, Captain?"

"Here he comes now," Smith gave a slight nod that saw Carman escort Captain Duguay from down below. Few of the crew had been aware of Duguay's presence, and Hargreaves kept them busy, loading the cargo, so nobody saw him emerge from below.

"You kept your word, Captain Smith," Dupon said.

"As you will keep yours," Smith reminded.

Dupon put a hard hand on Smith's arm. "Step aft with me, Captain."

The three captains stood at the taffrail of *Profiteur* as their crews transferred the spirits from ship to ship. Captain Duguay breathed deeply of the atmosphere of a French vessel once more.

"Le Manche smells sweet today," Duguay said, rubbing his hand on the mizzenmast. "She welcomes me with her laughter."

Smith nodded. From here, he could see both France and Great Britain, with the sea a highway connecting both, rather than a mobile moat protecting one from the tyranny of the other. Smith shook his head, wondering which monarch was the tyrant and which nation was the aggressor. From the sea, there was little to choose in the matter of kings,

"What do you have for me, Captain Dupon?" Smith asked.

"I will not give you any Dunkirk vessels," Dupon told him. "I know all their masters and most of their crews." He lifted his chin as if expecting Smith to explode in wrath or shoot him out of hand.

vere fine seamen, Smith knew, but the French of Brittany and he Channel ports matched them in all respects.

"Another sail, Captain!" Henry Ramsley called from aloft. By that time, the crew were weary of investigating every passing ship from a distance and sailing on without making a capture. The hands wanted a quick trip across the Channel to pick up an illicit cargo or a two-day cruise to snatch a French prize rather than an extended search in perilous waters.

Smith climbed aloft and extended his telescope. The ship was large, with three masts, and was moving slowly under easy sail.

Why the lack of sail, captain? Are you setting a trap?

As Smith focussed his telescope, he saw the vessel had been battered by heavy weather, with patched sails and new spars. She carried at least a dozen cannons, maybe twelve pounders, far more than *Maid of Kent*, but in wartime, many merchant vessels carried arms in case of privateers. Carrying guns did not mean the ship had the skill, or the will, to use them.

That's why you're moving so slowly, Smith thought. *You've had a rough passage, and your vessel is damaged. You're limping home to France. Sorry, Captain, but I want your cargo.*

"She's a whaling ship," Smith said and smiled. "Raise the French ensign, boys, and steer towards her."

"I understand that," Smith said. "Unless a Dunkirk vessel attacks me, I will treat them as if they were Christ's angels."

Dupon breathed out slowly in relief. "There is a vessel from La Rochelle due in Calais tomorrow with a cargo of rice and a whaling vessel arriving shortly after if they can avoid the Royal Navy's blockade."

"A whaling ship?" Dupon's words aroused Smith's interest. "Will she come from east or west?"

"She was fishing in the Greenland Sea," Marcel said. "The British have a convoy system from the ice down past the Shetland Islands and along their east coast. Our whaler will sail to the west of Ireland to escape the British cruisers."

"She'll come from the west, then," Smith's mind was busy with tides and winds, working out the probable route of the whaling vessel. "I have one more question to ask."

"What is that, Captain?" Dupon sounded unhappy giving Smith information about French shipping movements.

"Do you possess a spare flag?"

Dupon looked puzzled. "Only a French flag, Captain, and very tattered."

"All the better. I will pay a golden guinea for your tattered flag, Dupon."

"It is not worth half of that, Captain," Dupon sent a boy for the flag.

"It may be worth much more." Smith tossed over the guinea. When the boy, another of Dupon's sons, arrived with the flag, Smith passed him a sovereign.

"Look after that," he said.

Dupon was correct; hard usage had battered the flag, but it was still recognisably French. A white cross on a blue background, with the royal arms in the centre, the flag had a proud history.

"Thank you, Captain," Smith said as the ideas formed in his mind. He sniffed the wind. "It's a pleasure doing business with you."

With Duguay safely on *Profiteur*, and a fluky wind flicking the tops from the Channel waves, *Maid of Kent* sailed west. Smith ordered Henry Ramsley to the masthead as the lookout and hid his apprehension as he stood at the stern. The wind altered with every hour, mainly southerly but never steady, which necessitated frequent course alterations.

"What's happening, Captain?" Hargreaves interrupted Smith's train of thought.

"We're after a rich prize, Hargreaves, or we're wasting time that Sir Francis will question me about."

"The hands are wondering why we're not returning home with the cargo."

"Damn the hands," Smith said testily. "They've done better in this ship than any other in their lives."

"Yes, Captain." Hargreaves withdrew hastily.

"Sail ho!" Henry Ramsley called from the masthead, and Smith ran aloft with his telescope. Balancing on the crosstrees, he scanned the distant ship, saw she was a small snow, and dismissed her.

"She might make us a fine prize, Captain," Henry Ramsley suggested.

"No." Smith did not doubt that *Maid of Fife* could capture the snow, but the time taken might allow the whaling ship, a much larger prize, to escape.

"If you tell me what we're hunting, Captain, and leave me the spyglass, it'd be better."

"No," Smith said again.

After two hours, Smith replaced Henry Ramsley with his brother Jake and then, as dark closed in, sent Roper aloft. All the time, he remained on deck, overseeing every minute alteration to the ship's course, adding or changing her sails with every shift of the wind until the crew cursed the sound of his voice.

"We should have taken that snow," Henry Ramsley's grating voice sounded from forward. "She was begging to be captured,

and the captain ignored her. What are we doing, [...] time beating about the Channel?"

"You're right, Henry," Jake said. "Smith's no priv[...] too soft."

"Pipe down!" Carman's cracked voice sounded [...] making my ears bleed with your complaints. I'd keelhau[...] of you for mutiny if I had my way."

Closing his mind to the grumbles, Smith remained [...] hoping he had made the correct decision to pursue the [...] ship.

"It's too dark to see, Captain!" Roper shouted.

"I'll come aloft," Smith replied. "Mr Hargreaves, take [...] the ship. Follow the course I have set, beat back and forth[...] quarry must pass between the Goodwin Sands and the Fr[...] coast."

"Aye, sir," Hargreaves said doubtfully. "We don't want to [...] up shop on Goodwin Sands."

"Keep her safe, then," Smith said and ran aloft, sendi[...] Roper back down.

All night, *Maid of Kent* patrolled her beat, with Smith at th[...] masthead, scanning the night-dark sea for lights or the glint of moonlight on sails. Twice he thought he saw something, but each time it was only the sea, breaking white.

Am I wasting time? Should I have taken that snow? A ship in hand is better than ten at sea, and any prize money is better than none.

At the first gleam of dawn, Henry Ramsley came aloft again.

"Mr Hargreaves has sent me to take over, Captain," he said with false respect in his voice.

"Keep a sharp eye," Smith scraped a hand over his unshaven chin and returned to the deck. He cursed the stiffness in his limbs and hoping the whaling vessel had not slipped past in the night. He had another fear, for the French were bound to have seen *Maid* off their shore, and a French warship might slide through the Royal Naval blockade to investigate. The British

Chapter Twenty

S mith watched as the confused crew raised the blue-and-white cross.

"French?" Henry Ramsley queried. "We're not bloody French! Is the captain going to make us French?"

"Stow it!" Carman snarled. "The captain knows what he's doing!"

You've more faith in me than I have, Thomas!

With her French lines and the French flag fluttering from her mizzen, *Maid of Kent* stood towards the whaling ship.

"Hand me the speaking trumpet," Smith ordered as the two vessels closed. He could see the white blobs of curious faces on the French ship and knew her master would be scrutinising him through a telescope. A stray gust of wind blew the stench of whale oil toward him, reminding him why these vessels were known as blubber ships and why other ships avoided them.

The whaling ship master shouted an order, and a score of men rushed to her guns.

"Whaling ships carry large crews," Hargreaves warned, handing over the speaking trumpet. "She'll have forty or fifty men aboard, and we have only twenty-five."

"I am aware of that, Mr Hargreaves," Smith did not hide his irritation at the mate interrupting his train of thought.

Smith lifted the trumpet, feeling the metal cold against his lips. "Bateau ahoy — ship ahoy!" he bellowed, unsure how French ships addressed each other, so using the French equivalent of British usage.

"She has *Nantes* on her stern," Hargreaves murmured, with his telescope extended.

Smith nodded. "*Nantes* ahoy!" He waited until *Nantes'* master responded with a friendly hail.

"Come on board, Captain," Smith invited. "I'm afraid I can't send a boat. The Goddams destroyed it." He hoped the French still used the term "goddams" to describe the British.

Nantes' master scanned *Maid of Kent* again. He would recognise that she was French-built, but the place of origin meant little, with many ships captured and recaptured during the war. Wearing the enemy's flag was also a legal ruse of war, perfectly acceptable as long as the aggressor hoisted the correct flag before the actual fighting began.

"Is there a British ship nearby?" *Nantes'* captain asked anxiously.

"They have our coast under a close blockade, Captain. Come on board, and I'll give details." Smith found shouting in French a tremendous strain on his throat.

"Smile nicely until they're on board," Smith murmured to his men. "Then it's pistols and cutlasses and escort them to the hold."

"Aye, aye, sir," Hargreaves said with a grin. "We've done this before with the privateer."

"The crew of *Marie Blanc* were children. The whaling men will be less naïve." Smith warned.

Smith was not sure of his next move until he saw the French captain. Wearing a distinctive white hat, the captain steered his open whaling boat towards *Maid of Kent* while four seamen wielded the oars.

"Welcome, Captain," Smith ushered the whaling men on board. "Secure the boat and bring your men. We have brandy, wine, and rum." Only when all five men were in his cabin did Smith drop the mask.

"I apologise for the deception, Monsieur, but you are now my prisoner."

The captain opened his mouth wide. "But the flag! That is an outrage! It is against all the rules of the sea. I protest, sir, in the strongest terms," he spluttered. "You fly a French flag."

"I'll do worse than that, Captain," Smith warned him cheerfully. "Unless you do as I say, I'll kill one of your men."

The captain would have lunged forward if Smith had not thrust a pistol into his stomach. "Easy there, Captain."

"I will not!" the captain said.

Carman stepped inside the already crowded cabin with his cutlass in his hand.

"Waiting for orders, Captain," he said, grinning.

"Mr Carman," Smith spoke in French and then repeated his words in English. "Take away that man there," he pointed to the youngest of the French, "and cut his throat."

"Yes, Captain," Carman said, smiling as if he murdered stray seamen every day. Smith remembered Carman's past and wondered if he had chosen the wrong man, but it was too late. Helped by Jake Ramsley, Carman dragged the young Frenchman behind the mainmast. A moment later, there was a gurgling scream, and Carman returned, wiping the blade of his cutlass.

"Well, Captain?" Smith asked the white-faced whaling master. "Shall we dispose of another of your men?" He indicated a man in his late teens. "That fellow, I think."

The captain threw Smith a look of cold hatred. "What do you want me to say to my men?"

"How many are in your crew?"

"Thirty-six," the captain said sullenly.

"That's small for a whaling crew," Smith said suspiciously. "If you lie to me, Captain, there will be blood spilt."

"I lost six men in the ice," the captain explained. "A whale upset the whaleboat."

You've had an unfortunate season, Captain.

"Tell them we are hosting a celebration on board," Smith said. "Ask another six men to come across."

"I will not," the captain said. "You are a monster."

"I am," Smith agreed. "Mr Carman!"

"Captain?" Carman drew his cutlass and raised his eyebrows.

"That man next." Smith nodded to the young Frenchman.

"Non!" The French captain snarled. "I will do as you say, but under strong protest. You break all the rules of war, monsieur, and I will inform the authorities of your actions."

"You must do as you see fit, Captain. Now, call over your men."

With Smith at his side, the whaling master stood on the quarterdeck and shouted across to his ship.

"Any deceptions, monsieur, and I'll order all your men killed," Smith growled, wondering how much he was bluffing. He knew that the Ramsley brothers, and probably Roper and Carman, would kill any Frenchman without a qualm.

Within five minutes, two boatloads of Frenchmen came across, to be welcomed with handshakes and proffered bottles by *Maid's* crew, and then taken below and locked away.

"That leaves twenty Frenchmen on *Nantes*," Smith said. "They'll be wondering what is happening."

"Yes, Captain," Hargreaves said. "What do you plan?"

"I plan to capture the whole damned ship," Smith said. "She'll make us a pretty penny as a prize."

"Yes, sir. But how? *Nantes* still outguns us, and her crew must be suspicious."

Smith smiled. "A good hanging is in order."

"What do you mean?" Hargreaves asked.

Smith gestured to the French captain. "This fellow and I are of similar build, and his hat is quite distinctive, don't you think?"

Hargreaves struggled to follow Smith's train of thought. "Yes, Captain. Not many people wear a white hat."

"That's what I thought." Smith removed the French captain's hat. "You two!" he gestured to the Ramsley brothers. "Strip this fellow of his clothes."

Ignoring the Frenchman's protests, the Ramsleys obeyed, grinning and making obscene jokes. Smith exchanged the French captain's clothes for his own.

"Dress this fellow and take him below," Smith said. "Treat him gently."

"Aye, aye, sir," Hargreaves gestured to the Ramsleys, who hustled the French captain below deck.

"Now Hewitt will take me aloft at cutlass point," Smith ordered, ramming the white hat onto his head. "And tie a noose around my neck. You are going to threaten to hang me from the yardarm unless the whaling ship surrenders." Smith hid his unease at having a noose around his throat again. "The Crapauds will see the white hat and won't look any further."

"What shall I do then, Captain?"

"Order them to surrender." Smith knew that Hargreaves was an excellent subordinate but lacked the decision-making confidence to make a ship's master. "Give them three minutes and send ten men across, heavily armed."

"That will leave us nearly unmanned!"

"I know!" Smith said. "We're dancing with fate here, Mr Hargreaves, but what is life if not one great gamble?"

Balancing on the yard with the Channel wind picking up, Smith suppressed his shudder as Hewitt thrust him onto the mainsail yard arm. Hewitt removed Smith's hat and placed the noose around his neck. The touch of the rope brought back memories, and for an instant, Smith wished to remove the noose and sail away, leaving the whaling ship to its freedom.

"The hat!" Smith hissed. "Put the hat back on my head!"

"Yes, Captain," Hewitt crammed the white hat back. "Don't slip, Captain, for the love of God."

Smith glanced at the sea far below and forced away old memories. *Get on with it, Hargreaves.*

"We have your captain!" Hargreaves shouted in English. "Unless you surrender to us, I will hang him and all your men!"

Smith watched the consternation on the French ship as men shouted back or stared up at him.

"Don't let them hang my men!" Smith shouted in French. "The Goddamns have killed two already!" He hoped that confusion and the wind would disguise his voice sufficiently for the whaler's crew to believe he was their captain. After an arduous voyage from the Arctic, the hands would be too tired to look beyond the white hat.

Balancing on the yardarm, Smith turned away from the French ship. The wind carried snatches of conversation from *Nantes,* with men bellowing questions that Hargreaves ignored.

"You have one minute!" Hargreaves shouted, with the speaking trumpet giving a metallic ring to his voice. "One minute, and then your captain hangs!"

That's cutting it fine, Hargreaves. Send a boat across for the love of God. Take their ship before they organise themselves.

It seemed an age before Hargreaves sent a boat to the Frenchman, with the Ramsley brothers to the fore, yelling as they brandished cutlasses and pistols. The French were too stunned to resist as *Maid's* crew rounded them up with loud shouts, kicks, and blows.

"You're safe now, Captain," Hewitt said.

"Thank God!" Smith cast off the noose with a shudder and returned to the deck to retake command. When he looked up, he saw the noose swinging in the wind, dark and sinister against the sky.

"Get rid of that damned thing, Hewitt," Smith said. "I won't have it disfiguring my ship."

"Aye, aye, sir," Hewitt dashed back aloft as Hargreaves threw Smith a curious look. "We've captured the Frenchman, Captain," Hargreaves said.

"I know," Smith said, "I know. Have you handed the dead man back? The man Carman pretended to kill?"

"Yes, Captain," Hargreaves grinned. "The poor French captain nearly fainted with apoplexy when he realised the trick you played on him! I nearly thought he'd prefer his men to be dead!"

Smith nodded absently and rubbed a hand over his throat. He could still feel where the hemp had rubbed against his flesh.

Will I have the nightmare of the noose all my life?

As the captured *Nantes* was too large to fit into Kingsgate's minute harbour, Smith sailed it to Dover as a prize and completed the necessary documentation before contacting Sir Francis.

"You've captured what as a prize?" Sir Francis asked.

"*Nantes,* sir, a French whaling ship," Smith said. "She's a three-masted vessel of 356 tons, with a full cargo of whale oil and bone, the produce of eleven whales." He saw Sir Francis's face brighten with avarice.

"A full cargo?" Sir Francis repeated.

"Yes, sir," Smith said. "The ship alone is worth a great deal. She's less than two seasons' old and, except for some repairable damage from the Arctic ice, in excellent condition. The cargo will sell for many thousands of pounds."

"Good God." Sir Francis looked at Smith across the width of his desk. "Where did I find you? I must confess that I had my doubts about you, Smith. I have heard some queer rumours and some rather disturbing stories in which you play a prominent role."

"People will always talk, sir," Smith said calmly. "I am sure you will disregard the gossip mongers."

Sir Francis poured himself a brandy. "It appears I was correct to issue you with a Letter of Marque," he said.

"Thank you, sir," Smith bowed without a trace of irony.

Sir Francis leaned back in his chair and eyed Smith. "Where did you come from, Smith? There is something very familiar about you."

Smith had anticipated that Sir Francis would question him and had prepared his answers. "I sailed into Kingsgate as a young seaman, Sir Francis. You may have seen me in the harbour."

Sir Francis nodded. "That must be it. All right, Smith, you may go."

"Thank you, Sir Francis." Smith bowed and withdrew. He was aware of Lady Selby watching from inside her boudoir but did not respond.

Things are progressing slowly and steadily.

BESS WAS EQUALLY PLEASED WHEN SMITH TOLD HER ABOUT *Nantes*. "How much do we get?" she asked candidly.

Smith noted the word 'we'. "Our share will be in the high hundreds," he told her. "Perhaps a thousand pounds."

"A thousand pounds," Bess repeated the figure, which was beyond the imagination of most people. "What do you intend doing with it?"

"I'm going to buy the Spike." Smith poured them both a stiff tot of rum and watched Bess's reaction as she frowned.

"The Spike is only a ruin," she said.

"It has potential," Smith nearly told her he had wanted the Spike since he was a small boy.

"I didn't know the Spike was for sale," Bess said.

"It's not for sale yet." Smith lay back on the bed with the rum bottle in one hand and a glass in the other. "But it will be soon."

Bess knocked back her rum in a single swallow. "Who owns it? And how do you know it will soon be for sale?" She held out her glass for a refill. "Why do you want it?"

"I like the view," Smith answered the last question and ignored the rest as he poured more rum into her glass.

"What will you do with the ruin?"

"We will live there," Smith said and, in a rare moment of disclosure, added, "I've always wanted to live at the Spike."

It's the highest point in the parish. I can look down on the big house and know I am better than the Selbies.

"It's only a ruin," Bess reminded.

"It won't always be a ruin," Smith said. "You might like it when it's finished."

Bess sat beside him, bouncing on the bed, so he had to hold his glass high to prevent the contents from spilling. "Do you intend to rebuild the Spike?"

"Yes," Smith remembered his younger self clambering over the ruins, listening to his mother's tales of the parish as it once was, and imagining himself as the landowner.

"Someday, Mother, I will own this place."

"Of course you will, son," his mother had smiled and caressed his head. Smith's mother was always smiling until the day Sir Francis had arrested her husband.

"I'll make it as good as new, Mother, and we can live here together."

Smith's mother had laughed. "I will look forward to that day."

"It might be interesting to see it rebuilt," Bess scrutinised Smith through narrowed eyes.

"I have things to do first," Smith swirled the remnants of the rum in his glass.

Bess glanced at the bed. "Haven't you earned a rest?" she smiled. "Or a woman?"

"I'll rest later," Smith said. "And I only want one woman."

"Which one?" Bess demanded sharply.

"You," Smith placed the bottle and glass on the table.

"SIR FRANCIS IS IN THE CHESS ROOM WITH THE JUDGE," a footman said, barely looking at Smith. "He is not to be disturbed."

"Sir Francis summoned me," Smith reminded. "He said come at seven o'clock sharp, and it is that time now." He indicated the longcase clock in the corner of the hall. Sir Francis undoubtedly liked his clocks, for he had placed them at suitable locations throughout his house.

He must like his servants to work to a strict timetable.

"Yes, Captain Smith," the servant said, "but Sir Francis plays the judge at chess every Thursday afternoon. It's a tradition they have for years when they discuss the forthcoming cases at the assizes."

Smith nodded. "Show me into the room," he said. "I will wait there."

"I'm not sure," the servant hesitated between his fear of his master and this ship captain with the growing reputation and basilisk eyes.

"Show me in," Smith gave his most charming smile. "I won't disturb the game."

As the servant protested, Smith opened the door of the Chess Room and slipped inside. The room was nearly empty, with the shutters closed to keep out all extraneous noise and four multi-branched candelabras providing bright light for the chess table in the centre of the room.

Aside from the chess table with the board and two seats, there were two chairs near the door, the ubiquitous longcase clock, and a side table with a silver tray. A crystal decanter of port stood on the tray with two unused glasses.

Neither Sir Francis nor the judge looked up from the chess set as Smith slid onto one of the spare chairs. One glance assured him that he did not know the judge. It was not the man who had condemned him to death.

That's a relief, for if I saw that man, I'd shoot him out of hand and damn the consequences.

Smith had never seen such a chess set before. The board was two feet square and carved from hardwood, with alternative brown and white squares. Each chess piece was of ivory, hand-sculpted by a master craftsman, so the faces of each piece had a distinctive character. The queens looked down their royal noses at all the lesser pieces, while the knights rode chargers with an intensity matched only on the battlefield. The rooks appeared like mediaeval castles, the bishops held their croziers with saintly pride, and even the pawns glared across the board with individual features. Above all, the kings were uselessly regal as if they expected every other piece to sacrifice itself for the sake of royalty.

Smith watched the game and listened to the desultory conversation.

"You will hang Jenks, of course," Sir Francis said as he moved a pawn a single space.

"If the jury convicts him," the judge contemplated the board and moved a bishop as the clock ticked away the minutes.

"They will. I know each man." Sir Francis countered the judge with his queen. "They are all my tenants and know my opinion of the case. Jenks has been poaching on my land for years."

"Ah. Nice move, Sir Francis." The judge backed his bishop with a knight. "I have you in check. Jenks is not accused of poaching. He is accused of horse theft."

"Another of his hobbies," Sir Francis said. "And you do have me in check, My Lord." Sir Francis moved his king behind a pawn.

"Many of your tenants seem to be horse thieves," the judge said. "That is a hanging matter, of course, if the jury finds him guilty."

"Good," Sir Francis said. "And Lambert?"

"Seven years transportation to the American colonies for him. He won't survive, of course." The judge moved his second knight. "The climate in Jamaica will kill him, as it kills most transportees. I hope some planter gets the benefit of a few months' labour before Lambert dies. The rogue should do something useful with the life the good Lord, in His wisdom, granted him."

Sir Francis chuckled as if they were discussing some sporting event rather than the lives of unfortunate men. He captured the judge's knight with his queen. "I have you in check, judge."

"So I see," the judge stepped away from the game, poured himself a glass of port from a decanter and noticed Smith. "There is a fellow waiting for your attention, Sir Francis."

"That is Captain Smith," Sir Francis said, without looking up from the board. "He can wait, my Lord. It's your move."

The judge grunted and swallowed some port. "You've also been busy at the bench, I hear."

"I only have the minor cases, My Lord. I can't send them to the Americas or the gallows as you can."

The judge snorted. "No, mores the pity. That would save me the trouble. You deal with them as they deserve, I know."

"I do," Sir Francis said. "I whip them and pillory them as much as I can." He watched the judge move a bishop, smiled, and shifted his queen.

The judge grunted as he studied the board. "I know. You keep them in order. You even burned a smuggler to death, I hear." He shifted his queen's knight.

Sir Francis shook his head. "I can't take the credit for that, my Lord. I knew that Blackwell was smuggling, but I didn't cause the fire." He nodded towards Smith. "Captain Smith there was instrumental in ending that escapade."

The judge glanced up. "Indeed?" he said without interest.

Sir Francis moved his bishop and smiled. "And that's checkmate for you, my Lord."

Smith watched the fury on the judge's face and knew he did not like to lose at chess.

"Another game," the judge's mouth was taut.

"If you wish, my Lord. Shall we say a hundred guineas on the outcome?" Sir Francis remembered that Smith was in the room. "Oh, go away, Smith. It wasn't important."

"Yes, sir." Smith left without another word.

So Sir Francis still accuses people of horse stealing. The leopard does not change his spots.

AN OWL WHISTLED FROM THE FRINGES OF THE POLICIES, THE sound strangely melancholic through the trees. As moonlight gleamed on their white marble, the statues seemed to take on a life of their own, with shifting shadows suggesting movement. Smith waited until the servants extinguished the last of the Manor's lights and remained static for another hour to ensure that everybody was settled. He stepped forward, tapping the ground in front of him with a stout stick. As he entered an area of deep shadow, the stick touched the footplate of a mantrap, and the fanged iron jaws slammed shut, snapping the sturdy length of blackthorn in two.

The sound reverberated around the policies like the report of a pistol. Smith stood still, hoping anybody searching for the noise would mistake him for a statue. There was no response from Kingshunt Manor, no sudden light as somebody threw open shutters, only the lonely hoot of the owl. After two long minutes, Smith grunted and threw away the remains of his stick. He had fifty yards of open ground to cross without the means to test for mantraps.

"Enough creeping in the dark," Smith said. "Let's dance," he shifted the heavy sack on his shoulders and strode out with his back straight and his head high.

Sir Francis had added iron bars and shutters to every window on the ground floor, keeping the servants inside and any intruders, or male visitors, out. Rather than force open the bars and cut a hole in the shutters, Smith left his sack on the ground, tied it with a cord to his belt and began to climb. After a lifetime climbing the rigging at sea, the side of a house presented no difficulties, and Smith soon gained the upper storey.

Balancing on the stone sill of a window, Smith scraped away the putty from one of the upper panes and carefully placed the glass at his feet. He inserted his hand to unfasten the window, pushed back the catch, and slid the lower half open. It was the work of a moment to ease the glass pane inside the house and roll into the room. Once safe inside, Smith hauled up his sack, hand over hand, taking care he did not bang it against any of the shutters.

Smith waited for another moment to ensure none of the servants had heard him, then opened the sack. At the top lay a sealed bag of damp putty, which he used to replace the window-pane. Smith smoothed over his work, hoping nobody inspected the window too closely or noticed the smell of putty. Only then did he look around the room. It was a guest's bedroom, neat, clean, and devoid of character.

Lifting the sack, Smith turned the door handle and opened the door. The corridor was wood-panelled, hung with sporting prints and empty of people. Smith headed left and crept down the carpeted stairs to the great hall and then down again to the cellars. The lower level of stairs was of bare stone, curving slightly between unpainted plaster walls.

Smith stopped twice, thinking he heard movement, waited until the clock in the hall ticked away a minute, and continued. A mouse scampered past his feet, loud in the darkness. As he knew Sir Francis kept the cellars locked, Smith was prepared with a false key. Suzanne Hargreaves' contacts with the servants had proved useful.

Smith opened the first door, closed it behind him, and took the stump of a candle from his sack. Striking a spark from his pistol-shaped tinderbox, Smith lit the candle wick and waited until the flame pooled light around the cellar. Shelves of bottles alternated with kegs and hogsheads of wine and port, with a well-trodden path to the left.

That'll do for me, Smith thought and moved to the right.

Five minutes after he arrived in the wine cellar, Smith left, with the sack now empty and tied around his waist. He locked the door and returned upstairs, always watchful for wandering servants. Another false key allowed him into Sir Francis's study, where a book about chess lay carelessly on the floor, and a riding crop was draped over the back of a chair. Smith grunted at this evidence of Sir Francis's two hobbies, scraped a spark from the tinderbox on the shelf, and applied it to the candle in its brass holder. He allowed the soft light to grow before he stepped to the desk. It was a simple task to open the locks.

All three drawers were full of papers, documents, and letters. Tempted to read everything, Smith kept to the matter in hand and slipped the letter he carried into the bottom drawer before searching for land registration documents. He found them tied with a linen ribbon and scanned each page. Ignoring most of the legal terminology, he struggled with the expected Latin phrases yet still understood the gist.

"Not yours for long, Sir Francis," Smith said to himself. He could hardly restrain his smile as he left the study. As he descended the carpeted stairs, he heard female laughter and stopped, sliding into the side.

Who the deuce is laughing at this time of night? Everybody should be in bed, damn them.

The laughter sounded again, coming from the master bedroom. The laughter ended, and an educated male voice spoke.

"Again, my dear?"

That's Sir Francis, Smith thought and fought the mingled spasm of pain, hatred, and jealousy that ran through him when the woman laughed again. *Is that Becky laughing?*

A sliver of light showed the bedroom door was ajar, and, unable to restrain himself, Smith stepped closer and peered inside. In the soft glow of candlelight, Smith saw Sir Francis, naked as a newborn, pouring claret into two glasses, and a much younger woman watching.

That's not Becky!

When the woman flicked back the hair from her face, Smith saw her clearly.

She's barely more than a child.

Then Sir Francis handed the woman a glass, and they toasted each other, with the woman smiling as Sir Francis fondled her.

Smith moved away, with his mind busy. The scene had replaced any jealousy with even greater anger, which he knew he would later analyse.

So that's the way of it?

Smith moved to the bedroom where he had entered the house, closed the door, and stopped. Aware of the slow breathing in the corner, he pulled the pistol from his belt and backed against the wall.

"I thought it was you." Lady Selby's voice sounded low and calm through the darkness. "I'd recognise your walk in a November midnight."

"Good evening, Lady Selby," Smith hid his disquiet.

Lady Selby emerged from a corner of the room. "What have you been stealing, Mr Smith?"

"Nothing," Smith said truthfully.

"There's no need for the gun," Lady Selby put a slender finger on the barrel. "You know that I'm no threat to you."

"That's the truth." Smith ensured there was nobody else in the room before replacing the pistol under his belt.

"If you weren't stealing, what were you doing?" Lady Selby lit a candle and allowed the soft light to strengthen. She wore a short cape over her nightclothes while bare feet protruded from the hem of her dress.

"Something else," Smith said, as his gaze fixed on Lady Selby's face. Even with her hair in slight disarray and a loose thread hanging from her nightdress, she looked more elegant than any woman Smith had seen before. Smith fought the mixed emotions that crowded him.

"Don't tell me," Lady Selby put the candle on a chest and held up her right hand. "I already know."

"Oh?" Smith read the desperate hurt in her eyes.

"You looked into Sir Francis's bedroom."

"I did," Smith admitted.

"I don't think you were looking for Francis, so you must have been searching for me."

Perhaps I was, damn it. "Sir Francis was not alone," Smith said, holding her gaze.

"My husband is seldom alone in bed," Lady Selby told him. "And I seldom share it with him."

Leave this subject! "Have you deposited any money with the bank as I advised, Lady Selby?"

Lady Selby smiled bitterly at the change of subject. "We were not always so formal, Captain Smith. I have deposited as much as I am able without arousing suspicion."

"Add as much as you can."

"I suspect that you are the harbinger of change," Lady Selby said, holding his arm. "What are you planning, Abe?"

Smith flinched at Lady Selby's use of his given name. "Keep saving, Becky, for the love of God." Smith took hold of her slender arm for a moment, with the feel of her warmth bringing back a hundred memories. Then he pulled away and slid open the window. Lady Selby took hold of his arm and again called him by his given name.

"For God's sake, Abe, don't abandon me here. We were close, once."

Smith paused with one foot on the window ledge. "That was a long time ago." He turned and climbed back down, knowing he would weaken if he remained longer. He was aware of Lady Selby watching him long after he was out of sight.

Chapter Twenty-One

"**H**olden was here." The innkeeper looked at the mess within the Royal Arms. He spread his arms in dismay. "He and his boys wrecked my tavern and threatened my staff."

"So I see," Smith said. "Was anybody hurt?"

"Only me," the tavern keeper indicated his swollen eye. "But they scared my barmaid. They told her that unless I changed my supplier, they'd ruin her life and her reputation."

"I'll pay for the damage." Smith handed over five guineas. "If the account exceeds that, let me know. Tell your girl to remain at home for the next fortnight."

The tavern keeper frowned. "She needs to earn to eat."

"I'll pay her wages," Smith said, "and I'll send you a replacement."

"Holden will return and give her the same treatment."

"No doubt," Smith agreed. "Did Holden say when he would return?"

"Next week," the tavern keeper said. "With his delivery to me."

Smith nodded slowly. "Leave it in my hands." Mounting Rodney, he left the village of Snargate behind.

For the next few days, Smith toured the western fringe of Kent, visiting each inn, tavern, and public house that he supplied with spirits. He also passed some time with his private customers, ensuring them that he would deal with Holden before long.

"He's a dangerous man," the Reverend Tibbs told him, tasting his French brandy with evident appreciation. "He even threatened me, a man of the cloth."

"I'll ensure he does not harm you, Reverend," Smith said.

The Reverend Tibbs smiled. "We're all in God's hands," he said, "but sometimes I wish he would smite the Philistines hip and thigh rather than leaving such matters to us!" Tibbs tasted more of the brandy. "However, with men like you standing at God's right-hand side, my faith is restored."

Smith stood up and reached for his hat. "I've been called many things in my life, Reverend, but never God's right-hand man."

Tibbs finished his brandy. "I can see the goodness in you, Captain Smith. Oh, I know you are a rogue, but we all have some good in us. Except maybe Captain Holden and the French, damn their eyes."

"Thank you, Reverend," Smith gave a little bow. He did not smile until he left the vicarage.

A week to the hour, Holden's men returned to the Royal Arms. Smith stood in the shelter of a recessed doorway, watching as three undoubted bullies swaggered into the tavern. Each man carried a cudgel, and Smith guessed that at least one also had a pistol in his belt. The leading man had a keg under his left arm. A moment later, Hitchins rode up, dismounted, and tossed his reins to a waiting stable boy.

"Look after my horse, youngster," Hitchins said with a broad smile.

Smith slipped inside the Royal Arms and stood watching.

"We've come with the delivery from Captain Holden," the

first bully crashed his keg onto the counter. "The finest French brandy, so pay up, sharp!"

Hitchins remained at the rear, with one hand inside his cloak. He smiled at everybody in the taproom without noticing Smith standing in the furthest shadows.

Bess looked up from the counter with a bright smile. "We deal with Captain Smith," she said. "But thank you for coming. Please remove your keg and close the door as you leave."

"I've seen you before," Hitchins stepped to the counter, still smiling and with his hand hidden underneath his cloak. "You were with Smith at the Templar's Rest."

Bess dropped in a mocking curtsey. "That's correct, Mr Hitchins. May I remind you that you have strayed over the border into Kent?" she said. "You must have forgotten that Captain Smith warned you to remain in Sussex."

The smallest of the three bullies stretched across the counter and slapped Bess backhanded across the face. "We'll have less of your cheek, girl, or I'll take my whip to your back."

Smith felt the rage surging within him. *You'll pay for that, you bastard!*

Bess reeled back, put a hand to her face, and recovered. "I think it's time you left, Mr Hitchins, and take your blackguards with you."

"Where's the landlord?" Hitchins asked. "I do apologise for my man's rough behaviour, my dear young woman, but you did antagonise him."

"I'm here, Hitchins," the landlord passed Smith as he hurried to Bess's side. "Get out of my house."

Hitchins laughed and shook his head. "On the contrary, we are thinking of taking over your house," he said. "Captain Holden intends to buy the lease here and of the other properties in this part of his territory."

"Your Captain Holden should remain in Sussex," Smith said quietly. "And your men need a lesson in manners." He emerged from his doorway with a pistol in each hand. "Place your weapons on the counter."

Hitchins laughed again, with his voice as smooth as any lawyer. "We reckoned you'd be here, Smith, and made arrangements." He gave a long, piercing whistle. "That's why we brought a few more men with us." As the tavern doors crashed open, half a dozen men rushed in, all carrying long staves.

"A reinforcement of batsmen," Smith murmured. "And all ready to fight." He raised his voice slightly. "Drop your bats, boys."

Grinning, the batsmen allowed their staffs to clatter on the floor.

Smith jabbed Hitchins with his pistol. "You see, Hitchins, you're in Kent, and you employed local men. Kentish men. These lads prefer to work for a fellow white-horseman than a South Saxon." Smith stepped forward, handed one pistol to Bess, and searched Hitchins and his bullies, removing a weighty purse from Hitchins and a few silver and copper coins from the others. He also took the rings from Hitchins' fingers and the gold watch from his waistcoat pocket.

"Do you have anything else of interest, Hitchins?" Smith flicked back his cloak and removed a small pistol from his waistband. "Careful now. If that had gone off accidentally, it could have done a great deal of damage."

Opening Hitchins' purse, Smith emptied the contents onto the counter. Mostly golden sovereigns, the coins danced on the scarred surface and settled in an untidy pile.

Nodding, Smith divided the money into two unequal piles, with one approximately twice the size of the other. Pushing the larger pile towards the batsmen, he said: "Divide that among you, boys."

As the batsmen dived to claim their shares, Smith passed the smaller pile to the landlord.

"That's yours," he said. "For your trouble."

"What are you going to do with them?" Bess took Hitchins'

pocket pistol, checked the flint was secure, and pointed it at the man who had slapped her. "I can shoot this one," she said, touching her face with her left hand.

"We'll send them back to Sussex, with a message for Holden," Smith said. "You decide how they travel, Bess, living or dead." He lowered his voice and whispered in her ear, so she smiled.

"That will be fun," Bess said. She pulled back the hammer of her pistol, so the man who slapped her flinched and looked away.

"Strip," Bess said, smiling as she emerged from behind the counter. "All of you. Take your clothes off, every last stitch."

"Us too?" one of the batsmen asked.

"Not you," Bess said, looked the speaker up and down, and winked. "More's the pity." She watched as the Sussex men reluctantly obeyed, prodding them with the barrel of her pistol when they hesitated. Eventually, Hitchins and his companions stood in a hunched group, covering themselves with cupped hands.

"Not very impressive, are they?" Bess asked, walking around Hitchins and his men as the batsmen laughed.

Stopping in front of the man who had slapped her, Bess lifted her left hand and slapped his face, then a second time and a third.

"The Bible teaches us to turn the other cheek," Bess said and slapped him again as the man cringed before her. "I don't believe in the Bible."

The batsmen jeered, with most already spending their newfound wealth at the bar. They gave Bess advice, most of it obscene.

"Thank you for the suggestions, boys," Bess acknowledged the batsmen, then prodded her pistol into Hitchins' chest. "Get outside," she ordered.

The Sussex men had stabled their horses, with the teenaged stable boy looking nervous at the activity in his ordinarily quiet workplace.

"It's all right," Bess assured him with a charming smile. "Nobody will hurt you."

Smith followed Bess, still holding his pistols, watching for any sign of resistance from Hitchins and his followers. The commotion had attracted a crowd from Snargate, men and women who stared with a mixture of curiosity and amusement at the group of naked men.

"Take the saddles off these horses," Bess ordered, "and lead the beasts outside the King's Arms."

The stable boy obeyed, wordless and with his hands clumsy with nervousness. His eyes slid to the Sussex men and away again.

"There's a tale to tell your grandchildren," Bess said, smiling. She lifted a riding-whip from one of the saddles, swished it through the air. The Sussex men, stripped of all braggado as well as dignity, watched her in horrified fascination.

"Tie their hands behind their backs," Bess ordered, swishing her whip. "And mount them backwards on the horses, except that one," she pointed to the man who had slapped her. She watched the batsmen obey her, thumping the naked men roughly and painfully astride the horse's backs.

"Tie their feet together under the horses' bellies," Bess ordered cheerfully. "We don't want them falling off and hurting themselves, do we?"

The batsmen laughed again, as did the growing crowd, with some women offering to help.

"Now him," Bess indicated the man who had struck her. "I want him facedown over his horse, with his wrists tied to his ankles."

"What are you going to do?" The bully pleaded, with all his bluster gone.

"You'll see," Bess swished her whip suggestively.

When the batsmen obeyed, Bess thanked them with a curt-sey, asked one to hold the horse, and then slashed her whip across the man's back. She smiled at his yelp and struck again, whipping the man from his shoulders to his knees and back. The crowd cheered and laughed, encouraging her to hit harder.

"That's the way, girl! Teach him not to hit a lady!"

Eventually, she stopped, out of breath, admired her handiwork, and raised her voice.

"Right, ladies!" Bess shouted. "Send these men on their way!"

A dozen women rushed forward, cheering at this unexpected diversion, and Bess led by example, slashing at each man with her whip.

"I rather enjoyed that," Bess said, as a cheering, taunting crowd escorted Holden's men back in the direction of Sussex.

"I thought you did," Smith said.

"We let them off lightly," Bess said, flexing her whip. "We might have killed them all."

Smith nodded and began to fill his pipe. "No. What we did was better. Men killed in a fight retain their honour and their reputation," he explained. "Men who return stripped of their clothes and dignity, riding backwards and revealing their dishonour, do not. We've sent a powerful message to Holden and the Sussex gang, yet without committing a capital offence. People will talk of this afternoon's entertainment for years to come, and Hitchins and his men will be the butt of a hundred jests."

"What now?" Bess asked. "Will we return to Kingsgate?"

"No," Smith shook his head. "Now, we'll drive the message home. The Ramsley brothers, Thomas Carman, and Roper should be with us shortly. Would you care to ride along?"

Bess swished her whip once more. "Would you care to try and prevent me?"

Smith laughed. "Not I, Bess."

The Ramsley brothers brought Josh Roper and Thomas Carman. Riding hard, Smith led his small gang across the border into Sussex and clattered into Downfield, the closest village to Kent. The Cross-keys inn dominated the main street, spreading around a courtyard, with stabling for post-horses and the twice-weekly coach to London. The Cross-keys appeared a prosperous, respectable inn from the outside, with chips of black flint inserted in the mortar between slabs of chalk around multi-paned windows.

"Stay here until I call for you," Smith ordered, leaving his followers at the edge of the village. "Cover your faces."

Jake Ramsley nodded, produced an inch of tobacco, and bit into it as Carman put a small flask to his lips.

With his kerchief over his lower face, Smith dismounted at the stables, entered the Cross-keys, and asked for the landlord.

"That's me, sir," the man was stout, bald, and genial. "What will be your pleasure?"

"Mr Holden sends his compliments," Smith said, ensuring the pistols at his belt were visible, "and as from today, his prices have doubled."

The landlord paled as his smile faded. "Well, sir, you can tell Mr Holden that I will not pay his increased prices," he said. "Indeed, sir, I will not pay him a penny. Not a penny more, sir, and you may tell him that with as many compliments as you care to add."

"As you wish, landlord," Smith said, and having ascertained that Holden was the Cross-key's supplier, stepped to the door and whistled. The Ramsley brothers and their companions trotted up, dismounted, and crashed inside the inn, with Carman bristling with weapons.

"This insolent fellow is refusing to pay Mr Holden his dues," Smith said. "Show him what Mr Holden does to such fellows."

It was a task perfectly suited to the Ramsleys' talents. They began a wrecking spree that reduced the Cross-keys taproom to a shambles of broken furniture and smashed glass. When the other customers moved to interfere, Roper and Carman produced their pistols and held them at bay.

"As you were, cully!" Roper rasped as one man lifted a cudgel from the floor. "Touch that, and I'll part your fingers from your hand!"

Carman walked around the room, presenting the muzzle of a

pistol at the more prosperous of the customers. "Mr Holden would appreciate a contribution," he said, removing the men's purses and valuables. When one of the women began to harangue him, Carman lifted his mask and placed an emphatic kiss on her lips.

"That's your contribution, my sweeting," he said and moved on.

With a purple kerchief concealing her lower face and only her eyes visible below her tricorne hat, Bess stood at the door. She held her blunderbuss in both hands.

"That's us, boys!" Smith said when he was satisfied he had made an impression. His men left the inn.

"This is the most fun I've had since Teach!" Carman said, counting his takings.

Bess remained where she was until the others were outside before backing through the doorway.

"Bar the door from the outside," Smith ordered. "Roper, Carman, release the horses from the stables. We don't want anybody following us yet." He raised his voice so that the people inside the inn could hear him. "Back to the Templars, boys! We'll teach the bastards to respect Holden's Sussex gang."

From the Cross-keys, Smith rode hard to the village of Peasmarsh to continue the good work. The first tavern keeper denied being Holden's customer, so Smith left the place untouched. The second landlady was aggressive as she rejected Holden's apparent revised terms, so Bess gave her a couple of stinging cuts with her whip as the Ramsleys indulged in their enjoyable new pastime of wrecking public houses.

"That's enough," Smith said after five minutes of wanton destruction. "We've other places to visit."

"Come on, boys!" Jake Ramsley said. "Mr Holden wants his payment!"

Smith's gang visited five premises that evening and wrecked four, with the landlord in shock and the contents broken or strewn in the street outside. They left their mark from Rye to

Ewhurst Green and south to Brede, demanding money in Holden's name, robbing the wealthy, wrecking the taverns, and knocking down anybody who dared to resist.

"Holden's name will be infamous," Bess said as they returned to Kingsgate with the Ramsleys passing a bottle of Holden's brandy back and forward.

"More importantly," Smith said, "he'll lose money, and that's worse for him than losing men. He can always recruit batsmen and seamen, but it will take him months to regain his good name and rebuild his business."

"Is it finished now?" Bess sounded disappointed.

"Not quite," Smith said. "I have one last thing to do."

CYCLOPES GATHERING WAS A HALF-DECKED, THREE-MASTED Deal-built lugger, ideally suited to jinking across the Channel. Seventy feet long, she had a shallow draught to slide up the sloping shingle beach at the back of the Templar's Arms and a single three-pounder in the stern. At her side, *Cyclopes Gain* was an identical sister, with her master scraping barnacles from her clinker hull.

"Captain Holt?" Smith stood on the shingle with the wind blowing spray from the breakers over them both.

"That's my name," the captain confessed.

"My name is John Smith."

Holt looked Smith up and down. "I've heard stories about you." He continued to scrape the hull. "Are you planning to strip me naked, too?"

"No," Smith said. "I'm planning to save you."

Holt did not falter. "Save me from what?" He continued to scrape the lugger's hull.

Smith admired the man's phlegm. "I want to save you from a French prison, or Davy Jones' Locker."

Holt smoothed a rough hand over *Cyclopes Gain's* planking.

209

"That's a very Christian gesture, Captain Smith. Why go to the trouble to save me? We're hardly shipmates."

"Mr Holden doesn't seem to care about his men."

Holt continued with his work. "You've come to the wrong man, Smith. Step back; you're causing a shadow."

"I'm delivering a friendly warning, Captain Holt. Don't sail across the Channel for at least a week."

"I'll give you a friendly warning, Captain Smith." Holt did not turn to face Smith. "If you come within twenty paces of *Cyclopes Gain* a second time, you won't come a third."

"You're an honest man, Captain," Smith said. "Holden is fortunate to employ a man with so much loyalty."

Holt continued to work. He did not reply.

"Did you find out what you wanted?" Bess asked as Smith walked away.

"I did," Smith said. "And I want one of those Deal luggers."

Chapter Twenty-Two

July 1762

"Captain Smith!" Ruth was agitated as she approached Smith. "I have a letter for you."

"A letter?" Smith looked up in surprise. "Who the devil would write me a letter?"

Ruth shook her head. "I don't know, sir."

The fact that she addressed Smith as 'sir' warned him that Ruth was uneasy. "From where did it come, Ruth?"

"The Hounds Rest acts as a post office, Captain, as you know, but the landlord there doesn't have much to do with us," Ruth lowered her voice. "Sir Francis owns the lease, and the Hound's landlord is Sir Francis's man. So I send the boy over for any mail, once a week. This time, the Hound sent one of his servants to us."

Smith held out his hand. "Let's see it then, Ruth."

The letter was on poor quality paper, folded once, and sealed. Smith examined the device impressed on the seal. "Six martlets on a shield," he said. "That's the symbol of Sussex. I don't know from where he stole the seal, but somebody is sending us a warning."

"The boy said it was important," Ruth said.

Smith snapped the seal. "I'll read this out loud," he said. "I don't like secrets between friends and shipmates. Listen." He scanned the paper, smiling as he read.

"Smith, Damn you,

And God damn your purblind eyes, you bugger and you death-looking son of a bitch. You were fortunate that I was not present when you insulted and ill-treated my men, you murderous bastard. I would have driven you and your unnatural woman to hell, where you belong, you devil incarnate. I will send you into your kennel below, you hell hound, to bathe you in the sulphurous lake that is prepared for you, for it is time the world is rid of a devil like you.

You are no man, and your unnatural companion is no woman, but devils who will soon fall into hell, there to lie unpitied forever and ever which God grant of his infinite mercy, amen.

Captain William Holden."

"You seem to have annoyed him," Bess said as Carman gave a bark of laughter and raised his glass in salute.

"I believe so," Smith agreed. "I think Holden will retaliate now, ladies and gentlemen. We had better prepare for his return. Pray do me the honour of pinning this message to the wall, Ruth, so nobody is in any doubt of Holden's feelings toward me."

THE RIDERS CAME BEFORE DAWN, A SCORE OF DRAGOONS ON heavy horses, with three civilians in front. They rode through Kingsgate without pausing, and the echo of their hooves was like the devil's drumbeats between the ancient, crowded houses. From the village, they headed slightly inland and stopped at the lodge of Kingshunt Manor. When the lodge-keeper stepped outside to enquire their business, the civilians demanded that he open the gates to them.

"I cannot do that," the lodge-keeper said, blinking and with his bald head gleaming in the dark until the civilian in charge of the dragoons pointed a pistol to his face.

"Then you'd better stand still, my friend, or I'll introduce your brains to daylight." The civilian motioned to the nearest two dragoons. "You, corporal, and you, private, get inside and find the gate key."

The dragoons dismounted immediately, pushed open the lodge-house door and swarmed inside. Five minutes later, the corporal emerged with the gate key, elbowed past the keeper and opened the gate. The civilian replaced his pistol in its holster, kicked in his spurs, and walked his horse inside the grounds. His immediate companions following at his back, with the dragoons in a silent column behind them.

The second dragoon emerged from the lodge a moment later, with a bottle in his hand. He pushed the keeper aside, mounted his horse, and joined the others.

"We'll catch Selby unprepared," the leading civilian said, replacing his pistol in the holster inside his cloak.

However rapid the dragoons' movements, Kingsgate's intelligence service was faster. Used to watching for revenue cutters and the Impress service, the villagers had long since developed a system for knowing who approached Kingsgate.

A farmer on the edge of the Weald was first to see the horsemen and spread a white sheet over a prominent hawthorn bush. His neighbour saw the signal and hung a shirt from the side of his barn, which was a sign a coppice maker saw from three fields away. He lit a fire at the top of a nearby knoll, with the smoke rising into the summer sky.

The first time smoke had risen from that knoll, the Spanish Armada had threatened Queen Elizabeth's England, so people broadcast the warning across the county.

Before the dragoons reached the parish boundary, every man and woman in Kingsgate knew the potential danger.

"You'd best get to the lookout, Captain Smith," Ruth kept

her voice level. "That smoke might warn of a French landing or Holden and his men."

The lookout was an extension to the inn, an octagonal tower thrusting upwards from the roof, with windows facing every direction. The interior was furnished with a comfortable, padded chair and a brass telescope, with a bottle of rum to fortify the watcher. Smith ran up the ladder, pulled it up behind him, and lifted the telescope to sweep across the parish from the Spike to the western boundary and inland to the Weald. A minute later, he scrambled back down the ladder and thrust into his room.

"What's the to do?" Bess asked as Smith grabbed his hat, cloak, and pistol.

"We're dancing," Smith said. "It's all right, Mrs Martin, the Dancing Horse is in no danger."

"What's happening?" Ruth called, but Smith was already at the door.

"Wait for me," Bess rose to follow. "I said wait!"

Smith was on his horse before Bess arrived at the stables. "The boy's put your saddle on," he told her.

Bess nodded and mounted Anson, her grey mare. She rode side-saddle with the riding-whip in her hand. "Where are we going?"

"Kingshunt Manor," Smith told her. "The dragoons have arrived."

They left Kingsgate at a trot, tied up the horses at the edge of the policies, ignored the lodge house, and slipped over the boundary wall. Once inside the grounds, they ran through the open woodland to the house.

"Watch for man traps," Smith warned.

When they reached the fringe of the woodland, Smith put a hand on Bess's shoulder. "Wait," he said.

A pair of dragoons rode past with the heavy horses' hooves thumping onto the damp ground. The dragoons rode slowly, with the swords prominent beside the saddles and carbines loose in their buckets. When the dragoons passed, they left a sour smell of stale ale and sweat.

"Stay with me," Smith said.

"What's happening?" Bess asked. "Why are the dragoons here?"

"They're on the King's business," Smith said. He watched for a gap in the patrols and ran closer to the Manor, with Bess hitching up her skirts to join him. Smith heard the light patter of her feet on the closely mown grass.

Good girl! You've got grit; I'll grant you that!

Moving to the back of the house, Smith tested each window until he found one that was open and slipped inside. Bess followed, looked around at the décor, and dropped a small ornament into her pocket.

"A trinket to help me remember the day," she said, slightly guiltily.

"I doubt you'll forget it," Smith told her, moving towards the great hall. "Keep out of sight," he advised.

"I'm good at that," Bess automatically kept to the shadows, checking behind her every few steps. "I've never been in the Manor before."

"Watch out!" Smith stopped her. They stepped into a recessed doorway, listening.

"I don't care a damn who you are!" Sir Francis's voice sounded from the great hall. "I want you out of my house!"

Smith tested the door, found it was open, and ushered Bess inside the room before following her. He held the door open a crack, enabling him to see and hear what was happening. Bess peered over his shoulder, pressing against him in her eagerness to watch.

The tall civilian produced a document from inside his cloak, held it up, and tapped the crown on the head of the staff he carried. "These items give me the authority to search your house, Sir Francis, and arrest you if I must."

"Damn you, sir!" Sir Francis snatched the document, scanned it and stepped back. "Damn your authority!"

"If you damn my authority, you damn the king himself," the tall civilian said. "And that is treason."

Sir Francis sat with a thump on the carved wooden settle under his family portraits. "Good God," he said faintly as he read the paper. "This is outrageous. This document accuses me of treason to the king. My family have been loyal for centuries, sir! We fought for King Charles and suffered exile during Cromwell's years!"

The civilian rapped the brass tip of his staff on the floor. "My men will search the house, Sir Francis. You will remain with me. If you attempt to leave, I will have you secured, manacled, sir, and I'll drag you out in chains."

Sir Francis's face paled. "I am a magistrate, for God's sake, the king's authority in this parish. The Selbies have controlled this part of Kent for generations, ever since the Plantagenets ruled!"

"Which makes your transgression all the more serious," the civilian told him.

"Francis!" Lady Selby shook the hand of a beefy dragoon from her arm. "What's happening? What's the to do?"

"It's all a misunderstanding," Sir Francis tried to adopt a brave face. "I'm sure we can clear it up."

"You, sir!" Lady Selby approached the civilian. "Who are you, and what do you mean by invading our house with these soldiers?"

The civilian handed over his document. "This intimation will explain everything, Madam," he said, as calm as if he were speaking to an old friend in his gentleman's club.

"I don't care a damn for your piece of paper," Lady Selby tossed the document to the floor and kicked it into a corner in a fine display of temper. "Or your silly stick. I want you to tell me!"

The civilian gave a slight bow. "As you wish, Madam. Our

agents in France informed us that Sir Francis helped a notorious French privateer escape, thus endangering British commerce and putting the lives of British seamen at risk. Helping the enemy in time of war is treason, Lady Selby."

"Nonsense!" Lady Selby defended her husband. "Sir Francis would never do such a thing. He is the most loyal man you could hope to find."

"Come, Madam," the civilian said. "Sit you down. We do not take these actions lightly, I assure you. We checked with the Commandant of Sissinghurst Castle and found that Sir Francis signed a paper taking all responsibility for the French privateer."

"He did no such thing!" Lady Selby protested.

"We have the document," the civilian said softly. "And our agents in France tell us that Captain Duguay, the privateer, is back in Dunkirk and making hay with our commerce."

"Nonsense!" Lady Selby said.

"We have his signature," the civilian said gently. "On more than one document."

"Why would my husband do such a thing?"

"We don't know yet," the civilian said. "But I assure you that we will find out. We have men who are very skilled in extracting information from even the most reluctant of prisoners."

Smith felt Bess shift beside him and wondered what she was imagining.

"Sir! My Lord Graham!" The second civilian ran down the stairs, with his cloak billowing from his shoulders. "I found this in Sir Francis's desk, My Lord." He held up a folded piece of paper. "It's a letter, sir, written in French."

Lord Graham? Who the devil is Lord Graham? Some government man, for sure.

"In French?" the tall civilian, Lord Graham, asked. "Was it in plain sight?"

"It was not, My Lord," the second civilian replied. "It was concealed within a pile of estate accounts."

Lord Graham read the letter, shaking his head. "That seems

conclusive," he said. "A personal note from Captain Duguay the French privateer, an enemy of the king. It addresses you by name, Sir Francis."

"What are you saying?" Sir Francis snatched the letter. "I've never seen this thing before in my life," he said. "And I've never heard of this French fellow, Duguay, let alone met him!"

"That's surprising," Lord Graham said dryly. "All of Great Britain knows him as the most successful of French privateers, a man the Navy hunted for years. The loyal among us celebrated his capture with relief." Lord Graham showed some emotion for the first time as he leaned over Sir Francis. "And a man you returned to France, allowing him to resume his career as a predator of British shipping!"

"I'm damned if I did!" Sir Francis rose from his seat until two dragoons stepped closer. The corporal put a heavy hand on his shoulder.

"Your damnation, sir, is as certain as your guilt! Lord Graham agreed. "Come with me, sir, or I'll have you dragged from this house." Lord Douglas nodded to the corporal, who closed with Sir Francis again.

"Where are you taking him?" Lady Selby asked.

"I am taking him somewhere he can do no more damage to the king's cause," Lord Douglas replied. "We will hold him securely until his trial."

"My trial?" Sir Francis stood up. He looked dazed.

"Your trial, sir, and, I have no doubt, your condemnation before a jury of your peers," Lord Douglas said.

Everybody looked around as a dragoon sergeant trudged up the steps from the cellar. Dusty smudges showed upon the sleeves and knees of his uniform.

"Sir! My Lord! We found this, sir." The sergeant signalled behind him, and a trooper placed a keg on the floor and handed over a folded letter. The seal was unbroken.

"The writing on the barrel's in French, sir," the sergeant said, "and the letter was lying on top."

"What does it say, man?" Lord Douglas asked.

"It's sealed, sir," the sergeant said. "I thought it best to bring it to you."

"Quite right, Sergeant," Lord Douglas said. He snapped the seal, opened and read the document, and grunted. "I have here a message from your French friend, Sir Francis, with a keg of brandy as a thank you."

"I have no French friend," Sir Francis denied stoutly.

"Let me see!" Lady Selby held out her hand imperiously. Snatching the letter, she scanned it, with her eyes flicking from side to side.

"Do you read French, Madam?" Lord Douglas asked, with his eyebrows raised in amusement.

"I do, sir," Lady Selby replied in French. "And English as well. I don't believe this letter is genuine. My husband would never betray his country."

Still listening at the door, Smith nodded. "Well said, Becky. Defend your man." He felt Bess tauten against him.

"I commend your loyalty, Madam," Lord Douglas shared Smith's opinion. "If not your choice of man on whom you waste it. Unless you are also involved in this diabolical plot to help the King's enemies." He raised his voice. "Shackle Sir Francis and put him astride a horse!"

"Where are you taking my husband, sir?" Lady Selby asked again.

"To a place where he cannot betray his country," Lord Douglas said.

Too shocked to protest, Sir Francis gabbled meaningless words as the two dragoons fastened manacles on his wrists and led him away, leaving Lady Selby standing in the great hall. A circle of bemused servants stood at a distance.

Smith watched her, aware of her dejection, and for a second, he was tempted to offer his sympathy. *I didn't want to hurt you, Becky.*

"Serves her right," Bess whispered savagely in his ear. "Marrying that monster! I'll wager she was every bit as bad."

When one of the servants nervously approached Lady Selby, Smith pulled back and quietly closed the door. "We've seen all I need to see," he said.

Bess looked at him with her head tilted to the left. "You planned all this," she hissed.

"I did," Smith admitted.

"You arranged everything with Duguay merely to get Sir Franky arrested."

"I did." Smith agreed.

"You could have shot him."

"That would have been too easy," Smith said. "He would only have lost his life. Now he will lose his reputation, his position, and the respect of his peers."

Bess frowned. "The judge might not find him guilty."

"Mud sticks," Smith said. "And there is a chance he might hang." He put a hand to his throat, fingering the faint rope mark. "Hang by the neck until he is dead."

Bess narrowed her eyes. "That may happen," she said. "You're a devious man," she said.

"Come on, Bess," Smith took her arm. "Let's go home."

Chapter Twenty-Three

Bess was silent as they returned to Kingsgate, and she remained quiet for the remainder of that day. "If Sir Francis is hanged, you'll lose your position as captain of *Maid of Kent*," she said at last as they sat in their room in the inn.

"Is that what's troubling you?" Smith knew there was more. "You've less to worry about than you think. Do you know how ship ownership works?" He poured them both a tumbler of brandy.

"No," Bess admitted, downing half the brandy in a single swallow.

"A ship is divided into sixty-four shares," Smith explained. "And most vessels have more than a single owner. In theory, as many as sixty-four people can own one ship, although that would be a rarity."

Bess held the tumbler in both hands, with her grey eyes fixed on Smith.

"I've been purchasing shares in *Maid* as they came up for sale and persuading the share-owners to sell." Smith continued.

"You're a man of many surprises," Bess said. "How did you know when the shares are for sale?"

"Some were advertised in the press," Smith said. "They are

sold by public auction in coffee houses. Others I bought by a private bargain."

Bess sipped at the remains of her brandy. "You used the word persuading. Were the previous owners willing to sell?"

Smith's expression did not alter. "I had to ask quite forcibly sometimes, and in other cases, a handful of gold was persuasion enough."

Bess accepted Smith's explanation. "Who owns *Maid* now?"

"I am the major shareholder," Smith said, "and the managing owner, although Sir Francis still holds ten shares." He smiled. "I'll purchase them for a song when the court finds him guilty, and his lands and possessions are forfeit."

Bess's eyes sharpened. "You have everything worked out, John. But how will you know when *Maid's* shares are for sale?"

"Sir Francis's lawyer has a taste for French brandy, and his wife likes silk."

Bess lifted her glass in salute. "When were you going to inform me?" She leaned forward. "Were you ever going to inform me? I don't like secrets!"

"I have informed you," Smith said. "I have control of *Maid* and will continue to trade legally as well as smuggling. I'll find another magistrate to sign the Letter of Marque."

"How will you find cargoes?"

Smith smiled again. "Sir Francis is not the only landowner in England, and the Navy pays well to feed its crews. In times of war, landowners profit." He leaned forward. "What else is disturbing you, Bess?"

She shook her head. "Nothing at all," she said.

Smith knew Bess was lying.

"Is it that fellow Lord Graham?"

When Bess nodded, Smith explained. "I've never seen the man before, but I suspect he is one of the shady men in government service."

"The shady men?"

"Yes. You do know the government controls the postal service, don't you?"

Bess shook her head. "No. I've never sent a letter in my life."

"Ah," Smith said. "There are men in government that scan every letter going abroad and every letter that might pose a threat to the established order. They are a form of intelligence service, as are our diplomats in other countries."

Bess listened intently. "I had no idea," she said.

"I suspect that Lord Graham is the head of that government branch," Smith said. "He certainly works in that area."

Bess nodded, but Smith knew there was something else on her mind. Dark shadows lay behind her grey eyes. His suspicions were confirmed when they went to bed, and Bess quickly turned her back.

"I'm tired tonight," Bess said.

When Smith reviewed the events of the day, he could find only one explanation. *Bess heard me call Lady Selby Becky! Damn my loose tongue! Damn it to the pits! Now she is afraid Becky may take her place.*

Is she right to be afraid?

"DID YOU HEAR THE NEWS?" RUTH LEANED ACROSS THE breakfast table.

"The raid on Kingshunt Manor?" Bess looked up from her plate with dark shadows under her eyes.

"That's old news," Ruth said. "It's about your other friend, Holden of Hastings."

Bess looked at Smith before she replied. "What about him?"

"He's lost one of his luggers," Ruth said cheerfully. "The French captured *Cyclopes Gathering* and all her cargo."

"That's unusual," Smith spoke for the first time. "The French normally try to keep on good terms with the Free Traders. Holden must have done something to cross them."

"It was that privateer captain, Duguay," Ruth said. "The one who stayed with us for a few days."

Smith felt Bess's eyes fix on him as he replied. "Captain Duguay is an independent-minded man. He dances to his own tune, not the music King Louis chooses."

"Did you arrange that too?" Bess asked when Ruth bustled to secure another customer. "Did you have Duguay capture *Cyclopes Gathering?*"

Smith concentrated on his mutton chop. "I have some business to arrange across the Channel," he said. "I might be a day or two."

"We can be as long as we like," Bess said, with a sweet smile that sliced scimitar-sharp. "You've been keeping too many secrets, John, and I don't like being a partner on the outside."

That's because of the Becky word.

Smith nodded. "Have you been to France before?"

"No. The French are the enemy." Bess's voice was flat.

"They're the King's enemy, not mine," Smith told her. "Don't sing God Save the King when we're there."

Bess chewed mightily at her mutton. "I won't," she said, knowing she had won.

SMITH STOOD AT THE SPIKE, SMOKING HIS PIPE AND STARING out to sea. He watched the revenue cutters cruising offshore, one close to land and the other two miles out, daring the shallows of the Goodwin Sands.

"They're coming for us, now," Smith said, puffing blue smoke into the air. He produced his telescope and focussed on the closest cutter, where the officers clustered aft. As Smith watched, a stocky man with a short jacket took the cutter's telescope from its bracket on the mizzen mast and swept his gaze across the Kentish coast. He stopped when the telescope pointed at the Spike. For a minute, Smith and the stocky man studied each other, and then the stocky man turned away and spoke to the officer at his side. Smith continued to watch the cutter as it cruised along the coast until it furled its sails and dropped anchor fifteen cable's lengths off Kingsgate harbour.

Smith closed the telescope.

That man will be *trouble*, Smith thought. *I'll lay ten sovereigns to a queer farthing that he's Ambrose Grant. Matters are coming to a head.*

Leaving the Spike, Smith passed Kingshunt Manor without a glance and made his way to Kingsgate. As he had expected, the Preventative Service had sent a boat from the cutter. Now the stocky man and two of his colleagues were inspecting the vessels in the harbour.

"Good evening to you," the stocky man strode to Smith. "I am Ambrose Grant, Captain of *Charming Nelly,* a cutter of the Revenue service."

"John Smith, Master of *Maid of Kent,*" Smith shook Grant's hand.

"She's a fine vessel," Grant had steady brown eyes and a steel grip. "French-built, I'd say."

"You'd be correct, sir," Smith agreed.

"Would you care to allow me to board, Captain Smith?"

"Come on and welcome," Smith said. "This way, Mr Grant." Smith ushered the Collector onto *Maid,* noting Grant's quick inspection of her spars and rigging.

"Three masts for a coasting lugger? That will give you quite a turn of speed."

"It does, sir," Smith said. "We've had a couple of encounters with French privateers, and I have no desire to spend the remainder of the war in a French prison."

Grant smiled. "You are also relatively heavily armed, Captain."

"I have a Letter of Marque from Sir Francis Selby, the local magistrate, who owns some shares in *Maid.*" Smith guessed that

Grant already knew everything about his position, so he told the truth.

Grant looked up sharply. "You'll need a new certificate to be a legal privateer, Captain, now that Sir Francis is in custody. His official position is suspended, if not revoked."

"I have that in hand," Smith said. "I'll have the new letter of marque by tomorrow and fresh Protections for the crew. Sir Ralph Naylor is the closest landowner and has taken over Sir Francis's magisterial duties."

Grant moved with grace for a man of his build. "I'll have a look at your ship now I'm aboard," he said.

"Shall I accompany you?" Smith knew it was better to acquiesce with good grace rather than put up resistance.

"I'm sure you'll have work to do, Captain Smith," Grant said as he slid below decks.

Smith pushed tobacco into the bowl of his pipe and moved aft, where Hargreaves had been quietly listening to the conversation.

"Did I hear that was Ambrose Grant?" Hargreaves asked.

"You did," Smith confirmed. "A dangerous man, and sharp as a needle."

Hargreaves looked concerned. "He's the man who caught the Hampshire Hawkshaw gang, Robert Anderson from Montrose, and the Geordie boys."

"So I believe," Smith said.

"And Betty Totman from Essex," Hargreaves said. "He's bad news."

Smith puffed at his pipe, watching the Preventative men on the quay questioning all the elderly loafers and fishermen. "He is a very mobile man, is our Ambrose Grant."

"The government sends him wherever smuggling is particularly rife," Hargreaves sounded worried. "He never fails to catch his man."

"Thank you, Hargreaves," Smith said. "I am aware that Mr Grant is a very dedicated Preventative officer. We must ensure

"WHAT DO YOU INTEND TO DO ABOUT GRANT?" HARGREAVES asked as they sat in the taproom of the Dancing Horse.

Smith swirled his rum in the bottom of his glass. "I shall give our Ambrose what he wants," he said.

"I don't understand."

"Read that," Smith pointed to the newspaper that Ruth had pinned to the wall. At a time when few men and fewer women could read or afford a paper, it was common for an innkeeper to purchase a newspaper and put it on display. The more educated of the patrons would read out the news, and the others gathered round to listen.

"I'm not a scholar," Hargreaves admitted, which was a euphemism for illiteracy.

Smith nodded. "There is a piece in the newspaper about an outbreak of smuggling along the Kent coast. The Preventative men believe that the smugglers are associated with Sir Francis Selby, who was so lately arrested for treason."

"Oh," Hargreaves finished his rum with a single swallow. "How do they know that?"

Smith sighed. "Maybe one of our men has a loose mouth, but I don't think so. I believe Holden, or his smooth-faced friend Hitchins, passed on the intelligence because we damaged so much of his organisation."

Hargreaves sucked at his teeth. "Do you mean to give up the free trading? The boys will miss the income."

"Not a bit of it," Smith said. "I mean to give Grant a fine new smuggling lugger, which was once *Cyclopes Gathering*."

"The French have her," Hargreaves pointed out.

"I want her," Smith said, "and I mean to have her. She's a Deal-built vessel, fast, handy, and seaworthy."

Hargreaves leaned back in his seat. "Most Deal-built vessels Captain, but how can you capture her and then hand her ?"

Smith smiled. "Wait and see, Mr Mate, and all will be led."

he leaves the area with a notable success under his belt." He ignored Hargreaves' puzzled look.

Twenty minutes later, Grant joined them on the quarter deck. "Captain Smith," he acknowledged, "and Mr Hargreaves, I believe?"

"That's correct," Smith said. "Mr Hargreaves is the mate of *Maid of Kent*."

"So I believe," Grant had clearly learned about *Maid* before he visited Kingsgate. "I have heard many tales about free trading in this area, my friends."

Smith offered Grant a cut of tobacco. "There is a lot," he admitted.

"Your name was mentioned," Grant accepted the tobacco.

Smith grunted. "You are welcome to search the ship again or rummage in my home." He indicated the Dancing Horse. "I use my vast smuggling profits to rent a single room. Anyway, men will accuse a stranger of anything."

"That is true," Grant held the tobacco. "I presume the duty was paid on this item?"

"I presume it was," Smith said. "I purchased it from a peddler."

Grant put the tobacco inside his pouch. "I aim to stop smuggling from western Kent," he said.

"Good," Smith said. "Stop it from Sussex too, can't you? These damned free traders cause nothing but trouble for honest seamen. They befriend the French and put up taxes for the rest of us."

"Put up taxes?" Grant looked confused.

"Of course they do!" Smith puffed out aromatic smoke. "The king orders the government to stop the smuggling, so the government recruits the Preventative men, who need ships, wages, and uniforms and equipment. Who pays for that? Why sir, the government pays for that. And from where does the government get the money? From taxes and nowhere else! Damned free traders cost me a fortune in taxes."

Grant smiled. "You don't like smugglers then?"

"You're damned right I don't," Smith said. "And that fellow Holden is the worst of the lot."

Grant pounced on the name, as Smith had intended. "Holden?"

Smith looked away, muttering a curse. "I should not have said that."

"Come, come, Captain," Grant said. "It is the duty of every honest man to fight these traitors to the king."

"Maybe so," Smith said, "but this honest man doesn't want Holden to blow his brains out some dark night."

"Ah," Grant said. "I understand. I'll leave you, Captain Smith, and attend to other business." He left *Maid of Kent* with a spring in his step.

"That was neatly done, Captain," Hargreaves said. "Do you think you put him off the trail?"

"No," Smith said. "Our Ambrose Grant is too experienced to fall for a simple trick. But I might have sown a mustard seed of doubt. We'll see."

When *Maid of Kent* sailed on her next voyage, *Charming Nelly*, a revenue cutter, shadowed her, not coming close yet never straying out of sight. Ninety feet long and built to chase smugglers, *Charming Nelly* had a twenty-five-foot beam, a crew of thirty and carried a dozen guns.

"We have company, Captain," Hargreaves said.

"Let's see how good she is," Smith suggested. "Hoist all the sails, Hargreaves, and hang up the washing if it gains us an extra knot!"

"Aye, aye, sir!" Hargreaves grinned and gave a string of orders that had the crew jumping to increase the sails as Smith tried to lose his charming companion. The cutter remained in sight, dropping back a little but too persistent to give up.

"He's a good sailor, our Ambrose," Smith studied *Charming Nelly* through his telescope.

"There's a squall coming, Captain," Hargreaves said. "Shall we alter course when it hits?"

Smith considered for a moment. "No. Let's play the honest trader. Keep on course for Portsmouth. There's nothing guilty about a ship sailing fast, but altering course will undoubtedly raise Grant's suspicions."

"Aye, aye, sir," Hargreaves said and steered *Maid* into the heart of the foul weather, with the cutter temporarily invisible behind flying spray and dark clouds.

"Take in the mainsail," Smith said as the waves broke green over *Maid's* larboard quarter and washed, knee-high, over the deck. He stood on the quarterdeck, watching the hands at work. *Maid* lost much of her speed by sailing with topsails only, yet Smith hoped the squall might separate her from *Charming Nelly*.

"She's still there," Hargreaves said as *Maid* left the storm astern, and the cutter emerged five minutes later. "It seems th Grant does not trust us."

That complicates matters.

"There will be no free trading this voyage," Smith dec "We'll have to tighten our belts and polish our halos."

"Grant is a most persistent man," Smith said, as *Ch Nelly* cruised off Portsmouth when *Maid of Kent* unloa then followed her back to Kingsgate.

"Aye, no free trading this voyage, as you said," F grumbled. "Your friends in France will be wonde happened."

"They will," Smith agreed. When he extended and scanned the cutter, Ambrose Grant was in h his telescope watching *Maid*. As soon as Grant lifted a hand in greeting. Smith waved back, worthy adversary.

I hope. I'm juggling too many balls at one time here. If I succeed, my trip to France was not wasted. If I fail, I have squandered a great deal of money and time for nothing.

SMITH WAITED AT THE NORTHEAST OF THE GOODWIN SANDS, watching the tide change and the water alter colour. With every quarter-hour, the Sands became more visible, so he checked *Maid of Kent's* chronometer and the sails that speckled the Channel. To larboard, a busy Royal Navy sloop fretted over a small convoy she was escorting from London to Falmouth while a dozen fishing boats sailed homeward with the tide. To starboard, *Charming Nelly* watched *Maid*, never permitting her to escape observation.

"Grant thinks we're running a cargo," Smith said, keeping his voice casual.

"It's a dangerous game you're playing," Hargreaves lifted his telescope for the tenth time in the last hour, alternating between *Charming Nelly* and the fast-appearing Sands.

"A little danger adds salt to life," Smith said. He checked the chronometer and stepped away. "The tide is about right," he observed. "*Cyclopes Gathering* should be here shortly."

"Even if you're right," Hargreaves said, "things might not go according to plan."

"They rarely do," Smith agreed. "Then we alter the plan and devise something new. Here she comes, only fifteen minutes behind time!"

Hargreaves swivelled around and focussed his telescope. "By God, you're right, Captain." He looked at Smith as if he were some new Messiah come to save the Free Traders from the wrath of the Preventative men.

Smith gave a bleak smile. *If only you knew how much thought, planning, and sheer hard work I put into each of my schemes, Mr Hargreaves, you would not be as admiring.*

Cyclopes Gathering eased into plain sight, with her sails spread to catch the best of the breeze and a bone frothing under her forefoot. A quarter of a mile astern of her, a cutter was in full chase. Equally fast and with a skilled man at the helm, the Preventative vessel was closing the distance.

"*Charming Rachel,*" Smith said. "The third of the Charming trio."

"The Preventative men believe they have *Gathering* trapped," Hargreaves said. "With the cutter astern and the Sands ahead, they can't see any escape." He lowered his telescope. "Neither can I."

"Watch," Smith said. If he were a religious man, he would be praying now. As Smith had long since renounced belief in any deity, God or the devil, he preferred to observe. Now, he relied on his knowledge of tides, currents, and the capabilities of ships and men.

"I'm going aloft," Smith said and scrambled to the masthead. The wind was keener at nearly one hundred feet above the sea, with *Maid of Kent* looking very small beneath him and the yards stretching to a quivering end on either side. *Cyclopes Gathering* was approaching the Sands, where the sea swept between two tide-formed dunes. *Charming Rachel* was closer now, with a group of men clustered around a bow chaser right forward beside her bowsprit and a uniformed officer giving orders from astern.

Even as Smith watched, the gun crew fired, with the powder smoke jetting out around the orange muzzle flare. Smith saw an elliptical tear form in *Cyclopes'* mizzen, and then she returned fire from the six-pounder in her stern and eased onto the channel between the emerging dunes.

Charming Rachel followed to the edge of the Sands and then hauled her wind and altered her course, with her master preferring not to risk his vessel.

"Your draught's too deep," Smith murmured. "You can't catch my lugger, Preventative men."

Cyclopes Gathering eased through the channel between the

dunes, with her shallow draught and speed carrying her over the Sands. Smith waited until *Cyclopes* was three-quarters of the way across and under topsails only before he returned to the deck.

"Set the Royals, Mr Hargreaves. Intercept that lugger. I want to catch her before she leaves the Goodwin."

"*Charming Nelly's* still behind us, Captain," Hargreaves reminded.

"Let's give her something to watch," Smith suggested and raised his voice. "Man the starboard battery!" He waited until the crew was in position and ordered. "Load with powder only."

"What are we firing at, Captain? There are two Preventative cutters." Roper sounded confused.

"Neither, Roper. Aim at the lugger."

"That's *Cyclopes Gathering,* Captain!"

"Do as I order, damn your eyes!"

Standing at the wheel, Carman barked a short laugh, then shifted the quid of tobacco inside his cheek.

The guns thrust out from *Maid's* side, grinning black muzzles pointing towards the lugger as she swept over the Sands.

Smith waited, aware of the Preventative cutter astern and the rapidly shallowing water under his keel. He assessed the waves, waited until *Maid* was on the uproll, and shouted.

"Fire!"

The broadside roared out, rocking *Maid of Kent* and throwing a bank of grey-white smoke across the Sands.

Cyclopes Gathering slowed as if the crew had panicked under the supposed fire from *Maid of Kent*. She glided forward slowly, with her sails flapping, "like mother's washing line," as Hewitt said sarcastically.

"Take over here, Mr Hargreaves," Smith ordered. "Take *Maid* back to Kingsgate." He called up half a dozen men to man his gig and rowed across to the lugger. "Come on, lads! Get to *Cyclopes* before the Preventative men realise what's happening."

As the gig raced to the Sands, the lugger's crew abandoned the vessel, jumping onto the Sands in full view of *Charming Nelly*.

"Where are they running to?" Roper asked, but Smith did not reply. Instead, he nodded to a single-sailed boat that had appeared from the east.

"Who's that?" Roper asked.

"That's not your business," Smith said and steered for the lugger, keeping the gig in the centre of the channel. "Row, damn you! And don't catch a crab, or I'll have your hides!"

Within minutes, Smith led his crew onto *Cyclopes Gathering*. "If we hurry, there will still be sufficient water under the keel," he said. "We'll take her to Kingsgate. *Maid of Kent* will follow."

Smith sent Roper to the bow with a lead. "Sound the depth, Roper, and keep sounding until we're well clear of the Goodwin. The rest, get the topsails back up!"

Smith watched the water beneath the lugger, judging the depth by the colour. He saw *Charming Nelly* close with *Maid* and knew Grant would be watching everything he did.

"Come on, lads," Smith said, smiling. "It's time to do our bit for King and country."

CHARMING NELLY FOLLOWED AS SMITH BROUGHT *CYCLOPES Gathering* into the harbour and tied her up.

"Right, lads," Smith said. "That's you free, but keep your Protections handy." Jumping onto the quay, he hurried to *Maid of Kent*.

"All right, Mr Hargreaves?"

"All right, Captain. *Charming Nelly* was confused. He didn't know whether to follow us, you, or the longboat with *Cyclopes* crew."

"He stuck with you, I see."

"Every inch of the way, Captain," Hargreaves said. "And here he comes now."

Grant boarded *Maid of Kent* with a puzzled expression on his face.

"Captain Smith," Grant hurried across the deck. "I am at a loss to understand what occurred this afternoon. What were you about?"

"I was capturing a French prize," Smith explained. "*Maid* is still a licenced privateer."

Grant looked over *Maid* and then at her prize. "I don't believe the vessel is French," he said. "She is a Deal-built lugger, and I believe she is an English smuggler."

"English, Mr Grant?" Smith smiled as if the idea amused him. "Why no, sir. This vessel is as French as King Louis's pet toad. She was English once, but that damned privateer Duguay captured her recently. Now she is my prize." Smith sighed. "It's only a pity her crew escaped. I'd wager they were Duguay's men."

"The crew escaped," Grant agreed. "If they are French, we will soon hunt them down. A dozen Frenchmen will not survive in the English countryside. However, if they are English, they will merge with the local ne'er do wells, and we'll never see them again." Grant looked around as a company of Preventative men marched on board from *Charming Nelly*. "My men will rummage your ship for contraband and then search your prize."

"Naturally," Smith said. "Pray inform me what they find, sir. In the meantime, I will report my capture to the Navy." He enjoyed the look of mixed anger and confusion on Grant's face.

Chapter Twenty-Four

"John!" Bess stood at the window of their room. "Look at this!"

Smith was at the table, poring over a column of figures. "I'm trying to see if we can buy that Deal lugger," he said. "*Cyclopes Gathering* would be a useful addition to our business. We'll get a proportion of the prize sale, of course, but we have to pay the crew and maintenance as well."

"Never mind that now," Bess interrupted him. "A whole troop of mounted men just rode past. I'm sure the Ramsleys were with them."

"Damn them! I've nothing planned." Smith joined Bess at the window, quill in hand and with fresh ink spots on his cuff.

"The Ramsleys have," Bess said. "I heard whispers in the taproom while you were out at sea."

Smith tapped the feather of his quill on the windowsill. "I wish you had told me. What did the whispers say?"

"They were just rumours," Bess told him. "People were whispering that the Ramsleys would rob Kingshunt Manor. With Sir Francis locked up and only his wife and some servants at home, the Ramsleys will do what they like."

"The devil they will," Smith dropped the quill, turned, and lifted his pistol.

"Where are you going?" Bess stepped away from the window.

"To Kingshunt Manor," Smith lifted his hat and coat. "We've worked hard to build up our organisation. I'm not having a couple of blackguards like the Ramsleys jeopardise all our work."

"Leave them." Bess took hold of Smith's arm. "Let it be, John; it won't affect us. The Ramsleys are best left alone. They are capable of anything."

"I know they are." Smith left the door open as he ran downstairs. "Boy!" He roared. "Saddle my horse, and he'd better be in prime condition, or I'll have your hide!"

The lodge gates were open as Smith cantered through. He kicked in his heels, urging Rodney to greater speed as he approached Kingshunt Lodge's closed front door. A dozen horses stood outside the house, some grazing on the no-longer-immaculate lawn and others looking forlorn, as if unable to cope with their new freedom.

Smith heard the noise, the breaking of glass and rough male laughter coupled with a woman's high protests. He dismounted at speed, threw the reins over Rodney's neck, and bounded up the short flight of steps to the door. "Stand clear!" he roared, kicked the door open, and crashed inside the house.

The great hall was empty, except for a smashed mirror, the settle that lay on its side, and one shocked maidservant sitting against the wall, weeping. A hunting horn lay on the ground, looking useless and forlorn.

"Where are they?" Smith lifted the maid by her arms. She looked at him, with her eyes dazed. "Where are they?" Smith shook her roughly. The girl had a swollen lip, and blood trickled from the corner of her mouth.

"Everywhere," she said at last. "When I answered the door, they charged in and knocked me down."

Smith kicked the settle back upright and sat the girl down. "Where is your mistress? Where is Lady Selby?"

The servant shook her head. "I don't know, sir."

"Find somewhere safe and stay there until these scoundrels have left the house." Smith strode forward, glancing from left to right. "Ramsley!" he shouted. "Where are you?"

He heard a renewed bout of male laughter from upstairs and then a scream, quickly cut off. A man shouted, with the words unclear.

Smith swore. A male servant stumbled down the stairs with his shirt torn and blood dripping from his left hand. "Where is your mistress?" Smith asked.

The servant looked blankly at Smith, then collapsed.

Ignoring him, Smith tried to locate the source of the noise. "Ramsley!" he shouted again. "Where are you, Jake?"

The woman screamed again, and this time Smith was sufficiently close to trace the sound. He kicked open the drawing-room door to see Jake Ramsley stuffing a silver plate into a canvas bag while a second maidservant cowered, squealing, in a corner.

"What the deuce?" Jake Ramsley looked around. Even with his face blackened, he looked vicious. Smith withdrew immediately, cursing. He had not come to save Sir Francis's silver plate or look after his servants. He looked up, more by instinct than anything else.

Henry Ramsley and Roper were on the stairs, with Lady Selby between them. Ramsley was leering, with his left hand on Lady Selby's hip and his trousers awry.

Roper started when he saw Smith and dropped his gaze, while Mrs Selby was white-faced, with dishevelled clothes and her normally well-groomed hair a shambles.

"What happened here?" Smith tried to keep his voice under control.

Henry Ramsley laughed, meeting Smith's eye. "What do you think, Captain?"

"He lay with me," Lady Selby said and hardened her tone, despite the shock in her eyes. "This blackguard raped me."

"Will we always be friends?" Becky lay on her back, laughing at him through crinkled eyes.

"Of course we will," Smith said.

"Even when you're a grown man sailing the seven seas?"

"Even then," Smith told her solemnly.

Becky had smiled and closed her eyes. *"Promise?"*

"I promise," Smith said.

Smith saw Lady Selby as she was now, an unhappy wife with an unfaithful husband and assaulted by a violent man.

"I'll always be your friend," Becky told him solemnly. *"Whatever happens, and however far apart we are."*

"And I'll always be yours," Smith promised.

"Abel," Lady Selby said, biting her lip, and suddenly Smith saw young Becky pleading with him through Lady Selby's tortured eyes.

"You bastard," Smith said softly. He lifted his pistol, aimed, and fired in the same movement. As if time slowed down, Smith saw the passage of the ball as a thin black line extending from the muzzle of his pistol, emerging from the grey-white smoke and the orange muzzle flare. He saw the leer on Henry Ramsley's face alter to shock, and then sudden pain as the lead ball smashed into his face.

The ball splintered the cheekbone, and the soft lead spread, ruining Ramsley's right eye and entering the brain by way of the eye socket, carrying bone splinters and fragments of flesh in its passage. Ramsley did not have time to scream before he died, and Smith was running up the stairs.

Ignoring the already crumpling form of Henry Ramsley, Smith thrust the smoking barrel of his pistol hard into Roper's groin, grabbed the man's hair when he doubled up and, left-handed, threw him down the stairs.

"Abel!" Mrs Selby screamed again as Smith reached her side. He held her close, murmuring in her ear as the sound of the shot attracted the remainder of the raiders.

"I've got you," Smith said. "I've got you, Becky. You're safe now."

"Captain Smith!" Jake Ramsley emerged from the drawing-room and stared up at the body of his brother in disbelief. "You shot Henry. You shot my brother."

Smith stepped away from Lady Selby. "Yes." He felt for powder and ball to reload his pistol, but he had neglected to bring more ammunition with him. Roper stood up. Still holding his groin, he descended the stairs in a half-crouch and sat against the wall, moaning slightly. Smith heard the front door open but did not look around. The floor was ready, but any other dancers were superfluous. The main performers here were himself and Jake Ramsley, dancing to the music of gunfire.

"You bastard!" Jake Ramsley pulled a pistol from his belt. "I'll blow your bloody head off!"

Smith saw Lady Selby's mouth open as she prepared to spring down the stairs at Jake. "Stay out of this, Becky!" Smith eased her to one side and closed his fists. He measured the distance down the stairs, planning how to reach Jake and avoid his bullet.

"If you make another move, I'll blow your spine through the wall," Bess stood in the doorway with her blunderbuss in her hands.

"He shot Henry!" Jake Ramsley said, altering his attention from Smith to Bess and back. "He killed my brother!"

"And I'll kill you," Bess's voice was even as she crossed the hall to stand two feet behind Jake. "Then your mother will have two sons to mourn. Get out!" She gestured with her blunderbuss. "All of you!" She stepped back as Smith slipped down the stairs and grabbed Jake's pistol.

"I'm not moving without Henry," Jake Ramsley said. "I'll come for you, Smith," Jake said through gritted teeth. "We'll all come for you."

Smith reached Bess's side and looked back. Lady Selby remained where she was, standing on the stairs, shocked at the turn of events.

"Run," Smith ordered her quietly. "Grab what you must and run out of the house. Don't come back; don't even look back. Forget Kingshunt Manor and all it ever stood for."

I ruined Becky's life with my pursuit of Sir Francis.

Lady Selby held Smith's eyes for a moment, and then she ran. She looked neither left nor right as she sped down the stairs, passed Bess without a glance, and ran out of the front door to the cool night outside.

"Come on, John," Bess said. She backed out of the house, holding Jake Ramsley's murderous gaze while her blunderbuss ensured a safe passage.

Smith moved towards the door, paused for a second to lift the discarded hunting horn, and followed Bess.

"You murdered my brother!" Jake shouted.

"I always told you the Ramsleys were trouble." Bess poured them both a drink as Smith sat on his chair in their room.

"You did," Smith agreed. He tossed back the brandy and held out the glass for more. Bess filled it to the brim.

"Why?" Bess asked.

"Why what?"

"Why the concern for Lady Selby? You've only opened the door for a lot of trouble."

Smith drained half the glass. "We were close once."

Bess shook off her cloak and allowed it to slide from her shoulders onto the floor. "Were you lovers?"

"No," Smith replied, pushing aside the images of Becky's laughing young face.

"Are you lovers now?"

"No," Smith said again.

"Lady Selby wants you to be." Bess locked the door.

"I know," Smith emptied the glass. The spirits did not affect him. His head was as clear as if he had been drinking milk.

"You call her Becky," Bess said. "How much do you like her?"

Smith nursed his empty glass. "When I was with the Royal Navy," he said slowly. "I thought of her a lot."

Bess was silent for a long moment. "Do you want her?"

Smith crossed to the brandy bottle and refilled his glass, with the splashing spirits the only sound in the room. He did not reply.

I don't know the answer. If I didn't have Bess, I would not hesitate to snatch Becky back.

"I see," Bess said. "You can't have us both."

Smith only sipped at his brandy. "I don't want you both," he said.

"Do you want me?" Bess took off her clothes, aware he was watching. She slid off her final stitch and stood naked before him.

"Yes," Smith put his glass on the table. It was not hard to push thoughts of Lady Selby from his mind.

"Take me, then," Bess ordered, standing with her hands on her hips and the devil in her eyes.

They lay naked on the bed, intertwined in the soft afterglow of love, with the candles burned to stumps and a gentle wind caressing the open shutters outside.

"Where do you come from, Bess?" Smith asked.

"You've never asked that before," Bess said.

"I'm asking now." He stroked her leg. "From where do you come?"

"Why do you ask?"

"I'm interested," Smith replied and examined his motives. *I'm telling the truth, damn me. I want to know about this woman.*

242

"You've never cared before," Bess moved slightly further away. "Why the concern now?"

"Where do you come from, Bess?" Smith reached for his brandy, held the glass to Bess's lips, and watched her swallow.

"I'm damned if I know," Bess said. "I'm a child of the parish, an orphan, so my father could have been a passing one-legged seaman or the previous King George for all I know."

Smith sipped at the brandy, allowing the fiery sweetness to ease through him. "A passing seaman? Did your mother never tell you?"

"My mother?" Bess grimaced. "My mother was a dragtail, a bunter, a whore, or so people told me. I never knew her, anyway."

Smith did not request more details. "What's your last name? You've never told me that either."

Bess took the brandy from Smith and swallowed a mouthful. "My last name is whatever people wish to call me. I was told that a shepherd found me at the corner of a field. He looked after me as a baby, but when his wife died, he handed me to the church beadle."

Smith waited, but Bess said no more. "And?" He prompted.

"The beadle, Mr Moore, taught me to count, read and write, and used me as free labour." Bess drank more of the brandy. "I could use either of their names; Bessy Webb, the shepherd's daughter, or Bess Moore, the beadle's unpaid servant."

"Which do you prefer?" Smith asked.

Bess looked away. "I don't care. Later I went with a soldier for a while. I followed the drum in the last war when I was a youngster."

"How young?"

Bess screwed up her face. "Twelve or fourteen, maybe. I don't know. I acted as his wife, so I could also be Mrs Bess Cooper, although we never went through a marriage ceremony. When the camp fever took him, another soldier wanted me. His wife objected, and we fought. I had to leave the regiment after that."

"Why?" Smith asked. "Didn't you like the military life?"

"I liked it as much as I liked anything else, but I had killed the woman. I stuck her husband's bayonet between her ribs." Bess said. "We were in the Low Countries then, after the battle of Lauffeld, and I ran to the coast. I never caught scarlet fever, meaning I never ached for another soldier."

Smith waited for more, but Bess's eyes and thoughts were far away as she relived her youth. "Tell me more," Smith insisted, replacing his hand on her leg.

Bess started. "What? Oh, yes. I stowed away on an English ship, landed in Deal, and walked back to the parish. And here I've been ever since, and here I am now." She raised her arms. "All of me, God help you."

"Here you are, indeed," Smith said. "Captain Blackwell took you in, did he?"

"He did. He was a good man, in his way," Bess said. She sat up, cross-legged on the bed with her eyes clearing of old memories. "I'm always loyal to the man I'm with, John. I never cheated on any of them, and I won't cheat on you, as long as we're together."

Smith shifted his position, so he faced her. "My father was a seaman and a smuggler from Kingsgate. He liked women, any woman."

Bess laughed. "We might share the same father." She looked over at him, with her hand exploring. "Maybe that's why I felt a connection."

"Maybe it is," Smith said and returned to an earlier question. "When people ask for your surname, what name do you use?"

"Whatever name comes into my head," Bess said. "Sometimes I use Smith."

"Smith is a handy name. It's widespread and hard to trace."

"I thought so," Bess said. "But it's not your real name, is it?"

Smith considered for a minute, holding up the tumbler and looking at the dull glow of the guttering candle through the glass. "No," he said at last. "My name is not John Smith."

Bess held his gaze. "Who is Abel? Lady Selby called you Abel. Is that your real name?"

"Yes," Smith said. "I am Abel Watson."

"I've used Watson as well," Bess said. "Will you return to Watson?"

"That man is dead."

Which man is dead? You are alive."

"I buried that name along the coast," Smith told her. He watched as Bess stood to refill the glass, allowing his eyes to follow her smooth back and the curve of her hips, buttocks, and thighs. "Bring my pipe and tobacco too," he said.

Bess did so, biting off a chunk of tobacco for herself.

"I may return to Watson after," Smith said.

"After?" Bess faced him with her eyebrows raised.

"After," he repeated, patting the bed.

Chapter Twenty-Five

Wind, weather, and the passage of time had not been kind to the simple wooden cross, which had slipped to a sixty-degree angle in the soft earth. As Smith straightened the cross and firmed the soil at the base, Bess solemnly placed a bunch of flowers on the grave.

"Abel Watson," Bess read the carved name. "It must seem strange standing beside your own grave."

Smith shook his head. "The man who lies here was named John Smith in life. He was a good enough man, a reasonable seaman, and with as much personality as the name suggests. I'm doing him a favour by giving him my name."

Bess smiled. "You're an intriguing man, Abel Watson." She removed a handful of weeds, looked around, and tossed them over the graveyard wall.

"I'm John Smith now. As you see, Abel Watson is dead and buried."

"He died in a noble cause," Bess said, taking Smith's arm.

As they left the grave, a sudden wind scattered the flowers and knocked over the cross once more.

SMITH HAD EXPECTED TO BE CALLED AS A WITNESS IN SIR Francis's trial, so he and Bess had spent hours preparing his response to every possible question the lawyers could devise.

Bess had acted as a lawyer, firing a hundred questions at Smith, trying to trap him verbally, pushing him to his limit, testing his nerve and patience under pressure. Smith schooled himself to answer the questions without rising to any bait, keeping his voice low as he acted the honest shipmaster.

Now, Smith stood in court, with the be-wigged judge and legal men looking solemn and Sir Francis pale with prison-pallor but as arrogant as ever between two stern officials. Dressed in simple but clean clothes, Smith swept off his hat, so his short queue and plain ribbon pronounced his status and the light reflected from the brass buttons of his coat. Bess had helped him select his dress and schooled him in his demeanour and attitude.

"Remember," Bess had said. "You are not a smuggling captain nor a Royal Navy seaman. You are not Abel Watson, but Captain John Smith, a coasting captain, honest and slightly naïve."

"Yes, Bess," Smith adopted the part. "I am a loyal servant of the king, and of Sir Francis, rot his hide."

Smith remembered this room with its oak-panelled walls, the tall, dome-headed windows, and the thirty-six candles providing extra light. He knew there were thirty-six candles because he counted them, as he had done on his previous visit more than a decade previously.

The judge sat in splendour, his robes and wig proclaiming his status and power and his eyes assessing every man and woman who came before him. Smith gave a little jolt when he recognised Sir Francis's one-time chess partner and wondered if the previous acquaintanceship would prejudice the case.

It's too late to think of that now, and anyway, I could not influence the choice of judge any more than I could alter the tides.

The prosecutor strutted before Smith, with his gown nearly touching the floor and his fruity voice booming around the court.

"You are Captain John Smith!" The prosecutor announced.

"I am," Smith agreed.

The prosecutor faced Smith. "Sir Francis Selby of Kingshunt Manor, the accused, employed you as a shipmaster on his vessel *Maid of Kent*."

"He did," Smith kept his voice low and humble, as befitted a mariner out of his depth in these surroundings. The last time Smith had been in court, a judge had sentenced him and his father to death on Sir Francis's false accusation of horse theft. Smith fought the inclination to shift his neckcloth and touch the marks of hemp around his throat.

The prosecutor walked to the jury and back, increasing the tension inside the room. "Well, Captain Smith, after Sir Francis employed you as a shipmaster and put you in his debt, he abused your trust. I say he ordered you to carry Captain Marcel Duguay, a recently released French prisoner-of-war, an enemy of the king, and a very dangerous privateer captain, from Kent to France!"

The jury gave a little gasp at the prosecutor's words. One man in the public gallery muttered "shame," and another murmured "blasted traitor." Smith faced the prosecutor squarely, aware that every eye in the court was focussed on him. "No," he said. "Sir Francis gave me no such order."

"I must remind you, Captain Smith," the prosecutor said, "that you are under oath."

Smith lifted his chin. "I am a British shipmaster, sir," he said. "I trust you are not impinging my honesty." Before the prosecutor had time to reply, Smith addressed the judge. "May I have the Bible returned, your honour?"

The judge had recognised Smith as soon as he stood in the witness box. "The Bible?" The judge looked momentarily surprised. He was middle-aged, with a benign face and bright blue eyes. "If you wish, Captain Smith."

That took you by surprise, your Honour!

Smith took the Bible in both hands, kissed it in a dramatic gesture, and raised his voice to dispel any doubt. "I, John Smith,

Captain of *Maid of Kent*, do swear again that I shall tell the truth and have told the truth." Smith raised his voice further, as though he was addressing the hands on the foretopmast or calling to the Lord beyond the highest clouds.

"Sir Francis Selby did not command me to carry any passenger, French or otherwise, prisoner-of-war, or free man, across the Channel to France or any other part of the world." Smith saw the impact his words had on the jury and judge. "As far as I can judge, Sir Francis is as loyal a subject of King George III as he always was to King George II."

And, more importantly, Smith thought, *the jury will believe I have sworn a mighty oath that I am innocent of carrying Duguay across to France.*

As the jury nodded, Smith saw Bess in the audience, studying him and smiling faintly. At the back of the audience, white-faced and scared, Lady Selby also watched, with her expression a mask of puzzlement.

"And if anything I say about Sir Francis Selby is a lie," Smith lowered his voice in case he frightened the jury while he gripped the Bible ever more firmly. "May the good Lord strike me down with lightning and thunderbolts here and now, as sure as death!"

The room was stunned to silence. Only Bess knew that Smith was clearing himself and creating the appearance of an honest, loyal man, although Lady Selby may have her suspicions.

Sir Francis looked hopeful as he sat in the dock, with steel manacles around his wrists and a row of spikes between him and the remainder of the court. He nodded to Smith, grateful to have somebody on his side in a case that seemed stacked against him.

"Did the accused, Sir Francis Selby, ever mention Captain Duguay or any other French prisoner to you?" the prosecutor asked in an attempt to regain the initiative.

"Never," Smith retained his grip on the Bible.

"Did the accused mention any partiality to France or a desire to help the French king?"

"Never!" Smith raised his chin as if even mentioning such a thing insulted Sir Francis's honour.

"Yet, French brandy was found in Sir Francis's cellar, with a note — a personal note — from the notorious French privateer Captain Duguay."

"I heard that rumour," Smith admitted reluctantly.

"It is no rumour, Captain, but a plain hard fact. Can you explain that fact, Captain Smith?"

Smith frowned. "I am not privy to Sir Francis's cellar, sir," he said. "Perhaps somebody placed the brandy there." Smith hoped he did not influence the jury too much in Sir Francis's favour.

"Why would anybody do such a thing?"

Smith glanced at the judge as if for support.

The judge nodded. "You may answer the question, Captain Smith."

"I repeat," the prosecutor said, sensing blood, "why would anybody wish to place a keg of French brandy in the cellar, the locked cellar, of Kingshunt Manor?"

Smith lowered his voice and clutched the Bible as if his life, or his soul, depended on it. "I am a ship's captain, sir. I cannot answer such a question. Perhaps somebody had a grudge against Sir Francis."

"Who might that be?" The prosecutor was relentless.

Smith tried to look confused. "Perhaps one of the smugglers Sir Francis jailed."

"Men in jail cannot place brandy in Sir Francis's cellar," the prosecutor said, with a tone of triumph.

Smith saw Lady Selby and knew she understood. "Maybe a smuggler's friend, sir," he said. He faced the judge again. "May I add something that may help Sir Francis's case, Your Honour?"

The judge frowned. "It is the accused legal representative's task to help him, Captain Smith. You are here to answer questions."

"Yes, Your Honour. I meant no disrespect to the court." Smith looked away as if embarrassed.

The judge sighed. "Say what is in your mind, Captain."

"Thank you, Your Honour. Mr Ambrose Grant, the Preventative officer, asked me about local smugglers recently."

"Do you know of any?"

"Only the Sussex Gang. Captain Holden and his crew," Smith saw the judge scribble a note. "I know Sir Francis recently prevented a landing of smuggled brandy in his parish, and I believe that Captain Holden of Hastings hopes to move into Kent, Your Honour. Perhaps Holden is afraid of Sir Francis's activity and hoped to remove him."

"Your loyalty to your employer is commendable," the prosecutor said smoothly, clearly hating Smith more than any murderous rogue or Frenchman. "But I believe it stems only from fear of losing your position. If Sir Francis is imprisoned, transported, or hanged, you will lose command of *Maid of Kent*. I put it to you, Captain Smith, that you plead as much for your own security as for the accused."

Smith let that suggestion lie for a moment to increase the dramatic effect of his rebuttal. "I am the majority shareholder and the managing owner of *Maid of Kent*," he said quietly, still gripping the Bible. "I have come to this court to speak the truth before his Honour," Smith indicated the judge, "and my God, as an honest man should."

The prosecutor stepped back. "No further questions," he said.

Smith bowed to the jury, handed back the Bible, and joined Bess in the public gallery. Bess glanced behind her at Lady Selby, deliberately shifted closer to Smith, and took hold of his hand.

"You looked most convincing," Bess whispered.

"Let's hope it was not too good an act," Smith replied.

Despite Smith's appearance, all the evidence pointed to Sir Francis's guilt. With two letters from Duguay in the house, the keg of smuggled brandy, and the documents from Sissinghurst Castle, the defence could do little except call on Sir Francis's reputation and previous good character.

Captain Easton of Sissinghurst could not swear that the man in the dock was Sir Francis but admitted that the gentleman who left with Captain Duguay called himself Sir Francis and had plied him with ardent spirits from their first acquaintance.

"Do you believe Sir Francis's intended to befuddle you, sir?" the prosecutor asked.

"Undoubtedly, sir!" Easton agreed, eager to salvage his career.

The prosecutor recognised an ally. "Would you agree, Captain Easton, that Sir Francis was like a man with a secondary purpose?"

"Exactly so," Easton grabbed at the chance to free himself of any blame.

"Would you agree that Sir Francis acted like a man seeped in deviousness, such as a traitor to the king?"

"Quite so," Easton agreed.

When the defence tried weakly to object to the prosecutor's choice of words, the judge demanded a rebuttal.

"Take those words back, sir. The jury will disregard the prosecutor's unfortunate phraseology."

However, the damage had already been done. With Sir Francis's attempt to befuddle Captain Easton through drink proved to everybody's satisfaction save that of Sir Francis; the prosecutor continued with his character assassination. "How much drink did Sir Francis force on you?"

"A great deal, sir," Easton said.

"A great deal," the prosecutor repeated. "It would be honest British spirits, though, gin or rum?"

"Why, no, sir," Captain Easton said. "It was French brandy. Sir Francis admitted to me that he was partial to brandy. He told me that he and Duguay were friendly even before the present war."

"Indeed?" the prosecutor said. "Sir Francis admitted that he was friendly with one of the king's most notorious enemies. No further questions, sir."

The jury murmured while people in the public galleries spoke loudly and threw looks of hatred towards Sir Francis.

Private Watler was adamant that the prisoner was the same man who asked him all about Sissinghurst, with bribes of French brandy, while Sergeant Ogden was equally sure the accused was the gentleman who asked about Major Foss.

"A well set up gentleman, he was," Sergeant Ogden said. "Riding good bloodstock as well. I'd know him in a company of a hundred."

Smith shrunk slightly on his bench and lowered his face in case the honest sergeant realised his mistake.

Even such an apparently staunch partisan as Smith had to admit there could only be one outcome when the trial ended. The jury deliberated for less than an hour and returned their inevitable verdict of guilty of treason.

Smith felt Bess squeeze his hand while simultaneously hearing Lady Selby give a little sob.

"It is my painful duty," the judge donned his black cap to the gasps from the audience, "to find you, Sir Francis Selby of King-shunt Manor, guilty of treason in time of war. You wilfully enabled an enemy of the king to escape, thus putting the commerce of the nation and the lives and liberty of the king's subjects in danger.

"It is doubly painful in that you are a man of standing and position and a man who should be at the forefront of loyalty and an example to those of lesser degree."

Some of the audience nodded sagely at the judge's words.

The judge looked at Smith. "If you possessed the God-fearing loyalty of Captain Smith, Sir Francis, you would be a better man. Instead, you have chosen to exchange your loyalty and duty to the king for brandy. It is the sentence of this court that you be taken to the place of public execution in your parish and hanged by the neck until you are dead. Furthermore, you will be left there to hang in chains as an awful example of the penalty of treason and the terrible result of your crime."

As the audience shouted, clapped, or swooned in delicious

horror, the judge leaned forward in his seat. "And that's checkmate for you, Sir Francis, and a higher penalty than a hundred guineas!"

"No!" Sir Francis shouted as Bess squeezed Smith's hand. "I'm innocent! You have condemned a loyal man!"

As a pair of stern-faced guards nearly dragged Sir Francis back to his cell, some of the audience left, although most remained for the following case, a simple highway robbery.

"Come on, Bess," Smith led her to the congested bustle of the street outside, where wagons and drays rumbled beside the elegant coaches of the wealthy. Sir Francis's defence lawyer approached Smith, tapping a silver-headed cane on the ground as he held his cloak tight around his shoulders.

"Captain Smith," the lawyer said. "I believe we have unfinished business."

"We have," Smith led the lawyer to a quiet corner, where two parked coaches concealed them from the passing crowds. "Thank you." He handed over a solid purse.

The lawyer weighed the purse in an expert hand, opened the drawstring, and glanced inside. "And that concludes the deal. We shall not meet again, Captain." He walked away, leaving Bess wondering.

"Did you bribe Sir Francis's barrister?"

"Leave nothing to chance," Smith said.

"I wondered why he was so inept." Bess shook her head. "You're a devious, dangerous man, Abel."

"John," Smith insisted. "I am still plain John Smith, a bluff seaman from Kent." He took her by the arm. "Come along, Bess; I always feel dirty after dealing with lawyers, peers, and politicians."

Pushing through the crowd, Smith led Bess to the stables, where they had left their horses.

"You did it, then," Lady Selby had been waiting, sitting on a hay bale. She approached them with her back straight, and her head held high. "You had my husband condemned to death."

"A jury of his peers reviewed the evidence, listened to the lawyers' arguments, and came to their reasoned conclusion," Smith reminded. "And the judge sentenced him as the law required. A judge," he said, "who knows Sir Francis very well."

"You manoeuvred your revenge, Abel," Lady Selby said.

"You overestimate my powers," Smith told her.

"Did you report your rape to the authorities?" Bess pushed in front of Smith.

"That's hardly your affair," Lady Selby said.

Bess smiled. "I didn't think you had. Perhaps James Quinn, the parish constable, would believe you, but as the wife of a proven traitor," she said. "I doubt a court in the land would take your side. My advice to you is to leave the area and start a new life elsewhere."

Lady Selby looked down her nose at the smaller Bess. "I don't require your advice."

Bess gave a mocking curtsey and withdrew a step. "As you wish, my Lady."

"Where are you staying, Lady Selby?" Smith asked.

"I took your advice," Lady Selby emphasised the third word, glancing at Bess as she spoke. "I put money aside and leased Orchardholm, in the High Weald near Elmsted."

"An excellent choice," Smith said with a bow. "And, if I may say, you are well rid of a poor husband."

Glancing again at Bess, Lady Selby leaned forward and kissed Smith on the forehead. She was his equal in height and did not need to stretch. "I will seek to replace Sir Francis with a better man," she said. "Once I get rid of a contemptible encumbrance." She turned, flicked her skirt away from Bess, and walked smartly away.

"And that's the last we'll see of her," Smith said.

"Perhaps," Bess watched Mrs Selby retreating form. She glanced at Smith. "Perhaps." She was quiet on the journey home, yet her fingers were busy on her horse's reins.

Chapter Twenty-Six

September 1762

When Mother Ramsley pushed open the door and stepped into the Dancing Horse, Ruth reached behind the counter for her pistol.

Mother Ramsley lifted a hand. "There's no need for a weapon, Mrs Martin," she Ramsley said. "I only want to speak to Captain Smith."

"Here I am." Smith sat in his customary seat, with a pile of documents, ink, and a pen in front of him. "I've been expecting your visit, Mother Ramsley."

"What I have to say won't take long," Mother Ramsley said.

Smith nodded, placing a pistol on the table in front of him. Its mate sat comfortably under his belt.

"There's no need for the barker tonight," Mother Ramsley said. "Unless you choose to murder me, as you murdered my son."

"He was a rapist," Smith said. "I saved the hangman a job."

"There's no hanging for a simple rape," Mother Ramsley announced and faced Bess, who sat at Smith's side. "You'll have your blunderbuss."

"Loaded with swan shot and pointed at your belly," Bess assured her.

"We'll keep this clean and open between honest folk," Mother Ramsley said. "There's no need to bring in the parish constable or any other interfering outsider."

"No need at all, Mother," Smith agreed, expecting the inn door to open and the rest of the Ramsley tribe to erupt inside.

"You murdered my Henry," Mother Ramsley said. "So we will kill you, John Smith, and all that cling to you. We'll kill your woman if she remains with you, and we'll take over your organisation."

"You can try!" Bess told her.

Mother Ramsley ignored the interruption. "We will grind your name and memory from the parish, John Smith. When we are finished, nobody will know that you ever existed."

Smith had listened patiently. "Thank you for the warning, Mother Ramsley, but here is what will happen," he replied. "You will return to your home and bury your boy Henry in peace. He transgressed and paid the price, as we all must do, in time. Then you and your family will rant, rave, drink, and make wild threats, none of which you will bring to pass."

Smith sat up straight in his seat. "If you pit your family against me, Mother, you will lose. There will be more deaths, and you'll bury more of your sons, or they will bury you."

Mother Ramsley held Smith's gaze. "We understand each other, you and me, John Smith, as you call yourself. What must happen shall come to pass." She backed away, step by step, until she reached the outer door. "We'll meet again." She stepped outside, and the door quietly closed.

Hargreaves appeared from behind the inner door with a pistol in his hand and another in his belt. "She was not merely ranting, Captain. With the Ramsleys, it will be war to the knife, and the living will envy the tranquillity of the dead."

"That's true," Smith said. "You'd best be out of it, Hargreaves. You have a wife to consider." He raised his voice. "You too, Ruth. Bess and I will be leaving the Dancing Horse now; else the Ramsleys will burn it to the foundations."

Ruth shook her head. "Stay as long as you wish, Captain, and welcome. You pay your accounts on time and bring me good custom, which is more than the Ramsleys and their kind have ever done."

"It will be dangerous for you," Smith said.

Ruth produced a bottle of Jamaica rum and poured herself a drink before tossing the bottle across the room. Smith caught it left-handed. "We're Kent folk," she said. "We live with the Impress Service and the expectation of French raids. Our lives could alter or end at any time, and we're all seagoing folk here. I'm not putting out a friend for fear of a gang of cut-throats."

Smith lifted the bottle in salute. "You're a lady, Mrs Martin."

"I'm charging you for that bottle," Ruth said. "And I want your account paid in full before the sun sets tonight. Dead men can't pay their bills."

Smith was unsure if Ruth was jesting. "I'll pay it directly," he promised.

GALLOWS HILL ROSE AT THE NORTH-WESTERN EXTREMITY OF the parish and the end of Sir Francis's land. At a little over five hundred feet, it was not a high hill, but prominent that it formed an isolated spur of the Weald, made bald by generations of grazing sheep and a seemingly ever-present wind from the Channel.

Bess accompanied Smith as he rode to Gallows Hill, pushing his horse through the crowds that thronged to the spectacle, for it was not often they witnessed the execution of a landowner and gentleman.

"I thought traitors had their heads chopped off," a woman complained. "It's only a simple hanging." She twisted her head sideways and thrust her tongue out of the side of her mouth to demonstrate the results.

"Did you want to see blood?" her male companion asked.

"I can see a hanging any month I choose," the woman said. "They're ten a penny."

"They last longer than a decapitation," her knowledgeable friend consoled her. "And it will only happen once to Sir Francis, the treacherous dog."

"Maybe a drawing and quartering," the woman mused. "I have never seen one of them, with Jack Ketch hauling out the squire's innards and chopping off his manhood. Now that would be fun."

"Are you all right?" Smith asked Bess. "I hope a hanging won't upset you."

"I saw a thousand times worse at the aftermath of Lauffeld," Bess said soberly. "Thousands of dead and wounded men with arms, legs, and other things missing. I searched the wounded for friends and still remember what I saw."

"A hanging won't upset you, then."

"No," Bess said shortly.

Smith fingered his throat as he pulled Rodney to a halt. The place of execution reared above them, a simple construction of sturdy timber, raised above the hill, with a platform for the hangman and his customer. The gallows thrust upward, with a straight bar set at right angles to a vertical post, supported by a diagonal length of Kentish oak.

"Sir Frankie is a popular man," Bess looked across the heads of the mob that had gathered to witness the execution.

"Free entertainment," Smith tried to sound nonchalant. "Cheaper sport than a day at the races, if less bloody than bull-baiting or dog-fighting."

Augmenting the curious and the idle, Smith saw a gang of London pickpockets here to rob the yokels and flats. He also saw many of Sir Francis's tenants and one or two of his servants. Standing slightly apart, or waiting by their carriages, some of Sir Francis's hunting and chess cronies tried to ignore the mass of the people as they poured port into crystal glasses and betted on how long their erstwhile colleague would last.

"He's a stubborn man," one elegant dandy said, sipping at his port. "I give him a good twenty minutes struggle before he succumbs."

"Not him," a plump woman replied, adjusting her hat to ensure no sunlight blemished her delicate white skin. "He won't wish to amuse the tenants. He'll throw himself off the scaffold to die quickly. Ten guineas says he'll die within ten minutes."

"A guinea a minute? Is that all Sir Francis is worth?" A broad-shouldered country squire said, shifting behind the plump woman to pinch her backside. "Why, he was a good man on a horse, madam, a good man!"

At the opposite edge of the crowd, sitting side-saddle on a splendid grey horse, Lady Selby cast a lonely figure. She gave a little start as she saw Smith and lifted a white-gloved hand in salutation.

"Here come the redcoats," Bess said. "Ignore Her Ladyship. She is not your concern."

The authorities had decided that an entire infantry company was required to keep public order. The Kent Militia pushed through the crowd, tricorn hats at an identical angle, Brown Bess muskets secure in their hands, and three officers at their head, arrogant with their power and status.

"Make way in the King's name!" The captain in charge ordered. "I hold the King's commission, and I command you to make way!"

When the crowd ignored him, the captain drew his sword and used the flat of the blade of backs, shoulders, and buttocks, with his sergeants pushing with their halberds and the private soldiers dropping the heavy butts of their muskets on unwary toes. Eventually, the militia forced a passage through to the gallows, where they formed a hollow square, facing outward. The senior sergeant took forty men to keep the road open.

"Get back there, you dogs!" The sergeant pushed with his halberd. "Make way!"

"Stop acting the tyrant, Ned Clarke!" A woman shouted in

the sergeant's ear. "I've known you since you were a babe in arms!"

Sergeant Clarke looked momentarily nonplussed, then decided to ignore the woman and continued to harangue the crowd. "Make way in the King's name!"

"Here he comes!" Somebody shrieked. "Here comes the traitor!"

Smith saw Sir Francis at the foot of the hill, with an escort of dragoons around his cart. As a great yell erupted, ballad sellers began peddling broadsheets proclaiming Sir Francis's last words long before he had uttered them. Smith saw lords and ladies arrive in their coaches, with the drivers using their whips to obtain a position that provided the best view. Family men hoisted their children on brawny shoulders so they could watch the events, and always the pickpockets were busy, lifting everything from handkerchiefs to purses. Finally, the cart arrived, with dragoons snarling and kicking at the crowd, many of whom hissed and threw eggs and cabbages at Sir Francis.

Sir Francis faced the rear, with his wrists chained to a horizontal bar at the back of the cart. A chaplain stood at his side to give spiritual guidance in the last few moments of the condemned man's life.

"I remember the chaplain," Smith said. "He accepted my father's spirits and preached at him to repent his sins, with the smell of smuggled brandy on his breath and a smuggled silk kerchief around his neck."

"Canting hypocrite," Bess said, with her attention alternating between Smith and Lady Selby.

"Don't stray. I'll be back in a minute," Smith said and prodded his horse towards the cart. The dragoons watched him suspiciously as he approached until Smith raised a placatory hand. "I just want a word with Sir Francis," he said.

"Are you a relative?" A suspicious sergeant asked.

"A friend," Smith pushed past and spoke quietly to Sir Francis. "Keep your head up, sir," he said, patting Sir Francis's side. He withdrew a second later and returned to Bess.

"What were you doing?" Bess asked.

"This," Smith passed over Sir Francis's purse, which he had extracted from the condemned man's pocket.

"You devil!" Bess said. "Robbing the nearly dead!"

The noise abated as Sir Francis left the cart. The hangman unlocked the chains from Sir Francis's ankles and helped him mount the steps to the gallows, pushing him up to the platform. The crowd were hissing, with chants of "traitor" and "damn the French!" heard above the background noise.

Sir Francis faced the crowd, still with the manacles around his wrists, as the chaplain read to him from the Bible. His head was up despite the occasional egg or half-rotted cabbage that sailed past him.

"Don't leave this spot," Smith said to Bess. "I have something to do."

"What's that?" Bess asked, but Smith pulled Rodney away and pushed around the outside of the crowd to Lady Selby's side.

Lady Selby looked up. "You've left your little girl alone."

"I know." Smith ensured that Sir Francis was watching. "Kiss me."

"What?" Lady Selby looked at him as he leaned forward, put an arm around her shoulders and pulled her close. When she pecked his cheek, Smith frowned.

"Not an auntie's kiss. Kiss me with passion!" He placed his lips against hers and opened her teeth with his tongue. When he eventually broke the embrace, Sir Francis had sunk to his knees, staring. "I think I've hurt him," Smith said.

Sir Francis did not move when the executioner removed his neckcloth, exposing his throat to the tense cheers of the crowd.

"Hang the traitor," a woman shouted. "Make it slow!"

"Checkmate!" a man's voice sounded above the crowd. Smith recognised Jenkins, one of Sir Francis's servants, a man thoroughly enjoying his master's demise.

The executioner waited for a minute then pinioned Sir Francis's arms with a black sash.

"What's the hangman waiting for?" Lady Selby asked.

"His wages," Smith explained. "The more the condemned man pays the hangman, the easier his death will be."

"But Francis didn't pay him anything."

"I know," Smith said. "We distracted him when we kissed, and anyway, Sir Francis has lost his purse."

Lady Selby looked at Smith. "You intended that."

"Sir Francis fabricated evidence to have my father hanged," Smith reminded. "He had me half-hanged and sent into the Navy and took you from me. I vowed then I'd get even if I was spared."

Smith was a teenager again, watching as the judge donned the black cap and pronounced the fatal words. He had screamed, pleading for mercy for himself and his father, but there was no grace from the judge's graceless face.

"Hanged by the neck until you are dead," the judge pronounced.

"I'll get you!" Young Smith shouted across the crowded court. "I'll get even with you, Francis Selby!"

Sir Francis had laughed openly. "Not this side of hell, Watson. It's the noose for you and your father and destitution for your mother!"

Smith's mother pressed a handkerchief to her mouth to stifle her sobs as a burly court official hauled Smith away.

Smith shook himself back to the present. He moved closer to the gallows as the executioner produced a white hood, held it up, and threw it into the crowd. Eager hands grabbed at this splendid souvenir.

"Let them watch your face as you suffer," the executioner said to Sir Francis.

Smith came as close to the gallows as the militia allowed until a sweating corporal ordered him back.

"Sir Francis!" Smith pitched his voice above the babble of the mob.

The squire looked down at the same instant that the executioner slipped the noose around his neck.

"Do you remember me?" Smith asked.

Sir Francis licked dry lips, struggling to maintain his composure as he faced a shameful death. "You're Captain John Smith."

"I am Abel Watson. You hanged my father, Josiah Watson, and sent me into the Navy!" Smith waited until the hangman hauled Sir Francis to the raised section of the gallows and spoke louder. "You also married my girl, Sir Francis!"

The hangman put a hand on the lever, ready to level the platform and leave Sir Francis suspended by his neck. The corporal stepped forward, prepared to push Smith back into the now-silent, expectant crowd.

"My girl," Smith repeated, watching the anguish on Sir Francis's face, "and she'll be mine again while you're hanging in chains as a traitor."

Squire opened his mouth to speak as Smith added his final words. "And, Francis, Captain Duguay is my friend. I brought his note to your cellar."

The hangman pulled the lever and the platform levelled. Smith held Sir Francis's gaze for a moment, watching his eyes bulge and seeing the rope cut into his throat. "You die a reviled traitor, Francis Selby, hated by everybody."

Sir Francis gagged as the rope slowly strangled him, with his mouth foaming and his legs kicking for purchase that they would never find.

"Back you go!" The corporal pushed Smith away.

Behind Smith, the crowd were cheering, but he did not hear. He was a youth again, watching his father hang as his world dissolved in tears and tragedy.

Chapter Twenty-Seven

September 1762

The noose tightened around his neck, slowly choking him as the rough hemp burned into the tender skin of his throat. Smith tried to reach up, but with manacles around his wrists, he could not loosen the rope. His calls for help brought no response, and he kicked to alleviate the terrible pain in his throat and lungs.

Above him, Smith saw his father dying, with his eyes bulging, and his feet dancing on nothing. In front, his mother watched in horror, with her face the only thing Smith saw clearly in the featureless crowd.

"Mother!" Smith tried to shout, but the only response was a horrible gurgle as his tongue seemed swollen to twice its usual size. The crowd was in front of him, a sea of faces, shouting and gesticulating. The noise increased, a rising tide of sound that woke Smith from his nightmare.

Bess woke simultaneously, pushed back her hair, and blinked at Smith across the width of a pillow.

"What the devil?" Bess began. Sliding from the bed, she began to unfasten the shutters.

"No!" Smith put a hand on her arm. "Leave them." Lifting a pistol from the sideboard, he opened the door and padded along the corridor to the unoccupied room next door, with Bess a step behind him.

Striding to the window, Smith eased the shutters open and, keeping well to the side, peered outside. A crowd had gathered outside the Dancing Horse, fifteen youngsters, all waiting with stones in their hands as they shouted upwards at Smith's window.

"See the leading lads there?" Smith said quietly. "That's some of the Ramsley's brood."

"The little buggers!" Bess said, just as the most vocal of the children began to throw stones.

"Right!" Smith said, pointed his pistol in the air and fired. The sound of a gunshot stunned the crowd, which scattered around the street, boys and girls running for shelter.

"That showed them," Bess chuckled.

"They'll be back," Smith said. "That was only Mother Ramsley's statement of intent. She was letting us know that the war has started. From now on, Bess, we'd better be careful."

"I'll carry my gun," Bess promised.

Smith looked down at the now-empty street. "That would be best," he agreed. "Maybe you should leave the area until this clears up."

"No." Bess hooked her arm into Smith's. "I said before that I never cheat on my man, and I'll never leave him to fight alone either. I followed the drum against Johnny Crapaud and stood as French cannonballs battered our camp." She nudged Smith with her hip. "I don't think a few ragged Ramsleys will scare me away."

Smith closed the shutters and wafted away the worst of the powder smoke. "You're some woman, Bess."

Ruth was in the corridor when they returned to their room. "What was all the commotion?" She held up a brass holder with a stumpy candle and eyed Smith's naked body without interest.

"The Ramsleys," Smith brandished his pistol. "We chased them away with a warning shot."

"Was anybody hurt?" Ruth asked.

"Not this time."

"Goodnight, then." Ruth turned away with her nightdress billowing around her broad hips.

"Goodnight," Smith called after her. He reloaded his pistol immediately once he returned to his room, then locked the door. "Goodnight, Bess," he said and smiled when he saw she was already asleep.

SMITH WOKE TO FIND THE BED NEXT TO HIM EMPTY AND BESS'S pistol missing from its customary position. He lit a candle and dressed leisurely by its yellow glow before checking the time. It was five in the morning and still dark outside.

"Bess left half an hour since," Ruth emerged from her room with her hair an explosion and a cloak thrown over her night-clothes. "I thought it was you when I heard the front door open and close."

"The little minx!" Smith said, reaching into his snuff box. He did not like snuff but knew to partake of the powdered tobacco was a refined habit, so he chose to indulge.

"Are you going after her?" Ruth asked.

"No," Smith shook his head. "I have a cargo to deliver today."

"I'll get your breakfast," Ruth said. She looked over her shoulder as Smith followed her downstairs. "You'd best be careful today, Captain. Mother Ramsley made her intention clear yesterday, and she's not a woman to forget a grudge."

"Nor am I," Smith said.

Maid of Kent left with the morning tide, with half a dozen seagulls bidding them farewell and the smoke of Kingsgate drifting across the rooftops. Hargreaves was quiet, and Smith noted the pistol in his belt.

"Why?" Smith asked.

"In case of the Ramsleys," Hargreaves replied.

Smith nodded. "We'll leave them behind at sea. Ready aft." He gave his usual order.

"Ready aft, Captain," Hargreaves replied.

"Let fall! Sheet home!" Smith ordered, sniffing the wind. An offshore breeze eased *Maid of Kent* from the harbour as the hands scampered across the deck with the sheets. *Maid* woke up as the cordage moved and blocks rattled and groaned throughout the lugger. Smith glanced at the half dozen or so people standing on the quay, watching *Maid* lift her head to the first of the Channel rollers.

"Belay the tops'l sheets! Man the tops'l halliards." By now, Smith was accustomed to giving orders, yet the thrill of commanding his own ship was as great as ever. After years of running to obey orders, now he was in charge, and nobody, not even King George, could countermand his orders on *Maid of Kent*.

"Tend the braces! Hoist the tops'l!"

Smith heard the roar as the anchor cable was paid down to the chain lockers. He nodded his satisfaction. *Maid of Kent* was behaving herself, and all was well with his world. There were minor worries, such as prowling French privateers, Mother Ramsley and her tribe, Ambrose Grant, and Holden's Sussex Gang, but nothing he could not handle.

The Channel altered its mood to a stiff easterly that bowled *Maid of Kent* out of the Downs without incident. Smith did not sight a single unfriendly sail, and his hands behaved impeccably, with the ship not missing the Ramsley brothers in the slightest.

"Are you taking over all Sir Francis's customers?" Hargreaves asked as they left Portsmouth for the return journey.

"All of them except the tenants on the estate," Smith said. "The Crown has grabbed Sir Francis's lands and leased them to Sir Ralph Naylor."

"How about Lady Selby?" Hargreaves asked. "I know that you and she were friendly once."

Smith shook his head. "There's nothing for her."

"And the sons?"

"Disinherited. They get nothing."

Hargreaves nodded. "Such is the way of the world. Lady Selby won't thank you for impoverishing her boys."

"That is hard, I think," Smith said. *I had not intended to hurt Becky. I hope she took plenty of Sir Francis's money before he died.*

When the wind shifted again, Hargreaves bellowed orders to the hands, and *Maid of Kent* tacked eastwards along the south coast of Wight. "What do you plan?"

"Nothing," Smith said. "Set course southeast by east. We're picking up a cargo tonight."

"Aye, sir," Hargreaves said.

Smith lifted his telescope, glad to be back at sea and free of the complications on land.

BESS WAS WAITING WHEN SMITH RETURNED HOME WITH THE cargo safely stored in the cave and *Maid of Kent* back in the harbour.

"Where did you take the pistol?" Smith asked.

"The Spike," Bess said.

"And what did you shoot at the Spike?"

"Targets," Bess said.

Smith nodded. "I see." He hung up his dripping sea cloak and put his hat on the peg above. "Next time, tell me before you leave."

Bess poured them both a glass of rum. "Tomorrow," she said. "I'm leaving tomorrow."

Smith sipped at the rum, rolled it around his mouth, and swallowed. "Are you coming back here?"

"Maybe."

Maybe; what the deuce does that mean? Smith killed his surge of dismay. "Will you need money?"

"I have sufficient for my needs," Bess said cautiously. She

watched as Smith changed out of his seagoing garments into the long clothes he wore on land.

"I'll be gone for half an hour," Smith said. "Don't leave the room."

Bess nodded. "I'll stay here." She poured herself some brandy and opened the account books as Smith walked away and closed the door.

"Dress up," Smith said when he returned. "We're dancing tonight."

"Why?"

"It might be our last night together."

Bess nodded. "Where are we dancing?"

"In the taproom," Smith said. *If you're leaving me, Bess, I'll give you something to remember me by. If you're thinking of coming back sometime, then we'll dance to dare the devil.*

The fiddlers arrived at seven and struck up a slow melody as Ruth cleared the tables to the side of the room.

"Mrs Martin!" Smith handed her twenty guineas. "That's for the drink and any breakages. If the bill comes to more than that, I'll pay tomorrow or the next day."

"And tonight?" Ruth asked.

"Tonight, we dance our cares away," Smith said. *And damn the devil and the Ramsleys.* "Come, Bess, and take the floor with me."

The fiddlers struck up a jig, and Smith showed a lively pair of feet, with Bess matching him step for step while the regular customers watched. Within minutes, the noise attracted people from the Hounds Rest and seamen from the harbour. Soon the floor was crowded, with Thomas Carman holding the Widow Dodd in a close embrace and James Hewitt showing some fancy footwork he had learned in West Africa.

After an hour, Smith and Bess found a space at the counter to order refreshments, but the music continued, and more customers squeezed into the Dancing Horse.

"That's the Preventative men," Ruth said as Ambrose Grant

walked into the inn. Ruth reached under the counter for her pistol.

"Leave them be," Smith said. "They're safe in here tonight. Pass the word around." *Let's hope the Ramsleys stay away.*

The entrance of the Preventative men altered the atmosphere, with many of the free traders stepping back or reaching inside their tunics for hidden weapons.

"Keep the boys under control," Smith told Hargreaves. He stepped towards Grant with his hand extended.

"Welcome to the Dancing Horse, Ambrose! We've no rank or position in here. We are all just fellow men and women of Kent and our guests."

Grant took Smith's hand with a surprised smile on his face. "Thank you, Captain Smith."

"Tonight, I am paying for the entertainment and the rum and beer." He grinned. "No brandy, I am afraid. The Dancing Horse is a law-abiding inn." Smith hoped that Ruth would have the brandy well hidden from prying eyes.

"What's the occasion?" Grant asked, smiling softly as his gaze took in everybody and everything in the inn.

"I like to dance," Smith said.

"A hornpipe?" Grant asked and lowered his voice. "Or the Tyburn jig?" That was an allusion to the gallows at Tyburn in London, where many unfortunate men and women ended their life.

"A hornpipe," Smith replied. "Here's a partner for you," he motioned to Hargreaves' teenaged daughter, who came willingly, curtseyed to Grant, and led him onto the floor.

Ruth was watching, with one hand still underneath the counter. "Your new friend was quick to spot the brandy," she said quietly to Smith. "He asked where I got the French spirits. I told him that Holden was back and with threats."

"Good!" Smith leaned across the counter and kissed her. "And now, dance with me, Mrs Martin!"

There was little finesse in the dancing and nothing that

would be recognised in the elegant Assembly Rooms that were springing up the length and breadth of the country. However, there was a great deal of energy and noise. By nine that night, Dancing Horse's taproom was too full, so the dancers spilt onto the street outside, with the local vicar and Quinn the parish constable joining in. Sir Ralph Naylor arrived at ten, with half a dozen of his servants and his elegant wife, and by midnight most of the village and a great many of the farming folk of the parish joined in.

The Ramsleys have stayed away. That might be a blessing or a pity, for if the Ramsleys caused trouble, Sir Ralph and Grant would be valuable allies.

Although the night was dedicated to Bacchus, Venus also descended from whatever heavenly home she inhabited and spread her influence over many willing Kingsgate dancers. Courting couples took advantage of the general hilarity to find a quiet nook where they could indulge their passion, and Smith nodded his approval as he saw Thomas Carman escort the Widow Dodd to his cottage.

Smith did not know how often he was on the floor or what time it was when he eventually retired to bed. He only knew that Bess was in his arms that night, and when he woke, she was gone.

"She was more sober than you were." Ruth looked none the worse for her all-night dancing as she set about putting her inn to rights and counting the missing glasses and tankards. "Our Bess was always careful how much she had to drink."

"Damn her hide!" Smith took a draught of small beer to try to regain his clarity of thought. "I should have taken a belt to her long ago."

The landlady laughed. "I rather think that Bess would return the favour with interest."

Smith smiled sourly. "Isn't that the truth, now? She's some girl, is my Bess."

"Woman," the landlady corrected. "Bess stopped being a girl many years ago."

Smith nodded, unwilling to argue until his head cleared. "I'd better see if she's all right."

"She'll be up at the Spike," the landlady said. "She goes up there every morning you're at sea to practise her shooting."

"She's not there this morning," Smith said.

The landlady cocked her head, listening for the sound of pistol fire. "No," she said after a few minutes. "She's not. Where d'you think she might be?"

"Killing somebody," Smith said, as his mind began to clear, "or being killed. Tell the stable boy to get my horse ready."

With three pistols holstered beside his saddle and a pair under his cloak, Smith mounted Rodney, kicked in his heels, and left the village. Riding inland, he nodded to the corpse of Sir Francis that swung in its gibbet, surrounded by feasting rooks, and checked his pistols.

"Hell mend you, Sir Francis."

Smith rode at a fast trot, increasing to a canter when he approached his destination.

The house of Orchardholm stood on a spur of the High Weald, two stories high and four square to all the winds of the Weald. Orchardholm stared defiantly southward, with the morning sun glinting from its windows.

As Smith drew closer, he saw a lone horsewoman ahead of him, riding through the double wrought-iron gates.

Bess!

Smith spurred harder, but Bess was at the front door of Orchardholm before Smith entered the modest grounds. Anson stood at the foot of the stairs, nibbling the lawn with her reins trailing on the ground.

"Bess!" Smith shouted.

Bess ignored him, pushing through the front door and into

the house.

"Damn the woman!" Smith said and followed. Orchardholm's front door closed with a thump as Smith slid from his horse and bounded up the steps.

"Wait!"

Nobody heard or heeded Smith's shout. When he banged on the door, the sound echoed around the neat policies, disturbing a flock of nervous sparrows that rose, chattering in a cloud. Smith knocked again, and a smart footman answered.

"Yes, sir?" The footman adjusted his powdered wig.

"Let me in!" Smith tried to push past, only for the polite footman to block his path. "Let me in! I have to see Lady Selby."

"Who are you, sir?"

"John Smith. I am Captain John Smith. Lady Selby knows me."

The footman remained static in Smith's path. "If you will wait here, sir, I will see if Lady Selby is at home."

"You know damned well that she's at home, damn you!" Smith feinted left, then slid right, passed the footman, and strode into the house. The great hall was half the size of King-shunt Manor and nearly empty of furniture.

Smith jinked past a simple stone column. "Lady Selby! Bess!"

"Here we are, Abel," Lady Selby said quietly. "Bess is with me."

Bess and Lady Selby faced each other across the breadth of the hall. Bess wore her riding cloak and a man's tricorn hat, with her right hand tapping a riding whip against her thigh. Lady Selby was smartly dressed in a long green gown, with an elaborate hat and no jewellery save a pair of expensive emerald earrings that matched her gown.

"What's to do?" Smith looked from one to the other, still aware of the pounding of his head.

"You're the to do," Lady Selby said. "You can't have us both, Abel."

Smith stepped back as Lady Selby sent the footman away

with an imperious flick of her hand. "Perhaps I don't want either of you," Smith said.

"Oh, but you do," Lady Selby said.

"You want us both," Bess told him, "and neither Lady Selby nor I am inclined to share."

Lady Selby nodded an acknowledgement towards Bess, then removed her hat with an impatient snort. "This thing gets in the way."

Bess continued. "Lady Selby and I will decide for you."

"Is that the way of it?" Smith was aware of a crowd of curious servants behind him.

"I'll fight you for him," Bess told Lady Selby. "Winner takes all."

Lady Selby smiled, looking Bess up and down from the scuffed toes of her boots to the weather-battered tricorne hat. "Are you challenging me to a duel, child?" She sounded incredulous. "I was thinking of something more civilised, such as a game of chess."

"I don't play," Bess said.

"Of course not. It is a game of skill and finesse. I doubt there was much call for chess in your lovers' bedrooms," Lady Selby fired her opening volley. "Perhaps a hand of cards then? I take it you can count the pips?"

"Better than you, Rebecca," Bess said. "But after I won, you would still be tempted to steal my man."

"Your man, is it?" When Lady Selby shook her head, her emerald earrings sparkled in the morning light. "I've known Abel since he was a toddling child."

"And I know him as a full-grown man," Bess countered. "A duel. I contemplated shooting you out of hand, but this way, I give you a sporting chance."

Lady Selby gave a mocking curtsey. "That was very noble of you."

"This is crass stupidity!" Smith said. "I forbid any such thing! You are not duelling."

"Forbid?" Lady Selby faced Smith. "No, sir, you cannot forbid. You have no authority to forbid anything in my house, and I'd thank you to keep your orders to yourself, or I'll order my servants to throw you out of my property."

"Rebecca is correct," Bess said. "This affair is between her and me, and you have no say in the matter."

Damn her! I can command an entire crew of men, but I cannot control one woman!

"A duel it is then," Lady Selby said to Bess.

Bess nodded, dropped her whip, and produced two identical pistols from beneath her riding cloak and placed them on the side table. "Choose your weapon, madam."

Lady Selby laughed and shook her head. "I have never seen a duel before, let alone taken part in one, yet I believe the convention is for the challenged party to have the choice of weapons."

"Then choose," Bess indicated both pistols. "I assure you that they are identical, and both are loaded."

Lady Selby smiled. "I choose swords," she said.

Smith sensed Bess's dismay. *Oh, dear God! Becky is correct that the challenged party has the choice of weapons. What does Bess know about sword fighting?*

"I've never held a sword in my life," Bess admitted as the colour drained from her face.

Lady Selby raised her eyebrows. "Then withdraw your challenge, Bess whatever-your-name-is, and leave my house and this county." She leaned forward with her eyes narrowed. "Crawl away, little girl, with your tail between your legs."

When Smith stepped forward, Lady Selby faced him. "I told you, Abel, this is not your affair. This discussion is between Bess and me. You are the object, not the arbitrator."

"Swords, then," Bess agreed recklessly, pale under her unfashionable tan. "I can spit you as easily as I can shoot you. When and where?"

Lady Selby had recovered her poise. "What better time than the present, my dear?"

Chapter Twenty-Eight

September – October 1762

"Jack Milburn, the previous occupier of this house, was a cavalry officer," Lady Selby said casually. "He died at Minden, without ever drawing his sword in action." She smiled. "When the infantry was winning everlasting glory, the cavalry sat and watched. A stray cannonball took the head clean off poor Jack's shoulders."

"That's very interesting," Bess said.

"Jack's swords have never been blooded. They are virginal," Mrs said. "Unlike you, Bess, I would imagine."

Bess took a deep breath.

Don't let her rile you, Bess!

"I hope your sons like being disinherited," Bess retaliated sweetly. "Poverty will challenge their characters."

Both women wore long, loose skirts and a tight tunic, with their hair pulled back to hang in a tight tail down the back of the neck. Lady Selby produced two swords. Long, with a curved blade, they looked wickedly dangerous.

"My lieutenant's cavalry sabres." Lady Selby held one in each hand. "Heavy for a woman to wield, but the only pair of equal blades in Orchardholm. Choose, my dear."

Bess lifted both, tested them for weight, and selected one. She held the sword clumsily, with the weight pulling at her wrist.

"You don't have to do this!" Smith said.

"Keep out of our affairs," Bess told him.

"Damn you both! I'll have no part in it. You're a pair of hell hounds, and I want nothing to do with either of you!"

Yet Smith watched every movement of both women, with his head full of memories and his mouth dry with worry.

"This way." Lady Selby led them outside the house, with the servants following like a human tail. Behind the stables was an area of lawn, which the gardener kept pristine with long sweeps with his scythe. Russet-leaved trees stood sentinel all around, as they had for generations, while beyond the woodland, the fertile fields of Kent rolled away towards the sea in the dim distance.

Smith had little appreciation of the beauty of the county as he watched the drama unfold. The women stood opposite each other. Bess had her sword balanced on her right shoulder, and Lady Selby held the hilt in her right hand with the tip of the blade in her left.

"You servants!" Lady Selby raised her voice sharply. "You'll have work to do, and you'd better get to it, or I'll have your hides!"

The servants fled, with the women lifting the hems of their long skirts to run faster and the men holding onto their wigs.

"One has to keep the servants on their toes," Lady Selby revealed a side to her that Smith had never seen before. "Now, child," she addressed Bess, "whenever you are ready."

Bess responded with a rush and a powerful swing that would have parted Lady Selby's head from her shoulders had she not parried with an upraised blade. The force of Bess's swing forced Lady Selby to withdraw, but she managed to hold the sword for a long second and then began a series of attacks that pushed the smaller woman back, step by reluctant step until they completed a circuit of the lawn.

By that time, Bess was panting with exertion, with a sheen of perspiration on her face, while Lady Selby was as calm and relaxed as if she was strolling around her garden picking roses. Smith watched without visible emotion as Bess countered another controlled attack, holding the sabre two-handed.

Lady Selby stepped back. "You're a spirited little creature," she said. "I'll grant you that."

"And you are skilled with the blade," Bess allowed, panting for breath.

"If you give up now," Lady Selby suggested, "nobody will think the worse of you."

"He's my man," Bess said. "Nobody's ever treated me better." She attacked with a rush, hoping to catch Lady Selby off guard as she slashed, thrust, and swung.

Lady Selby stepped back, parrying each blow with skill. However, the sheer force of Bess's assault forced her to retreat. Bess held her sword in both hands, grunting with every stroke, alternating her attack from head-high to a downward jab to Lady Selby's feet, then a thrust to her middle.

"You're tiring," Lady Selby blocked Bess's blade and pushed her aside. Both women stepped back. A sheen of sweat had formed on Bess's forehead while Lady Selby was also breathing heavily.

"As are you," Bess pressed forward in a wild attack that gave Lady Selby an opening. She smashed Bess's sable sideways, darted inside her guard, and brought the edge of her blade down Bess's face, from the corner of her eye to her chin. As Bess yelled and dropped her sword, Lady Selby slashed sideways. The long blade caught Bess's right hip, slicing through her skirt and layers of petticoats to lay open the flesh across the hip and upper thigh. Bess shrieked again and fell, holding the open wound.

Lady Selby stepped forward and placed the point of her sabre against Bess's chest. "Give in, child, or I will finish it."

Smith stepped forward. "That's enough," he ordered. "Damn you both for a pair of bitches!"

"It's not ended yet!" With blood covering her face and her

voice taut with pain, Bess sat up. Removing her hand from her hip, she suddenly lifted her sword and thrust upwards. The point of Bess's blade penetrated Lady Selby's stomach, and Bess twisted and ripped upward, gasping with effort.

Lady Selby died there, lying in a welter of blood on the grass, with the wind caressing her and a gentle rain washing her face.

"You're my man, John Smith." Bess thrust her sabre into the grass. "I won you fair and square."

"You did," Smith said. *There was never any doubt, you little witch!* He uncocked the pistol he had up his sleeve. "Now, let's tend to your injuries before you bleed to death."

RUTH WAS USED TO DEALING WITH WOUNDS AND HELPED carry Bess to her room. They laid Bess on the bed and stripped her bare.

"What a mess!" Ruth said.

"Get me spirits, a needle and thread," Smith ordered. "And quickly. She's lost a lot of blood on the journey here."

Bess lay, face down, moaning slightly.

"This will sting like the devil," Smith said and applied the spirits to the wound across her hip. He grunted as Bess writhed but remained nearly silent. "Brave girl. Now lie as still as you can." He stitched her wounds together with a skill that any country doctor would have envied as Bess made little mewing noises.

"Where did you learn to stitch like that?" Ruth watched through critical eyes.

"I was a surgeon's mate in the Navy for a while," Smith told her. "Now, Bess, I'm going to dress your face."

Together, Ruth and Smith turned Bess on her side.

"It's not as bad as it looks," Smith said. "It's a shallow cut that will leave a scar, but the eye and nose are undamaged." He dabbed on brandy, asked Ruth to hold Bess's head still and stitched again. "There you are, Bess, my girl. You'll have an interesting scar to show to your grandchildren."

"Where's Bess's opponent?" Ruth asked.

"I'll bury her tonight," Smith said.

Ruth nodded. "Was it Lady Selby?"

"It was."

Ruth grunted. "The authorities might ask questions." She examined Bess's wounds with a critical eye. "I'll send the boy to the doctor," she said. "Bess will undoubtedly run a fever now."

"Thank you, Ruth. I'll bribe the servants to say Lady Selby rode to London," Smith said. "They didn't know her well, and I'll give them a choice of accepting my gold or my lead," he touched his pistol.

"Both can be very persuasive metals," Ruth agreed. "Go and do what you have to do. I'll look after Bess. You're lucky that the authorities hanged Sir Francis. Nobody cares what happens to the wife of a disinherited traitor."

RUTH'S PREDICTION PROVED CORRECT. BESS TOSSED AND sweated through a fever, despite, or because of, the doctor's potions and bleedings. For a while, Smith thought Bess might join Lady Selby in an early grave. However, she was a fighter with a constitution toughened by adversity. Bess pulled through with a shipload of curses and a glower for misplaced sympathy.

It was six weeks before Bess left the bed. She had lost weight, so she was wan, drawn, and permanently out of temper.

"Stand aside, John! I'm not lying in bed all day when there's work to be done!" Bess rose, staggered, recovered, and limped around the room. Rather than surrender to weakness, she swore at the tightness of her leg and the scar on her face.

Every day, Smith wondered how many cargoes he was missing and when Holden or the Ramsleys would act. He sent Hargreaves to Portsmouth in *Maid of Kent*, worried about his ship, then looked at Bess and knew he could not leave her to suffer alone.

"You're back with us then," Smith had barely left the room while Bess recovered. Now, she perched awkwardly on a chair, peering into the mirror that Ruth had thoughtfully provided.

"I'm back," Bess pushed back the hair from her face. "I look like one of the church gargoyles, and my leg is scarred forever, but I'm alive."

"Let's see if you can walk around the room," Smith offered his arm.

"I can walk without your help!" Bess snapped. She shifted her legs sideways, hid her wince of pain, and rose from the chair.

Smith caught her before she fell.

"Let go! I'm all right!" Bess recovered her balance, shook Smith away and walked to the door and back. "You see?"

"I see," Smith said. Lady Selby's sword had left a livid scar across Bess's left cheek. Smith's stitch marks remained, puckering the skin even after the doctor had removed the thread. Bess could never have been called classically beautiful, but, as Smith told her, she was certainly striking.

"If Lady Selby had won," Bess gasped as she sat at the mirror, perching uncomfortably to avoid the wound on her right hip and thigh. "Would you have remained with her?" She examined her face and began to disguise her scar with a careful application of powder and potions.

"Lady Selby would not have won," Smith told her.

"She was damned close to victory!" Bess snapped.

Smith tapped his pistol. "If Lady Selby looked like killing you, I'd have shot her."

Bess looked around from the mirror. "You constantly surprise me," she said.

"You shouldn't be surprised," Smith scolded. "I told you before that I have one woman at a time. You are that woman."

"Even now?" Bess rose and stood sideways at the mirror, examining the raw wound that disfigured her right hip and thigh.

"Even with a face like a monster and," she indicated her scar, "that? It's hardly appealing, is it?"

Smith knelt at her side and kissed the scar. "It's an honourable wound gained in fighting for me. Every time I see your battle trophies, I will remember that you put your life in danger for me."

"You are an extraordinarily strange man," Bess said. She waited until Smith stood again. "Now you have me, and Sir Francis and Lady Becky are gone, have you finished what you came here for?"

"I have hardly started," Smith said. Throwing up the sash, he peered out of the window at the building work at the Spike. "I've made a beginning, Bess, and laid the foundations. We've astonished the village. Next, we will astonish all of Kent."

If the Ramsleys don't kill me first, Holden doesn't take away my business, or Ambrose Grant doesn't catch me smuggling. I have to guard against all three possibilities, yet I can hardly leave the Dancing Horse with Bess incapacitated. I only hope my plans are working out.

Chapter Twenty-Nine

November 1762

"Captain Smith!" Joseph Mitchell had been running for hours. Despite the beginning of the winter frost, beads of sweat furrowed the dirt on his face and created dark patches under his armpits.

"Yes, Mitchell?" Smith looked up from the deck of *Maid of Kent*, where he had been altering the rake of the masts.

"William Holden's coming, Captain," Mitchell gasped, holding onto the rail for support. "And he's bringing an army with him."

"I wondered when he would act," Smith said quietly. *He's been gathering his men while I've been caring for Bess.* "How big an army?"

"About two hundred men, Captain Smith, maybe more. He's got a company of horsemen and a whole mod of batsmen on foot. They've crossed the frontier from Sussex, and they're already in Kent, marching towards Kingsgate."

Smith nodded. "Thank you, Mitchell. I'd better prepare to meet them." He raised his voice. "Mr Hargreaves!"

"I heard, Captain." Hargreaves was in shirt sleeves. "I'll get the crew together."

"Roper!" Smith shouted, and Roper appeared.

"Yes, Captain?"

"Fetch Mr Skinner and two carts. Tell him that Holden has crossed the frontier."

"Yes, Captain," Roper hesitated. "Will Skinner know what the message means, Captain?"

Smith nodded. "Skinner knows what to do."

"Yes, Captain."

Smith stepped into his cabin and lifted a brace of pistols from the desk. Thrusting them under his belt, he swung off *Maid of Kent* and onto the quay.

"Good luck, Captain," somebody shouted as Smith strode to the Dancing Horse, where Ruth was busily putting up the external shutters.

"You've already heard, then," Smith said.

"I've heard," Ruth said, slotting the final shutter in place. "Try to keep any trouble away from the Dancing Horse, Captain."

"I'll do what I can," Smith mounted the stairs and entered his room. Bess lay face-down on the bed, still bandaged from hip to knee.

"How are you?" Smith asked.

"How do I look?" Bess asked over her shoulder.

"Scarred and still beautiful," Smith told her. "Holden is coming to town. I want you to keep out of his road."

Bess looked around. "I was thinking of jumping out of the window and running down the road to greet him." She shifted her leg slightly, gasped, and winced. "This time, John, you'll have to fight without me."

"You'll be a loss," Smith said seriously. "Stay put." He kissed her, lifted a pair of holstered pistols from the side table, and strapped them around his body.

"That's four pistols," Bess said.

"Five including the gun up my sleeve," Smith told her. He added a powder horn, a dozen spare balls, and a knife, considered for a moment and lifted his telescope and the hunting horn he had liberated from Sir Francis's hallway.

"Try to come back alive," Bess said.

"I'll do my best," Smith replied. "I can't promise."

I'll miss Bess. It was always good to know she had my back with her blunderbuss. Still, she should be safe in the Dancing Horse. It's sheer bad luck that I was looking after Bess when Holden was preparing to attack so that I couldn't gather the men together.

"Captain!" Ruth was waiting for him at the foot of the stairs, holding the Dancing Horse flag in her hands. "John, or Abel if you prefer."

"Abel?" Smith was taken aback.

"Abel Watson. I knew you the moment you stepped in my inn." She thrust out the flag to him. "Here, Captain, fight under the old banner of Kent. The Dancing White Horse."

"Thank you, Ruth." Smith took the banner. "Invicta," he spoke the old Kent slogan. "Invincible."

"Invicta," Ruth said. "Come back to us, Captain." She returned indoors.

Mounting Rodney, Smith folded the flag on top of his saddle and rode westward, out of Kingsgate. As he passed along the street, he saw the villagers putting up their shutters.

"Don't let the Sussex Gang get here, Captain!" A woman called out. "We don't want their sort in Kingsgate!"

"I'm behind you, Captain," a voice sounded. Hargreaves rode clumsily behind him on an ancient mare. "I'm not much of a horseman, Captain."

"Sailors on horseback, eh?" Smith said. "You don't have to come, Hargreaves. Holden's men will outnumber us, and your family needs you."

Hargreaves nodded. "I know. I've put the word out, as we arranged." He glanced at Smith. "If you had spent less time with Bess, you would be better prepared."

Smith hauled on the reins, slowing his horse. "She's saved me more than once."

"Yes, Captain," Hargreaves looked away.

Smith heard footsteps behind him. "*Maid of Kent!*" a man

shouted and ran from his cottage to join them. Hewitt nodded to them as he hefted a staff. A cutlass gleamed naked under his belt.

"With you, Captain!"

"*Maid of Kent*," another voice replied as two more crewmen left their homes to join Smith.

"With you, Captain Smith!" Thomas Carman ran to join them. Old in years, his eyes danced like a youth with the prospect of excitement. "It's like the old days, Captain, when I sailed with Blackbeard Teach!"

"Thanks, lads," Smith said. *Now we are six strong against two hundred of Holden's men.*

A hundred yards from the village, a group of men merged from the left, each holding a long staff.

"We heard the Sussex men were coming," A tall spokesman said. "The batsmen are with you, Captain!" they formed into a rough column, four abreast and six long, and every ten steps, they rapped their staffs on the ground.

"Your army is growing," Hargreaves murmured.

Smith nodded. "I want Holden," he said. "I don't want a war with casualties to innocent people." He remembered the fortifications of Louisbourg, the crash of cannon and the high yelling of the men. Young Perkins had died there, screaming, with his intestines sliding from his body. Smith had watched him die, then ran on, with Sinclair falling at his side with both legs shorn off at the thighs. He had seen too much blood, death, and agony to seek more, yet he had not coerced any of the men with him today. They joined him willingly, fully aware of the consequences.

Hargreaves freed Smith from his thoughts. "Are you considering a duel with Holden?"

"I want him dead. I don't care how."

Columns of smoke coiled skywards in the west, merging to form low clouds smudging the horizon. Smith lifted his head. "Damn you, Holden."

"What the devil?" Hargreaves wondered. "What's that?"

"Holden and the Sussex gang," Smith said. "He's torching my clients, claiming Kent as his own."

"The devil he is," Hargreaves said.

"I'll teach him who the devil is," Smith increased his speed. "Come on, lads! The bastards are burning our profit!"

The men's growl was an ugly thing, full of menace toward Holden's Sussex gang.

The drumming started then, distinct across the frost-bitter fields, combined with the sound of a distant mob.

"Holden's men are marching to the tuck of drum," Hargreaves said. "He thinks he's James bloody Wolfe!"

"Wolfe died on the Plains of Abraham," Smith reminded. "Maybe Holden will die on the Plains of Kent."

Smith glanced over his shoulder, estimated he had thirty men behind him, and led them up a slight rise to a small copse of wind-stripped elm trees. The landscape rolled out before them in a succession of low hills, frost-rimmed and picturesque under the late autumn sun. Adding to the atmosphere, a skein of geese passed overhead, calling in a melancholic chorus as a mist drifted in from the Channel.

"We'll meet them here." Smith knew this area well. The ridge faced due west, with a gentle slope behind and a steeper rise in front, which Holden's army would have to climb before reaching Smith's men. Smith had the advantage of position and height as some compensation for the disparity of numbers. The drumming continued, an ominous harbinger of war.

"Hargreaves!" Smith handed over the White Horse flag. "Find a pole and hoist the flag. We're going to proclaim our identity."

"Aye, aye, Captain!" Hargreaves said. Within ten minutes, the White Horse rose above Smith's little army.

"Do you envisage a full-scale battle?" Hargreaves sounded nervous.

"Maybe," Smith said.

Smith looked around his men. More had arrived in ones,

twos, and small groups, boosting his numbers to around fifty. *If only I had more time to prepare.* He looked ahead, where the Sussex men were now in view. For every man he had, Holden had four, and then young Mitchell ran to Smith, panting.

"Captain!" Mitchell nearly collapsed at Smith's feet. "It's the ship. *Maid of Kent* is on fire."

This day is not going well.

Smith looked over his shoulder and saw another column of smoke rising from the direction of Kingsgate. His mouth twitched as he fought his anger. "*Maid's* insured," he said. "We'll build another." He focussed his telescope towards the village, then saw two carts jolting over the rough track, alternately appearing and disappearing as they drove into pockets of mist.

Smith nodded. *That's more like it. Come on, Skinner. Get these bloody wagons moving. We're still vastly outnumbered, but if you reach us, we have more of a chance.*

When Smith shifted his gaze further back and adjusted the telescope, his mouth twitched a second time. A group of people were leaving the village, a quarter of a mile behind the two carts.

"Things could get lively," Smith said.

"What's happening?" Hargreaves sounded nervous.

Smith passed over the telescope. "Use the spyglass. Look who is leaving the village."

"I can't make them out in the mist," Hargreaves complained. "Wait, Captain, I see them now. It's the Ramsleys," Hargreaves' voice was flat.

"Mother Ramsley promised revenge, and here she comes now. I'll wager it was the Ramsleys who set fire to *Maid of Kent* and informed the Holdens that I was concentrating on Bess."

Hargreaves produced his clay pipe, thrust it in his mouth, and promptly bit through the stem. "Bugger!" He watched the bowl drop to the ground. "What are we going to do, Captain?"

Smith pulled a pipe from his pocket and handed it to Hargreaves, dismounted, and stamped his feet, right then left. "I'm going to talk to the men," he said, smiling.

Mounting a rock, Smith called the men to him, raising his hands for silence. He ignored the increasing clamour of the drums.

"Men of Kent," he said. "I thank you all for your loyalty and your friendship." The men cheered, with the batsmen knocking their staffs on the ground in unconscious imitation of the advancing drums. "You hear Holden's men approaching?"

Some of the men nodded; others roared a challenge while a few looked solemn. Carman lifted his cutlass in the air. When Hewitt shouted the old Kent slogan, "Invicta!" others took up the chant until Smith again held up his hands for silence.

The noise ended, except for the drums of Sussex and the beautiful call of a solitary blackbird. Smith continued, feeling like Harold before Hastings, which was fought only a few miles away.

"The Holdens are greater in numbers than us," Smith shouted. "If any of you wish to leave, then go now, and nobody will blame you." He waited, fully aware of how much moral courage it took to admit fear in front of one's friends. When one man hung his head and sidled away, Smith felt only admiration, despite the subdued hisses from some of the crowd.

"There walks a brave man," Smith said without a trace of irony. The crowd cheered, not understanding, and the batsmen recommenced their hammering on the ground.

"All right!" Smith held up both hands. "You are all fools, and I am the greatest fool to have caused this commotion." Only he knew how much truth was in that statement. "Men with muskets or fowling pieces form a line in front. Batsmen take position in the left flank behind the musketeers. Men with pistols, take the centre." Smith waited until his little army organised itself.

I wish I had time to gather more men!

"Crew of *Maid*, I want you on the right flank, behind the muskets."

As Smith made his dispositions, he glanced behind him, where the column of smoke marked the funeral pyre of his ship.

The Ramsleys had taken a shorter route than the lumbering carts and were fast approaching the rear of his army. Mother Ramsley led from the front, a formidable figure with her sons immediately behind her. The nephews and more distant relatives followed in a ragtag mob of dangerous men, all intent on avenging the murdered Henry.

"Carman," Smith said quietly. "I need your experience here."

"Yes, Captain!" Carman grinned, with his eyes as bright as a teenager's.

"Take half a dozen of *Maid's* crew and slow down the Ramsleys." He touched Carman's arm. "Take care of my men, Thomas. Skirmish and retreat and don't lose anybody."

"Aye, aye, Captain!" Carman said, grinning.

"Use the mist as your ally, Thomas."

"I know how to fight, Captain!" Carman assured him.

The drumming seemed to dominate everything as if Holden's two drums had multiplied tenfold and Holden's army had donned the scarlet uniforms of British infantry.

"Here they come!" Roper shouted. Smith's army gave a terrific yell and waved their staffs, cutlasses, and muskets in the air as the Sussex men emerged from a patch of thick mist. Tendrils of grey moisture wafted among them, seeming to increase their numbers and render them even more formidable.

"White horse!" Hewitt roared in a defiant challenge. "White horse of Kent! Invicta, you bastards!"

"Sweet God and all his angels," Roper said. "There are bloody thousands of them."

Smith agreed, removing all expression from his face as he looked towards the enemy. Holden's army spread out around the base of the ridge, overlapping the Kent men on both sides. The drums stopped, and silence descended on the frost-bright fields as the mist began to lift. The blackbird still sang a lone sound of sanity as the White Horse banner drooped, and men wondered why they were here and not safe at home.

Smith thought he heard an echo of the drums high in the shredding mist.

"Captain!" Mitchell said urgently. "Over to the left!"

"What?"

"There, Captain!" Mitchell pointed.

Another force spread across the fields along the Sussex-Kent border, dimly seen as it ghosted from copse to copse.

"Who the devil?" Smith wondered. "Has Holden got even more reinforcements?"

"God knows, Captain."

"Send Mitchell to find out who they are," Smith ordered, and then other events took his attention as Holden stepped in front of his men with Hitchins at his side.

"Smith!" Holden roared. "Captain John Smith!"

"William Holden!" Smith met Holden's shout. "You are on our border!" He lifted a hand to quieten the swelling growl from the Kent men.

"Send your men away, Smith! Save their lives!"

Smith heard a crackle of gunfire from behind and knew that Carman had made contact with the Ramsleys. "Face me, Holden, man-to-man, and we'll settle this business without anybody else getting hurt."

The Sussex men took up Holden's laughter, so his entire rival army mocked Smith's words.

"You suggest that I give up my advantages?" Holden laughed again.

Fifty yards apart, the rival smugglers' gangs faced each other, Smith's men of Kent and Holden's much larger Sussex gang.

"They're going to charge us!" Roper said, with his voice rising in near panic. He glanced over his shoulder towards Kent.

"That other mob is getting closer!" Hewitt said.

Smith could see them now, maybe thirty strong and advancing at speed across the fields. There seemed something strange about them, but with the last of the drifting mist and the distraction of Holden's army, Smith could not make out what. More gunfire sounded from the rear and a chorus of shouts.

"The Ramsleys are pushing Carman back!" Hargreaves sounded worried.

"We can't do anything about that," Smith said. He heard the clatter of wheels and the two carts pulled up on the hill, with Skinner halting in the shelter of the wood. Smith nodded in satisfaction. *Carman has slowed the Ramsleys. Now that the carts are here, we have a better chance.*

"Good man, Skinner," Smith said. "Send one cart to the left wing and the other in the centre."

"Yes, Captain," Skinner chose the central position himself and ordered the second cart to the left flank, where the western slope was the most gentle.

"What are you going to do with the carts?" Roper asked. "Hide behind them?"

"You'll see," Smith said. *You're ready to run, Roper. You won't be part of my crew much longer. If I still have a crew after today.*

Holden gave an order, and the drums recommenced their rhythmic tapping. The Sussex men advanced, keeping their line intact. They outflanked the Kent force on both sides and lapped around the sides of the hill, nearly surrounding Smith's men. If the Ramsley's succeeded in getting past Carman's gallant band, the encirclement would be complete.

"Load!" Smith roared. "Musketmen! Kneel and face the enemy! Pistol men, get ready to repel boarders! We'll fire one volley, then charge!"

The lads look nervous. Who is that third force? I might start the ball now in case they are on Holden's team.

Smith stepped forward, a lone, slim figure in front of his men, with the wind flapping his cloak around his calves and the hat pressed firmly on his head.

"Holden!" Smith shouted. "Call off your men! Call off your men and return to Sussex, or the day will go ill with you!"

The mysterious third force was closer now so that Smith

could make out what they were. As he waited for Holden's response, Smith focussed his telescope on the newcomers. He started as he saw their determined stride and the broad skirts that brushed against the ground as they advanced.

Mrs Hargreaves! It's Suzanne Hargreaves and the Kingsgate women.

"Charge!" Holden roared. "Charge, men, and we'll take the free trade of all Kent. We'll all be rich men, lads!"

Suzanne Hargreaves' women arrived then, running in a yelling mob at the rear of the Sussex men, throwing stones and wielding an array of weapons from simple broomsticks to staffs, agricultural flails and even a cutlass.

Now! Now's the time, with Suzanne distracting the Sussex gang and Carman still holding the Ramsleys.

Lifting the hunting horn from around his neck, Smith blew a long blast. The call resounded loud and clear above the roar of the men, distinctive even at a distance.

The horn invoked an immediate response as people emerged from the back of both carts, throwing off the canvas covers to reveal a swivel gun in each. In the cart closest to the centre of the line, Bess and Ruth aimed the gun directly at Holden and Hitchins, while the swivel on the left flank pointed to the mass of the Sussex gang. At that range, the swivel would kill and maim a dozen men or more.

Smith blew the horn again. "Your last chance, Holden! One more step, and we'll blast you to oblivion!"

Holden stopped, staring at the swivel that pointed towards him, with Hitchins shifting behind him to seek cover. He turned around as Suzanne's gallant band crashed into the rear of his men, causing consternation.

"Permission to fire, Captain?" Bess aimed the swivel, which was a larger variety of blunderbuss.

"I thought I told you to stay in bed!" Smith stepped forward beside Bess.

"When did I ever do as somebody orders me?" Bess was white-faced, with the scar livid across her cheek.

Holden's mouth worked without words, unsure what to do as Bess aimed the gun directly at him. The men nearest to him began to drift away from the threat of the swivel.

"One step," Ruth said, "and I'll blow fragments of you all the way back to Sussex."

Smith knew that nothing was decided yet. The Sussex men still outnumbered his force, and one mad charge could determine the day. Suzanne's women had rammed into the back of Holden's force, knocking men down and pulling some away from the main Sussex Army, but not in sufficient numbers to equalise the odds. Smith pulled two pistols from his belt and waited for Holden's next move.

The drumming began again, from outside the fields, accompanied by the high trilling of fifes. Even before Holden could act, a group of horsemen cantered between the two forces. Suzanne's women stopped their attack and stepped back to watch.

"About bloody time," Smith said.

Ambrose Grant rode at the head of the horsemen, flanked by Riding Officers and with a troop of dragoons at his back.

"What the devil is happening?" Hargreaves asked.

Grant rode directly to Smith, pulling his horse to a halt in a display of horsemanship impressive for a seaman. "Where is he, Captain Smith? Where is Holden the smuggler?"

"That's your man," Smith pointed directly at Holden. "And the fellow at his side is Hitchins, a sneaky, nasty piece."

"We'll take care of them now, Captain," Grant pointed to the column of Kent Militia that marched around both flanks of the Sussex Gang. "Thank you for your assistance."

"Can I shoot him now?" Bess asked, aiming the swivel.

"No, Bess. Allow Captain Grant to take over now. Our work here is complete." Smith smiled. "The music has stopped, and this particular dance has run its course."

Ruth helped Bess down from the cart as the militia advanced with fixed bayonets, surrounding and disarming the Sussex gang.

"You bastard!" Holden screamed. "I'll kill you both!" Pulling a pair of pistols from beneath his cloak, he began to run up the hill towards Smith.

Bess was first to react, pulling the pistol from within her cloak and firing, with Smith and Grant half a second behind. The force of the three balls knocked Holden off his feet, so he fell backwards, still holding his pistols.

"He was going to kill you, Captain Grant," Bess said.

Grant nodded. "Not with you around," he stared at Holden's crumpled body. "I've never shot a man before."

"The first is always the worst," Smith put an arm around Bess. When he looked behind him, the Ramsleys were in full retreat, with Carman's band in pursuit. The body of Mother Ramsley lay on the ground, with Jake lying crumpled at her side.

"Have you turned informer?" Hargreaves asked as they sat in the taproom.

"I used the Preventative service for our ends," Smith told him. "Holden intended to take over our business. Now, we will expand into Sussex and control the Free Trade along half the South Coast, from the North Foreland to Selsey Bill."

"Ambrose Grant is no fool," Hargreaves said. "He must know what's happening."

"Grant has another feather in his cap with the execution of Holden and the capture of his gang," Smith said. "He is rising up the Preventative ladder, rung by rung, and every success sees his masters take more notice of him." Smith put down his rum. "It's not hard to control men, Hargreaves. All you have to do is find their motivation and help them towards their ambition."

"In other words, give them what they want," Hargreaves said.

"Or what they think they want," Smith said. "Grant wanted

to capture a notable smuggler in this area, and now he has, he'll move away."

Hargreaves smiled. "When you returned to Kingsgate," he said. "I thought you were your father's son. I thought you only sought revenge for his execution."

"You believed that was my motivation?" Smith made room for Bess beside the fire. She sat gingerly, favouring her still tender hip.

"I did," Hargreaves said.

"Maybe it was, then," Smith spoke, as much musing to himself as replying to Hargreaves. "But a man always needs a purpose, or life becomes stale. Simple men have simple requirements. Give them drink, women, tobacco, and a snug berth for the night, and they are happy. The more complex the man, the larger his purpose and the more distant his horizon."

Hargreaves nodded, only partly understanding. "What's your horizon, Captain?"

"It's always shifting, Hargreaves. My horizon shifts outward with every success, and my demons drive me to sail on through fair wind or foul."

"Here's to a fair wind," Hargreaves raised his glass.

"A fair wind," Smith said, "confusion to the enemy, and the next horizon."

"The next horizon," Bess said, smiling.

About the Author

Born in Edinburgh, Scotland and educated at the University of Dundee, Malcolm Archibald writes in a variety of genres, from academic history to folklore, historical fiction to fantasy. He won the Dundee International Book Prize with 'Whales for the Wizard' in 2005.

Happily married for 35 years, Malcolm has three grown children and lives in darkest Moray in northern Scotland, close by a 13th century abbey and with buzzards and deer more common than people.

To learn more about Malcolm Archibald and discover more Next Chapter authors, visit our website at www.nextchapter.pub.